DRAGON SCALES

To Amy

DRAGON SCALES

❖ A JELF ACADEMY NOVEL ❖

JENNA E. FAAS

SPARKS AND CINDERS PUBLISHING
PITTSBURGH

First published by Sparks and Cinders Publishing 2022

Dragon Scales. Copyright © 2022 by Sparks and Cinders Publishing

All rights reserved. No part of this publication may be reproduced, stored, or transmitted in any form or by any means, electronic, mechanical, photocopying, recording, scanning, or otherwise, without written permission from the publisher. It is illegal to copy this book, post it to a website, or distribute it by any other means without permission.

This novel is entirely a work of fiction. The names, characters, and incidents portrayed in it are the work of the author's imagination. Any resemblance to actual persons, living or dead, events, or localities is entirely coincidental.

Jenna E. Faas asserts the moral right to be identified as the author of this work.

First U.S. Edition

Cover art and formatting by Damonza

Editing by Alexandria Groves

ISBN 978-1-956207-05-7 (hardback)
ISBN 978-1-956207-03-3 (paperback)
ISBN 978-1-956207-05-7 (ebook)

Dragon Scales

1: Long Days of Summer 1
2: The Lake 10
3: Waiting for the Doorbell 18
4: Return to Jewel Caverns 25
5: Meeting at the Leaf and Lily 35
6: The Girls 42
7: It is Not Okay to be Different 59
8: Forbidden 71
9: Calling Charms and Compatibility 80
10: Dragon Eggs 92
11: Emily's Future In-Laws 103
12: In the Hands of the Gods 121
13: A W.A.S.P. Attack 129
14: A Shocking Return 138
15: Missing Memory 148
16: Preparing for a Wedding 154
17: The Best Christmas Present 165
18: The New Year's Eve Party 179
19: Peer Pressure 189
20: Thistle 200
21: Discovered 210
22: Love Is All That Matters 219
23: Birthdays Are Anything but Happy 232
24: A Fateful Mistake 248
25: Disagreement and Deception 258
26: A Disturbing Discovery 267
27: Code Red 279
28: A Special Day 294
29: A Tea Leaf Prediction 305
30: The Final Betrayal 315
31: Painful Preparations 323
32: The Wedding Day 335
33: The Doyle Mansion 343
34: Up in Flames 352
Acknowledgements 362
About the author 365

*For my son, Clayton, the light of my life.
You have motivated me to achieve my goals, so
I can show you that anything is possible.
I am so proud to be your mom, and I will
always support you with all your dreams.*

xoxo
Infinity and Beyond

1
Long Days of Summer

THE SWELTERING SUN radiated down on my back as I worked. It was so hot outside that I could see the heat waves in the air across the field. I wiped the sweat from my brow and continued to dig the shovel into the hard ground. Ever since I had returned for the summer, Marie assigned me more outdoor chores. Marie was my stepmother, and ever since my father passed away, she treated me like a slave. She even moved my bedroom into the attic. Marie hated me because I looked like my mother, who passed away when I was only one year old. She had always been jealous that my father loved my mother more.

However, that wasn't the only reason Marie couldn't stand me. Not only did I look like my mother, but I also had her "special" talent; I could move things with my mind. Marie thought I was a freak and told me she would throw me out if anyone found out about what I could do. What she didn't know was there were other people just like me. I was a pixie. Pixies could move things with our minds and create charms from rocks and minerals. Marie was also unaware that I was attending a school called the Jelf Academy. This school taught pixies how to manage their magic. Marie believed she was sending me to a school to learn etiquette, so I could become the perfect respectable servant. If she ever found out the real purpose of the Jelf Academy, she would stop me from attending and follow through on her threat.

The Jelf Academy was such a special place for so many reasons. First of all, it was the school my mother had attended. I instantly felt connected to her once I had started attending. The academy also made me feel as if I finally belonged. It had become my home. However, there was a third and most important reason I had to finish my five years at the Jelf Academy. My mother hadn't passed away because she had been sick. She had been murdered by an evil group known as the World Association for the Slaying of Pixies, abbreviated W.A.S.P. These people hated all pixies and intended to eliminate them one by one. My mother had been a very powerful pixie, so the W.A.S.P. had rejoiced when they had defeated her. They didn't know about me when they ended her life.

The W.A.S.P. recently gained information from the pixies they tortured that I would be responsible for dismantling their organization. Since I was my mother's only child, it made sense for the prophecy to be about me, which currently made me their primary target.

I was not in immediate danger since the W.A.S.P. knew nothing about me. They believed I went by my mother's last name, McCalski, instead of Fitzgerald and that I was being raised by pixies. For once in my life, I was thankful I lived with Marie. Unfortunately, my safety was temporary because it would only be a matter of time until the W.A.S.P. discovered my actual whereabouts. That was why it was essential for me to attend the Jelf Academy. I needed to know everything about being a pixie in order to defend myself if I was ever found. I tried not to think about being hunted by the W.A.S.P., but I couldn't help always looking over my shoulder.

I couldn't wait to be back at the Jelf Academy to start my second year. Since Marie knew nothing about the magic school,

Dr. Tweedle, the headmaster, always transported me to the academy. A year ago, he appeared in my life and explained who I was and my abilities. He was the one who changed my world around, and I'll be forever grateful for that.

I was accepted at the Jelf Academy of Magic, but not everyone in the pixie community had accepted me. Last year, I had to prove I was worthy of remaining in the pixie world. Since it's illegal for pixies to have relations with humans, there had never been a student who was half-human before. Fortunately, I had been able to convince the pixie government of my abilities. The fact that the W.A.S.P. was hunting me also helped my case. I would be less likely to expose the pixie world now that my life was in danger.

I continued to work in the field and tried not to think of the potential peril that could befall me. Soon, I was interrupted by Robert, the only friend I had at the manor. Robert was the auburn-haired boy Marie had hired to work in the barn and help with the horses. Unfortunately, he was paid with room and board and forced to live in the loft above the horses. He used to live with a man named Mr. Wicker, who was actually worse than Marie. He never spoke to me when he first began living at the manor. I thought it was because he didn't like me, but that wasn't the case. Since then, Robert and I have grown closer and have become friends. He eventually told me that Mr. Wicker didn't allow him to speak, and if he did, he would be punished.

"Good afternoon, Jane," he said to me as he approached. "I see Marie has you doing outdoor chores again." He shook his head as he inspected them. "A lady shouldn't be out in the sun doing a man's job."

"Haven't you heard? I'm not a lady," I replied with a chuckle. Robert looked at the ground, ignoring my comment.

"When you're finished cleaning up dinner, do you want to come down to the lake again?" Robert asked, referring to the small lake in the woods on the manor's property. Sometimes, if Marie and her children were preoccupied, I would sneak down to the lake. It was the only relaxing thing I could do at the manor. Moreover, it was refreshing after a long day of working under the sun.

"We'll have to see, Robert. It depends on Marie. Sometimes she has me working well into the night," I replied.

Robert looked sympathetic. "You start school again soon, don't you?" he asked with an upset look. Robert told me before that he missed me when I was gone. I wished he was also a pixie, so he could attend too.

"Yes. I will be picked up from here in a week to begin my second year!" I said excitedly.

"How much do you have left to learn about etiquette? I can't believe you have to go to that school for five years," he replied.

"Oh, I couldn't believe how much there is to learn either," I lied and instantly felt guilty.

I always hated lying to Robert. I wished I could tell him the truth, but since humans were not allowed to know of the pixie world, I would be jeopardizing my position when I had just worked so hard to prove myself. Any human could belong to the W.A.S.P., so you couldn't trust anyone. My mother took that risk and broke that rule for love.

"You'll have to tell me all about it then," Robert chuckled, breaking my thoughts.

"Yes, sure," I replied noncommittally. I hoped Robert wouldn't ask me.

I finished the tilling with the shovel and followed Robert to the barn. It was the hottest part of the day, and I was using most of my energy to keep myself cool. Pixies had the ability to change their body temperatures. We just had to stay focused on the task, which was sometimes hard to do. Your mind had to be able to multitask.

My body ached all over, and it was such a relief to enter the cool barn. I hung my shovel on the wall next to the others and took a deep breath. I knew I would have to get back up to the house to help with dinner, but I found myself sitting down on a bale of hay. I hadn't realized how tired I was.

"Would you like some water?" Robert asked me.

"Sure," I sighed. It felt so good to sit, and my throat was so parched.

He handed me a bucket full of water. I cupped a handful and brought it to my lips. Robert stood watching me intently. I tried not to spill water down my dress because sometimes his firm gaze made me nervous, and I felt self-conscious for no reason. I didn't know why he made me feel that way. He was just my friend.

"Thank you," I said, handing the bucket of water back to him.

He smiled at me as he took the bucket from my hands, and, again, his brown eyes met my violet ones. I quickly looked down at my hands because I could feel my cheeks reddening. Sometimes that look of his made me react funny. Finally, I looked back up at him and smiled.

"I should head back up to the house. I know Marie will want me to help with dinner. She's probably already mad that I'm not up there already slaving away," I sighed as I got up from the hay.

"Hopefully, I'll see you tonight at the lake," Robert said.

"I'll have to see what Marie is doing and if I can sneak away or not," I replied.

He smiled again as I left the barn. My legs burned as I walked up the slightly inclined terrain that led up to the side of the house. I had worked very hard today and had exhausted myself. I walked around the back of the house and entered through the kitchen door.

"Where the hell have you been?" This was the greeting I got from Ellen, the cook. Her mousey brown hair was concealed beneath a cobalt bonnet, and her apron was ruffled over her round stomach.

"I just finished my work in the field," I replied, used to her tone with me.

"Wash your hands immediately and get over here!" she yipped.

I inwardly sighed as I washed my hands in the sink and joined her in preparing dinner. Ellen told me to begin boiling the corn on the cob and then instructed me to cut all the kernels off the cobs. Apparently, Marie didn't want to bite it off the cob today. The hot corn burned my fingers as I held it upright with one hand and cut off the kernels. Of course, Marie would think of this as a punishment for me. I was almost certain she sat around all day and thought of things I could do that would make my life miserable.

After I finished, I added butter to the bowl and stirred it until mixed well. Then, I helped Ellen finish the preparations by taking the rolls out of the oven and placing them on a nice dish. Marie always wanted to have dinner served in the best china, no matter the day. When the chicken was finished roasting, we carried the food out to the table. Marie, Emily, and Preston were usually seated at the table when Ellen and I served dinner. We never had to call them down to the dining room. I always wondered how long they sat there.

Marie sat straight in her chair as if a metal rod had been inserted in her spine. Her midnight hair, streaked through with gray, was always in a severe bun, and she always wore a stern look on her face. I had never seen her smile or laugh. When she did smile, it always seemed cold and malicious, not genuine. Marie probably had been pretty when she was young, but her cold demeanor overshadowed any features I would consider beautiful. Even her gray eyes matched the stoniness of her heart.

Emily was like a carbon copy of Marie. She had the same black hair, and her eyes were also gray. Emily wasn't distasteful to look at, but she lacked inner beauty like her mother. Emily delighted at anyone's misfortune, which was the only time she laughed. Making my life miserable was one of Emily's favorite activities. Another favorite of hers was verbally insulting me to make me feel insignificant and beneath her. Of course, I didn't listen or believe anything she said, but what she said was hurtful. Soon, I wouldn't have to worry about Emily's verbal insults because she would be married next spring. After that, she would move in with her new husband, Drake Doyle.

I couldn't say I would be upset to see her go, but I would have more chores to do as the wedding drew nearer. Marie and Emily already told me I would be slaving away at the favors and other decorations needed for the wedding. Then, I would act as a server to the guests at Mr. Doyle's house, where the wedding would be held on the wedding day. I couldn't wait for the whole thing to be over.

As I laid out dinner, I glanced at Preston. His appearance was so unlike his mother and sister that it would've been easy to think he was adopted. But that was until you got to know him. His personality was the same, if not more malicious. Preston was fourteen years old, but he acted like he was still a child. He would throw temper tantrums when he didn't get his way. His green eyes always had a mischievous glint, and his bright orange hair was always messy. Preston was never able to sit still for long. Compared to Marie and Emily's posture, his was quite the opposite. For as ridged as Marie was, it was hard to believe she let Preston act the way he did. I always assumed these traits came from his father, Marie's first husband, who was missing and believed to be dead.

Ellen placed the roasted chicken in the middle of the table, and I put out the bowls of corn and potatoes. I returned to the kitchen to bring out the rolls and butter. Preston was already digging into his meal like an animal when I returned to the table. I tried not to laugh because Marie complained about my manners but didn't say anything about Preston's. As soon as I placed the rolls on the table, he snatched one and stuffed the whole thing into his mouth. I turned away, disgusted. Back in the kitchen, I waited in case I was summoned for anything. I wouldn't be able to eat my dinner until they were done. I got whatever was left.

I waited patiently, and when they were finished, I started clearing off the plates. Preston had made a mess, so I needed to get the mop. How he had gotten food all over the floor was beyond me.

I swear it amused him that I would have to scrub the floors after dinner. What other fourteen-year-old would act like that? I put the dishes in the sink and then filled up a bucket so I could mop the dining room floor. I had the bucket halfway full when I heard my name being called.

"Jane! Where are you? Why do you disappear every time I need to talk to you?" Marie's harsh voice echoed outside the kitchen. I stopped what I was doing and went back into the dining room. Marie sneered when she saw me. "There you are."

Where else would I be besides cleaning up after dinner? I looked at her, waiting for the commands she was sure to give me.

"Emily and I will not be home this evening. We were invited to Drake Doyle's mansion to discuss plans for the wedding. His mother will also be there to help us with the planning," she stated with a roll of her eyes. "I expect you to clean up this mess. The floor is so sticky. I expect it to be mopped." She looked at me as if the floor was my fault.

"I was just getting the mop, ma'am," I replied.

"Good. Make sure this floor shines. Perhaps a wax would also do," Marie said with a nasty smile. I nodded at her in understanding. "It better be perfect when we return home. I don't know how late we'll be, but you better get to work," she commanded me and then turned on her heel to leave.

She thought she was making my job harder by commanding me to wax the floor. Unbeknownst to her, she was actually making it easier on me by leaving the house. Since she wouldn't be home, I could use a pixie charm called the *quick complete charm*. This charm allowed me to move faster than a human and complete the chores quicker than I usually would. I learned to master this charm last year. Since then, I have kept small amounts of the charm in tiny bottles that I always carried with me.

I listened to make sure everyone was gone. All the hired help should've retired to the servant's quarters by now, so I would be able to use the charm. I went into the kitchen to finish up the dishes the human way just to make sure. Finally, I reached into my pocket and pulled out a bottle full of maroon-colored dust. The charm was made entirely of garnet. I tapped some of the dust onto my hand and then sprinkled it over my body. The familiar sensation tingled in my limbs. I could feel my muscles tighten with energy straining to be used.

I rushed around the dining room, rolling up rugs and moving furniture, to clear the floor. My muscles felt good now that I was moving quickly. Using the charm gave me a boost of energy without exhaustion afterward.

Within five minutes, I had the floor mopped. My hand moved in wide fast circles as I waxed, and I managed to complete the task within a half hour. The *quick complete charm* was starting to wear off as I rolled out the rugs in their usual positions. My muscles twitched, and I finally relaxed. I sat down on the floor with my back against the wall and glanced at the grandfather clock. It was only eight o'clock. Marie and Emily were gone for the evening, and I deserved some fun.

2

THE LAKE

THE NIGHT AIR felt hot and humid against my skin. I trudged down the small hill toward the back gardens. Beyond them lay the woods. The small lake was not very far. I could hear the sound of insects making their night noises as I walked through the gardens. The sun was just beginning to set on the horizon, shining an array of colors across the sky. The flowers in the garden were beautiful in the soft light.

The woods stood before me, a mass of dark greens and black shadows. When I entered beneath the leafy green branches, it felt slightly cooler, but it was still humid. I picked my way over sharp sticks and stones, heading in the direction of the lake. The forest at dusk was incredibly breathtaking and peaceful as dim shafts of light shone through the trees from the setting sun. I felt my body start to relax despite the heat.

When I got to the lake, my clothes stuck to me, and I knew how wonderful it would be to swim in the cool blue water. There was no sign of Robert yet, and I paused to appreciate the beauty of the scene in front of me. The water looked crystal clear, and I could see all the rocks at the bottom. Tall pines surrounded the lake, making the area seem secluded, which was precisely why I liked coming down here. I pulled off my sweat-soaked dress, kicked off my shoes, and slid out of my stockings. I laid them on one of the rocks and entered the lake in my underclothes.

At first, the water felt cold, but as my body got used to it, the water felt great. I swam out to the middle of the lake and floated on my back. I gazed at the sky and watched the clouds and the tops of the pine trees towering over me. A flock of birds flew into my line of vision, and I watched them soar over the treetops and disappear. How wonderful it would be to be a bird, I thought. You could fly away from your problems and land in a better place than the one you left. This summer, I had felt like a caged bird waiting to be set free.

I closed my eyes and put my hands underneath my head as I continued to float on the water. I only had to survive the week, and then I'd only see my stepfamily on the weekends. I was happy summer was almost over. This thought was a calming one. I relaxed in the water and felt the tension in my muscles disappear. I thought about all the new things I would be learning in the upcoming year. I couldn't remember if I would be getting a new class. I was excited to find out. However, I knew this next week would drag by since I was eager to get it over with.

The crunch of a stick snapped me out of my daydreams. I sat up in the water and glanced at the woods around me. My stomach dropped when I didn't see anyone. An animal could have made the noise, but it would be foolish of me not to be cautious. Thoughts of the W.A.S.P. remained at the forefront of my mind. I sank into the water, so only the top of my head was visible. Treading water slowly, I tried not to make a sound as I scanned the forest around me. My heart raced in my chest, and I breathed deeply to calm myself.

Relief flooded my body when Robert walked out of the woods. I moved, and Robert spotted me.

"I didn't think you were here," Robert called out. "I didn't see you out there."

I swam toward him. "I was just floating. After a day of hard work, the water feels great," I replied.

I couldn't help glancing down as Robert removed his shirt. I felt my cheeks redden, and I didn't know why. I had met Robert at the lake for a swim over the summer, but I still blushed at his undressing. I glanced at him from beneath my eyelashes and saw his broad chest muscles. Around his neck was a tarnished silver chain. Dangling from the chain was a silver ring. Robert had confided to me that he had been separated from his family when he was young. He had roamed the streets until Mr. Wicker picked him up. Since he was so young and scared, he didn't have a choice. The only object he had to remind him of his family was his father's ring, which he wore around his neck. As far as I knew, he never took it off. Robert told me that he intended to find his family if he ever had the resources. I felt sorry for him and wished I could help him somehow. At least his family might still be alive.

I looked down again as Robert unbuckled his belt. To prevent my eyes from looking, I lay on my back and continued to float again. The sky was growing darker with each minute. Robert and I always swam in the lake at night, so the darkness didn't bother me. Before Robert came to the manor, I used to swim in the lake alone. I was very familiar with the surrounding woods and could probably make it back to the manor blindfolded.

I heard a splash and looked to see Robert in the water, swimming toward me.

"When did you get down here?" he asked me.

"Only about five minutes before you did," I replied

"I'm glad you decided to come. I only have a few days left with you before you return to school. I guess Marie had something important to do," Robert said.

I smiled at his first statement. I guess he did miss me when I was away. "Yes. Marie and Emily went over to Drake Doyle's house to meet with his mother. They were going to discuss some plans for the wedding," I grimaced.

"I bet you can't wait until that wedding's over," Robert replied.

"Yes. I'll have one less nuisance to look after. I'm counting the days until Emily's gone. I'll no longer be her personal slave. May the gods have pity on Mr. Doyle's servants when they have to deal with her," I sighed.

"Gods?" Robert asked questioningly.

I bit my tongue. Just last year, I found out that pixies believed in gods and goddesses. I had decided to worship the pixie religion because I had wanted something to believe in. I hoped there were superior beings who controlled our universe. If we had lived a kind-hearted life, we would be able to live with Cian, the god of the dead, in his beautiful kingdom when we died. I hoped this was true because I wanted to see my mother when I died.

"It's just an expression," I shrugged, thinking quickly.

"Well, yes. Emily's extremely hard to handle," he laughed, accepting my explanation.

"Tell me about it," I grinned.

"Marie told me I'll be coming along to help serve the guests. Apparently, this joyous event will occur at the Doyle mansion," Robert replied.

Marie and Emily had already informed me about the location of the wedding. I had been surprised to hear that it wasn't taking place at the manor. Supposedly, Mr. Doyle's house was much grander, and that's why it had been the chosen location.

"I'm so excited to see the house Emily incessantly brags about," I said sarcastically.

Robert smiled and playfully splashed at me, "At least you will be rid of her, and that's all that matters," he stated.

I splashed him back, and he dove beneath the water to avoid it. Before I knew it, he was tugging at my ankles and pulling me under. I was able to take one deep breath right before he dragged me down.

I opened my eyes under the water and saw a murky outline of him swimming to the surface. I kicked my legs to swim toward him. Robert broke the water's surface, and I playfully jumped on his shoulders to send him back under. We both resurfaced laughing.

"I love the sound of your laugh," Robert said. "I wish you would laugh more often."

"I wish I would, too," I said, blushing again. "But there's never much to laugh about."

Robert gazed at my face intently. "No more depressing conversations tonight. I'd like to have a good week with you. How about a race around the lake?" Robert asked.

I nodded my head, and with that, we took off. I had taught myself to swim and had become what I considered a strong swimmer. I was able to keep up with Robert, but soon it became clear that Robert had more stamina than I. He made it back to the starting point, and I got there a few minutes later. I turned on my back and began to float, trying to catch my breath.

"I beat you, Jane," Robert gasped as he turned on his back and floated beside me.

"I let you win," I said jokingly.

"No, you were trying your hardest," he laughed.

"Okay. You beat me," I replied.

As we drifted, we fell into a comfortable silence, looking at the stars as they popped out brightly against the black sky. I was able to pick out some constellations I had learned in Zodiac Signs. The moon was almost full, and it cast a lovely glow over the forest. It felt like we were in our own world, and no one else existed. I pondered on whether I would mind that so much.

"Do you think I'll ever be able to find my family?" Robert asked, breaking the silence.

"I don't know, Robert. Maybe you will someday," I replied.

"Sometimes, I stare at the night sky and wonder if they're

looking at the same sky thinking about me. I know that sounds silly, but I hope they haven't forgotten me," he sighed.

"I'd want to believe that my son was alive," I replied.

Robert sat up in the water, and so did I. "Come on. Let's dry off. It's getting late, and you don't know how long Marie and Emily will be gone," he said sadly.

I swam behind him to the shore, and we crawled up on a boulder. My skin felt chilled as the beads of water dried. It felt good because it was still humid even though the temperature had dropped.

"Sometimes, I look up at the stars, hoping there is a better place we go to when we die. I hope my mom's watching over me from that other place," I stated.

"There has to be someplace better than this. If not, life's the biggest joke," Robert replied darkly.

I glanced over at him and noticed how beads of water fell across his sun-tanned chest, how his muscles stood out beneath his skin, and how he had a fine line of freckles across his nose. His brown eyes captured my violet ones, and I felt like Robert had a way of looking into my soul. He looked at me as if I was the only person on earth. This thought made my cheeks redden again, and I was grateful for the moon's pale light.

"We should be heading back," I said as I leapt off the rock, reaching for my clothes.

"Yeah, I wouldn't want you to get in trouble. I'll walk you back," Robert said as he also slid off the rock.

I dressed quickly, now self-conscience of his gaze. I turned my back to him as he gathered his clothes and stared at the moon, wondering what time it was. Hopefully, it wasn't too late, and Marie and Emily were still out. Usually, when I was with Robert, I always managed to lose track of time. I heard Robert clear his throat, and when I turned around, he was dressed.

I turned to the woods, ready to head back, when Robert

extended his hand to me. We had never held hands before. "It's dark. I figured we could lead each other back," was his explanation. I reached out my hand and clasped his warm damp one. His fingers were shriveled from being in the water so long, and somehow, they slid perfectly into the spaces between mine. He grasped my hand tightly, and I followed him into the woods.

Even though I was familiar with the pathway back, I felt comfort in the warm feel of his hand against mine. The trees, which were formerly green, were now black. I would've been scared if I wasn't so familiar with the woods. My eyes were beginning to adjust to the darkness, and I continually glanced down to make sure I didn't trip. I didn't want to embarrass myself in front of Robert.

A chill went down my spine when we were halfway through the woods. I got the odd feeling that I was being watched. This wasn't the first time I'd felt this way. I clutched Robert's hand tighter and walked closer to him.

"Jane, what's wrong?" he asked me.

"I just got this very strange feeling, Robert, like we're being watched," I replied.

"I'm sure it's just because of the dark. It's probably nothing," he said as he squeezed my hand.

"No, I feel like something sinister is out there. I just got a chill down my spine," I said anxiously.

Robert chuckled. "Don't worry. Nothing too bad could be in these woods."

I froze. Of course, Robert wouldn't be aware of the possible dangers, not necessarily for him but for me. I couldn't ignore the nagging feeling in my stomach. I knew I might have to choose between flight and fight. I'd rather get out of the woods than expose what I really was to Robert or whoever was watching us.

"Are you okay?" Robert asked, looking into my eyes.

"Could we please get back to the house quickly?" I asked nervously.

Robert must've seen the fear in my eyes because he nodded, and we picked up our pace. My anxiety grew stronger, and it felt like something was going to jump out and grab us at any moment. I pumped my legs harder and was almost pulling Robert along. My fear abated a bit when we broke the tree line, but I didn't slow down. I didn't stop until I reached the barn. Robert let go of my hand, and I took deep breaths, trying to slow my racing heart.

"What was that all about?" Robert asked between gasps.

"I can't explain it," I replied. "I felt like we were in danger." I continued to breathe heavily.

"What could possibly be in those woods?" Robert gasped.

I shook my head. "I don't know, but I never felt that way about the woods when I was younger. Maybe I just imagined it," I lied to make Robert feel better.

"I think the darkness of the woods just got to you," Robert said, gently touching my arm.

I nodded, though I knew what I had felt in the woods was real. Robert smiled at me.

"I better head back to the house before Marie returns," I said, sadly glancing at him. His eyes found mine, and once again, I felt flush with color. I prayed he would mistake it for exertion.

"Good night, Jane," he said, reaching for my hand and squeezing it. "If Marie keeps us apart this week, enjoy returning to school."

"Good night, Robert," I replied as I squeezed his hand back. I couldn't believe how much I would miss him. I still held onto his hand as I turned to go. Slowly, his hand slipped out of my grasp. Robert's eyes looked at me sadly, and I turned away and walked toward the house, feeling guilty for leaving because of who I was.

3
Waiting for the Doorbell

The morning sun's rays fell across my face, waking me up. I groggily rubbed my eyes, shielding them from the light. Then, rolling over on my mattress, I sat up and stretched. Dust flitted in the light from the window as I looked around the attic. The old furniture was covered with white sheets to protect it from the dust.

Further back in the attic, clothing bags hung from the rafters containing some items that belonged to my mother. I didn't want Marie to rid of them, so I snuck them into the attic. When my father died, Marie had been determined to get rid of anything personally connected to my parents. Thankfully, I'd been lucky enough to save some precious mementos.

I rubbed my eyes again. When I realized that today was the twenty-first of August, excitement coursed through me because Dr. Tweedle was supposed to arrive. I flew off the mattress and headed down to the kitchen to get some water so I could wash up. I needed to be presentable today. It was a good thing I had woken up early, giving me enough time to properly get ready. I needed to be presentable today. Quickly, I carried two buckets of water back up to the attic to fill the small tub in the corner. I carefully poured one bucket at a time into the metal tub. When I stuck my toe in the water to test the temperature, it wasn't as warm as I would've liked, so I heated it with my magic.

When I got it to the temperature I wanted, I slid into the tub and proceeded to wash my hair. I tried to move as quickly as possible because I had to help with breakfast. I scrubbed my skin, stood up from the tub, and mentally dried myself off. Once dressed in clean clothes, I dug around in my hidden supply for my mother's ivory combs. I combed all the knots out of my long blonde hair and gazed at my reflection in the hand-held mirror. My violet eyes glittered in anticipation. I was ready to be back at the Jelf Academy.

When I got down to the kitchen, Ellen looked utterly frazzled. "Where have you been? You know Marie doesn't like waiting. Get over here and help me!" she demanded.

I joined her at the stove and began frying the bacon. The delicious smells of the food rose from the frying pan, and I inhaled deeply. I felt my stomach growl as I flipped the bacon, leaning away from the grease splashes. Ellen began making the over-easy eggs, and I split the bacon onto three plates for Marie, Emily, and Preston. As Ellen finished up, I got out a large tray to carry the food upstairs. Ellen flipped the perfect eggs onto the plates as I filled up three glasses of orange juice. With the help of magic, I discretely lifted the full tray. I made my way up the steps, telling myself that soon I would only have to serve them on weekends.

Still balancing the tray with my mind, I raised my other hand to knock on Marie's door.

"Come in," Marie's sharp voice rang through the door.

The room was dark since the green curtains were still drawn. Light flooded the room once I pulled them back, causing Marie, who was still in bed, to cover her eyes.

"Why couldn't you open those slower? You almost blinded me!" Marie complained.

As she shuddered away from the light, I brought her plate to her bedside. Marie's room had a sickening assortment of greens with emerald walls and a lighter green canopy and bedspread. All the furniture, including the fireplace mantel, was a dark brown mahogany. The floor was hardwood of the same rich brown with two decretive green rugs. Marie's room was beautiful, and she also had the largest adjoining bathroom. This room used to be the room she shared with my father, but she had it redone when he passed away.

Marie looked at the food, scrutinizing it. Then, she nodded her head. "Deliver Emily and Preston their breakfast. Then, you can begin making the beds and cleaning the rooms."

I nodded as I picked up the breakfast tray, leaving her room to make my way to Emily. Following the same procedure, I knocked on Emily's door and entered when I was demanded to do so. Emily's room was done in the color red, which always reminded me of blood. Emily delighted in the color, claiming it made her porcelain skin look lighter and her black hair darker. Like her mother, she was still in bed when I entered.

"What if I don't want eggs today?" she sneered.

"I'm sorry, Emily. Ellen makes the decisions for the menus. I'm only in the kitchen to help with what she's preparing," I replied. I held my breath as I waited for angry remarks.

"Drake has many cooks that work for him and a fully stocked kitchen. At every meal, you can choose exactly what you want to eat. It's a shame our kitchen isn't run this way. I'll have to speak to mother about this issue," she said snootily. I breathed a sigh of relief and moved on to Preston's room. Emily was only being difficult because she wanted to brag about Mr. Doyle's cooks.

I knocked on Preston's door and entered his room with my final plate. Preston's room was the blue room of the house. The walls and bedspread were baby blue, and he had a wall-to-wall white carpet on the floor. I was disappointed to see clothes strewn about the room.

Preston was sitting up in his bed when I entered, wearing his mischievous grin. What was I in for today? I couldn't believe how childish he was at fourteen. I placed his breakfast on the table next to his bed, watching his eyes light up.

"Oh goodie, I get to eat eggies for breakfast!" Preston exclaimed.

I tried not to roll my eyes as I exited his room and headed back to Marie's. When she summoned me in, she was almost done with her meal.

"Go to my closet and get out my comfortable blue dress. I have finances and bills to go over all day, so I will most likely be in the office," Marie demanded.

The office that she spoke of used to be my father's, where he used to manage his business, and I hated to see her seated behind that large oak desk. I laid out the outfit she had described and collected her plate. Emily was finished as well, but when I went for Preston's, I was dismayed to find that he'd spilled egg yolk all over his sheets. Now I would have to wash his bedding. He chuckled deviously as he watched my reaction. Then, he leapt from the bed like a wild animal and ran into his bathroom. The door slammed loudly behind him. I sighed to myself as I collected the remaining dishes.

I quickly washed the dishes and passed on breakfast. I knew I would have a lot of work to complete before Dr. Tweedle arrived, whenever that was. He never sent word. Rushing up the stairs, I started with Marie's room. I couldn't use my *quick complete charm* because the door was propped open, and I knew Emily and Preston were still upstairs. Besides, Marie could come up at any time. So, I focused on Dr. Tweedle's arrival, which lifted my spirits as I made Marie's bed and dusted off the furniture. Soon, I was humming to myself as I made Marie's room look perfect.

"What are you so happy about?" Emily's voice interrupted my thoughts. She was standing in the doorway with her arms crossed over her chest.

"Today seems like a good day," I replied. I didn't want to tell her I was returning to school because I knew she'd try to make my day miserable.

"Don't worry. It won't be such a good day when you get to my room," she laughed as she turned to walk down the stairs. What had she done now? I felt my heart sink a little, but I refused to let her get me down. By this evening, I would be far away from here.

I finished up with Marie's room and then took a deep breath as I headed across the hall to Emily's. Emily wasn't joking. She was trying to make my life miserable. She'd been in her closet and thrown every article of clothing she owned on the floor. The worst part was Emily had a walk-in closet, so the clothes were in large mounds around the room. I began picking them up and neatly hanging them back on the hangers. Emily was such an ungrateful person. She had many pretty outfits, yet she threw them around like they were rags. Some of my clothing were rags, yet I hung them up.

It was a little bit before ten o'clock when I finished with Emily's room and moved on to Preston's. The first thing I did was strip his bedding and take it down to be washed. Thankfully, I didn't have to clean the clothes and bedding most of the time. Marie had a few special servants to do that. Sometimes she would assign me the laundry, but I was sure she wouldn't. I returned to Preston's room with another set of sheets and a new comforter. I continued to dust and sweep the room until I was sure it was perfect. I had just swept the last of the dust into the dustpan when I heard the bong of the doorbell echoing throughout the house. Could that be Dr. Tweedle?

I tried not to be overly excited as I dumped the dirt into the trash bin and exited Preston's room. Before I got to the top of the grand staircase, I heard my name being called.

"Jane, come to my office right now," Marie's voice cried. I quickened my steps, not wanting to look so happy.

Marie was seated at the big oak desk facing me when I entered the office. In a chair opposite her was none other than Dr. Tweedle.

"You called for me, ma'am," I said as I bowed to her and walked into the room.

"Can you please explain to me why he is here?" Marie said rudely as she mentioned to Dr. Tweedle.

"Dr. Tweedle's here to collect me. I have to get my school supplies since I start school this week," I replied softly.

"Oh, I almost forgot about that. I really don't see why she has to go back," Marie said, making my heart pound wildly in my chest. Mentally, I would die if I couldn't return to the Jelf Academy.

"You must've seen an improvement in her," Dr. Tweedle suggested.

"Well, Jane does do her work without complaining and seems to be getting things done faster than she used to...."

"You see, my school is making progress with her," Dr. Tweedle replied.

"Yes, I can assume so, but that doesn't change the fact that I'll be planning my daughter's wedding very soon and will need all the help I can get. Jane has volunteered to help with most of the preparations," Marie said icily.

"Jane will return every weekend like last year, and I'm sure she'll work twice as hard," Dr. Tweedle said, glancing at me with a raised eyebrow.

"Yes, ma'am. I'll do everything that you ask of me," I replied, taking Dr. Tweedle's glance as my cue to speak.

Marie sat quietly for a few minutes with a malicious smile. I could see the wheels turning in her head, thinking what the best option would be to make my life awful.

"I'll allow you to return but know this: you'll barely have time to rest. You'll, once again, make up for the work you'd be doing if you were here. I don't want any complaints. Don't give me a reason to regret sending you," Marie said.

"Thank you, ma'am. You won't regret this. I promise," I said, bowing to her.

"In that case, I must take Jane to collect the supplies she'll need for the year," Dr. Tweedle stated as he got to his feet.

"Very well. Be prepared to work hard when you return. If I see any signs of incompetence, I will reconsider," Marie replied, gazing at me with her stone-cold eyes.

I nodded with my eyes downcast and then turned to exit the office. Dr. Tweedle followed me out, but Marie didn't even show us to the door. I quickly rushed to the attic to grab the small suitcases I'd already packed. Then, I joyous came back down the stairs. I tried to suppress my excitement as I threw open the front door. It took everything I had not to sprint out into the brilliant sunshine. I was finally escaping this place, at least for a little while.

4
Return to Jewel Caverns

As soon as we rode down the lane away from the manor, Dr. Tweedle reached into his pocket and extracted an envelope. It was beige with large black letters addressed to me. "Here's your list of school supplies. Of course, we'll be going to Jewel Caverns," Dr. Tweedle stated, handing me the envelope.

I grasped it excitedly. I couldn't wait to see what I would need. Plus, I loved Jewel Caverns, an all-pixie city that was cut into a cave. I had been in awe of seeing it for the first time last year, and I hadn't been there since then. I flipped the letter over in my hand and opened it at the seam.

> *Dear Jane Fitzgerald,*
>
> *I am eager to welcome you back for your second year at the Jelf Academy of Magic. Enclosed is the list of books and items you will need for your classes which begin the last week of August. As headmaster of the Jelf Academy of Magic, I wish you well and anticipate your return.*
>
> *Sincerely,*
> *Dr. Oliver Tweedle*
> *Headmaster.*

I flipped to the next page of the letter, which had the list of school supplies.

School Supplies:

- Restock the 12 astrological gemstones
- Restock any ingredients in your pixie dust case if needed
- Thick protective gloves
- Astrological charts
- Additional materials such as notebooks, pencils, etc.

Books:

- *Mixing Stone Powders Volume II*- Randolf Talc
- *Decoding the Crystal Ball and Other Means of Fortune Telling*- Moon Shadowveil, Master Seer
- *Magical Creatures of the World*- Natalie Tame
- *Ancient Pixies: History and Culture*- Kristina Woodrow

Optional:

- Small pet to keep in your dormitory

I finished looking at the letter and folded it back up into the envelope. I could tell a new class was added by looking at the materials, something revolving around magical creatures. This was definitely going to be an interesting year. I could hardly wait!

When Dr. Tweedle rounded the corner out of the manor's driveway, he instructed me to hold on tightly. Then, he pulled out his pixie dust case from his pocket and grabbed a pinch of pixie dust to use for a *teleportation charm*. I hadn't learned how to make that yet, but I was used to being teleported. I watched as Dr. Tweedle threw the dust into the air. Then, everything went black. I clung to Dr. Tweedle's coat sleeve as I felt the cloud of dust enclose us. My feet felt like they had lifted off the floor, causing me to clasp Dr. Tweedle's sleeve tighter. Soon enough, the feeling went away.

⚘

A humongous wall of rock stood in front of us. I didn't know precisely where the Jewel Caverns were located due to them being hidden from the human world. However, I guessed they had to be somewhere deep in the wilderness. Dr. Tweedle climbed out of the carriage and searched the rock wall until he found the lever that opened the cavern. Once he found the rocky lever, Dr. Tweedle pulled it up and a tunnel opened in the rock before me. Quickly, Dr. Tweedle got back in the carriage and steered us into the opening. We were thrust into blackness again for only a moment before tiny dots of light started to appear in the distance. As we continued down the tunnel, the specks of light became slightly larger until they were floating over our heads.

Floating in the balls of light were small creatures that looked like tiny humans. They had wings and emitted the light that surrounded them. These creatures were called sprites and were typically found in caves, forests, and even underwater. As they brightened the way ahead, we followed them down the tunnel, which grew more expansive as we went along.

Suddenly, we saw a bright light near the end of the tunnel. The new light illuminated the stalactites and stalagmites in the cavern, and I marveled at their forms. Then, the cave opened up further into a big, open chamber. The road we were on spiraled down to the bottom of the mountain, and the ceiling had an opening that let sunlight into the cavern. Along the route, shops were cut into the rock wall, and pixies were shopping for different things.

Dr. Tweedle drove the carriage down the spiraled road.

"I already went to the pixie bank to pick up your allotted kryptos and coodles for your school supplies," Dr. Tweedle said.

"Thank you," I replied, adding the money pouch to my bag. Pixie money consists of kryptos and coodles. Kryptos were in bills like dollars, and they had their worth printed on them. There were three types of coodles: magnus, beezle, and splick, and they were all worth a different value. Silver splicks were the smallest and least valuable. Five splicks equaled one beezle. The beezle was a medium-sized golden coin, and four of them were the same value as a magnus. The magnus was platinum and the largest of the three coins. Five magni equated to a krypto.

Dr. Tweedle steered us to the first shop, *Jewels and Powders,* where different rocks and minerals were sold. It was the place I could get all of the supplies for charms. I climbed down from the carriage and crossed the road with Dr. Tweedle. He helped me by holding the bags of minerals while I added the required amount. I also needed to refill the ingredients in my pixie dust case, a special box that stored all the minerals.

As Dr. Tweedle and I moved around the shop, I looked up and saw a familiar face. Betty Ann Barber had just entered with a man who appeared to be in his early fifties. She flipped her hair over her shoulder, flashing her fake smile in my direction, and started walking toward me. Would she dare to be nasty even with Dr. Tweedle present?

"Hello, Jane," she exclaimed in her fake voice. "It's so good to see you."

"Hello, Betty Ann," I replied smoothly.

The man accompanying her came toward us. He walked through the room as if he owned the place. His clothes were very neat, and I could tell they were expensive. He was well built and had short salt and pepper hair.

"Who is this, sweetheart?" he asked Betty Ann.

"Daddy, this is Jane Fitzgerald," she said in a sickeningly sweet voice, emphasizing my last name.

"Oh, of course," he replied with a glint in his eye, looking down his nose at me. "Hello, Oliver. How have you been?" he said, turning to Dr. Tweedle.

"I've been quite well, Arnold," Dr. Tweedle replied. "Just helping Jane collect her school supplies."

"I didn't know that you were responsible for Jane's school supplies. Doesn't that show favoritism?" Arnold Barber asked.

"I'm not buying her supplies. Jane has a fund set up by her late father. I am merely transporting her to the shops," Dr. Tweedle replied coolly with enough authority that any further discussion on the topic was impossible. Betty Ann continued to stare at me with a nasty smirk on her face.

"Well, that's very generous of your time, Oliver. Betty Ann and I must be on our way if we hope to accomplish all our shopping. Goodbye, Oliver…Jane," he said, nodding to both of us with a smile just as fake as Betty Ann's. As they walked away from us, Dr. Tweedle got in line at the cash register. I put all my items on the counter. The clerk totaled the amount and put the items into paper bags. I paid her the correct number of kryptos and coodles and then headed on our way.

"How about we take a break for some lunch?" Dr. Tweedle suggested.

"That would be showing favoritism, wouldn't it, sir?" I replied.

Dr. Tweedle chuckled, looking over at me. "I know it's not proper to show favoritism among my students, but between you and me, you're one of my favorite students. Your mother was one of my favorites, too, and you remind me so much of her. Don't think me too old a fool not to notice the falsity of the Barbers. Friendly backstabbers, I'd call them; they smile at you while sticking a knife deep into your back. However, the Barbers have made quite a few handsome donations to the Jelf Academy of Magic, so I suppose I should be grateful."

"Yes, sir," I replied, but I couldn't help smiling.

"Okay then, let's pick a place to eat," Dr. Tweedle said, taking the reins.

We stopped at a tiny saloon for lunch, and Dr. Tweedle ordered two ham sandwiches with water.

"I've made arrangements for you to stay at the *Leaf and Lily Inn* again," Dr. Tweedle stated as we waited for our food.

"Thank you. Irene was so wonderful the last time. I would be delighted to see her," I exclaimed. Irene Dimple was the owner of the *Leaf and Lily Inn*. She had attended school with my mother. The last time I had stayed at the inn, Irene had told me a few things about her that I'd never known.

"There's also a surprise awaiting you at the *Leaf and Lily Inn*," Dr. Tweedle replied.

"What is it?" I asked excitedly.

"If I told you, then it wouldn't be a surprise, would it?" Dr. Tweedle chuckled.

Our lunch finally arrived. The food tasted so good after a summer of leftovers. When we finished, we climbed back into the carriage to make our way to our next destination.

"Thank you so much for lunch. I really appreciate it," I told Dr. Tweedle as he steered the carriage toward *Paper and Ink*.

"It's no problem at all, Jane. I hope you enjoyed it," he replied.

"Yes, sir. It was one of the best meals I've had all summer," I said.

Dr. Tweedle parked the carriage and helped me down. We entered *Paper and Ink*, one of the best pixie bookstores with the largest selection of books. Walking around the shop, I picked up the books on my list, pausing briefly to look at other titles. I was always curious to learn more about the pixie world, and I wished I had the funds to purchase additional books.

"Where are we headed next?" I asked Dr. Tweedle.

"Well, we don't have to go to Mr. Murray's clothing store this year since you already have your school uniforms. So, we're going to a shop you've never been to," Dr. Tweedle replied.

Dr. Tweedle drove down toward the bottom of the cavern. We stopped at a shop cut into the rock at the end of the spiraling road. The sign hanging outside the shop was bright green with letters that spelled out *Creature Features*.

Dr. Tweedle held the door open for me. An animal smell overpowered me as soon as I walked through the door. Looking around, I saw all different kinds of cages filled with some of the strangest animals I had ever seen. Some of the animals were bird-like with feathers, and other animals were small with fur reminding me of rodents. But, as I walked around the shop, there was only one animal I recognized: a cactus cat. The only reason I recognized it was because Josefina had gotten one last year for Christmas.

"Before you get carried away with the animals," Dr. Tweedle started, "we only came in here to pick up the protective gloves on your list."

I nodded as he led me over to a wall covered with gloves. I didn't have enough money to even consider purchasing a pet anyway.

"These are some of the best protective gloves they have," Dr. Tweedle said, motioning to a selection of gloves. "You'll need something tough."

I picked a pair of black gloves that went all the way up to my elbow since he had emphasized the need for protection. I wondered why I would need them.

A big man with large muscles was standing behind the counter. His black hair was tied up under a red bandanna, and one of his light blue eyes was covered by an eye patch. Upon further inspection, I saw that he had scars that looked like scratches up and down his arms. I was slightly nervous about walking up to the counter.

"Good afternoon, Pete," Dr. Tweedle said, addressing the man.

"Good day, Dr. Oliver. What can I help you with today? Are you finally interested in some of my dangerous creatures?" he laughed.

Dr. Tweedle laughed back. "No, Pete. I'll have to pass yet again. Only helping a student collect her school supplies today."

I stepped up to the counter and laid down the gloves.

"Now, I know I've only got one good eye, Dr. Oliver, but am I seeing a ghost?" Pete asked.

I blushed, knowing exactly what he meant. A conversation like this had occurred many times since I entered the pixie world. So many people confused me for my mother, and I was slowly becoming used to it. People also tended to believe that I was as talented as my mother, but I wasn't so sure about that.

"No, Pete, this is Rachel's daughter, Jane Fitzgerald," Dr. Tweedle replied.

"I had no idea Rachel had a daughter," he stated.

Pete picked up the gloves I was buying and slipped them into a bag.

"I'll bet you're starting your second year," Pete said with a crooked grin. "I know what you'll need these for."

"Now, that's enough, Pete. You wouldn't want to spoil anything for Miss Fitzgerald," Dr. Tweedle scolded.

"Alright, Dr. Oliver. I'll keep quiet. That'll be ten kryptos and thirty-five coodles."

I dug into the envelope and pulled out the exact amount. Pete gave me the bag with the gloves, and I thanked him.

"Have a good day, Dr. Oliver. Maybe next time you'll be interested in purchasing one of my creatures," Pete called after us as we left the shop.

The air outside smelled ten times fresher than it had in the shop. We crossed over to the carriage, and Dr. Tweedle helped me in.

"That man's always trying to get me to purchase one of his animals," Dr. Tweedle said, shaking his head. "It's been a long day, and we have finished shopping for everything on your list. So, let's get you over to the *Leaf and Lily* so you can have time to relax before dinner. I'm sure you'll want to see your surprise, too."

I nodded in excitement. I wondered what could be waiting for me because I didn't have the faintest idea. Dr. Tweedle steered the carriage back up the road toward the *Leaf and Lily*. The inn was also cut into the rock wall, but it was very homey. Candles glowed in the rock windows, making the inn look inviting. We entered the *Leaf and Lily*, and a small bell above the door tinkled to alert our entrance. Irene Dimple's face lit up when she saw me. Her blonde hair hung in a braid down her back, and her light blue eyes shone with excitement. She glided toward me and embraced me with the biggest hug I had ever received.

"Hello, Jane. How have you been?' Irene exclaimed. "Welcome! I'm glad to have you."

"I'm glad to be staying here, too," I replied as she released me from the hug.

"Come now. Let me show you to your room." She reached for some of my bags.

I followed Irene up the carved stone steps to the second floor. She led me to a room similar to the one I had stayed in before. Instantly I remembered how comfortable the bedding was here, and I couldn't wait to relax.

"I'm preparing dinner in the kitchen. I'll let you know when it's ready. So go ahead and get settled," Irene said as she put down my bag and exited the room.

"Well, Jane, now that we're all done shopping, I'll be on my way. Plus, I'm sure your surprise will keep you occupied." A loud knock sounded at the door. He smiled. "I'm sure that's it right now."

Dr. Tweedle headed to the door to open it. He was almost overtaken by the whirlwind of three familiar figures. I stood in complete shock as I was converged on by Josefina, Miguel, and their older brother, Juan.

"Oh, Jane! I am so happy to see you! I was so worried about you all summer. I had no idea if you were okay. There was no way of finding out," Josefina exclaimed breathlessly as I received the second biggest hug of the day.

"I'm fine," I chuckled at her enthusiasm. Josefina could be so dramatic sometimes, but under the circumstances, it was reasonable. I was number one on the W.A.S.P.'s agenda.

"Jane, I'm going to leave now and let you reunite with your friends. I'll see you at the academy tomorrow," Dr. Tweedle said.

I disentangled myself from my friends and stepped out into the hallway with Dr. Tweedle.

"Thank you so much for taking me today. I appreciate it," I told him.

"You're welcome. I'll see you tomorrow." He waved goodbye to me as he went down the steps. Then, I returned to my room. There was a lot of catching up to do.

5
Meeting at the Leaf and Lily

Josefina nearly leapt on me again when I re-entered the room. "How was your summer? I hope Marie wasn't too awful. Has dreadful Emily started planning her wedding yet? You have to tell me everything!" she exclaimed.

"Josefina, let Jane breathe. I'm sure she'll tell you everything. You've only seen her for a few minutes," Miguel scolded.

"I know, but I've missed her so much," Josefina whined playfully.

"I missed all of you too. I want to tell you everything and hear about what you did as well," I replied.

"Of course, but you go first," Josefina exclaimed.

I was about to begin telling the Martinezes about my horrible summer when a knock sounded on the door. The door slowly opened, revealing Irene. "Oh good, you've been reunited! I'm sorry to interrupt, but dinner's ready in the dining area downstairs," she announced.

"Thank you, Irene. We'll be down in a moment," I replied.

Juan and Miguel headed toward the door. They must've been hungry because they moved quickly down the hall. Josefina and I followed behind them. Josefina reached out to take my hand, and as soon as her hand touched mine, her reaction was immediate.

"My gods, Jane. What has happened to your hands?" Josefina flipped my hand over to examine the palm.

Looking at the palms of my hand, I noticed the rough spots and callouses. Josefina traced them with her fingers and looked up at me, distraught.

"I was about to tell you what I did all summer," I replied. "Marie had me working outside most of the time."

"Outside!" Josefina shouted. "No lady should be working outside!"

"As I told Robert, apparently, I'm no lady," I stated.

"Jane, you know that's not true. Don't worry; I'll give you one of my herbal lotions," Josefina exclaimed as she clasped my hand.

Irene was placing food out on a buffet when we walked in. Juan and Miguel were already seated at the table, so we joined them. As I sat down, I looked around the dining room. At the other tables, pixies were waiting on dinner to be served. A young couple with a toddler was on one side of the room. The parents were entertaining the child by levitating their silverware. I couldn't help but envy the child a bit with the loving parents.

On the other side of the room was an elderly couple. The man was reading a newspaper, and the woman was paging through a magazine. Even though both pixies were reading, I noticed an aura of comfort around them. Instantly, I felt sad because my parents would never experience growing old together.

"So, Jane, you were going to tell us about your summer," Josefina said, pulling me back to the conversation at our table.

"Yes," I replied, grateful that she had interrupted my thoughts. "Marie had me working very hard this summer. She loved assigning me outdoor chores."

"This summer was so hot and humid," Miguel commented.

"I know. It took most of my energy to keep myself cool," I exclaimed.

"That sounds horrible. I couldn't imagine working outside all day," Josefina said.

"The only good thing about the work was that I spent time with Robert. He always manages to make the work fun," I replied.

"Isn't he the boy who works in the horse stable?" Miguel asked. I hadn't told Miguel about Robert, but since Josefina and Miguel could communicate telepathically, I was sure she had told him.

"Yes, but Robert isn't a little boy. He's a year older than us," I pointed out.

"I know Robert is your friend, but you have to be careful. He's a human," Josefina said as she patted my hand.

"I know, but not all humans have evil intentions toward pixies. Robert wouldn't hurt me. Don't forget, I'm half-human, too," I replied in a voice that I knew came out harsher than intended. It upset me that Josefina thought all humans were dangerous. She didn't even know Robert.

"I'm sorry if I upset you, Jane," Josefina said in a soft voice. "I'm just worried. You need to be extra careful since the W.A.S.P. is already hunting you."

"I know. I'm sorry too," I replied as I rose from my seat to go to the buffet. "He's the only friend I have there."

Josefina nodded her head sympathetically as we stood in line. Wonderful smells wafted up and tickled my nose. I had almost forgotten how excellent Irene's cooking was. Her food was even better than Ellen's, so I loaded my plate with turkey, mashed potatoes, and corn. My mouth watered as I also added a homemade biscuit. It was very hard to act like a lady when I hadn't eaten this good in a while.

It wasn't long before Irene stopped at our table to see what we thought about dinner. We all couldn't compliment her enough. The food was delicious.

"All of you remind me what it was like to head back to school," Irene said with a smile. "I couldn't wait to see my friends after being separated from them for the summer."

"It seemed so long since I've seen everyone. Those three months dragged by. I'm so glad to be back," I replied.

"Your mother always felt the same way," Irene said, patting my hand. "She loved the Jelf Academy. It was like her second home. She always hated to leave it."

I was sad Irene couldn't stay at our table and tell me more about my mother. She had other tables and guests to attend to. Maybe there would be a time when I could ask her everything I wanted to know about my mother. Irene was one of the few people I knew that had actually been friends with my mom.

"I'm sorry to ask since I've been out of the pixie world but was Lena ever…. found?" I asked with hesitation. Lena was a friend of the Martinez family who had gone missing last year. The W.A.S.P. was responsible for her disappearance.

"No, the pixie authorities have yet to find anything," Miguel said sadly.

I looked down at my plate, disheartened by the news. It had been three months, and the hope of finding her alive was minimal.

"Lena's alive," Juan stated loudly, talking for the first time since I had seen him.

"Juan, we all know you want to believe that Lena's alive. Believe me, we do too, but it has been three months," Josefina said sadly, gently touching his arm.

"No, I know she's alive. She's not dead. I would know if she was dead!" Juan insisted. "She would never leave me this way without a goodbye."

Josefina and Miguel looked over at me with sad expressions on their faces.

"Lena might be alive somewhere," Miguel said, patting his brother on the shoulder.

Juan finally calmed down. I looked at him sympathetically. Juan had loved Lena very much even though they'd never officially courted. My heart wrenched in my chest to see him this way. I felt sorry I had brought it up. We finished eating in silence and then climbed the stairs to our rooms.

Miguel and Juan were sharing a room, and it had been decided that Josefina would stay with me. We said good night to the boys and closed the door.

"I'm sorry about Juan," I stated. "I would've never mentioned Lena if I had known."

"It's okay, Jane. Juan needs to realize that Lena's gone, as hard as it is to accept. I don't even want to accept it myself, but I have to face reality," Josefina sobbed. "Juan has been so different. Since her disappearance, he's in denial and doesn't want to believe she's gone. I wish he would snap out of it. If he keeps it up, people will think he's crazy."

"No, Josefina, I don't think so. People will know Juan is grieving. They'll understand," I reassured her.

"I sure hope so, but you haven't been around him all summer," Josefina wailed.

I put my arms around her to comfort her. I knew how much she was grieving. I know she felt like she had lost a sister. Josefina stopped crying after a while and pulled back to look me in the face.

"I'm sorry, Jane. Today was supposed to be a happy day. I didn't mean to make you upset or push my problems on you," Josefina said, wiping the tears from her eyes.

"It's okay. Everyone's grief-stricken about Lena. I was insensitive to mention it, but I was hopeful too," I replied.

"Let's talk about something different," Josefina said. "Tell me about Emily's wedding plans? Has she made any yet?"

"That isn't a happy topic either," I replied teasingly.

"Yes, it is!" Josefina insisted. "Once Emily is married, she will move out, and there will be one less person that makes your life miserable."

"That's true," I giggled. That was one of the things I was most excited about concerning Emily's wedding. "They're having the wedding at her fiancé's mansion. Emily brags about it all the time, which is sickening. So far, I haven't done anything concerning the wedding, but they have been finalizing the plans with the groom and his mother."

"What are the in-laws like?" Josefina asked.

"Drake Doyle's handsome. I know he must be wealthy because Emily wouldn't have agreed to the marriage, and neither would Marie. I wouldn't trust him as far as I could throw him, though. He has a mischievous glint in his eyes which makes me weary. As for his mother, I have yet to meet the woman. If she's anything like Marie, this wedding will be my personal nightmare. I can hardly wait," I stated sarcastically.

Josefina laughed at my description. "Don't worry too much about it, Jane. Things are going to be better this year." I could tell she was trying to be positive.

"You are ridiculously optimistic; you know that? The W.A.S.P. wants to find and kill me. My stepfamily hates me. Plus, I'm on the verge of being tormented by this wedding. Only you would say that things are going to be better this year. I guess that's why I'm friends with you. You keep me positive," I replied. "I'm lucky to have a friend like you. You keep me moving ahead and looking for the good things."

Josefina smiled. "That's what friends are for."

"You never really described your summer," I stated, sitting down on the bed.

"It wasn't very exciting. My family was constantly worried about the W.A.S.P. after what happened to the Rodríguezes. My mother was so concerned she hardly ever let us out anywhere. She was also worried about you. I explained about the note found with Lena's family. I only told her because I was so nervous about you. She would like to meet you someday, and, if it weren't for Marie, we would have you over for Christmas this year," Josefina sighed.

Marie would never let me spend Christmas at a friend's house, I thought sadly.

"My summer consisted of being caged in the house, but it was okay. The W.A.S.P. really scares me, and ever since Lena disappeared...." Josefina let the thought hang in the air.

I got up from the bed and reached into my bag for my nightclothes. Then, excusing myself, I went into the bathroom to change.

Once in my nightclothes, I leaned on the sink and splashed water on my face. When I looked up into the mirror, my startling violet eyes stared back at me. Thoughts of Lena clouded my head, and I wondered what else had happened this summer. How many pixies had the W.A.S.P. murdered that I didn't know about yet? Would other classmates be missing when I returned? I shuddered as I pressed a towel against my face. Please, Gods, don't let that be true.

I finished up in the bathroom quickly and tried to push the terrifying thoughts from my head. When I re-entered the bedroom, Josefina was already in her nightclothes and under the covers. She looked up at me and smiled weakly.

"I'm sorry I brought up Lena again. I can't help thinking about her," she said, looking down at the comforter.

"That's okay because I can't either. It would be stupid for us to forget that she's gone," I replied. "We should get some sleep, though. Tomorrow's the first day of our second year."

Josefina nodded in agreement. I climbed into the other bed and reached over to lower the goblin fire lamp on the table between the beds.

"Good night, Jane," Josefina mumbled into the darkness.

"Good night. I'm so glad that you're staying with me at the *Leaf and Lily*. It was nice to see you a day early," I replied.

I rolled onto my side and focused on drifting off to sleep.

6

THE GIRLS

I WAS RUNNING AS fast as my legs could carry me. My breath came in short gasps as I pushed myself to go faster. I knew something was closing in on me. Beads of sweat ran down my face, and my hair felt like it was soaking wet. Branches from trees smacked me in the face, and I realized I had entered the woods. I swatted them away from me as I continued to run.

As I gazed about my surroundings, I felt the familiar eerie feeling move into my chest. The woods seemed so normal. Suddenly, I realized I was in the woods outside the manor. Whatever was chasing me was getting closer, and I tried to pump my legs even harder. I was flying through the underbrush, but it didn't seem like I was getting away. Suddenly, my foot became entangled in sharp branches on the forest floor. My upper body was still in motion, and I felt myself propel forward onto the ground. My whole body hurt from the impact. I struggled to get back to my feet. By the time I rolled over, it was already too late.

As a figure in a dark hooded robe approached me, I felt a chill down my spine. I tried pushing backward to crawl away, but he converged on me, grabbing hold of my legs. I tried to kick, but he had such a firm grip. The hooded figure crawled up my body until he was pinning my arms. His hand reached up toward the hood as if he would pull it off and reveal himself to me. When the hand touched the hood, I braced myself. Who was underneath? Why did he stir such fear in me?

All of a sudden, I heard my name being called. It sounded like Josefina. I felt something roughly shake my shoulders, and I blinked in surprise. When I opened my eyes, Josefina stood above me, light streaming in from the window. I reached up to rub my eyes. The dark figure was gone.

"Jane, are you okay?" Josefina asked. "You were breathing heavily and moaning in your sleep."

I sat up and looked at her concerned face. "It was just a dream. I'm fine," I said, smiling to reassure her.

Josefina looked doubtful, but soon her expression faded into a smile. "You're going to want to get out of bed if you don't want to miss the carriage to the Jelf Academy."

I quickly pulled off the covers. Hopping out of bed, I grabbed my school uniform and headed to the bathroom. I hurried to wash and dress. I tried my best to suppress the dream I had just woken up from. Why were they chasing me? Why did I feel so afraid? Did the dream mean anything at all? I shook my head and splashed water on my face. Then, putting on my purple school uniform, I glanced at myself in the mirror and nodded my approval.

As I exited the bathroom, Josefina entered it. I quickly set to work getting all my belongings together. I neatly put all my books in my bag and double-checked the room for any other items. My clothes were already packed in the other small bag I had brought, so I put both bags near the door. Once Josefina was finished in the bathroom, we went down to breakfast.

Juan and Miguel were already sitting at a table and helping themselves to the breakfast buffet. The food smelled delicious. My stomach rumbled in response. Josefina and I went over to the buffet and piled our plates with pancakes, bacon, and smoked sausage. I poured maple syrup over all of it and sat next to Miguel.

"There you girls are. We wondered when you'd be down for breakfast," Miguel said.

"We can't help it. We need to be presentable for our first day of school," Josefina replied.

"That's silly. Everyone remembers what you looked like last year," Miguel stated, shaking his head.

"That may be, but we need to intimidate the new first years," Josefina joked.

We finished our breakfast and went to collect our belongings. As I picked up my bags, a noise startled me. A cat with shimmering fur hopped through the window and padded over to Josefina.

"Oh, Coco, my girl. I was afraid you wouldn't return on time," Josefina cooed as she bent down to pick the cat up.

Coco was Josefina's cactus cat, and I wondered where she'd gotten to. I reached over to let Coco smell my fingers before scratching behind her ears. "Hi, Coco. Where have you been?" I asked.

"I let her out to hunt and explore. I figured she wouldn't like to be caged all day. I'll have to put her in the cage for the trip," Josefina responded. She lowered Coco into the cat-sized cage and closed the door.

"Are you ready to go?" I asked, and she nodded.

We picked up all the bags, and Josefina double-checked the room before heading downstairs. Juan, Miguel, and Irene were waiting at the bottom of the stairs. The boys had their bags stacked next to the door, ready to go for the carriage. Josefina and I placed ours next to theirs.

"I bet you're very excited to begin your second year. I was always anxious to get back to school when I was your age," Irene exclaimed. She smiled at me as she patted my shoulder.

"Yes," I replied. "Thanks for everything."

Dragon Scales

Miguel, who had been watching the front window, announced that our carriage had arrived. Juan picked up two of our suitcases and headed outside to put them into the carriage. Miguel began helping as well. As I bent down to pick up my smallest bag, I noticed that all the Martinez were already outside. I could hear Coco's snarls and hisses as her cage was jostled about.

Irene touched my arm again. I turned to look at her and saw concern written over her face. "Be careful, Jane," Irene told me. "There's been an increase of W.A.S.P. attacks this summer. I worry about you, especially since you live among humans."

"I'll be fine, Irene," I insisted. "You should be careful too." Irene's husband was taken by the W.A.S.P. many years ago, so I refrained from telling her about the W.A.S.P.'s threat.

"Don't worry about me, dear. I hardly ever leave the Jewel Caverns. I'll be safe here." She pulled me in for a hug. "Good luck at school this year. I hope to see you soon."

"I'll always stay here when I'm in Jewel Caverns. I wouldn't want to stay anywhere else," I told her, backing out of her hug. "Goodbye, Irene."

I gave her one last look before I walked out the door to the carriage. The Martinezes were already inside, and I sat on the seat next to Josefina. Miguel was across from her, looking very angry and annoyed. I noticed he was holding his thumb and pressing a tissue against it. I gave them a puzzled stare.

"Miguel hates Coco," Josefina huffed.

"Your damn cat stabbed my thumb," Miguel said roughly, pulling away the tissue to expose a pinprick oozing blood.

"You made her nervous because you shook her cage. Cactus cats become defensive when they're distressed," Josefina muttered.

"Well, it really hurts," Miguel said, pressing the tissue back on the wound.

"I know. You've been projecting the pain," Josefina sighed.

"You can feel his pain?" I asked Josefina surprised. I thought twins could only exchange thoughts, not feelings.

"Yes, we know when each other is in pain. Sometimes we subconsciously transmit our emotions or feelings to each other. Miguel isn't purposely trying to hurt me. It just happens in extreme situations. It's easier to block Miguel from speaking inside my head than it is to block how he's feeling," Josefina explained.

"I don't know how Josefina feels every second of the day, but if it's an intense feeling, then I'll know," Miguel replied.

I nodded my head in awe. It was amazing what pixie twins were capable of.

"When we were babies, if Miguel was upset and crying, I would cry, too, just because I knew he was in distress. We drove our mother crazy. Juan was only three when we were born, so she had three small children to take care of," Josefina said. She looked toward Juan, but he was staring out the window. He hadn't said much since I had arrived yesterday. Juan was never this quiet.

A silence lapsed over the carriage, and we all looked out the windows at the ground below. The winged white horses pulling the carriage were swiftly gliding over the landscape.

Soon, we were landing in a meadow full of other winged horses and carriages. Other students were milling around between the carriages. Everyone seemed excited to see their friends. When our carriage landed, Josefina and I hopped out and began pulling the luggage out of the back. Miguel joined us, still holding the tissue to his thumb.

"You can grab your cat this time," Miguel stated.

Josefina reached up and gently pulled Coco's cage from the carriage. The cat purred softly and rubbed Josefina's hand. Miguel sighed in aspiration and shook his head. I glanced around to see if Juan had gotten out. He had, and I noticed him scanning the field as if he were searching for someone, searching for Lena. Josefina and Miguel caught my gaze and slowly shook their heads. The three of us unloaded the bags while Juan stood looking around the open meadow. After some time, he joined us at the back of the carriage, waiting for the cloud to drop.

Suddenly, a loud voice to the right called Josefina's name. She turned to face the noise, my gaze following hers. Three plump-faced girls were approaching us. The one in the middle had pale blonde hair while the other two were brunettes, their hair almost the same color as chocolate. At first, I had thought they were all related, but as they drew closer, I realized the only similarity was their round faces.

"Hello, Josefina," the middle girl said.

"Hi, Marley," Josefina replied with a small smile.

"Are you going to introduce us?" she asked, turning to me.

"This is my friend, Jane. Jane, meet Marley Thornton, Candi Vaughn, and Bellony Sandhu," Josefina said, pointing to the blonde first and then the two brunettes. "They're my neighbors and the girls I grew up with. This is their first year."

"We aren't just neighbors. We're best friends," Marley gushed in a fake-sounding voice.

"We've known Josefina since she moved onto our street. That was right after your father discovered the gem mine, right?" Candi said in a know-it-all voice.

I smiled warmly at them, but a strange feeling came over me. I didn't know why, but they seemed a little snobby. I tried to press that thought away because, after all, these were Josefina's childhood friends.

"Who are you going to share a room with?" Marley asked, looking hard at Josefina.

"Well, I was going to share with Jane again. Besides, the school likes you to share a room with someone from your year," Josefina said softly.

"I guess one of us will be on the outs," the brunette named Bellony said.

"I'm sorry," Josefina replied. She glanced down at her hands.

Miguel motioned to the sky before anyone could say anything else, and we watched as the cloud descended. A line began to form, so we picked up our belongings. Marley, Candi, and Bellony followed the Martinezes, constantly chattering away about their excitement to start the Jelf Academy.

"I'm so happy to be away from home," Candi said. "My mother's absolutely unbearable. Ever since my dad left on a business trip, my mom has been so controlling."

"I know. My parents barely let me out of the house this summer. All they could talk about was the stupid W.A.S.P.," Marley complained.

I couldn't believe what I was hearing. They didn't sound worried about the W.A.S.P. at all. Hadn't they heard about the deaths that had occurred?

Soon, it was our turn to board the cloud. Riding the cloud was one of the weirdest sensations I'd ever experienced. The cloud felt light and springy under my feet. Josefina's friends followed us onto the cloud and immediately began bouncing around.

"Wow, it's so soft and bouncy," Marley said, jumping up and down.

"Yes, this is fun," Bellony replied, also starting to bounce as the cloud ascended into the air.

Their bouncing made me nervous. I was trying to keep my balance as they continued to cause the whole cloud to vibrate. I was relieved when we finally made it to the top, and I was able to hop off it.

In front of me lay the school with its large white turrets capped with blue shingles. It looked like a fairy tale castle. Every time I looked upon it, I felt my heart soar.

"Oh, I expected it to be so much larger," sighed Candi in a very dull voice.

I turned around. Candi had her arms crossed and a grimace

on her face. In fact, Marley and Bellony looked like they agreed with her.

"It's much bigger inside," Josefina said optimistically. "Wait until you see the dining hall."

The Jelf Academy was one of the biggest buildings I had ever seen. What had they expected? Our group trudged toward the school. Soon, instead of clouds, we were walking on the grass that surrounded the school. Flowers and trees were planted around the grounds. A barn-like structure stood to the left. The white double doors swung open before us, revealing the entrance hall. The large staircase swept upward, and standing on the stairs was Dr. Tweedle.

"Good morning, students," he greeted. "All first-year students should report to the dining hall to receive their schedules and the rules. All other students can report to the fourth floor to receive room assignments and schedules. Help the first-year students find the classrooms throughout your day."

"I'll see you later," Josefina told Marley, Bellony, and Candi as they headed toward the dining hall. I waved at them, but they didn't acknowledge me. Instead, they kept walking toward the dining hall, talking to each other.

Josefina and I climbed the stairs to the fourth floor. The first-year rooms started in the east wing on the third floor and continued onto the fourth floor. Josefina and I would probably be placed on the fifth floor since those rooms were for second years. When we were far enough up the stairs, I turned to Josefina.

"It was nice to finally meet your childhood friends. You didn't talk about them too much last year," I said.

"I know. They're just friends I spend time with occasionally. I've known them since I was eight years old when we moved into our new house," Josefina replied.

"According to Marley, you're the best of friends," I chuckled.

"Marley thinks everyone's her best friend," Josefina stated.

We reached the fourth floor and saw a line going up to a desk with Mr. Withermyer behind it. Mr. Withermyer was the Charms teacher, and even though he was the youngest teacher, he was also the most callous. I knew he didn't like me, but I didn't know why. Perhaps, it was because I was half-human, or it had something to do with my mother.

The line moved up, and we came closer to Mr. Withermyer. He was wearing a black jacket that was as dark as his hair. He always seemed to have a scowl on his face. I had never seen him smile. I would consider him handsome if he didn't always look so menacing. As I glanced at him, he happened to look up, and his green eyes caught mine. He held my gaze, and it felt like his eyes were burning into me. I could've sworn I saw his face relax for a second, but then he scowled again. I quickly looked down. The line moved up again, and soon we were in front of Mr. Withermyer.

"Miss Martinez and Miss Fitzgerald," Mr. Withermyer said curtly. He flipped through the papers in front of him and pulled out two envelopes with our names on them. "In these envelopes are your schedules. I assume you want to share a room again."

"Yes, sir," Josefina replied as we each took our envelopes.

Mr. Withermyer wrote our names on a sheet next to a room number. "Your room number is 224," he told us. "You may leave any personal items there, but don't be late for class."

We thanked him and headed to our room. Instead of having a key, the door had a panel that scanned and memorized your handprint. We arrived at our room. I placed my hand on the panel and felt a pinch. Suddenly, I heard a voice coming from the door.

"Jane Fitzgerald, 5'2", 110 pounds, violet eyes, blonde hair, English and Polish descent, a second-year student at the Jelf Academy, and granted access to this room for the year."

When the voice finished talking, Josefina stepped up. When the panel pinched her, she jumped backward, and the voice began speaking again.

"Josefina Martinez, 5'6", 120 pounds, brown eyes, black hair, of Mexican descent, a second-year student at the Jelf Academy, and granted access to this room for the year."

The door slid open. The room had a soft white carpet on the floor, and the walls were a lilac color. It was similar to the one we had last year. Through a doorway on the left, we had a private bathroom. I picked one of the beds, tossing my bags onto it. Josefina placed Coco's cage on the ground and opened the latch. Coco sprung free of her confinement, stretching leisurely before hopping onto Josefina's bed.

I sat on my bed and opened the envelope Mr. Withermyer had given me. Inside was a welcome back letter written by Dr. Tweedle. Behind it was a paper that showed my class schedule.

Charms- 8:00 a.m.-8:55 a.m.
History of Pixies- 9:00 a.m.-9:55 a.m.
Zodiac Signs- 10:00 a.m.-10:55 a.m.
Lunch- 11:00 a.m.-12:30 p.m.
Magical Creatures- 12:35 p.m.-1:30 p.m.
Earth Catastrophes- 1:35 p.m.-2:30 p.m.
Predicting the Future- 2:35 p.m.-3:30 p.m.

I sighed when I saw that Charms was my first class. What an awful way to start the day. At least I got to get it out of the way. The next class wasn't any better. History of Pixies was taught by Mr. Collyworth, the most boring teacher at the Jelf Academy. Well, my mornings were going to be stressful and dull.

"Do we have the same schedule?" Josefina asked as she got up from her bed.

"Charms is going to be brutal first thing in the morning. Then, I have a History of Pixies," I replied.

"I don't have History of Pixies as my next class," Josefina frowned as she sat down beside me. "I have Earth Catastrophes after Charms."

We exchanged schedules with each other. I saw that Josefina had Charms first, but she didn't have History of Pixies next. Instead, she had it while I had Predicting the Future. We had Zodiac Signs and Magical Creatures together, but she had Predicting the Future when I had Earth Catastrophes. I wondered what Miguel's schedule looked like.

"I don't like that our schedules aren't the same," Josefina said, passing mine back to me.

"Me too," I replied.

"Let me ask Miguel about his schedule before heading to Charms," Josefina said.

She sat quietly as she contacted Miguel.

"He has Charms with us and History of Pixies with you," Josefina said after a few minutes. "He doesn't have Zodiac Signs with us or Earth Catastrophes. We all have Magical Creatures together. He said he got a new roommate, but we'll have to discuss it at lunch."

I glanced at the pixie clock on the night table and jumped off the bed. Josefina taught me how to read the clock last year. The earth rotated around the sun, and the shadow on the planet showed what time it was. It was actually more accurate than a human clock.

Josefina and I left our room, heading for the second floor in the west wing. Today's classes were only supposed to be introductions to the courses.

Once Josefina and I made it to the Charms classroom, we fell silent before walking into the room. Mr. Withermyer hated talking and would punish anyone who did. So we quietly took our seats. Mr. Withermyer sat at his brown desk in the front corner of the room. He looked around, analyzing the class. His green eyes happened to catch mine as they had done earlier. I looked down right away.

As the bell rang, he got up from his desk, crossing the room to close the door. Before he could, Betty Ann and Miguel came into the room. Mr. Withermyer didn't even glance at Betty Ann, but he scowled at Miguel. Miguel quickly plopped down beside Josefina. Mr. Withermyer cleared his throat once he shut the door.

"Good morning, class. For those of you who thought the first year of Charms was difficult, you better prepare yourself. This is a class where you will have to work hard and study. So, if you were planning on slacking, change your mind this minute. Charms are fundamental for pixies as they are part of our everyday life."

Mr. Withermyer began pacing the front of the room.

"The ability to create and use charms is what makes us pixies. If you cannot do this, you are no better than humans." His eyes glanced toward me, making my face flush. Mr. Withermyer was obviously insulting me. I narrowed my eyes at him, knowing he was trying to insult me.

"Tomorrow, you will have a pre-test on a few charms you learned last year. I am going to hand out a study guide with the name of each charm for you to go over. Be thankful I am even doing this for you. So, you can look up these charms for the remainder of the class and familiarize yourself with them again. When the bell rings, you are dismissed."

Silently, I flipped open my old Charms book and started looking up each charm. Mr. Withermyer was known for giving us tasks without a full explanation because he wanted us to figure them out on our own. Although I usually figured out how to complete each charm, I hated being under pressure. I hadn't practiced any charms over the summer, so I dreaded the pre-test. Before I knew it, the bell rang. I collected my books and threw them into my bag.

Miguel was waiting for me as I left the classroom. "We have History of Pixies together. Unfortunately, Josefina has to go to Earth Catastrophes," Miguel stated.

"I know," I replied.

"Josefina thinks we were split up in History because I helped her too much last year," Miguel laughed.

"It's definitely going to be strange to have classes without the both of you," I sighed.

We made our way to the History of Pixies classroom, located on the first floor of the west wing. Miguel wanted to sit in the front of the class, so I reluctantly followed. Miguel loved this class, which I couldn't understand.

Mr. Collyworth strode into the classroom wearing brown pants and a tweed jacket. He had on his typical round spectacles.

"Good morning, class," he said very slowly. "This is History of Pixies, and as second-year students, we will be learning about ancient pixies. We will discuss the first pixies who were nomadic, but we were the first to create civilizations in Mesopotamia and Egypt. We will also discuss pixie religion and where it originated from. I will assign you a god or goddess when we get to that section. You will do a report on them and share some of their mythological stories with the class," Mr. Collyworth stated.

"We have so much to go over this year. I am sure you will all be very interested in the origins of our pixie society. I would like you to look over the first chapter in your books tonight. Nomadic pixies had so much to discover about the world, and we will discuss how the first charms were discovered," Mr. Collyworth droned on.

Even though Mr. Collyworth had a very nasally voice and talked really slowly, I felt a glimmer of hope. Learning about ancient pixies and their culture interested me. Maybe this year, I wouldn't feel compelled to fall asleep.

"It's a shame we don't have time to begin a lecture today, so prepare for tomorrow," Mr. Collyworth said just as the bell rang.

I stuffed my books in my bag and pulled out my schedule to see what I had next. At ten o'clock was Zodiac signs, which was with Josefina but not Miguel. As we were about to part ways, I said goodbye to him and headed toward the grand staircase. Zodiac Signs was on the third floor, which meant I had to fight my way past hordes of students on the stairs before turning into the west wing.

Suddenly, I thought I had heard my name. It was faint, and I wasn't sure if I had heard correctly. Glancing around, my eyes made contact with Taylor Miller…

"Hello, Jane. How have you been?" Taylor asked me in the same wispy voice that had called my name.

Taylor Miller had untamable blonde hair that frizzed out in every direction and always had on shabby clothes. She had pretty blue eyes that were always hidden behind square glasses. Everyone in our class thought she was strange, but she wasn't. Taylor was extremely smart but so shy. I thought Taylor was sweet and saw her as a vulnerable little sister who needed protection.

"I'm fine. How was your summer?" I asked her.

"Oh, it was just alright," she said quietly. "Are you heading to Zodiac Signs?"

"Yes. Josefina is in that class too," I replied.

"It's good to know someone. At least you're not in my Charms class," Taylor said.

"Taylor, I said I was sorry about last year. I didn't know my charm would cause that reaction. I didn't even want to use my charm on you," I apologized.

Taylor smiled at me, a rare occurrence for her. "It's okay, Jane. I was just joking."

I smiled back at her, startled by the thought of Taylor joking. We climbed the next set of steps to the third floor and entered the Zodiac classroom. Josefina was already seated, so I sat down next to her. Taylor took the seat on the other side of me.

"Hi, Taylor," Josefina greeted brightly.

The desks in the room were arranged in a circle and had star charts on the walls. The ceiling was black with tiny pinpoints of white light. Without the light, the ceiling turned into the night sky.

Mrs. Harris walked into the classroom and entered the center of the circle of desks. She had her bright red hair pinned up and wore a white dress with a yellow flower pattern. She spun around the circle, looking at each student with her cornflower blue eyes.

"Good morning, class. Welcome to your second year of Zodiac Signs. This year, we will look at comparisons between compatibility. This class explains how to connect with each other depending on their signs. Some combinations work better than others. By tomorrow, I would like you to familiarize yourself with the zodiac. That will be all for today. As soon as the bell rings, you can all be dismissed for lunch."

I noticed Taylor pulling out her Zodiac book from last year and started to flip through it. I pulled out my book as well and began looking over the zodiac.

"I'm going to drop my books off in our room," Josefina said to me at the end of class.

"All right. I'll follow you," I replied, slinging my bag over my shoulder.

The Jelf Academy gave students an hour and a half for lunch. We had time to switch our morning books out for our afternoon ones, eat lunch, socialize with friends, or relax.

The dining hall greeted us with the loud buzz of many voices. The tables were filling up while Josefina and I worked our way toward the buffet.

"Miguel already saved us seats," Josefina told me.

After we got our food, Josefina led me to Miguel. Surprisingly, Juan was also at the table. He looked even more depressed than yesterday. Juan continued to pick at his sandwich as we took our seats.

"How were your classes? I have hardly seen you today," Josefina asked Miguel.

"They were fine. History of Pixies is going to be awesome this year! We are learning about ancient pixies and their cultures. Sorry to spoil it for you, Josefina," he laughed as she rolled her eyes at him.

"At least we have Magical Creatures class together after lunch and…." Josefina was cut off by a loud voice behind us.

"Oh gods, Josefina! You better have saved us a seat."

I turned around to see Marley flanked by Bellony and Candi. I had almost forgotten Josefina's childhood friends.

"Yes, you can sit with us," Josefina replied.

Marley squeezed rudely into the small space between Josefina and me while Candi squeezed in on the other side. Bellony must have realized she wasn't going to fit on this side of the table, so she sat next to Juan on the other side. This caused Juan to glance up from his sandwich.

"Where is Lena going to sit?" he mumbled.

I looked sympathetically toward him. Josefina reached across the table to touch his hand. Juan kept glancing at Bellony as she began to eat her lunch. Juan shook off Josefina's hand, grabbed his tray, and stalked away from our table. We watched him return his tray and leave the dining hall.

"Doesn't he know that Lena is dead?" Candi asked callously.

"Juan's having a difficult time with Lena's disappearance. Since she hasn't been found, he still has hope. He was really in love with her," Josefina explained.

"There's no way Lena's alive. The W.A.S.P. never keeps anyone alive," Marley shrugged. Didn't they know how close the Martinezes were to Lena? Why would they talk about her like that?

"We like to remain hopeful," Miguel said, glaring down the table. He got up and took his tray. "I'll see you in Magical Creatures," he said to Josefina and me.

Josefina scooted down into Miguel's spot giving me more room since I had been squeezed like a sardine between Marley and Candi.

"So, Josefina, how are classes? I bet second-year classes are more interesting," Bellony asked excitedly.

"It's hard to say since it's only the first day," Josefina replied.

"Oh, my gods, History of Pixies makes me want to die. I can't survive an hour in that class every day," Marley gushed.

"Since we're in that class together, we should start passing notes," Candi said.

"American pixie class was pretty boring," Josefina agreed.

"I found some of the topics fascinating," I said.

"Really?" Marley sighed. "I don't think there will ever be anything interesting about that class."

"Mr. Collyworth just drones on and on. Why do we need to know about pixie history anyway?" Candi complained.

"I don't know why…." I started but was cut off mid-sentence by Marley.

"Well, at least this food's okay," she stated.

I looked down at my sandwich and continued eating. Marley, Candi, and Bellony described their first three classes, but they only addressed Josefina. All their questions were explicitly directed toward her.

"You'll have to help us study since you already took these classes. Oh, and you must warn us about the different teachers," Marley demanded.

I looked up at the clock on the wall and saw that lunch was almost over. However, I still needed to get my books for the second half of the day, so I stood up.

"Lunch is almost over," I announced, but no one looked up. I stepped over the bench and away from the table. Josefina finally looked up at me.

"Is lunch over already? You don't have to wait for me, Jane. I'll just meet you at the Magical Creatures classroom. I believe it's on the right side of the building," Josefina replied.

"Okay, I'll see you out there," I said, turning away from the table. While I walked away, I heard their conversation resume, and Marley laughed loudly.

7
It is Not Okay to be Different

The Magical Creatures classroom was located on the lawn to the right side of the building as you exited the front doors. Trees surrounded a padlocked area, and rows of desks faced the fence under the trees. Miguel was already there, so I slid into a chair next to his.

"Where's Josefina?" he asked quizzically.

"She's finishing up her lunch with Marley, Candi, and Bellony," I replied

Miguel made a face. "Those three," he mumbled, shaking his head. "There's something I can't stand about them."

I didn't reply. I didn't know the three girls well enough to agree with him, but I did think some of the things they said had been rude.

I looked around and saw Mrs. Rowley crossing the lawn toward us. She stopped in front of the fence, turning towards the desks. "I'll wait just a few more minutes before I start," she said. I was surprised to see that Mrs. Rowley taught Magical Creatures as well as Gemstones 101. She was a small older woman with gray hair and green eyes. I couldn't imagine her handling magical creatures. As usual, Betty Ann arrived late. She walked across the lawn and plopped down in the back of the classroom. I sighed inwardly. Where was Josefina?

"Alright, class, I think it is about time to begin," Mrs. Rowley stated. "In this class, as the name suggests, we will be studying magical creatures. This padlock behind me will hold whatever animal we are studying, so we can observe the real creature instead of looking at artistic pictures," Mrs. Rowley paused, looking toward the back of the classroom. Josefina was coming up the aisle of chairs, and she slid into the seat behind me. "So glad you could join us, Miss Martinez," Mrs. Rowley said.

"Sorry, ma'am," Josefina quickly muttered.

"What was I saying? Oh, yes. We'll be able to study real animals. Some will be safe to interact with, while others won't be. Sometime during the year, we'll be doing a very exciting project, but I don't want to reveal too much just yet. The deliveries I'm expecting will determine when we will start.

"Tonight, you can page through your book to get an idea about what kind of magical creatures we will be studying. I'm so glad to see all of you again. I hope this class is one all of you will enjoy. You may read until the bell. Have a nice evening."

I began looking through my Magical Creatures book. Some of the animals were so fantastical I could hardly believe they existed in real life. I could already tell this class was going to be my favorite. Mrs. Rowley was one of my favorite teachers, so I was glad she was the one who taught the class.

Miguel and I got up from our seats when the bell rang and turned to face Josefina.

"I can't believe you were late," Miguel said.

"Only a little bit," Josefina said, shaking him off. "Besides, it's the only time I've ever been late."

"I'm on my way to Earth Catastrophes," I said.

"We both have Predicting the Future," Miguel said.

"Okay, I'll see you back in the room after class," Josefina said sadly.

I walked in the opposite direction of the twins to get to Earth Catastrophes. It was on the opposite side of the school under a large willow tree. I was grateful to see Taylor sitting beneath the tree when I arrived. I slid into the seat next to her.

"Hello, again," Taylor said in her wispy voice. Our Earth Catastrophes book from last year was on the desk in front of her. It was opened to section two. Mr. Laruse said we would use the book for the next three years. I pulled mine out of my bag and placed it on my desk.

"I see that you're already reading," I commented.

"Actually, I'm rereading," Taylor replied. "I read over the summer."

"I wish I could've had time to read," I laughed.

"You're not making fun of me, are you, Jane?" Taylor asked with a sad expression on her face.

"Of course not, Taylor. I wish I had the free time. Unfortunately, my stepmother wouldn't allow it," I replied.

"That's strange. Why wouldn't she want you to read your schoolbooks?" Taylor asked.

"My stepmother doesn't even know I attend a pixie school. She thinks she's sending me away to an etiquette school. She would throw me out of the house if she knew the truth," I said.

"Your stepmother isn't a pixie?" Taylor asked, confused.

"No, she's human," I stated.

"Jane, I had no idea that you lived with humans. That's so dangerous! I mean, I knew your father was human, but I didn't realize your stepmother was one as well," Taylor exclaimed. "So, you had no idea you were a pixie until you came here?"

"Not until Dr. Tweedle came to get me. I always knew I had

magic, but I thought I was an abomination. I didn't know there were so many others like me," I replied.

"Wow, Jane, I didn't know. Since you were so good at charms, I just thought someone had been training you," Taylor stated.

"I'm not that good. Last year was beginner's luck," I chuckled.

Our conversation was interrupted by Mr. Laruse running across the lawn. His blonde tufts of hair stood out on both sides of his balding head as the papers he carried blew out of his hands. He had to turn around to pick them up. When Mr. Laruse finally stood in front of the class, he smoothed back his hair and laid the papers on his desk.

"Good afternoon, class. Welcome to Earth Catastrophes. I'm sure you're all excited about your first day at the Jelf Academy. We are going to start with chapter one. I'm glad you all found the outdoor classroom. Most first-year students have difficulty with that."

Taylor and I looked at each other in confusion. Then, Taylor raised her hand. "Excuse me, Mr. Laruse. This is a second-year class."

He paused to glance around the classroom. "Why yes, it is. I wondered why some of you looked so familiar," Mr. Laruse chuckled. "I am so sorry for the confusion. We'll start in the book's second section. Earth Catastrophes class includes more than weather events. It's also comprised of other disasters that can occur on the Earth. Does everyone know what else we will be predicting?"

Taylor's hand shot in the air. "Predicting forest fires, earthquakes, volcanic eruptions, and tidal waves," she recited.

Mr. Laruse nodded his head. "Yes, those and so much more," he replied. "Look through section two of the book to get an idea. This year's going to be great! You won't believe the number of dangerous things we can predict! You can save lives when you know how to predict a disaster!" he said excitedly.

Mr. Laruse went on about the importance of his class until the bell rang.

"I'll see you all tomorrow," he said, dismissing us.

I collected my supplies. "Where are you headed next?" I asked Taylor.

"I have Predicting the Future," she replied.

"Me too. Do you mind if I walk with you?" I asked.

"No, of course not."

We crossed the lawn together and entered through the large white front doors. The Predicting the Future classroom was on the second floor in the east wing. As we walked down the hall, I heard a familiar laugh. I looked up. My stomach dropped as soon as I spied Thomas Whitmore at the end of the hallway. I had met Thomas last year in this very hallway. At the time, he had seemed sweet and sincere. He had blonde hair, beautiful blue eyes, and was well built. I had thought he was someone special, but then I found out he was courting Betty Ann.

Last year, Thomas and Betty Ann had pulled a terrible prank on me. He said he wanted to take me to the Harvest Festival, the fall dance at the Jelf Academy. At the dance, Thomas and Betty Ann publicly humiliated me. Now, I couldn't stand the sight of him.

Luckily, I was able to duck into the Predicting the Future classroom before he glanced my way. The classroom was circular and stepped like a theater. Down in the center of the room was a crystal ball, and instead of desks with chairs, there were pillows to sit on. Taylor and I picked a row closer to the front and sat down. Other students started to fill the room. I looked behind me to see who else was in class. A boy named Brian Nickles and a girl named Lacey Stevenson were in the class. Both of them had been in my Charms class last year. Unfortunately, Betty Ann was also in this class and was sitting down with her group of friends at the back of the room.

Suddenly, the lights in the room dimmed, and a fog began to appear. Behind the crystal ball, the beaded curtains began to sway. Soon, Ms. Crescent stepped out from behind them. Ms. Crescent had long brown hair and green eyes. She wore lots of beads and medallions around her neck and a ring on every finger. Around her waist was a shawl covered in coins, and when she walked, they rattled. Ms. Crescent reminded me of a gypsy.

"Good afternoon, class. This will be a wonderful school year," Ms. Crescent said in her wispy voice. "Predicting the Future will become more important considering what has been happening recently. Predicting the future correctly could mean life or death," she said dramatically, throwing one hand over her forehead.

"Knowing what to avoid is just as good of a defense as knowing how to create protective charms. Charms cannot prevent death but knowing how to predict the future can. The things I will teach you will be very valuable."

Ms. Crescent spun through the fog dramatically, glancing around the lecture hall. The charms on her wrist made little tinkling noises. "This week, we will review all the predicting tactics you learned last year, including tarot cards, palm reading, and auras. In the time remaining, you can practice palm reading with a partner. If anyone needs my assistance, I will be in my office. Have a wonderful evening, and be prepared for tomorrow," Turning on her heel, she quickly disappeared through the beaded curtain.

Taylor and I quickly agreed to partner for the palm reading exercise. For the remainder of the class, we flipped through our books, trying to come up with an acceptable reading. I was surprised by how talkative she was. Last year, Taylor had kept to herself. I was glad to see that she was coming out of her shell.

When the bell rang, I was glad classes were over. I got up from the pillow, said goodbye to Taylor, and headed back to my room. As I opened the door, Coco jumped down from Josefina's bed to greet me. I scratched behind her ears, and she rubbed up against my legs. Josefina had not returned yet, so I opened my bag and started putting my books away. Since I had time to waste before dinner, I found my Zodiac book for Mrs. Harris's assignment. I was a Pisces, the two jumping fish since my birthday fell between

February 20th and March 20th. Flipping through the book, I came to the page that described the traits of a Pisces:

> *A person born under the sign of Pisces tends to be a kind- and good-hearted person. They are creative, adventurous, and mentally ambitious. Pisces easily absorb knowledge and are open to new ideas. They are dedicated to their friends. They will lie to save their friends' feelings or obtain some alone time for themselves. People with the astrological sign Pisces are generally shy but are good at sorting out other people's problems and giving advice. They love to investigate and obtain knowledge, and they can figure out how others are feeling. Pisces sometimes become depressed and believe that the world is against them. They are emotional but also easygoing. Usually, they wait to be asked before revealing their opinions. They typically suffer from nerves and hate to be tested publicly. The best calming color would be different shades of purple.*

I contemplated the description and tried to compare it to myself. I was a kind and devoted friend. I could be creative, but I never had the opportunity to do anything that required it. Marie hardly let me have any free time and never allowed me to practice a skill. I enjoyed learning. As for thinking the world was against me, how could I not since it appeared to be true?

My reading was soon interrupted by loud noises behind the opening door. Josefina was not alone. Marley, Bellony, and Candi were with her. All three girls were talking loudly while Josefina listened. Josefina's three friends sat on her bed, practically throwing Coco off of it. She hissed, flashing her spikes for a second before darting into the bathroom.

"Hello, Jane. What are you reading?" Josefina asked quizzically.

"The Zodiac Signs book," I replied, closing it.

"You have homework already?" Marley asked disgustedly.

"It's not really homework. Mrs. Harris wanted us to review the zodiac signs," Josefina told her.

"We're going to learn the zodiac signs, too," Bellony said.

"Maybe we should have a study group. Then, we could learn them as you review," Marley suggested.

"Yes. Would you like to meet in the library after dinner?" Josefina asked.

"Okay," Candi replied while the other two girls nodded.

"Jane, would you like to join us? We can review together," Josefina suggested looking up at me.

Josefina's friends twisted around on the bed, finally acknowledging me.

"I guess Jane can come too," Marley sighed.

"Sure. I'll join you," I replied. "Are you ready to go to dinner?" I directed my gaze at Josefina.

Josefina glanced at the clock on our bedside table. "Wow, it's already dinner time." She crossed the room and looked at her reflection in the bathroom mirror. She fixed her hair and turned to smile at me. "I'm ready to go."

Once I got up, Marley, Bellony, and Candi quickly followed. I allowed them to exit the room before me, so I could close the door. The three girls surrounded Josefina as they walked down the hall while I was left following behind. I couldn't quite hear what they were talking about. They hadn't stopped talking from the minute we left the room.

I felt entirely left out of the conversation by the time we sat down. Marley, Bellony, and Candi huddled around Josefina, forcing me to sit on the opposite side of the table. I was relieved when I saw Miguel approaching. He was with a boy that had neatly cut brown hair and big brown eyes. He had freckles across the bridge of his nose and a heart-shaped face. His clothing was impeccably neat, and his hands looked like they had never done hard work.

"Hello, everyone. I would like to introduce you to my new

roommate, Andrew Smith. This is my lovely twin sister, Josefina, and her best friend, Jane Fitzgerald," Miguel said, staring at me. "Marley Thornton, Candi Vaughn, and Bellony Sandhu are the other girls. They are our neighbors from home."

Miguel had not made a point to tell Andrew who was who out of the three girls. As they politely said hello, I heard Miguel whisper to Andrew something about how he could hardly tell them apart.

Miguel sat beside me while Andrew sat next to him. "Nice to meet you all," Andrew said in a voice higher than I expected.

"Do you like your new roommate?" Marley asked with a chuckle.

I saw Andrew blush. "Yes, I do," he replied awkwardly.

"I think Andrew and I are going to get along fine," Miguel said, smiling.

"We have many things in common," Andrew agreed.

"Like what?" Bellony pressed.

"Andrew is just as interested in history as I am," Miguel countered.

"It's so nice that you and your roommate will get along," Candi said darkly. "Marley and Bellony decided to share a room, so they left me out. Unfortunately, I don't think I will like my new roommate. Oh no, here she comes," Candi sighed.

I turned around to see a beautiful girl with hair so light it almost looked white. She had a broad smile and looked excited to see Candi. She had the lightest hazel eyes I had ever seen and a tiny physique. When she drew closer, I thought her ears looked slightly pointed.

"Hi, Candi. I've been looking all over for you," she said in a musical voice.

"Hello, roommate," Candi said briskly, turning away from the girl.

"Aren't you going to introduce me to your friends?" she asked sweetly.

"Friends, this is my roommate. Roommate, these are my

friends," Candi replied before turning away again. Marley and Bellony chuckled while Josefina glanced at Candi. I thought Candi was being very rude, so I got up from the table and extended my hand toward her.

"My name is Jane Fitzgerald. It's very nice to meet you."

She grasped my hand with her small one. "I'm Isabelle O'Leary, but my friends call me Izzy," she replied.

"It is nice to meet you, Izzy," Josefina said with a smile.

"Would you mind if I joined your table?" Izzy asked.

Candi sighed loudly, but Josefina and I were already nodding our heads. Izzy must have sensed the hostility coming from Candi because she came around to sit next to me.

"I'm glad to make new friends. This is my first year at the Jelf Academy," she said as she pushed a strand of her silvery hair behind her ear. I saw that her ear was definitely pointed. She looked even smaller sitting next to me. Her bone structure was like a tiny bird's. Izzy was precisely how I would've imagined a pixie before discovering that I was one.

Upon Izzy's arrival, Marley, Candi, and Bellony fell silent. They didn't speak to Izzy unless she directly asked them a question. Their answers were always short. Josefina and I talked more to prevent awkward silence. Miguel and Andrew talked mostly about history class, which had the three girls rolling their eyes.

When we finished dinner, I headed up to my room to retrieve my Zodiac Signs book. I told Josefina I would meet them in the library, and she asked me to grab her book as well. Quickly, I entered our room, found both books, and shoved them into my bag. I slung the bag over my shoulder and raced down to the library. I was glad that we were getting a head start on our studies. I just hoped I would see a better side to Josefina's friends. So far, they had all acted very shallowly.

As I quietly entered the library, Miss Pierce, the librarian, looked up from her desk. She had dark brown eyes that were hidden behind a pair of thick glasses. Her mousy brown hair hung limply around her shoulders. I headed deeper into the library, looking for Josefina. I found her sitting at a table towards the back. There wasn't an empty chair, so I had to grab one from another table.

"You're hidden back here," I exclaimed in a whisper.

"I picked this table because it's the farthest from Miss Pierce so that we can talk above a whisper," Josefina replied. Miss Pierce didn't allow anyone to be loud in the library.

Spreading out my book in the middle of the table, I flipped to the page where the zodiac descriptions began.

"Candi, I've wanted to ask, what's wrong with your roommate's ears? They were pointed. How abnormal!" Marley asked.

"Yes, she is abnormal. Her father married a leprechaun, and she is the product of that. She told me all about it in the first five minutes of meeting her. It would be something I'd want to hide," Candi sighed.

"Pixies are allowed to marry other magical beings?" I asked. I wondered if it was just as frowned upon as marrying a human.

"Yes, unfortunately, it is allowed. Pixies can marry leprechauns, werewolves, vampires, and even mermaids, though I don't see how that's possible," Marley chuckled.

Werewolves and vampires also existed? No one had mentioned them before. "Yes, technically, there is no law. I wouldn't want to, but it's probably because those other races have magic," Bellony chimed in. "They wouldn't tell the W.A.S.P. about us."

"I think pixies should be able to marry whomever they want," I replied.

"I wouldn't want to be involved with other races," Marley said disgustedly.

"I'm sure the other races have great qualities. All humans aren't dangerous either," I said.

"How would you know that?" Candi asked snidely.

"Because my father was human, and he was a wonderful man," I replied angrily.

All three girls gasped and looked at me with wide eyes. "You mean to tell us you are half-human?" Marley spat out after a while.

"Yes, my mother was a pixie, and my father was a human."

"Josefina never told us that about you," Bellony said.

"Being a human doesn't define who Jane is, so I never thought it was necessary to mention it," Josefina said. "Jane is such a good pixie; you wouldn't even know her father was human. Her mother was Rachel McCalski."

"Rachel McCalski, the youngest pixie to ever work for Waldrick the Great?" Bellony asked in astonishment.

"The one and only," I said, trying not to sound annoyed.

"Why don't we start reviewing like we came to do? I'm sure we're making Jane uncomfortable by talking about her parents," Josefina suggested, and I was grateful.

I glanced down at my book and pointed to the picture of Capricorn. "The sign of Capricorn is the head of a goat with a fishtail," I explained.

I flipped through the book, looking at every zodiac sign, but Marley, Candi, and Bellony were unusually quiet. They didn't say much and blankly stared at the pictures. Not long into studying, the girls announced they were leaving. Josefina and I stayed longer to study, but I couldn't help thinking it was strange they had left so early. After all, weren't they the ones who had suggested having a study group? They had started acting weird after I told them my father was human. They seemed disturbed that Izzy had a leprechaun for a mother, and that was supposedly permitted. Marrying a human was illegal, so I could only imagine how much disdain they had for me now.

8
Forbidden

THE FIRST WEEK at the Jelf Academy went by in the blink of an eye. Before I knew it, I was out in the hot midday sun, doing a grand cleaning of the house. Marie said she wanted it done to prepare for the fall and winter months. My task was to hang rugs over a clothesline and beat the dust from them. After that, I needed to roll them up and take them inside. It was hard work. Not only were the rugs heavy, but the dust particles in the air were also constantly making me cough. I had to keep putting the collar of my dress over my nose.

I stopped my beating for a few seconds to take several gulps of fresh air. After a few more breaths, I turned back to the rug I was currently working on, the dining room rug, one of the larger ones at the manor. After a few more hard hits, I decided the carpet was good enough. I began rolling it up and subtly levitated it onto my shoulder.

I was suddenly startled by the noise of someone clapping. Spinning around, I saw Robert standing behind me.

"I have to admit; I'm quite impressed. That rug's probably too heavy even for me to carry," Robert commented. "Here, let me give you a hand." He raced over to me and grabbed one end of the rug. I shifted my hold to the other side.

"Thank you for your help," I replied. We walked slowly and carefully into the house to avoid tripping over the front steps.

"Where does this rug go?" Robert called.

"In the dining room," I replied, steering the rug through the front hall.

"This rug is heavy even with two people. How did you manage to lift it all by yourself?" Robert asked.

"With personal willpower," I replied. "Marie wanted me to get this task done, so I had to find a way to do it."

Once we entered the dining room, Robert helped me lower the rug to the floor. I started to unroll it back into its proper place. Before I could object, Robert was on his hands and knees helping me.

"You don't have to help me with this, you know? This is my responsibility," I told him.

"I know, Jane, but when are you going to understand that I want to help you?" Robert said, moving the dining room table back into the center of the room. I grabbed the chairs and set them where they belonged.

"Robert, I don't want you to be punished."

"Maybe if I help you shoulder the punishment, it won't seem that bad," Robert replied with a chuckle.

"Whom should I be punishing?" Marie asked as she glided into the room.

"No one, ma'am. I was just helping Jane carry this heavy rug," Robert stated.

"Good afternoon, Robert," Marie said snidely. "I don't remember assigning you the job of beating rugs."

"You didn't, ma'am. The rug looked cumbersome, and I'm sure she was having trouble lugging it into the house."

"How nice of you, but you shouldn't be doing it if I did not assign you the chore. You should be doing what I brought you here to do. Are you undermining my authority?" Marie snapped at him.

"No, ma'am," Robert replied, hanging his head.

"Then I suggest you get outside and complete the chores assigned to you. I'm sure Jane can handle this by herself," Marie said, smirking at me.

Quickly, Robert walked out of the dining room. Marie spun around to stare at me with narrowed eyes.

"How sweet, the little farm boy, running to your aid. Did you ask him to abandon his chores? Don't think pretending to be weak and playing with that boy's emotions will get you out of your chores."

"I didn't ask him to help me. I was handling the rug on my own. He offered to help and wouldn't take no for an answer," I told her.

"If I ever see that boy helping you with something I did not assign the both of you, I swear I'll have you working twenty-four hours straight. I might even consider canceling your weekly trips to that stupid school. Do I make myself clear?"

"Yes, ma'am," I replied.

"Emily, Preston, and I are dining at Mr. Doyle's house this evening. That gives you lots of time to complete all of the rugs upstairs. Now, get to work. I'm trying to build your character by giving you all these chores. That simply won't work if someone else is doing them for you. I expect all the rugs to be done by the time I return tonight."

Marie turned on her heel and left the dining room. I sighed and continued working. Building my character? I wanted to laugh. It was more like trying to kill me. If I wasn't a pixie, I would never be able to complete any of her chores. I knew Robert's help would lead to something like this. I tried to tell him, but he wouldn't listen. Since Marie wouldn't be home, I had to visit the barn and tell him what she said.

I could hear the three of them getting ready as I climbed the stairs. I was surprised Preston had been invited. How would he act at Mr. Doyle's house? How would Marie be able to cover up his actions? As I imagined the scene that could unfold, Emily's bedroom door burst open.

"Didn't mother tell you we were going out?" she shrieked. "I need you to help me right now!" She stormed back into her bedroom.

I was conflicted. I needed to finish the rugs, but was I allowed to help Emily get ready? What would be the lesser of two evils? After some contemplation, I decided to see to Emily's needs.

"What is taking you so long, Jane. What part of 'I need you to help me,' didn't you understand? Drake cannot see me looking less than perfect. Plus, his mother is also going to be there. The awful hag," Emily complained.

I was surprised to hear someone was making Emily's life miserable. Could there possibly be someone worse than Marie and Emily? I just couldn't imagine that. I grabbed a brush and began doing Emily's hair.

"A braided hairstyle spun into an elegant bun will do. Do not let a strand of hair be out of place," Emily commanded.

I hoped they weren't in too much of a hurry. Emily was demanding a complicated hairstyle. It was going to take a while if she wanted it to be perfect. So, I began to intricately braid her hair, hoping she would be satisfied.

"Soon, I will have you work on my wedding invitations. Drake and I are finalizing our list. As soon as we agree, you'll be doing all the busy work: addressing, sending, and even making my invitations," Emily told me.

I could hardly wait, I thought sarcastically as I twisted the braids together.

"Weddings are supposed to be a lot of work. As the bride, I don't want to be under too much stress, which is why you'll be doing all the hard work. After all, isn't that what sisters are for," Emily said with a nasty chuckle.

I didn't comment. It was better not to say anything.

I was finishing up the last touches on Emily's hair when Marie burst into the room.

"Are you ready to go yet? We are going to be late!" Marie stated in her cold voice.

"Sorry, mother. When I told Jane I was going to Drake's house for dinner, she insisted I look my best. I tried to tell her I didn't have much time, but she insisted," Emily squealed.

I stood there, stunned by her accusation. I couldn't care less what she looked like.

"I have just finished. She's ready to go," I replied, bowing to Marie.

Marie smirked, turning toward Emily. "Let's go, so we're not late," Marie demanded.

Emily frowned at me as she rose from her vanity chair. She glanced at her reflection and examined her hair. "I guess this will have to do," she sighed as she waltzed out of the room.

"Don't forget to finish the rugs," Marie said, turning towards me. She marched from the room, and I followed to ensure I didn't need to assist with anything else. To my surprise, Preston was ready and waiting by the door when we entered the great hall. I didn't even have to find him and force him out of the house.

"Preston, I'm glad to see that you are ready to leave," Marie commented. She also wasn't used to him being prepared.

"Yes, mother. I am looking forward to Mr. Doyle's house. We had a conversation at our last meeting, and I'm eager to continue it," Preston responded.

Marie beamed at Preston. "I am glad you're finding common interests with Emily's fiancé."

I opened the door, and they exited down the pathway. It was a relief to see them go. Once the door was closed, I checked the house to see if the servants had finished with their day. When it seemed like no one was around, I decided to use the *quick complete charm* on the rugs.

I finished in record timing but had to stop to catch my breath afterward. Although Marie hadn't given me a list, I still went around to check the house, making sure everything looked perfect. I didn't want to be up to the early hours of the morning cleaning whatever she thought was wrong. Upon completing my walk-through, I decided to visit Robert.

The back door in the kitchen creaked as I opened it. The night air was humid, and it felt like it was compressing my body once I stepped outside. Night noises of crickets and animals filled my ears as I moved away from the house. I hesitated for a moment to let my eyes adjust to the dark. The stars glittered above my head, and I briefly studied the sky for any zodiac signs. There were so many stars that I soon gave up and continued to the lumbering black shape of the barn. I could see a soft glow from a lantern in the loft window. Robert was still awake.

My fingers touched the wooden side of the barn as I worked my way to the doors. I could feel the places where the paint had chipped, and I carefully moved along, trying to avoid getting a splinter. Soon, my fingers came in contact with the cool metal of the door hinge. Flipping the latch, I pulled on the handle. If I thought the kitchen door was creaky, it was nothing compared to the barn doors. I shuddered against the piercing sound that sliced through the silence of the night. I slipped through and stepped onto a pile of hay that crunched under my feet. The light in the loft shifted, causing me to pause by the door.

"Jane? Is that you?" I heard Robert's voice and saw the lantern being raised. Some horses whinnied, moving in their stalls as the light shone down on them.

"Yes, it's only me," I replied, shielding my eyes from the bright light.

"Come on up," he said, putting the light back down. "I'm guessing Marie is out, or you wouldn't be here."

"The whole family went over to Mr. Doyle's house for dinner," I stated as I climbed the rungs of the ladder.

When I made it to the top, Robert positioned the lantern, illuminating both our faces.

"How mad was Marie since I helped with that rug? I'm sorry if I caused you any extra grief," Robert apologized.

"Marie was furious. It's actually why I came to visit. I needed to tell you her new rules," I replied.

"New rules?" Robert asked with a questioning look on his face.

"Yes. Marie doesn't want you to help me with chores she hasn't assigned you. The only time you can help me is when we are assigned the same chores," I told him.

"That's ridiculous. Those rugs were too heavy for you to handle by yourself. How can she expect you to do those kinds of chores?" Robert growled.

"I don't know, Robert. She said if you help me again, I'm going to be punished for it," I replied.

"What are you supposed to do? You could've killed yourself today. You could've lost your footing because of the weight of that rug. Chores like that can result in broken bones, a broken neck, or worse," Robert was practically yelling.

"My death would probably be a relief to her," I muttered.

Faster than I could comprehend, Robert roughly cupped my face between his hands. "Don't you ever say something like that," he cried passionately. "Nothing about your death would do anyone any good. It would tear me apart if something happened to you." He softened his grip and gently rolled his thumbs over my cheekbones. My heart fluttered as his chocolate brown eyes stared into my violet ones. Robert leaned closer to me. "Please understand,

Jane. I'm happier because of you, and I couldn't bear to lose you," I heard him whisper.

With his hands still touching my face, Robert leaned into me and planted his lips against mine. I closed my eyes, feeling myself sink into him. Robert's lips were so soft and warm. I felt heat flush over my body as he began to move his lips. With his hands, he tilted my head to an angle that suited him better and continued to kiss me. Butterflies seemed to be moving around in my stomach, and when Robert finally pulled away from me, I sat in a daze. My eyes opened slowly. I saw Robert smiling at me, and I let myself fall into his chest, relishing in the feel of him. Then, all of a sudden, my mind snapped awake.

What had I done? I just kissed a human. I was breaking the most important law. My head fell into my hands. Why did I have these feelings about Robert? Why did he make my heart pound and the blood race through my veins? This was forbidden. I shouldn't have kissed him back. A raging conflict began in my mind. I knew I couldn't be with him, but my heart rejoiced at the feel of his lips.

"Jane, are you alright?" I heard Robert ask with concern. I lifted my head to see him gazing at me. "I'm sorry if I frightened you, but I can't be sorry for kissing you. It's been all I've wanted to do for quite a while. I've been too scared before, but I'm not anymore. I care about you, Jane."

My heart dropped into my stomach. These were words I'd been longing to hear. Instead, it felt like my chest was being torn apart. "We can't," I uttered as I jumped to my feet.

Robert looked like I had struck him. "What do you mean we can't?" he asked, sounding hoarse.

"We can't be together," I repeated with a sob.

"Why? Is it because you don't want to?" he looked at me with a hurt expression.

I shook my head as tears streamed down my face. Turning, I

headed for the loft ladder. "We are not allowed to be together," I uttered with my foot on the first rung.

Robert was now on his feet. "It's Marie, isn't it?" he asked. I continued to climb down the ladder until I reached the bottom. "Is this one of her new rules?" Robert asked. I didn't answer him as I wiped tears from the cheeks he had so gently touched. "Jane, please don't leave until you answer me," he pleaded.

I stopped and turned toward the loft. Robert was holding the lantern as he gazed down at me. "My heart wants to be with you, but I simply can't," I choked out, wiping the tears away again. I turned back to the door, preparing to leave.

"I don't care what Marie says. I'll never stop caring about you. I will secretly help you whenever I can, and I'll do my best to protect you. I'm sure we can find a way around this," Robert called after me as I exited into the night. He would never understand that there wasn't a way around it. I could never change what I was, and we could never be together.

9
Calling Charms and Compatibility

I RETURNED TO THE Jelf Academy in a daze. Robert's confession of his feelings had sent my mind whirling, and it was hard to concentrate on anything else. Every time I closed my eyes, I saw Robert staring back at me. I would imagine his hands caressing my face and the soft feel of his lips against mine. At times, I found myself pausing whatever I was doing and gently touching my lips, convincing myself that his kiss had been real. Whenever my mind drifted to the kiss, I reminded myself that I could never kiss him again.

I was quiet when Dr. Tweedle came for me, and I hoped he wouldn't notice. I was so relieved when we reached the academy without any questions. However, Josefina would be able to look right at me and instantly know something was off. Even though she was my best friend, I wasn't ready to tell her about Robert. I had to think of another reason for my mood if she decided to question me. My mind was quickly thinking of excuses while I climbed the stairs to my room. Perhaps I could say Marie and Emily were extra hard on me over the weekend. I decided that would be my excuse as I reached the door to my room. With a heavy heart, I lifted my hand and placed it on the panel.

What I found inside my room was unexpected. Not only was Josefina there, but Marley, Candi, and Bellony were also. I was startled to walk into a room full of people and definitely not in the mood for them.

"There she is. We were wondering when you'd get back," Josefina exclaimed.

"Hello, everyone," I said smiling, hoping it didn't look fake.

Marley, Candi, and Bellony gave me small nods. Then, as if I hadn't even arrived, they instantly returned to their conversation. At first, I was disappointed at their lack of acknowledgement, but it allowed me to slip into the room without Josefina noticing something was wrong. I took my time putting my things away and pretended to be interested in the conversation. However, I was finding it hard to concentrate. Shifting on my bed, I moved into a more comfortable position, my eyes beginning to feel heavy. Within a matter of minutes, I let them fall closed.

✦

Opening my eyes, I saw Robert's smiling face. He looked so happy to see me and pulled me into his arms. His embrace was warm and welcoming. I instantly felt safe. I leaned back to look into his deep brown eyes as he pushed a strand of hair behind my ear. The feel of his rough hands in my hair made me smile and lean into his touch. Robert lowered his face toward mine and soon felt the touch of his lips again. They were just as soft as they were when we first kissed. When it ended, I looked into his eyes again.

"Robert, I already told you. I'm not allowed to be with you," I insisted, putting my hand on his warm muscled chest. My hands betrayed me as they relished the feel of him under my fingertips.

"Jane, I don't care. I want to be with you, and I know you want to be with me. I can see it in your eyes," Robert replied.

"Robert, you know I care about you. My heart flutters when you are near," I admitted, feeling my face start to blush. "But I can't care for you in that way."

"Why not, Jane? Nothing can stop the way you feel. So why try to fight it?" Robert questioned.

"It's because of who I am…what I am," I replied.

Robert's facial expression became confused. How could I tell him what I meant by that? Suddenly, I felt as if someone was shaking me. Robert was still holding me in his arms, so I was confused. Ignoring what I had just felt, I gazed back into Robert's eyes and prepared to explain myself. However, the shaking occurred again. Robert's face started to fade from my vision, and his arms didn't feel as tight around me. Slowly, he seemed to be slipping away from me, and I reached for him. My world was starting to shake now. Fear clenched in my stomach as Robert disappeared, and I couldn't stop him. There was nothing I could do…

"Jane," I heard a distant voice cry. It wasn't Robert's and sounded female. "Jane, please wake up."

My eyes snapped open, and Josefina's face came into view. She was sitting on the edge of my bed with her hand on my shoulder. She looked relieved when her eyes met mine.

"Good morning, Jane. You had me worried. You were talking in your sleep for most of the night. It's time to get up."

Slowly, I sat up. My whole body felt warm and damp. I had broken out into a sweat while I was asleep. I rubbed my eyes and looked around the room. There was no trace of Robert. He had only been a dream. It had all been a dream despite it feeling so real.

"What was I saying?" I asked, rising from the bed.

"You must have been having a bad dream. You kept saying 'no' and 'I can't,'" Josefina replied.

It wouldn't be the first time Josefina caught me having a bad dream. Hopefully, she came to her own conclusions so I wouldn't have to make something up. I went into our bathroom to freshen up and chose my school uniform from the closet. After I finished dressing, Josefina and I headed down to breakfast. I was happy Josefina hadn't asked me what the dream had been about.

"So, Jane, what can't you do?" I heard Marley snicker as she quickly squeezed between Josefina and me. "You were thrashing around an awful lot."

I had forgotten that I had fallen asleep while they were in the room. "We eventually had to leave because you kept talking," Candi commented. She said it in a way that seemed to imply I had been bothering them.

"Are you going to tell us?" Bellony asked.

"What was so important?" Candi questioned with a smirk.

I scowled at them. "It was nothing. I didn't know you three were so concerned with my dreams," I replied.

Marley, Candi, and Bellony stopped talking to me, which was fine by me. I didn't know why they had to be so demanding. I knew they only wanted to find something to make fun of. I was so relieved when breakfast was over. I needed to get away from them for a while.

My relief was short-lived once I remembered Charms was my first class. Mr. Withermyer was sitting behind his desk when Josefina and I arrived. He had a smirk on his face, causing my body to shudder. He obviously had something difficult planned for the class. I quietly sat down next to Josefina and pulled out my *Mixing Stone Powders Vol. II* textbook. I needed to concentrate and push thoughts of Robert out of my mind. When the entire class had filed in, Mr. Withermyer got up from his desk, and words started to appear on the board behind him. Two words had been written: *Calling Charm*.

"Today, class, I decided to go easy on you. You are going to create the *calling charm*. Its creation is similar to the *See All Charm* but with an extra ingredient. As second-year students, you should be able to create a *See All Charm*, so adding another step should be easy," Mr. Withermyer said, gazing around the room.

"The *calling charm* is used for communication. By putting the charm in water, we can channel energy toward the person we wish to communicate with. At the front of this room, there is a bowl of water. I have also stationed another bowl in Dr. Tweedle's office. The objective is to use a *Calling Charm* to contact Dr. Tweedle. You will have to concentrate on Dr. Tweedle and the office itself to be able to make a connection, that is if your charm has been created correctly."

Some students looked confused, while others looked excited. Brian Nickles raised his hand. "Sir, what if we've never been to Dr. Tweedle's office?"

Mr. Withermyer smiled his small sly smile. "It can still be done. However, I'm sorry to say it will be harder for those of you who have never gone to Dr. Tweedle's office."

Half the students in the room looked outraged, but no one spoke a word. Everyone was smart enough to know that Mr. Withermyer would deal out a much worse punishment for being disruptive than botching the charm.

"You may now begin. You have thirty minutes to complete the charm," Mr. Withermyer commanded.

Quickly, I grabbed my book and flipped to the index to find the charm. The ingredients for the charm included tiger's eye, azurite, and marcasite. The first two were used in the *See All Charm,* and the instructions looked similar. First, I had to use the mortar and pestle to grind up the stones until I had a cup of each. Then, I had to use my mind to heat the mixture. Had Mr. Withermyer been telling the truth when he said he was going easy on us?

I finished the charm before our time was up. Glancing around the room, I noticed Betty Ann finishing up her charm. She looked up and winked at me. There was no doubt she had copied me again. Why couldn't Mr. Withermyer see what she was doing? I needed to disguise what I was doing in the future.

Mr. Withermyer stood up from his desk. Josefina wiped the

sweat from her brow and turned to me. She looked nervous and tired. Miguel looked just as frazzled.

"Who will be the first to test their charm?" Mr. Withermyer asked as he paced the room. "I noticed Miss Fitzgerald was the first to finish. Perhaps she should go first. Apparently, she was so confident she decided not to use the full amount of time I allotted."

Taking a deep breath, I collected my charm and headed toward the front of the room. I tried to push my nervous feelings away as I neared the sparkling bowl of water. Slowly, I stepped up to Mr. Withermyer's desk and took a pinch of my charm. Closing my eyes, I concentrated on Dr. Tweedle's appearance. I thought of his gray beard, oval glasses, and warm smile. I pictured him in his office, seated behind his large desk, surrounded by baby blue walls. When I had the image fixed in my mind, I opened my hand and dropped the pixie dust into the water. As I opened my eyes, I watched as the water swirled around to create the image I had seen in my head, but with a few minor differences.

"Well, Dr. Tweedle is visible, but can he hear and speak to us?" Mr. Withermyer asked.

"Dr. Tweedle, can you hear me?" I called into the bowl, feeling absolutely ridiculous.

Dr. Tweedle shifted in his chair and looked up from his work. A smile spread across Mr. Withermyer's face when he didn't respond right away. "Dr. Tweedle doesn't appear to have heard you, Miss Fitzgerald. It seems you have only created a *See All Charm*," he sneered.

Suddenly, Dr. Tweedle's blue eyes looked right at me. "Ah, Jane, is that you?" Dr. Tweedle's voice rang into the room. "What a pleasant surprise."

"Just practicing my *calling charm*," I replied, looking up from the bowl to smile at Mr. Withermyer.

"Very well, Jane. I'm glad to see you have completed the charm correctly. I can see and hear you perfectly."

"Thank you, Dr. Tweedle. The next student will be attempting soon," Mr. Withermyer exclaimed. Then, before I could even say goodbye to Dr. Tweedle, Mr. Withermyer dipped his hands into the water, making Dr. Tweedle disappear. He then evaporated the water and magically refilled it.

"You may now be seated, Miss Fitzgerald," Mr. Withermyer growled at me. I gave him one of my most winning smiles before I left the front of the room. He had obviously been disappointed by my success.

Once I was seated, Mr. Withermyer called up the rest of the students to test their charms. Many of the other students' charms did not go as well as mine had. There were problems distinguishing sound on both ends. A small percentage of students only created the *See All Charm*. Only a few had completed the charm correctly, including Betty Ann, not to her own merit.

I was happy when the class was over, and I headed to History of Pixies. Mr. Collyworth continued his lecture on ancient pixies. They were believed to be nomadic people who traveled throughout present-day Europe and the Middle East. These pixies were the first to discover charms. With the discovery of the *fire charm*, they could sustain their civilization. When humans discovered what the pixies could do, they worshipped them as gods or kings. Despite Mr. Collyworth's droning voice, I was interested in the lecture. It was amazing to learn about the origins of pixies. I tried to imagine what it would have been like to live back then. This class was more enjoyable than American Pixies had been. When the class ended, I was slightly disappointed. I had been so consumed by the information that the time had flown by.

My mind was still on ancient times when I arrived at Zodiac Signs. Taylor and Josefina were already in the classroom, so I sat in the empty seat between them.

"Hello, Jane. How are you today?" Taylor asked softly.

"I'm good. How are you?" I asked in return.

"I'm fine. Just worried about my Charms class today," she replied.

"You should be," Josefina spoke up. "You have to create a *calling charm* and be able to contact Dr. Tweedle. I hope you've been to his office because the charm is easier when you can also picture the surroundings," Josefina complained.

"I've been to Dr. Tweedle's office, and it was still difficult," I stated.

Josefina laughed. "Jane, is anything complicated for you? You complete every charm with the ease of a professional."

"No, I do not," I replied. "I have the same difficulties everyone else does. I honestly have no idea what I'm doing half the time."

"Sure, that's why all your charms come out perfectly," Josefina chuckled.

Before I could reply, Mrs. Harris walked into the classroom. "Today, we will discuss general compatibility between the zodiac signs. First, I'm going to have you move to a corner of the room that represents your sign. I have labeled each corner with an element: air, water, fire, and earth. Use your book to determine what element your sign is under, and then move to that corner," Mrs. Harris instructed.

I already knew I was a Pisces, so I moved to the water corner. I was surprised when Taylor followed me.

"What's your sign?" I asked her.

"I'm a Cancer. My birthday is at the end of June," she responded.

Josefina had moved into the air corner because she was a Gemini. As I glanced around the room, I saw Betty Ann in the fire corner. I wondered what her sign was. When the class had separated into the four corners, Mrs. Harris addressed us again.

"In your groups, find out the signs of all the other members. I'll give you a few minutes."

There were five students, including myself, in the water corner. Besides Taylor, I didn't know the names of the two boys or the girl.

We stood there staring at each other for a moment, but finally, the girl spoke up.

"My name is Victoria Swan," she said, pushing back a loose strand of her strawberry blonde hair and gazing at each of us with her powder blue eyes. "I'm a Scorpio."

Taylor and I made our introductions, and then the boys took their turns. One of the boys was Evan Foster. He had a square jaw with short brown hair and was athletic built. He announced he was a Pisces. The other boy was Jonathon Hillman, the skinniest boy I had ever seen. He lacked muscle tone, and his black hair stuck out at odd angles. The glasses on his face were a tad crooked, as were his teeth because spittle flew from his mouth when he said he was a Cancer.

"Now, according to compatibility, the people in your group have the most in common with you," stated Mrs. Harris, cutting off the side conversations, "such as similar interests and feelings. We will start by comparing water signs to the others.

"Water signs are the complete opposite of fire signs. These signs might not get along with each other. I'm not saying that it never happens and that you shouldn't have a relationship with people of opposite signs. I'm just telling you that these two signs tend to disagree. Fire signs tend to be less sympathetic toward the sensitive water signs, while the water signs tend to 'put out the ideas of the fire signs. As water puts out fire, the same thing figuratively occurs in relationships between water and fire signs," Mrs. Harris stated.

Water and fire were contrasting elements. It would make sense that Betty Ann was a fire sign since she constantly opposed me, but I guess I had the power to "put out" her cruelty.

"Next, we'll compare water and air signs. These two elements are more compatible than water and fire, but not by much. Think of it as a bird and a fish falling in love. Where would they live? These signs can get along, but the connection is not as strong. Earth signs are more compatible with water signs. These two elements work well together since they are not opposing elements," Mrs. Harris said.

She continued explaining the other elements' compatibility with each other. My mind had begun to wander as Mrs. Harris continued to explain. I was happy when we were dismissed for lunch. As I put my books back in my bag, Jonathon approached me.

"Jane, didn't you think it was an interesting lecture today?" he commented. I nodded as I continued to pack up my supplies. "It's good to know that Pisces signs are compatible with Cancer signs," Jonathon stated.

I slung my bag over my shoulder and looked at him. "Yes, this class has been interesting so far. Please excuse me. My friend is waiting on me," I replied as I gestured toward Josefina in the hallway.

"That was a fascinating lecture, but I don't know if I believe that compatibility stuff," Josefina commented. "According to compatibility, we shouldn't get along as well as we do."

"Mrs. Harris did say there are exceptions," I replied.

Josefina smiled at me. "Maybe you're right, but it could also be that some unknown pixie made up the compatibility rules."

We were still discussing compatibility by the time we got down to the dining hall.

"What are you two talking about?" Miguel questioned as he and Andrew joined us.

"Whether the compatibility between zodiac signs is real or not," Josefina replied.

Both boys looked at each other with raised eyebrows.

"You'll find out all about it in Zodiac Signs today," I told them.

"I think compatibility between signs is a made-up concept," Josefina explained.

"We haven't had the class yet, so I'll decide then," Andrew said with a smile.

"Who is making decisions, and about what?" I hadn't even noticed that Marley had approached us until I heard her voice.

Marley and her posse would track Josefina down like hound dogs whenever we weren›t in class.

"Nothing, Marley. It will be another year before you find out anyway," Miguel said, scowling at her.

"Never mind him, Marley. We were talking about the compatibility between zodiac signs," Josefina said apologetically.

Miguel rolled his eyes. He tapped Andrew on the shoulder, and they both walked off to the buffet.

"Whatever," Marley said as she watched them go. "I'm sure it's boring anyway. So, did anything interesting happen today?"

"We had to create a *calling charm* in Charms today. It was hard, but Jane was one of the few who completed it correctly," Josefina said.

"Of course!" Candi said, smirking at me. I wasn't sure, but it didn't seem like a compliment.

"But I thought you lived with humans?" Bellony questioned.

Marley elbowed her in the arm. I looked at them suspiciously. What did Bellony mean?

As if to read my mind, she began talking again. "Well, I was just wondering how you are so good at charms if you grew up among humans. Do they know you're a pixie? You know that telling a human about pixies is against the law."

"No, they don't know I'm a pixie," I replied, now annoyed with their questions. "I study my charms book."

"Her mother is Rachel McCalski. Her talent is in her blood," Josefina chuckled, sensing the tension and trying to lighten the mood. "Let's get something to eat before lunch is over."

I allowed Marley, Candi, and Bellony to go in front of me so I could lag behind. I was trying my best to like Josefina's friends, but most of the things they said were very offensive. They spoke whatever came to their minds and didn't care whether they sounded imposing or impolite. Josefina noticed that I was trailing, so she fell back to walk beside me.

"I'm sure Bellony didn't mean anything by her questions. Most pixies have never interacted with humans. I'm sure they're just naturally curious. They probably didn't mean to pry," Josefina said.

I nodded and smiled at her. "She wouldn't intentionally be rude to me, right?"

"Sometimes, my friends don't think before they speak. I knew you'd understand," Josefina stated as she draped her arm over my shoulder.

I just smiled. However, I wasn't entirely sure whether I understood or not.

10

Dragon Eggs

THE WIND GENTLY stroked my face as I headed across the lawn. Looking at the scenery around me, I noticed the leaves were changing color, and there was a slight chill in the air. Autumn was on its way.

When I arrived at the Magical Creatures classroom, Mrs. Rowley was standing by the fence with a giant smile on her face. I wondered what we were going to be learning today. She looked excited to begin. Along with the other students, I crowded around the fence, eagerly waiting for Mrs. Rowley to start.

"Good afternoon, class! Today is a special day. A turn of events happened, allowing us to begin our class project much earlier than I expected. I'm sure this is a project you'll all enjoy."

I heard Betty Ann sigh with annoyance behind me. Mrs. Rowley simply ignored her and continued speaking.

"In the crates behind me are dragon eggs." A slight murmur of excitement and curiosity went through the crowd. "The point of the project is to raise a dragon egg until it hatches. Once all the dragons have been hatched and matured, we'll be able to release them back into their natural habitat. This project will teach you about dragons and allow you to interact with them safely. I've received enough eggs so that each of you will receive one."

Most of the students looked elated about the project, but a few looked uncertain.

"Aren't dragons dangerous?" Betty Ann protested. "I'm sure my mother and father would be distraught to learn that I died at the Jelf Academy."

Mrs. Rowley chuckled. "Contrary to popular belief, dragons are not dangerous unless provoked, which is true for just about any species on the planet. Dragon hatchlings are no bigger than a family dog. Plus, your protective gloves will save you from any injury they could cause at this stage. So, don't worry, Betty Ann. You're not going to die from these little ones."

All the students started to chuckle with relief. It seemed everyone was a little worried.

"Once I open these crates, I expect everyone to civilly go about choosing their eggs. After you've made your selection, you'll open your book to the chapter on dragons and start building a nest," Mrs. Rowley instructed.

When all crates were opened, we could see the tops of the dragon eggs. There was a spectrum of different colors and sizes. On Mrs. Rowley's cue, we were allowed to make our way toward the crates. At first, everyone tried to remain calm, though it didn't last very long. Before I knew it, students began to walk faster and eventually started to run. Despite Mrs. Rowley's rules, the picking process became pure pandemonium.

I noticed Betty Ann nudging her way forward to get the upper hand. I decided to slow down. I refused to fight my fellow classmates to get an egg; whatever egg was left was meant to be mine. Calmly, I waited for the students in front of me to choose. Betty Ann walked away from the group, carrying one of the bunch›s most enormous and shiniest red eggs. She had a satisfied smirk on her face. I just shook my head and rolled my eyes. Of course, she got the one she wanted.

I was the last of the students to approach the eggs. Josefina and Miguel had managed to work their way through the crowd. All the crates appeared empty. Then, just as I was beginning to think there weren't enough eggs, I spotted a flash of purple in one of the boxes. When I peered inside, I found a small violet egg. Gently, I picked it up from the box and instinctively held it close to me. Even though the egg was half the size of Betty Ann's, I wasn't disappointed. There was a reason this egg was left for me.

Betty Ann decided to circle around so she could walk by me. "Jane, it seems like you got the runt of the litter," she said snidely. "Don't worry. I think you got the perfect egg. Since it's so small, the dragon will probably turn out abnormal like just you," Betty Ann chuckled to herself and turned to walk away. Just when I thought she would leave me alone, she turned back around. "Who am I kidding? You'll probably kill your egg before it even gets a chance to hatch."

I hugged my egg closer to me while I stared Betty Ann down. "I'd worry about your dragon biting your hand off since you had to choose the biggest one. I hope you know what you're doing," I yelled back at her.

I joined Josefina and Miguel on the other side of the field. Josefina had a green egg, and Miguel had a blue one. Both eggs were glossy and medium-sized. The twins were hunched over their books, flipping through them to find the chapter on dragons. Josefina looked up at me as I approached, staring at the small egg in my arms.

"Jane, why did you wait until everyone had chosen an egg? You should've elbowed your way in. You didn't have to settle for the last one," Josefina said.

"I didn't settle for this egg," I replied, hugging the egg close again. "This is the egg I wanted." Crouching down, I laid my egg in the grass and pulled out my book to begin reading. According to the text, dragon eggs had to be protected even though they were encased in a tough shell. They had to be kept warm at all times but not too hot, or they could receive burns. The chapter also mentioned that dragons were usually the color of the outside of their shells, which meant that my dragon would most likely be purple. If that wasn't fate, I didn't know what was.

Once I was done reading, I set out to build the nest. To collect whatever materials we needed, Mrs. Rowley allowed us to go into the copse of trees on the side of the school. I looked around the field and moved to an area where no one had chosen to build. I began my nest by digging a small hole just big enough to fit the bottom half of my egg.

After I placed the egg in the hole, I searched among the trees for something to finish my nest. I found a pine with needles littered around the base deep within the woods. When I touched the needles, they felt so soft on my hand that I decided to collect a large handful. When I returned to my egg, I dropped the pine needles into the space between the egg and the hole's edge. Stepping back from my nest to inspect it, I realized I needed to find something to place on top of the egg to protect it from cold nights. I reentered the trees and found some large leaves that felt like velvet.

On my way back, I accidentally stumbled over a couple of black rocks. As I brushed myself off, I took another look at the stones. Bending down, I picked up one of the rocks and turned it over in my fingers. It was smooth and warm from being in the sun all day. This type of rock would probably radiate heat off during the night. I collected several before heading back to my nest. Once I placed the leaves on top of my egg and the stones around the edge of the hole, my nest was complete.

Everyone else seemed to be finishing up when Mrs. Rowley called us over. "I see that everyone is just about finished. Over the next few months, we'll be raising our dragon eggs. We will start with a lecture in each class, and then, in the remaining five minutes of class, you'll tend to your eggs. As you do that, I would like you to keep a journal about any changes you notice in the egg and if you made any changes to the nest. Today's entry will be about what you used to originally build the nest and any details you have noticed about the egg you've chosen. For the next few days, I will continue to lecture on dragons. However, since the dragons will take some time to hatch, we'll be discussing other creatures before they hatch. With that being said, you are now dismissed. I'll see all of you tomorrow."

Once I collected my things, I said goodbye to Josefina and Miguel. I then walked across the lawn to Earth Catastrophes. I didn't want to leave my egg, and I was disappointed the class had passed so quickly. When I reached the Earth Catastrophes classroom, Taylor was waiting in her usual seat.

"Dragons are interesting, aren't they?" she asked me as I sat down.

"How did you know I've just come from Magical Creatures?" I asked in amazement.

"Oh, I've just been studying Predicting the Future in my spare time. I feel like I should be taking advanced classes on the subject," she said in her whimsical voice.

"Wow, you're really good at it. I just got my dragon egg," I replied in awe.

Taylor laughed unexpectedly. "No, I'm just kidding. I saw you walking over here from that direction. This morning, I had Magical Creatures class, so I already knew about the dragons."

"I wouldn't have pegged you as the type to joke around, Taylor," I replied. "You're always so serious."

"It's something new I've been trying out. Besides, I feel a little better this year now that I have a few friends," she said, smiling at me.

I smiled back at her as I pulled my book from my bag. It was nice to know she considered me a friend.

Mr. Laruse came bounding across the lawn toward us like he did every day. It was hard to believe that the man was late all the time. As much as I tried to concentrate on his lecture, my mind kept shifting back to my dragon egg. I hoped I'd made the nest warm enough.

It was even harder to concentrate on Predicting the Future. Ms. Crescent seemed very calm when we entered the classroom. She was seated at the front of the room on her pillow with her legs crossed and eyes closed. Even as all the students entered the room, Ms. Crescent didn't open her eyes. It wasn't until Betty Ann came charging in loudly that her eyes fluttered open.

"Oh my, I had not realized that class was about to begin," Ms. Crescent explained as she got up from her pillow. "Today, we will begin the art of meditation, which involves a lot of concentration. Please be seated on your pillows and find a comfortable position."

Once everyone seemed to look comfortable enough, Ms. Crescent began speaking again.

"This class will be silent. We must have complete quiet to concentrate because it's very easy to become distracted by our minds. Has everyone found a comfortable position?" Ms. Crescent asked. Everyone answered with a nod. "Good. Now, please close your eyes and try to clear your mind of all thoughts. I know this might sound simple, but it's much harder than you think. Don't let your mind wander. Let your mind go completely blank. This is the art of meditation. If it is done correctly, you can escape your body to receive visions of the future. We will attempt this until the end of class. If any of you receive visions, please write them down in your notebooks. We will discuss them tomorrow."

Once Ms. Crescent stopped talking, she closed her eyes. I followed suit and tried to do as she instructed. I breathed in deeply and shifted my weight on the pillow beneath me. As I sat as still as I could, time seemed to move so slowly. The more I tried to concentrate on not thinking, the more my brain noticed observations about the room. I could hear everyone breathing, and I could tell that the window was opened slightly because a slight breeze tickled my cheeks. Then, my mind ended up reverting to memories. I saw my father's face. His blonde hair and blue eyes shone as he stared at me. He looked healthy; not like he had been the last time I'd seen him. I didn't think this was the type of vision Ms. Crescent had been talking about. My father was in my past, not my future.

Reluctantly, I tried to clear my mind again. Think about nothing, I told myself, but was that even possible? Instead, I found myself thinking about my breathing, imagining the air moving in and out of my lungs. I was failing miserably at this. No matter how hard I tried, my mind constantly shifted to something else.

Soon, I just gave in to my wandering mind. I couldn't wait to go back to the Magical Creatures classroom. The time seemed to go faster as I thought about the egg and before I knew it, Predicting the Future was over. Every student rose sleepily from their pillows at the sound of the bell. Ms. Crescent didn't hear the bell because she remained on her pillow with her eyes closed. Quietly, I collected my supplies and hurried into the hallway.

I made my way through the halls, heading back to my room. When I put my hand on the panel, I was relieved to see that Josefina was the only one there.

"I couldn't wait for that class to be over," I huffed and hulled my bag onto my bed.

"History's my last class, and you know I always want to be out of there as soon as possible," Josefina replied.

I sighed. "After that exercise in Predicting the Future, I was almost ready to fall asleep."

"You didn't like meditation?" Josefina asked.

"I didn't understand meditation. I guess I'm going to have to make up a vision to write in my notebook," I replied.

"I didn't get any visions either, but I thought meditation was peaceful."

"How did you clear your mind? I couldn't stop thinking. My brain wouldn't allow it," I said.

"I don't know. There was a point when I couldn't hear anyone else in the room. It almost felt like I was in there all alone," Josefina stated.

"Sounds like you were doing it correctly," I said.

"I'm not sure, but in Ms. Crescent's class, you can never be sure of what you're doing. Are you almost ready for dinner?' Josefina asked.

"Yes. I'm ready."

I was so happy to be done with classes that I had forgotten entirely about Marley, Candi, and Bellony. As soon as we got down to the dining room, the three girls were instantly at Josefina's side, pushing me out of their way. I decided to hang back while they bombarded Josefina. Since the beginning of the school year, Josefina and I hadn't spent as much time together as last year. I was sad, but I hadn't said anything to Josefina because I didn't want to upset her. I had almost tuned them out by the time we had gotten to a table. I wondered if that was what meditation was like.

Miguel and Andrew sat next to me when they reached the table. Miguel made a face when he noticed the girls huddled closely around Josefina. He glanced at me and rolled his eyes. I tried to stifle a chuckle.

"So, Jane, how was your day? I loved the Magical Creatures class. I think I might enjoy it as much as History," Miguel told me.

"I loved that class, too. I can't wait to get back to my dragon egg," I replied.

"Predicting the Future is the stupidest class I've ever been to," Andrew piped in.

Suddenly, Josefina's end of the table started to pay attention to our conversation.

"Predicting the Future is not a stupid class!" Josefina said angrily. "You just don't understand it."

We were all taken aback by how mad she sounded.

"You think History is stupid, and I never get mad at you over it," Miguel replied.

"History is stupid," Marley said snidely. "Anyway, Josefina, do you want to go to the library with us tonight to help us study Predicting the Future?"

Josefina agreed, and Marley, Bellony, and Candi went back to ignoring my end of the table. I ate the rest of my dinner while listening to Miguel and Andrew discuss their favorite periods in pixie history.

When dinner was over, the girls told Josefina they would meet her in the library. After they left the dining hall, Josefina suddenly turned to me.

"Oh, Jane. I'm so sorry. I didn't even ask you if you wanted to go with us. You can join us if you want to," she offered.

"No, it's okay. I have some other homework that I need to finish," I replied.

"I'm sorry that the girls take up most of my free time. I promise we'll spend time together, just the two of us," she said with a smile.

I nodded. "With us not being in every class together, I feel like we don't see each other as often," I admitted.

"I know. I'm sorry. Maybe the five of us can do something fun?" she suggested.

I agreed politely, even though I wasn't thrilled by the idea. These girls were Josefina's friends, and perhaps I should try to get to know them better before I passed judgement on them. Josefina left the dining hall to get her books, and I finished cleaning up my dinner plate.

Leaving the dining hall, I heard my name. The voice was coming from the library. I backed up to the open door and was about to go in until I distinctly heard Marley's voice.

"I don't understand how Josefina is friends with Jane."

"I know," Candi chirped in. "She's wearing a used uniform. I can tell. I bet she got it off the clearance rack at Timothy Murray's."

I heard all three of them laughing. I felt my cheeks go red.

"Josefina was poor for half her life, so maybe that doesn't bother her," Bellony replied.

"That's not even the worst part about her," Marley exclaimed. "She's worse than your roommate, Candi."

"Yes, at least my roommate is only tainted by leprechaun blood," Candi snickered.

"Jane's father is a filthy human. My parents told me Rachel McCalski had disappeared, but I never knew it was because she married a human. How disgusting! I would never sink so low," Marley said.

I felt anger begin to rise in my chest.

"I hate how she seems to be good at everything," Bellony complained.

"How do we actually know she's a talented pixie? Josefina claims that she is, but have we ever seen it with our own eyes? I'm sure she isn't. Josefina is just being nice. She's always too nice to unfortunate people. You know Josefina can be stupid sometimes," Marley cackled like a witch.

My blood felt like it was boiling. I would've liked to go in there and show them how good of a pixie I was, but I quickly backed away from the library door instead. I didn't head for my room because I didn't want to run into Josefina. She would instantly know that something was wrong. How could I tell her what I had overheard?

My feet began leading me outside onto the front lawn toward the Magical Creatures classroom. I found the spot where I had made my nest and sat down in front of it. I felt water drip down onto my hands, making me realize that I was crying. Wiping the tears from my face, I stared down at the tiny purple egg.

"Don't worry, my little egg," I said aloud. "I'll take care of you and protect you. I won't let you end up like me. I know what it's like to be alone and uncared for. I won't let that happen to you."

I touched the smooth shell and thought about heat coursing through my hands. I transferred the heat to the egg to keep it warm in the cool night air. I sat outside for the rest of the evening. Soon, I began to feel better from sharing the company of another living creature who also seemed to be unwanted by everyone.

11

Emily's Future In-Laws

THE DAYS GREW colder as the weeks flew by. I didn't tell Josefina what Marley, Bellony, and Candi had said. I pretended that nothing was bothering me and came up with excuses when Josefina asked me to do something with the girls. Instead, I would sneak outside to spend time with my egg. Rather than talking to Josefina about my concerns, I found myself talking to the egg while I warmed it with my hands. Soon I began to feel guilty about leaving it on the weekends. When I came back, I always found time to sneak out and take care of it.

As autumn progressed, flyers were hung all over the academy announcing the Harvest Festival. First and second-year students were not allowed to attend the dance unless invited by an upperclassman. I had been invited to the dance last year by Thomas Whitmore, and he and Betty Ann ruined the experience. I didn't care to be invited this year. Josefina still wished she would be invited, but the only person we knew who could take her was Juan. However, Juan wasn't the same. He still hoped Lena would be found and always kept an empty spot at our table if she returned.

During this time of year, the mood around the school was

enlivened by the upcoming Harvest Festival. Despite my bad experience, the students' disposition was infectious as I overheard conversations about picking dresses and who was escorting whom. A few weeks before the dance, Thomas approached me at lunch. I didn't see him coming, so I couldn't exit the dining hall.

"So, Jane, would you like to go to the Harvest Festival with me and relive our wonderful night together?" he snickered.

"Thomas, why don't you leave me alone? Taking me to the dance must have been the best time of your life since you can't stop talking about it. Don't let Betty Ann know that you would rather have me on your arm."

"You took Jane to the Harvest Festival?" Marley said in disgust, whipping around to look at Thomas.

"Jane wasn't a perfect dance partner. I couldn't keep her out of the punch bowl," Thomas chuckled.

"What you did to Jane was awful and immature. Go away, Thomas," Josefina replied.

He laughed nastily, but I was relieved when he finally walked away.

"So, what happened?" Candi asked, leaning across the table and looking right at me.

"Nothing significant," I said shortly. I continued eating, refusing to say anything else.

"It must have been important if you went with Thomas Whitmore. I'm surprised he even went with you. He seems so attached to Betty Ann Barber," Bellony commented.

I kept looking down at my food. I didn't care to explain it. I sensed all three of them staring at me intently, expecting me to continue the story. I tried to finish lunch quickly to get out from under their prying eyes.

It soon became apparent that Thomas was escorting Betty Ann to the dance this year. In every class I had with her, she talked loudly about the Harvest Festival, bragging about how expensive her dress was. I was almost relieved when I began packing my bag to return to the manor the weekend of the Harvest Festival.

※

Dr. Tweedle was waiting for me in the grand hall, and from there, we left. Once we arrived at the manor, I wished him a good weekend before climbing the stairs to the front door. With a deep breath, I knocked with the heavy metal knocker.

"What took you so long to get back here today?" Marie said snidely when she finally answered the door.

"I'm not any later than usual, ma'am," I replied.

"Hurry up and get in this house. You have a lot of work to do. Mr. Doyle and his mother are coming for dinner tonight," Marie screamed.

She grabbed my arm roughly and pulled me through the door. "Take that filthy bag of yours up to the attic and get to the kitchen as fast as possible."

I pumped my legs as fast as I could up to the attic and dumped my bag onto the mattress. Then, without hesitating, I flew back down the steps and headed for the kitchen. Ellen barked orders at me the moment I walked through the door.

"Get to setting the table, girl," Ellen said. "It's about time you got here."

I sprang into action, laying out the china and silverware. Marie would murder me if the table wasn't flawless. I wondered what Mr. Doyle's mother would expect. I knew Marie would want to try to impress them. He seemed like a wealthy man and would probably expect the best.

I was almost done setting the table when Marie burst into the room. My body froze as I watched her eyes scan the room. She walked over to the table and inspected each place setting. Her hands closed around one of the china plates, and she lifted it so I could see it.

"This is the best china we have?" she asked.

"Yes, ma'am. I cleaned off my father's best for this evening," I replied.

Still holding the plate, she sauntered toward me. "Did I not marry your father?" she asked, which confused me.

"Yes, ma'am," I replied. What point was she trying to make?

"Then, what was his became mine, and since your father is dead, all of this is mine." She gestured to the plate and then the whole room. "Don't ever refer to anything as being 'his' again. Your father is dead."

"Yes, ma'am," I replied, keeping my head down, so she couldn't reprimand me for staring.

"Good, now put MY plate back on MY table and make sure MY dining room is ready for dinner. I expect you to stand by to serve us. Make sure your hands are clean and your clothes are neat. Do not disgrace me in front of my soon-to-be-in-laws." Marie shoved the plate into my hands before leaving the room, and it was amazing that I didn't drop it.

When I was satisfied with the table, I went into the kitchen to see if Ellen needed help with anything.

"I'm almost done making dinner. Just make sure the table is perfect and do everything Marie asks you to do," Ellen said, shooing me from the kitchen.

Since there wasn't anything else at the moment, I went back to the attic to make myself presentable. I uncovered my mother's old set of combs and combed my hair, tying it into a neat braid. Gazing into the small hand-held mirror, I checked my appearance and straightened my clothes. When I was sure Marie would be satisfied, I headed down to the front entrance to await my next assignment.

I had made it to the landing on the stairs when a knock sounded on the door. Marie glided down the hall and opened the front door with a flourish.

"Welcome to my home," Marie said in her fake voice as she stepped back from the doorway.

"Good evening, Mrs. Fitzgerald," Mr. Doyle said smoothly. He stepped into the front entryway with a short woman on his arm. She wasn't particularly glamorous, but she had an air that portrayed elegance and authority.

"You opened your own door?" were the first words out of Mrs. Doyle's mouth. "Don't you have a doorman?'

Marie's smile fell off her face, and her mouth gaped open. She didn't even have to say anything; her face made it evident that she didn't have a doorman. I rapidly moved to the front door to try to save the situation.

I curtsied to Mr. Doyle and his mother, giving them a huge smile. "Welcome. May I take your coats?" I asked. Mrs. Doyle looked startled at first, but a grin broke over her face.

"Finally, someone who has some manners," she huffed as she shrugged out of her coat and tossed it at me. "I'm glad to see that you have at least one servant who knows proper etiquette."

Mrs. Doyle couldn't have said anything better. Marie looked so taken aback that she stood frozen in the doorway. I almost laughed because for Mrs. Doyle to compliment my etiquette was priceless. Finally, Marie unfroze when Emily's voice boomed down the staircase.

"Drake, darling. I'm so glad you're here!" She flew down the stairs toward him. I tried not to roll my eyes as I watched her melodramatic act. Emily ignored Mrs. Doyle as she fawned over her fiancé. Moving to the closet to hang up the coats, I watched Mrs. Doyle. Her tiny black shoe made a tapping sound on the marble floor, and she crossed her arms over her chest. Obviously, she wasn't happy about being ignored.

"We have a lovely dinner planned for this evening. Please follow me to the dining room," Marie said, recovering and taking charge. She looked at Mrs. Doyle with the same hard eyes she used when looking at me. I could tell she hated her. Marie couldn't stand looking like a fool or having someone question how she ran her household. Mrs. Doyle had done both within two seconds of her arrival. Marie walked down the hallway toward the dining room with her back perfectly straight and her head tilted up to the ceiling. Emily clung to Mr. Doyle's arm, and he smiled down at her while his mother scowled at them.

Slowly, I walked behind everyone, trying to prepare myself mentally for whatever would go on at dinner. I had a place set for Preston, but I was uncertain if he would be there. A part of me prayed that he would behave himself, but the other part of me wondered what the Doyle's would do or say if Preston acted as he usually did. Somehow, I was afraid I would get blamed. I needed to make everything run smoothly for this dinner.

I quickly walked ahead of the party, so I could hold open the door of the dining room. Mr. Doyle pulled out a chair for his mother first, and I saw Emily's smile fall from her face. At that moment, I realized this dinner wasn't going to run smoothly no matter what I did. There was so much tension between these three women that I felt I was already treading on thin ice.

"Jane," Marie's voice rang out in the room. "Where is Preston? Go retrieve him so we can begin dinner," she said, aspirated as if I should've known Preston wouldn't arrive on time. I should've preplanned this and told him.

"Yes, ma'am," I replied with a bow. I quickly left the dining room and headed straight for the stairs. I wondered if he hadn't come down because he knew I would be reprimanded for it. Maybe if I was lucky, by the time I convinced Preston to come down, the women in the dining room would've already killed each other.

"Preston," I called at the top of the stairs. I waited in silence, hoping to hear an answer. Of course, he wasn't going to answer. I stalked down the hall to his bedroom and tried the doorknob, not even waiting for him to open the door. I knew Marie was timing me by how fast I could get him to come down to dinner. The doorknob refused to turn, and my heart sank. How did I get him to open the door? I balled my hand into a fist and pounded as hard as I could on the bedroom door.

"Preston, dinner is ready," I screamed. "Your mother would like you to come down to the dining room now." I paused and waited for a response. I couldn't hear through the door, so I raised my fist and banged again. "Preston, open this door right now! The Doyles have arrived, and it is imperative for you to come down," I repeated. This was ridiculous. When was he going to act his age? I pounded on his door until my hand felt numb. Just as I was about to give up and return to the dining room with the bad news, Preston opened his bedroom door. He had a massive grin on his face and mischief in his eyes. His messy bright red hair made him look demented.

"Oh, Jane. What a surprise! What are you doing outside my door? I was just on my way to dinner," he said with a chuckle.

I just stared at him as he started down the steps. If I could have punched that smug smile off his face, I would have.

"Jane," Preston said, turning to face me on the stairs. "My mother is probably wondering where you are." He raced down the stairs and swung around the bottom of the balustrade toward the dining room. Down, I went after him, knowing that I would probably be in trouble when he arrived in the dining room. I managed to enter only a few seconds after Preston.

"Jane, what was taking so long?" Marie snapped. "We are all very thirsty."

I picked up the water pitcher and refilled everyone's cup without pausing. Whatever halted conversations resumed as I worked my way around the table.

"We have already agreed to have the wedding at your manor instead of having it here. So Emily should be allowed to invite whomever she wants," Marie was saying.

"The house belongs to my son. Therefore, he has every

right to look over and eliminate people from the guest list," Mrs. Doyle replied.

"You insisted on having the wedding at your son's manor. Emily and I compromised and agreed to it because it's what you wanted it. If Emily was to have her wedding here, she could invite whomever she wanted. It would be best if you compromised on this, or we might need to change our minds about other things," Marie said with authority.

Marie had met her match because Mrs. Doyle's face read disgust, and she looked ready to fight her position. The wrinkles on her face became more profound, and she sat up straighter in her chair. As soon as her mouth opened, her son cut her off.

"Mother, please calm down. Of course, Emily can invite whomever she likes. After all, it is our wedding, and I want my Emily to be happy," Mr. Doyle replied, reaching over to grab Emily's hand. She looked over at him as if he were a genie that could grant her every wish.

"Drake, the larger the guest list, the bigger the dent this wedding will make in your bank account," Mrs. Doyle protested. "Who knows how many people 'your Emily' will invite," she said, very snippy.

Marie's eyes narrowed as she stared at Mrs. Doyle. This was how she looked right before throwing Mr. Wicker out last year. Mr. Doyle spoke up before Marie had a chance to. "Mother, I don't care how much this will cost me. I have the money. I would do anything to make Emily happy."

I almost gagged as I finished pouring the water. I moved off to the side of the room until I was summoned again. This was just what Emily needed: another person to give her everything she wanted.

"I always knew you were a good man," Marie said, smiling wickedly in Mrs. Doyle's direction.

I left the tension-filled room and popped into the kitchen to help Ellen bring out the food. I was able to eavesdrop on the conversation as I brought out the roasted chicken and rolls.

"Drake, the larger the guest list, the more servants we have to pay," Mrs. Doyle was saying.

"I've already decided to bring a few of my servants," Marie said haughtily.

"Which servants would they be? You don't even have a butler to open the door."

Marie looked like she had been slapped across the face. "I have plenty of servants. How dare you discredit my household?" Marie barked.

I noticed Mrs. Doyle's cup was no longer full, so I took the water pitcher to refill her glass.

"Well, I hope you bring this girl," Mrs. Doyle said, motioning to me. "She seems to be the only one who works around here."

Marie looked startled by the fact I had received another compliment. "Yes, I am going to bring Jane, though I don't know what you see in her."

Mrs. Doyle didn't respond to Marie, but she began picking off the best pieces of chicken for herself. While everyone filled their plates, I went around filling glasses. The food smelled so good, and I tried to ignore my rumbling stomach as I moved back to my place.

"This chicken is delicious," Mr. Doyle commented after taking his first bite.

"Not the best I've tasted, but good enough. At least you have a satisfactory chef," Mrs. Doyle replied.

I watched as Marie continued to glare at Mrs. Doyle. If Mr. Doyle weren't so rich, I wouldn't doubt that Marie would call off the wedding. It took everything Marie had to control her temper, but you could see the anger reflected in her eyes. I could only imagine what was going on in Marie's mind. She wanted her daughter to marry the wealthiest man she could find, but she couldn't stand his mother. Marie never wanted to be in the presence of someone she couldn't stand, let alone someone she couldn't control.

"Drake, we still need to get flowers. I'm thinking roses. I want the bouquets to be huge. I won't settle for anything less. I also just changed my mind about our cake. I no longer want Ellen to make it. I know that you have better chefs than my mother, and I must have the best of everything," Emily demanded.

Mrs. Doyle rolled her eyes with no effort to hide it. It didn't go unnoticed. "This is my wedding," Emily continued. "People only get married once, and I deserve the best."

"Yes, of course," Mr. Doyle said, flashing his smile.

"Drake, darling, do you know any seamstresses that could make my dress? I want something no one else has or will ever have."

"I hope the dress will be white," Mrs. Doyle said.

"Mother! Why would you say such a thing?" Mr. Doyle gasped while Marie slightly choked on her food.

"Are you suggesting that my daughter is not pure?" Marie said, her voice raised.

"No, I'm not suggesting. I'm just making sure," Mrs. Doyle replied, her voice just as threatening.

"Mother, please. Emily is nothing short of perfect. You have nothing to worry about. Mrs. Fitzgerald and Emily have invited us for this wonderful dinner, and it is not right for you to insult them in such a way."

"I apologize," Mrs. Doyle said, but I could tell she was not sorry. "Young women don't always protect their virtues these days."

"Your concern is unnecessary. Emily has never been alone with any man," Marie said snidely, looking down the table at Mrs. Doyle.

I had to admit; that it was fun watching Marie suffer discomfort in her own home. I could tell she was just itching to toss Mrs. Doyle out into the cold. The Doyles must have more money than I thought for Marie not to lose her temper with this woman.

Slowly, I retreated into the kitchen but kept close to the door to hear the conversation.

"I believe we were talking about my white dress," Emily continued with what I was sure was a pout. "Do you know anyone who could help, Drake, darling?"

"I will contact my associates in London and Paris. I want only the best for my future wife," Mr. Doyle replied.

"Oh, how wonderful to have my dress designed in the latest fashions!" Emily exclaimed, talking extra loudly so I could hear her in the kitchen.

"I will contact them tomorrow. With the wedding being less than nine months away, I need to get someone here as soon as possible," Drake stated.

Emily practically squealed with delight. I could imagine her devious smile.

"Drake, perhaps I'll commission a dress for the wedding as well. You'll have to let me know when these designers will be arriving," Mrs. Doyle commented. "It's my only son's wedding, after all."

I entered the room just in time to watch Emily's face fall. I tried to keep my face neutral as I walked around the table, refilling glasses and clearing plates. Mrs. Doyle was doing a number on both Marie and Emily, and I couldn't help but thoroughly enjoy it. It was highly entertaining to watch these women at each other's throats.

"That sounds like a splendid idea. Perhaps I shall order a new dress as well," Marie said snidely. I watched as Emily's face turned darker. She was expecting to be the only one in the latest fashions. I chewed on my lip to keep the smile off my face.

I disappeared into the kitchen with the dirty cutlery, finally letting the smile spread over my face. I placed the dishes in the sink and turned around to find Ellen staring at me.

"You better wipe that smile from your face before serving dessert," she said sternly.

"Sorry, ma'am," I said nervously. Ellen had never told Marie about my shortcomings, but that didn't mean she was always nice to me.

"I know it's funny watching them squirm at their own dinner table," she said with a smile and a wink. "Now, get back to work!" Ellen shoved two desserts into my hands and nodded toward the dining room.

I brought the apple pies to the table and served the Doyle's first since they were our guests.

"Do they not have sorbet?" Mrs. Doyle questioned.

"Sorry, Ellen has made apple pie for this evening," Marie remarked, seeming appalled that Mrs. Doyle would dare to place a dessert order.

"Not as a dessert." Mrs. Doyle seemed just as affronted. "Have you not heard of serving a palette cleanser between courses?"

"Mother, please eat your pie," Mr. Doyle interrupted, but it was already too late. I could tell Marie was humiliated. Mrs. Doyle had a knack for implying that Marie was stupid. Inwardly, I laughed at Marie's apparent lack of knowledge of fancy dinner service.

I returned to the kitchen after serving the rest of the pie. Everyone at the table was silent. I noticed that Preston had not had his typical dinner outburst for the first time. What sort of spell had Mrs. Doyle cast over the family? Marie and Emily were on edge, and Preston was on his best behavior.

I was almost sad when it was time for the Doyles to leave. I escorted them to the front door and helped Mrs. Doyle into her coat. Bowing deeply to them, I opened the front door.

"Have a pleasant evening, ma'am," I said as Mr. Doyle escorted his mother from the house and into the waiting carriage. I closed the door behind them and retreated to the kitchen to finish cleaning up. I kept my head bowed as I shuffled past Marie and Emily, who had remained in the dining room. They were so consumed in their conversation that they didn't even notice me.

"How dare that woman!" Marie howled. "She insulted us since the moment she walked in the door."

"She is awful, mother. I simply cannot stand her," Emily shrieked.

"How dare she question your virginity? The nerve of her!"

"She has wanted to control this wedding since the very beginning. I simply cannot let her, mother!" Emily wailed. "She will never let me have everything I want. Now the horrid old hag wants to try and upstage me in a designer dress!"

"Make sure Drake gives you exactly what you want. Don't let that evil woman have any say at all. To come into my home, making demands and trying to humiliate me is completely unacceptable, and I won't stand for it again," Marie huffed.

"I hope she dies before I make it down the aisle," Emily said, her voice fading as they moved out of the dining room.

I knew Emily was a terrible person, but I was still surprised to hear she hoped for someone's death. I began cleaning the dishes, deciding against magic because I didn't know if anyone would burst into the kitchen. After dealing with Mrs. Doyle, Marie and Emily were upset, so I had to be sure to do everything right this weekend. Just the sight of me would probably set them off. I had my enjoyment at their discomfort, but now I would surely suffer for it.

The sound of the back door opening almost made me drop the plate in my hand. Robert was standing in the doorway, and my heart jumped in my chest. I had been avoiding him and hadn't seen him since the day he kissed me.

"Hello, Jane," he said softly with a smile.

"Robert," I replied hesitantly.

"I've just come for my portion of dinner," he said, crossing the room to the remaining chicken.

I continued washing dishes as he sat down at the kitchen table. I was so nervous my hands were shaking. Would he bring up the last time we'd seen each other? Would he still want to be my friend? My heart would break into a thousand pieces if he stopped talking to me.

"I saw that the Doyles were here this evening," Robert commented. "I watched their carriage pull away down the drive."

"Yes, Mr. Doyle and his mother were here for dinner," I replied as I finished with the dishes. I started putting them away when Robert spoke again.

"So, what was Mr. Doyle's mother like? Emily's engagement happened almost a year ago, and it's the first time I've seen her here."

Putting the last of the dishes away, I sat at the table, helping myself to what was left of the meal. I was so happy that Robert was talking to me like everything between us was normal.

"You should have seen it, Robert," I said in an excited whisper. "Mrs. Doyle had Marie and Emily on edge the entire night. It was the most entertaining dinner I have ever seen."

Robert sat on the edge of his seat. "I know how Marie hates to be uncomfortable. She must have hated it."

"Both Marie and Emily hate Mrs. Doyle, but they can't tell her off because they don't want Mr. Doyle to call off the wedding. Marie had opened the front door when they arrived, and Mrs. Doyle was appalled that we don't have a butler. You should have seen Marie's face! Then, Mrs. Doyle complimented me. I thought Marie was going to explode."

"I guess that school is paying off."

"What?" I asked, confused for a moment. Then, I remembered. "Yes, the look on Marie's face was worth it, and it only got worse from there. Emily mentioned her wedding dress, and Mrs. Doyle made comments implying that Emily was not a virgin. For a moment, I thought both Marie and Emily were going to leap up from the table and choke her."

"I'm liking this woman more by the second," Robert said with a smile.

"So then, Mr. Doyle calms Emily down by telling her he will commission the best seamstress in all of Europe to design her dress. Mrs. Doyle pipes in again and says she would also like to order a designer dress. Emily was so mad I could almost see her boiling inside. After dinner, Mrs. Doyle complained that there wasn't any sorbet in between courses to cleanse her palette. It made Marie look like she had no idea how to have a proper dinner party. I'm sorry you missed it," I laughed softly.

"Let me help you clean up the rest of this mess, and perhaps we could head out to the barn so we don't have to whisper. They'll be retiring to bed soon anyway and won't even notice," Robert suggested.

I paused to consider his offer. Would it be foolish to push my luck by spending time with Robert? I had missed him, and I was glad he wasn't mad at me.

"Fine, you can help me, but I can't stay out too long. Marie and Emily are already in a bad mood, and I'd hate to be the one they take their anger out on."

Robert helped me clean up the platter, and then we did a quick cleaning of the rest of the kitchen. We snuck out the back door when everything looked perfect and headed across the lawn. It was pitch black outside, so Robert felt around for the locks to open the doors. Once we were inside, Robert found his lantern, and within seconds, he had lit a fire. The soft glow illuminated the inside of the barn, and the horses stirred slightly in their stalls.

"Climb up into the loft. I'll hand the lantern to you," Robert instructed.

I climbed up the wooden ladder and reached down. While Robert climbed up, I found a hay bale to sit down on. He cleared hay from a spot on the floor. Taking the lantern from me, he placed it between us.

"We can at least laugh openly up here."

"I had to bite my lip to keep from smiling when I refilled everyone's glasses."

"I can't believe Marie didn't throw her out. Anyone who makes a fool of her or her children gets the third degree."

"I know. I was just as surprised. Mr. Doyle must have a lot of money. That would be the only reason they put up with Mrs. Doyle. Besides, Mr. Doyle gives Emily everything she wants. Why would they want to ruin it?"

"How was Preston throughout all of this? Did he act how he typically does at dinner?" Robert questioned.

"No. Surprisingly, he was on his best behavior. He actually ate with silverware, and not a shred of food ended up on the floor. I don't know why he behaved so well. Nothing about this evening was normal," I replied.

"I wonder if both of the Doyles will be invited for dinner again," Robert mused.

"I don't know. I overheard Emily tell Marie that she hoped Mrs. Doyle would die before the wedding," I said.

Robert shook his head as he shifted his position on his bale of hay. "Emily would do whatever it takes to get what she wants."

"Yes, and I am sure it will be grander than any of the parties ever thrown for her. I wonder how much work they will subject me to. Emily has already hinted at writing out the invitations for her. Judging by the conversation this evening, the guest list will be huge."

"Don't worry about it, Jane. I've told you before that I would help you whenever I could."

"Robert, that's how I got in trouble before. Unfortunately, you can't help me. I've already told you about Marie's new rules," I cried.

Robert surprised me by leaning across the space and taking my hands in his. "I've told you before that I don't care what Marie says. I care about you, and I have difficulty believing that you don't care about me."

"Robert, I…"

"Jane, I want you to be honest with me. If you don't have feelings for me, then just say so. If the kiss didn't mean anything to you, then just tell me, but if the only reason is that you don't believe we can be together, then I don't want that as an excuse. How can you let other people control your feelings? Marie controls everything else. How can you ignore your heart?" Robert demanded.

"Robert, it's more complicated than that." How could I tell him that it was more than just Marie?

"Don't make excuses. How is it complicated? You either care about me, or you don't. Other people have no control over your feelings," Robert said, gripping my hands tighter.

He was right. No one could tell me how I felt about Robert. No matter what pixie society or anyone else said, I deeply cared about Robert. My mother had followed her heart despite the consequences. Did I dare to do the same?

"Robert, I do care about you, but...." Robert raised his finger to my lips, silencing me.

"Then that's all that matters. No one has to know," he replied, replacing his finger with his lips.

He dropped my hand and ran his fingers through my hair. "Jane, you don't know how much you mean to me," he said, resting his forehead against mine. "Ever since I came here, my life has been so much better because of you."

"You are the first person who has ever cared about me here," I said, looking into his eyes. He kissed me again, and I moved closer. Robert pulled me onto his lap and held me tight.

"I've dreamt of holding you," Robert said, pushing a strand of my hair behind my ear.

I could feel myself starting to blush, so I ducked my head. Robert's arms felt so good around me. I rested my head on his shoulder, and he kissed my forehead. For the first time, I felt safe outside the Jelf Academy. My heart pounded with happiness. I pushed thoughts of pixie society out of my head. All I had at the manor was Robert, and I was not going to push him or my feelings for him away.

Robert and I sat holding each other until I realized it was time for me to head back. This had been the most romantic and memorable night of my life. I didn't want to leave him, but I couldn't risk Marie noticing I was missing. Before I could climb down the ladder, Robert pulled me to him and kissed me again.

"I'm going to miss you even more now that I know you feel the same as I do," Robert whispered as he wrapped his arms around me.

"I'm going to miss you, too. This might be the first time I won't be as happy to return to the Jelf Academy. I never imagined you could care about me in this way."

"Jane, I've cared about you from the moment I met you," Robert replied as he tucked a strand of hair behind my ear.

"I thought you hated me initially," I chuckled softly.

"Hardly. I hadn't talked to anyone in years. I was afraid to say the wrong things. Talking with you saved my life. For the first time since I was a child, I finally feel like I found a little piece of home."

"You're all I have here, too, Robert." I leaned in to kiss him again. "I am sorry that I have to go."

Slowly, I backed away from him and made my way down the ladder. On my way back to the manor, my mind instantly went to the pixie society, causing my heart to clench. I was breaking their rules, and I couldn't tell if I was finding a home with him or destroying one.

12

In the Hands of the Gods

Returning to the Jelf Academy was abnormally hard this time. I had to hide the fact that my mind was elsewhere. As I thought of Robert slaving away, my heart broke for him. For the first time, I felt guilty about attending the academy. Josefina was consumed with Bellony, Marley, and Candi, so she didn't notice how distracted I was. Even Miguel was spending more time with his roommate, Andrew. With both twins occupied, I found myself alone, dreaming of Robert and spending my free hours with my dragon egg. As far as I could tell, no one else had visited their dragon outside of class. I was concerned with the changing weather and continued to add materials to the nest to keep the egg warm. Perhaps it was crazy but talking to the unborn dragon made me feel better. I felt compelled to care for the egg since no one had cared for me during my childhood.

The weeks flew by, slowly inching toward mid-terms and the Christmas holiday. I tried to spend as much time with Robert as I could when I was at the manor. It was harder to leave him each time, and I kept trying to find excuses for why I should be in the barn. I almost hoped Marie would have another Christmas party so Robert could be asked to serve again.

Emily had almost finalized the wedding guest list, and I knew she would make me write out the invitations. Emily was looking forward to the week of Christmas because it was when the European seamstresses would arrive to design her wedding dress. I knew I would be involved with the measurements since Emily couldn't resist an opportunity to brag.

Studying for my mid-terms was also in the back of my mind. I couldn't let my schoolwork suffer. I needed to stay focused.

Before I knew it, the first week of December had arrived. I hurried down to breakfast and saw Josefina was already sitting with Candi, Marley, and Bellony. I was stunned that she hadn't woken me up. I grabbed a plate of waffles and a cup of hot chocolate before joining them. There was barely any room, but I managed to squeeze in.

"Good morning, Jane. The girls wanted to meet early so I could help them organize their notes for the upcoming mid-terms. You got in so late last night I figured you could use the extra sleep." Josefina rushed to explain.

"It's okay," I replied even though it wasn't. It was beginning to bother me that Josefina had grown so distant. She did everything the girls asked her, though it sometimes affected her schoolwork. I was concerned but was too afraid to talk about it with her. I didn't want her to be angry with me or think I was a jealous friend. It was just upsetting that we weren't spending as much time together. I didn't know how to tell her that, so I quietly ate my waffles and listened to their conversation.

It was such a relief when the bell sounded for classes to begin. While Josefina and I walked to Charms, I listened to her prattle incessantly about her weekend. I decided that I wasn't going to tell her about Robert. I thought Josefina would be the one person I could share everything with, but now, I wasn't so sure.

Upon entering the Charms classroom, I noticed Mr. Withermyer had a new charm written on the blackboard: *Illuminating Charm*. I sighed deeply, knowing today wouldn't be a lecture, and flipped through my book to find the instructions. The ingredients were a mixture of gold, silver, copper, and platinum. I pulled those materials from my case and organized my workstation. From the looks of the instructions for the charm, it appeared that all metals had to be melted and combined in a particular order at varying degrees of heat. Once all the metals were mixed, they had to be chilled back to a solid, then ground down to create fine dust.

Combining the metals didn't seem difficult. It was converting them back into a solid that would prove to be complicated. My mind whirled, hoping to develop a solution before class officially began. What could I use to chill the metal?

Suddenly, I remembered that Mr. Withermyer instructed us to create an *ice charm* a few weeks ago. It was a more complicated version of a *fountain charm*, which required marble to turn the water to ice. Quickly, I flipped back through my book to the *ice charm*. I wondered if adding more marble to the recipe would make the ice colder and solidify the metal. It was worth a try. In Mr. Withermyer's class, you either completed the charm perfectly or failed.

I began taking out materials for the *ice charm* but hid them beneath one of my flipped-over mixing bowls so Betty Ann couldn't copy me.

"Good morning, class," Mr. Withermyer said, his voice booming throughout the silent classroom. "As you can see, you'll be making an *illuminating charm* today. Can anyone tell me the purpose of this charm?"

Everyone nervously glanced around, hoping not to be called on. "Miss Stevenson, could you please enlighten us?"

Lacey Stevenson nearly jumped out of her seat. "Yes, sir," she stuttered. "An *illuminating charm* creates light. I believe we can use it instead of a candle or goblin fire."

"Correct. I will give you forty-five minutes to create this charm. In the last ten minutes of class, we will extinguish the lights so your charms can be tested. You may begin."

I began melting down the correct amount of each metal in separate bowls. Following the instructions, I mixed the copper and silver first, paying close attention to the heat level. Gold was to be added next, followed by platinum. After mixing them properly, I began to work on the *ice charm*, hoping my hunch was correct. I made sure to hide my workstation from the rest of the class because I could feel Betty Ann's eyes on me. I knew she would be analyzing every step I made.

I mixed my *ice charm* in another bowl, deciding to double the marble in hopes that it would give the effect I wanted. I was pleased to discover that the mixture had yielded ice, and I hoped it was cold enough to solidify the metals. Grabbing the bowl of liquid metals, I placed it directly on top of the ice and watched with delight as they started to harden.

Checking the clock, I realized I had ten minutes left to grate the metal into pixie dust. I always liked to finish my charms several minutes before Mr. Withermyer told us to stop. I sifted through my tools and began grinding down the solid ball. Within a few minutes, I had my combined metals down to dust, and I waited patiently for Mr. Withermyer to instruct us to stop.

Mr. Withermyer's voice broke the silence. "Now, I want everyone to stand up and form a line between the worktables. We will begin the testing."

As I entered the line, I hoped my risk with the ice had paid off. Even though I knew Mr. Withermyer wouldn't compliment me, it would make me so happy to be successful. I always felt like I had to prove myself in this class since I knew he didn't like me.

Waiting was torture. I wished my turn would be over already. Finally, I was in front of Mr. Withermyer. When the room returned to complete darkness, I grabbed a pinch of the charm and threw it into the air in front of me. Instantly, a bright light flooded the room. The light was so bright that Mr. Withermyer stepped backward and shielded his eyes.

"Okay, Miss Fitzgerald. You can return to your seat," was all he said even though my charm had cast the brightest light so far.

My idea must have worked, and I was proud of myself for figuring it out. Josefina and Miguel were both able to accomplish the charm, but their lights hadn't been as bright as mine. Josefina leaned over and whispered to me.

"How did you get yours so bright?"

"I'll explain after class," I whispered out of the side of my mouth.

Soon, the bell rang, and I quickly explained to Josefina what I had done.

"How did you know that adding more marble to the *ice charm* would affect the temperature?" Miguel asked while we walked to History class.

"I didn't. It just made sense to me," I replied.

"You amaze me. You always do so well in that class, and Mr. Withermyer doesn't even care to notice," he stated.

"Mr. Withermyer hates me."

"Mr. Withermyer hates everyone. Don't take it personally."

"No. I know he does. Last year, I overheard him talking to Dr. Tweedle. He knew my mother somehow."

"Mr. Withermyer is so young, though. How could he have known your mother?" Miguel asked.

"How old is he?" I asked.

"I think he's in his early thirties."

"You're right. My mom was twenty-two years old when she passed away. She would be around thirty-eight if she were still alive. Mr. Withermyer would've arrived at the Jelf Academy a year or two after my mother had left it. I don't see how he could have known her unless they were neighbors. However, that doesn't explain why he doesn't like me."

Miguel shrugged as we walked into History of Pixies. "Are you sure you overheard Mr. Withermyer correctly? Maybe they were talking about something else."

I shook my head. "No. I know what I overheard, Miguel."

Mr. Collyworth entered the room, causing me to fall silent. I didn't want anyone to know I had been eavesdropping on Mr. Withermyer and Dr. Tweedle. Mr. Collyworth looked at the blackboard, and the words *Pixie gods/goddesses* appeared. When the class was seated, Mr. Collyworth began.

"Today, class, we are going to begin discussing pixie religion. By the end of the lecture, I will assign each of you a god or goddess to complete a report on. In lieu of a mid-term exam, you will write a paper and give a presentation the week before the holiday break. I suggest taking this assignment very seriously.

Today, I'll introduce you to all twenty gods and goddesses, but I won't go into much detail. That will be your job in a few weeks.

"First, we will begin with the four elemental gods and goddesses: Adharin, Kyla, Aden, and Lana. Each deity represents one of the four elements: air, water, fire, and earth. Adharin is the god of the air and sky. Kyla is the goddess of water and the sea. Aden is the god of fire and volcanoes, and Lana is the goddess of the earth and nature. These four gods and goddesses are the most powerful and the center of our faith," Mr. Collyworth said.

I wrote the information in my notebook. Learning about the gods was fascinating to me. When studying in the library, I came across a book about the gods and goddesses. I hadn't spent much time reading it, but I was familiar with some of them.

"There are sixteen secondary gods and goddesses representing other aspects of life," Mr. Collyworth droned on. "I will put them up on the blackboard, so you can copy them down." Behind him, the blackboard shimmered, and names and descriptions appeared.

Cillian- god of war
Karenza- goddess of love
Ciarra- goddess of night and the moon
Heulfryn- god of day and the sun
Steren- goddess of the stars
Cian- god of death
Deidra- goddess of pain and sorrow
Brew- god of farming
Teulu- goddess of family
Cythre-god of mischief
Leigh- goddess of health and medicine
Galline- goddess of wisdom
Bodd- god of enjoyment
Ceifa- goddess of the arts
Neg- god of messages
Chysgan- god of sleep and dreams

Mr. Collyworth spoke briefly about each god before calling us up to his desk to assign the god or goddess we had to research.

"Miss Fitzgerald," Mr. Collyworth called out.

I made my way to his desk. "Miss Fitzgerald, the goddess I would like you to research, is Karenza."

I put a star next to her name in my notebook. I couldn't help feeling excited to be assigned Karenza. Since I was falling in love with Robert, I wanted to learn as much as I could about her.

∽

I was happy when lunch flew by because I couldn't wait to tend to my dragon egg. All the dragon eggs were growing in size, and each day we documented the changes in our journals. Once the dragons hatched in January, we would raise them for a month before releasing them into their natural habitats. My heart hurt when I thought about it. Who would I talk to once my dragon was gone?

Mrs. Rowley began her lecture on Gwilingis, which looked like tiny black dogs. I knew a little about Gwilingis because Miguel had received one as a pet last Christmas. However, my mind kept wandering to the spot in the field where my egg rested. I couldn't wait for the lecture to be over so I could tend to my dragon.

In the last five minutes of class, I fixed my dragon's nest and applied heat to the egg. I hoped it was warm enough and that I was doing the right thing. When the bell rang, I promised my egg I would be back in the evening before heading to Earth Catastrophes.

It was no surprise that Mr. Laruse was a few minutes late. He immediately began a lecture about earthquakes, not pausing to say hello. I wasn't sure how we would be able to sense an earthquake since we were so far above the ground. Taylor and I exchanged glances, and I was sure she had been thinking the same thing.

Suddenly, I noticed movement from the direction of the school. Dr. Tweedle was rapidly crossing the lawn. His face was cloaked in sadness.

He approached Mr. Laruse's desk, causing Mr. Laruse to pause mid-sentence.

"Mr. Laruse, I need you to collect your students and bring them to the dining hall immediately."

Before Mr. Laruse could respond, Dr. Tweedle was already marching back to the building. Fear sliced into my heart, making it beat rapidly. Once again, Taylor and I locked eyes. She had gone completely pale, and her hands were shaking. The fear in her eyes matched my own. What had happened?

13
A W.A.S.P. ATTACK

Once every student had been herded into the dining hall, a very shaken Dr. Tweedle approached the podium. He cleared his throat several times. Finally, after adjusting his glasses, Dr. Tweedle began to speak.

"This is the most devastating announcement I have ever made. I have received news that the W.A.S.P. has attacked a village primarily composed of pixie families. This is the first time the W.A.S.P. has gleaned enough information to attack an entire village. Several well-known pixie families were murdered, while some pixies have been reported missing. As a few of you may have noticed, some of your classmates did not return last evening. I will now read the last names of each family affected by this horrible event."

Dr. Tweedle paused as he rifled through the papers in front of him. The W.A.S.P. had invaded a village, and the number of deaths was worse than ever before. I couldn't believe what I'd just heard, and my head began to spin. Dr. Tweedle's voice resounded in the quiet dining room.

"The names are as follows: the Bradys, the Burchfields, the

Caseys, the Gallaghers, the Johnsons, the Richmonds, and the Smiths," Dr. Tweedle concluded, his voice strained with emotion.

The dining room erupted into cries. Many students appeared to have known the families. Looking to my right, I noticed that Miguel's roommate, Andrew, had fallen to the floor weeping. I suddenly recalled that his last name was Smith. Had his parents been attacked, or was it another family member?

"Classes will be canceled for the rest of the day. We will have a memorial service after dinner this evening," Dr. Tweedle said, concluding his announcement.

Since I was shocked by the news, I didn't realize Dr. Tweedle had stepped down from the podium and headed right toward me.

"Jane, could I please see you in my office?" he asked, taking me by the arm.

I nodded, not even questioning why he would want to see me. In a daze, I walked beside Dr. Tweedle to his office. He gestured to the blue sofa as he released my arm. Then, he took a deep breath before speaking to me.

"Jane, the W.A.S.P. has left a message in the village. The society demands the whereabouts of Rachel McCalski's child. You have been keeping your powers a secret, haven't you?" he asked with concern in his cornflower-blue eyes.

I noticed the letter on his desk, the wax seal of the W.A.S.P. facing up: an actual wasp inside a hexagon.

"Yes, sir. I rarely use my powers at the manor," I said as my mouth went dry. I felt like I couldn't breathe.

"You haven't told anyone about being a pixie?" Dr. Tweedle questioned.

"No, sir. No one knows."

"Okay, I just needed to know. It is imperative that you keep to the pixie rules for your own safety."

Instantly, I thought of Robert and felt guilty. I hoped it didn't show on my face. I hadn't told Robert anything about the pixie world, but I talked about the school. At least that was one rule I hadn't broken.

"I am very concerned. The village was not far from the manor. I'm not telling you this to scare you, but you need to be aware. As far as I can tell, with the context of the message, the W.A.S.P. still has no idea whom it is looking for. The pixie officials are trying to keep the message a secret for your safety. Only a select few know what the W.A.S.P.'s real agenda is. The fewer people who know about it, the better. Your safety is our number one concern," Dr. Tweedle said.

My mind was swimming. Exactly how close was the village to the manor? Was it my fault all those pixies had died? I felt tears well in my eyes.

Dr. Tweedle got up from his desk and knelt in front of me. He patted my hands, and I looked up at him. "You must not think this is your fault," he said, reading my mind. "The W.A.S.P. has been killing pixies for hundreds of years. We have just never seen them discover so many pixie families at once."

"Dr. Tweedle, how could the W.A.S.P. believe I'd be responsible for their downfall? I'm only a seventeen-year-old girl."

"I don't know, my dear. Your mother was a very talented pixie. One of the best pixies this school has ever seen. She was offered an internship with Waldrick the Great while still attending the Jelf Academy. Her last two years of school were the busiest of her life. We actually rearranged her classes around her job. She worked so hard to keep the pixie society hidden from the W.A.S.P."

"So, it must have been a shock when she married my father," I replied.

"I didn't find out until after her death, but yes, it had been quite a shock for me. Your mother disappeared right after graduation from the Jelf Academy. No one had seen or heard from her. She even stopped going to her job. Everyone assumed the worst, but her body was never found. It wasn't until that fateful day over a year later that I discovered the truth," Dr. Tweedle said, staring off pensively.

I couldn't believe my mother had just disappeared without telling anyone. Would I be able to do that if Robert asked? How could I disappear and not tell Josefina or Miguel? Could I go the rest of my life without ever seeing them again? Could I hide what I was from Robert forever?

"I just wanted to let you know. I never want to leave you in the dark with anything that concerns you. Please be incredibly careful at the manor. You never know who could be watching," Dr. Tweedle warned, getting to his feet.

I stood from the sofa and headed for Dr. Tweedle's office door. Fear sliced through my heart, but I was glad that Dr. Tweedle had warned me. Was the nearness of the village just a coincidence, or did the W.A.S.P. really know something about me?

I moved quickly through the halls. The Jelf Academy had come under a veil of silence. It appeared everyone had retreated to their rooms. The shock of today's announcement seemed to permeate through the walls. Seven families had died. My heart ached for everyone's loss.

I placed my hand on the panel beside the door of my room, and it slid open. I shouldn't have been surprised, but I was still taken aback to find Marley, Candi, and Bellony in my room.

"Jane, where have you been? We saw you leave the dining room with Dr. Tweedle," Josefina questioned.

I gave her a look, which I hoped conveyed that I didn't want to discuss it in front of the girls. "It was nothing," I replied. "He just wanted to discuss some of my class reports." I couldn't think of a better lie. My mind was still not functioning properly.

"Oh, not doing so well in your classes?" Marley said, mocking concern in her voice.

"No, just the opposite, in fact. Dr. Tweedle said if I keep up the good work, I might become Valedictorian when I graduate," I responded, wiping the smug looks from their faces.

Josefina's face still held a look of concern, but she didn't say anything. I unpacked my schoolbooks and put them on the shelf above my desk. I couldn't concentrate on any assignments, and I hoped the teachers would understand in lieu of today's events. I sat down on my bed, unsure of what to do next. It was always so uncomfortable for me when the girls were in my room. Why did they have to be here every day?

Josefina must've sensed how I was feeling, and I'm sure she wanted to find out what really happened in Dr. Tweedle's office because she rose from her bed and addressed them.

"Do you mind if we catch up at dinner? I'm feeling very drained from today's announcement."

The girls looked disappointed, but they all exited the room. I breathed a sigh of relief. Once they had been gone for a few minutes, Josefina turned to me.

"Are you going to tell me the truth now?"

"I will if you promise not to say a word to anyone," I said slowly. Dr. Tweedle didn't want too many people to know, so you can't say anything to anyone except Miguel," I added.

"I won't tell a soul but Miguel," she swore.

"This is very serious. I mean it when I say I don't want anyone to know, especially the girls," I said, looking toward the door. They were the last people besides Betty Ann and Thomas that I'd want to trust with this information. They'd probably hand me over to the W.A.S.P if they got the chance.

"Jane, I would never tell anyone a secret you wanted me to keep," Josefina said.

"Dr. Tweedle called me into his office to talk about the W.A.S.P. attack. They left a message demanding my location. They are still actively hunting for me though they still know nothing about me. Dr. Tweedle told me the attack took place in a village not far from the manor. I have no idea if the W.A.S.P. is getting closer to finding me."

"Jane, you shouldn't go back to the manor. It's not safe!" Josefina wailed as she tugged on an unraveling string on her blanket.

"I have to go back. I don't have anywhere else to go."

"I'll contact my mother. I'm sure she wouldn't mind if you stayed with us."

My mind went to Robert. No matter how dangerous, I couldn't leave him there. It would kill me if I never saw him again. "No, I couldn't. The manor is my home. All my memories of my father are there."

"I'm scared, Jane. This is the greatest number of pixies to be killed by the W.A.S.P. at one time. They discovered a whole village of our people. Humans are dangerous no matter who they are. I wish there was a way for you to stay away from them."

"Not all humans are dangerous. My father was a great man," I snapped.

"You know that's not what I meant," Josefina sighed.

"I'm sorry. I'm just overwhelmed by everything. I know the W.A.S.P. is horrible, but I hate how everyone jumps to that conclusion. Everyone seems to forget that I am half-human."

"I didn't mean it. I'm sorry. It's hard to think differently when you are raised to believe all humans are the enemy. History has proven that our interactions with them are hardly ever ideal."

"Wow, you actually remembered something from History of Pixies," I teased, softening my tone.

"It's hard not to when that's all Miguel thinks about. Speaking of Miguel, his roommate, Andrew, lost some family members today."

"Oh," I said sadly.

"Yes, it was his aunt, uncle, and younger cousin."

"That's terrible. I can't help but think this is all my fault," I replied.

"Jane, it's not your fault at all. The W.A.S.P. would go after pixie families whether they were hunting you or not."

"Dr. Tweedle told me the same thing, but I can't help feeling that way."

"Please don't. Anyway, it's almost time for dinner. We should head down and grab something to eat before the memorial service."

The dining hall was extremely quiet when we entered. Not many people were talking, and if they were, it was in hushed voices. Josefina and I got in line with our trays and solemnly selected our entrees. We saw Miguel, Andrew, and Juan and made our way in their direction. Miguel tried to get Andrew to eat something, but he just pushed the tray away and laid his head on the table. We whispered our condolences and then ate quietly.

The silence didn't last long. Within a few minutes, Josefina's friends were headed to our table. They had been laughing about something which was highly inappropriate. What could they possibly find funny? Miguel looked up and gave them a nasty glare. "Do you mind? Andrew, and many others, lost family and friends today. Could you please lower your voices?"

The girls looked affronted but stopped their banter. When it was apparent that Josefina wasn't in the mood to engage in conversation, they remained quiet for the rest of the meal.

When dinner was over, all the students gathered in the great hall as we waited for the memorial service to begin. The teachers started to hand out candles of goblin fire to every student. Mr. Withermyer approached us with candles in his hand. "Miss Fitzgerald, Miss Martinez," he said as he handed us each one. He looked very disturbed, and I wondered if he had known any of the families. Mr. Withermyer glanced at my face a few seconds longer before he moved off into the crowd of students. I wondered if he knew about the message the W.A.S.P. had left. What if he was blaming me for the deaths?

Dr. Tweedle climbed up to the podium. Once every student

had a candle, he began speaking. "We are going to move outside for tonight's memorial service. If all of you could go to the willow tree at the Earth Catastrophes classroom, we will begin there."

Slowly, everyone moved to the front doors and onto the front lawn. In the darkness of the night, the tiny lights of the goblin fire glowed brightly and looked like a sea of stars as we made our way toward the giant willow tree. No one spoke, and the silence of the night remained. We all gathered around Dr. Tweedle, who stood at the tree's base.

"We gather here this evening to remember all the pixie families that have lost their lives to the W.A.S.P.," he began once everyone had arrived. "We pray to Cian. May he open the gates of his kingdom and welcome those pixies with loving arms. May they find everlasting life within the golden walls of Speura. Also, we pray to Deidra; may she lift the pain and sorrow from our hearts and heal them with the knowledge that our loved ones are in a better place. Let us pray to Teulu for protection for all our people from this evil organization. May Galline give us the wisdom, and may Cillian give us the strength to find a way to prevent these horrible attacks and put a stop to them in the future.

"Almighty pixie gods, protect us from harm. Keep us safe from evil forces and shine your light upon us. Let us grow and love one another as you love us. Sustain our bodies and our minds with physical and spiritual nourishment. Please help us find forgiveness in our hearts for those who have wronged us and fill us with compassion for our fellow pixies. May you lead our souls to the kingdom of Speura and grant us eternal life," Dr. Tweedle said, concluding the prayer. I felt tears forming in my eyes, and I noticed many others were crying.

Dr. Tweedle called for a moment of silence, causing everyone to bow their heads. I watched my goblin fire candle flicker in my hands. My heart went out to everyone who had lost someone. I thought of my father and the last time I had seen him. No matter the circumstances, the death of a loved one was never easy, nor did it ever go away.

When the memorial was over, Dr. Tweedle instructed us to head back inside. Teachers stood at the door to collect our goblin fire candles. As Josefina and I waited in line to reenter the school, I heard a familiar voice behind me.

"Can't we move any faster? I had more important things to do than attend this memorial service."

Turning my head, I saw Betty Ann talking to her friends. "The next time the W.A.S.P. decides to kill someone, can't we receive the news in the morning, so all of our classes can be canceled? What good is it to receive the news when we only have two classes left in the day?"

I bristled inside. Betty Ann was a disgusting person. I couldn't believe what I was overhearing. Josefina had turned her head around as well. I grabbed her arm before she could do something she'd regret. "Forget her," I whispered. "It's not worth it. She's just trying to bait someone into a fight. That's all she's looking for. Just ignore her."

Josefina nodded as we shuffled closer to the Jelf Academy, trying to distance ourselves from Betty Ann. I hoped someone else would tell Betty Ann off. I was sickened by her comments. I didn't understand how anyone could be so heartless and show so much disrespect. Evil existed in both humans and pixies; of that, I was certain.

14

A Shocking Return

Snow began falling in large flakes as I looked out the library's windows. The week before Christmas break meant every day would consist of studying and mid-term exams. I had risen before the sun and gone to the library to study my notes and make final corrections to my oral report on the goddess Karenza. Though I had worked very hard on it, I was nervous about presenting in front of the class. Writing the paper had been so much easier.

I glanced at the library clock and realized it was time for breakfast. Collecting my papers, I headed to the dining hall. Since I was one of the first to arrive, I filled up my tray and sat at my usual table. I pulled out my notes, continuing to study them while I ate. It seemed like a long time before Andrew, Miguel, and Josefina came down. I was surprised to see Josefina alone. Andrew hadn't had an appetite since his family's passing. Miguel had been trying to force him to eat something for the past two weeks, but he would only nibble at the food Miguel brought him.

"So, Josefina, where are your three shadows this morning?" Miguel asked.

"Stop being mean, Miguel. Marley, Bellony, and Candi are not my shadows."

"They follow you around everywhere. I never see you without them," he replied.

"I'm sure they're off studying somewhere. They do have their first-year mid-terms this week," she replied. "I remember being very stressed about my first exams."

"Well, I have my presentation on Karenza today," I chimed in.

"I'm presenting mine on Cian, too. When do you present?" Miguel asked.

"As soon as the class begins."

"My history presentation isn't until tomorrow," Josefina said with distaste. She hadn't been too happy about being assigned Brew, the god of farming.

"I'm nervous since I'll be the first to present, and this counts as our mid-term grade. I don't want to fail in front of the class," I said.

"What are you failing?" Marley's brash voice echoed as she and the other two shadows made their way to our table.

"Thank the gods you're here!" Miguel exclaimed with feigned excitement. "We were beginning to worry."

Marley looked confused by Miguel's comment, but it didn't deter her from sitting at the table. Josefina gave Miguel a nasty look. She was probably yelling at him in her mind, and I tried to stifle my smile.

"These exams are killing me," Candi said, ignoring Miguel's comment. "Charms class is so complicated. We have that test tomorrow. Mr. Withermyer never goes over how to complete a charm correctly."

"We have so much studying. Josefina, would you like to join us in the library this evening?" Bellony inquired.

"Yes, I have to study for my history report. Jane, would you like to join us?" Josefina asked, turning to me.

"I'm not sure. I think Taylor mentioned something about

studying for Earth Catastrophes," I lied. I didn't want to go to the library with them, and I needed an excuse.

"Okay, maybe another time," Josefina said, looking disappointed.

Breakfast ended, and I headed off to Charms. Mr. Withermyer lectured about our upcoming mid-term, and I was relieved we were only taking notes. My mind was consumed with thoughts about my presentation. When the bell rang, my heart jumped into my throat.

Quickly, I raced to the History classroom, so I would have time to get organized and look over my notes again. My pulse raced, and I felt anxious. I never felt this way in Charms when we had to test our charms in front of the class, but I hardly had to speak when I did that. This was different.

Mr. Collyworth entered the classroom right behind me. "Are you ready, Miss Fitzgerald?" he asked me.

Slowly, I nodded before collecting my notes and heading toward the front of the classroom. I placed my report on Mr. Collyworth's desk before taking a deep breath.

"For my report, I had to research Karenza, the goddess of love. She is the daughter of Lana, goddess of the earth, and Adharin, god of the sky. She also has a twin sister named, Teulu, the goddess of marriage and family. Teulu and Karenza are the last children of Lana and Adharin, but since Teulu was born minutes before, Karenza is the youngest. Karenza is frivolous, vain, a daydreamer, and loves drama. She was blessed with the gift of love from her parents. With this gift, she influenced pixies to find romantic love. When pixies found their soul mates, they praised the goddess for their happiness.

"However, Karenza could be capricious, and soon she felt dissatisfied. She decided to use her powers for her own entertainment. Karenza played with pixie emotions and cast many *love charms*. Pixies began to fight over the affairs of the heart. These conflicts caught the attention of Cillian, god of war since many pixies prayed to him. This drew Cillian to earth, and when he saw Karenza's beauty, he immediately fell in love with her. Karenza was also smitten since Cillian was handsome and had a muscular physique. When these two deities were married, they caused many conflicts resulting in pixies praying to them. Karenza would haphazardly cast her love spells, which spewed jealousy and started wars in the name of love," I said, pausing for a moment.

"One of the most memorable wars that began over love occurred in what is now Italy. King Matteo was pompous and didn't believe in love. Karenza placed a love spell on Queen Bella, causing her to fall in love with Prince Lorenzo, a visiting prince. Lorenzo smuggled Bella out of her kingdom and returned to his father's land. When King Matteo discovered his queen was missing, he summoned his army, and they laid siege to Prince Lorenzo's kingdom. This war was called the *strith fiú*, which roughly translates to War for the Lady. This battle was one of the largest in the ancient world and is known for the biggest armies and the most deaths. King Matteo decimated the city and claimed it for his own. Prince Lorenzo was killed, and Queen Bella was dragged back to her home kingdom where she went mad with grief."

"The other gods and goddesses were angry with Karenza and Cillian for wreaking havoc on earth. For all the destruction they caused, the lovers were forced to remain in the gods' kingdom. Karenza was no longer allowed to influence pixies and directly interfere for her own amusement. The elemental gods greatly reduced her powers. Before Karenza left earth forever, she secretly left instructions for the *love charm*. Pixies were able to cast the charm, but they weren't as powerful or long-lasting. Even though Karenza is confined to the heavens, she still finds ways to interfere with pixie romance. Sometimes she casts weakened *love charms* or listens when pixies pray to her. She might not answer every prayer, but when a pixie falls in love, they've probably been hit by Karenza's pixie dust raining down to earth."

"The symbol of Karenza is a heart, and her mineral is jade.

Both are used to honor the goddess when asking for her help," I concluded.

The class applauded, and Mr. Collyworth said I could return to my seat. I was glad it was finally over. Mr. Collyworth then called Miguel up to the front.

"Cian, the god of death, is the ruler of both Speura and Ifrinn and the son of Lana and Adharin. These kingdoms of the afterlife are two sides of the same coin. In Speura, pixies are granted peace and pleasure for living a good and moral life. This kingdom is rumored to be surrounded by ivory walls, and the streets are paved with gold. Everything is perfect there, and pixies can live in eternity with family members who have also made it into the golden kingdom.

"Ifrinn, on the other hand, is dark and gloomy. Pixies who have behaved despicably are sentenced to eternity for their crimes. It is a place of punishment and servitude. The punishment in Ifrinn is seclusion and physical labor. Once sentenced to the halls of Ifrinn, there is no escape," Miguel said, taking a moment to shuffle through his notes.

"His appearance is described as having black hair and piercing blue eyes, and his personality is usually morose. However, his wife, Leigh, goddess of health and medicine, always brings him out of his moods. He is symbolized by a monolith, and his mineral is onyx. His mother, Lana, made him ruler of the afterlife since he is the eldest child. Our actions ultimately decide where we'll spend eternity, so Cian is not to be feared. His only job is to record what he observes on Earth.

"When a pixie is born, a book titled with their name appears in Cian's library, organized by years. At the end of a pixie's life, their book calculates what kingdom they will spend eternity in, and then the book disappears from Cian's shelves. Cian awards stars when a pixie does good deeds. He marks the book with an X when a pixie does something horrible. By the end of a pixie's life, if the stars outweigh the Xs, the pixie will be sent to Speura.; If there are more Xs, they will go to Ifrinn.

"Pixie heroes of the ancient world have tried breaking into both kingdoms to bring the deceased back to the mortal world. No one has ever succeeded. Once Cian, or in other words, death, has come for a pixie, there is no escape. There are instances when pixies can return to the mortal world for a short time. These are what we call ghosts. None of the sources I researched are entirely sure how this happens. Sometimes, living pixies can call upon the dead, but it's never a guarantee they'll respond. Every pixie will eventually meet Cian, and hopefully, Speura will be your place in the afterlife," Miguel concluded.

Did my mother have enough stars to get into Speura?

My day seemed to fly by once History of Pixies was over. My other classes consisted of mid-term reviews. As soon as I saw Taylor, I asked her if she wanted to study with me this evening. I was relieved when she agreed because I wasn't lying to Josefina.

Before dinner, I decided to go over Charms. We had learned six charms: *fountain, ice, drought, illuminating, calling,* and *undoing*. I wondered if Mr. Withermyer would choose any of these or if he would choose something we'd never done before but should theoretically know how to do.

After putting charms away, I organized my folders and pulled out the classes I shared with Taylor: Zodiac Signs, Earth Catastrophes, and Predicting the Future. Hopefully, we'd cover them all tonight.

Josefina returned to the room, thankfully alone. "The girls caught me in the hall after my last class. They wanted to go over their Predicting the Future notes. I'm glad we just have to turn in our meditation journals this year instead of palming reading and tarot cards."

"Honestly, I don't think my journal is great. I haven't mastered the art of meditation or received any visions. All I can think of are things that happened in the past," I replied.

"You have to keep trying, Jane. I'm sure something will come to you."

"I don't know. I can't focus, and my mind wanders too much. I don't even know how to receive a vision with meditation."

"When I was home, I tried meditation. I didn't see anything. Instead, I kept getting feelings of great joy. It felt like something outstanding would happen soon," Josefina exclaimed.

"For you, that would be Christmas," I joked. "For me, I'll be working hard at Marie's Christmas party and things for Emily's wedding."

"I wish you could come home with me for Christmas. My mom is so excited to meet you."

"Marie would never let that happen, whether I had chores or not. It was hard convincing her to let me attend the dance last year, and I needed Dr. Tweedle's help."

"Maybe next year," Josefina said, looking hopeful.

"Maybe, but I don't think she'd let me go for a whole week. She had a hard time accepting a weekend. I still can't believe she let me attend this school. I don't know what Dr. Tweedle slipped into her tea that day, but it must have been powerful. Marie never does anything unless she can see the benefit for herself. She thinks I'm training at an etiquette school."

"What are you going to do when we graduate?" Josefina asked.

"I haven't thought about that yet. That day feels so far away."

"Surely you won't stay at the manor. You'll be a fully trained pixie, and with your talent, I'm sure you could secure any job you wanted."

"When the time comes, I'll figure it out," I replied.

Josefina glanced at the clock on her bedside. "Dinner has just begun."

I stood up from my desk and followed Josefina out the door. "What are you studying with Taylor?" Josefina asked. "Earth Catastrophes, right?"

"I pulled out Zodiac Signs and Predicting the Future as well in case we can get to all three subjects."

"The girls will want me to go over Predicting the future, but I need to make sure I'm prepared for my History of Pixies presentation tomorrow. I'll probably go over my notes in between helping them with their homework."

"They're always asking for help with their homework," I commented.

"Yes, but they just want to make sure they're doing everything correctly."

"You don't do the homework for them, do you?"

Josefina gave me a look that made me regret asking

"No, I just help them. Sure, when they get stuck on an answer, I'll tell them what it is, but I make them think. I don't know why you don't study with us. Every time I ask you, it always seems like you have something else to do. I know the girls can be a bit much, but it seems like you don't even want to know them."

It was on the tip of my tongue to tell her what I overheard weeks ago, but I clamped my mouth shut. Josefina seemed angry, and I didn't want to make it worse. The way she defended them had me wondering. Why didn't she notice that they had never made an effort to invite me? They constantly interrupted me when I was talking or made condescending remarks. Why didn't Josefina see any of those things?

I decided to apologize instead. "I'm sorry if I seem busy, Josefina. I didn't mean to imply anything. I know you like to help everyone."

"That's okay, Jane. Maybe you can join us next time."

"I'll clear my calendar for the next study group," I said, forcing a smile. If it was essential to Josefina, I would act like I was trying.

When we arrived at the dining hall, Miguel and Andrew were sitting with Juan, who was farther down the table. This year, he was keeping his distance since Marley, Candi, and Bellony had been crowding our table.

"Josefina! There you are. You've been getting to the dining hall so much earlier than us," Marley said as the three girls walked toward the table.

"We're still going to study tonight, right?" Candi asked.

"Of course. We'll go to the library after dinner," Josefina replied.

"Is Jane coming, too?" Marley asked with a frown on her face.

"No, I have another study group to attend," I commented, but the girls were already ignoring me. They were too busy craning their necks to see what was on the menu.

As I selected a few pieces of turkey and some mashed potatoes, I listened to the girls complain about tarot cards.

"There are so many. How are you supposed to memorize all those meanings plus the meanings for when the cards are reversed?" Bellony whined.

"Don't worry. I'll show you a trick for memorizing the cards," Josefina said.

"Josefina, will you also help us prepare for our Charms midterm?" Marley asked as we sat down. I sat closer to the boys, so they all crowded around Josefina. Miguel and I locked eyes, and I knew what he was thinking.

"That's going to be hard since Mr. Withermyer is so unpredictable. You can never guess what charm he'll pick, so you must study everything for his class."

"Jane, good job on your report this morning," Miguel commented.

The girls looked down to our end of the table as if we were bothering them.

"Thank you, Miguel. I enjoyed yours as well. I'm glad my presentation is over. It's one less mid-term to worry about."

"Do you know when the test for Magical Creatures is?" Miguel asked.

"I believe that's on Thursday," I replied.

"Josefina," Marley said, her obnoxious voice growing louder. "Do you know how to do the *See All Charm*? That one is so hard to master."

I couldn't believe she was trying to talk over us. I chuckled because the *See All Charm* was one of the only charms with multiple ingredients in the first-year lessons. No wonder they were having a problem. They couldn't handle more than one thing at a time.

Suddenly, there was a commotion near the doors of the dining room. I craned my neck to see what was happening. Standing at the entrance was a girl covered in dirt from head to toe. She had a fear in her familiar eyes, but I couldn't place where I had seen her before. The loud noise sounded at my table, pulling my eyes away from the girl.

Juan had jumped up from the table and ran toward the girl. He had the happiest expression I had ever seen, and that was when my mind jolted to alert.

"Lena! Lena! I knew you were still alive! I knew in my heart that you would come back to me!" Juan cried, coming closer to the distressed-looking Lena.

Every eye in the dining room had turned to face the scene. Once Juan reached Lena, he wrapped his arms around her. Tears of joy were streaming down his face. He stepped back to look into Lena's eyes.

"Who are you?" she cried right before fainting in his arms.

15

MISSING MEMORY

Lena was immediately taken to the hospital wing, and I followed Josefina and Miguel to the third floor. The three of us were in complete shock. We couldn't believe she was alive. We sat stunned in the waiting room, patiently awaiting news about Lena. Juan had insisted on staying by her side the entire time.

"This is a miracle!" Josefina exclaimed.

"We had given up hope, and Juan was right," Miguel replied.

"I wonder what happened. Did she escape the W.A.S.P.?" I commented.

The infirmary door swung open, and Juan came out. "She's sleeping soundly for now. They promised to tell me when she awakens. I knew she was alive. My intuition told me not to give up on her."

"We're so sorry we didn't believe you," Josefina said, hugging her older brother.

"All that matters is Lena's alive," Juan said with a huge smile.

We all took a seat, wanting to be there, when Lena opened her eyes. I thanked the gods that she was alive. She had been missing for almost seven months. How had she survived for so long?

Loud voices sounded outside in the hallway. Suddenly, Marley, Candi, and Bellony burst into the nurse's office.

"What's going on, Josefina?" Marley asked obnoxiously.

"Was that Lena?" Candi asked.

Nurse Adelina looked up from her desk behind the sliding glass window. She had a scowl on her face, and I knew that the girls were being entirely too loud.

"Yes, that was Lena. She must have escaped from the W.A.S.P. We're waiting for her to wake up," Josefina replied.

"Are you still going to help us study?" Bellony whined.

"We really need help with Predicting the Future," Marley complained.

Nurse Adelina rose from her desk and pushed open the glass window. "If you cannot keep your voices down, I will have to ask you to leave," she said sternly.

Juan gave the girls a very nasty look. If he could've, Juan would've thrown them out himself.

"Girls, I'm sorry. I'm going to have to cancel. I need to be here for Lena."

"I guess we'll have to study Charms without you. That test is tomorrow. We really could have used the help," Candi said, rolling her eyes.

"Maybe we can study with you before the Predicting the Future mid-term. That's on Thursday. Hopefully, nothing else comes up," Marley stated as she turned on her heel and strode out of the nurse's office. Candi and Bellony followed her.

Suddenly, I remembered that I had asked Taylor to study tonight. "I'll be right back. I need to tell Taylor that we have to cancel our study group."

I quickly left the hospital wing and headed for the library. I hoped that Taylor would be there since I wasn't sure of her room number was. Miss Pierce glanced up briefly over the top of her glasses when I entered. Frantically, I began searching the tables for

Taylor. I didn't want her to think I lied when I told her I wanted to study. Finally, I heard her soft voice calling my name. "Jane, I'm over here."

I turned in the direction of Taylor's voice and found her at a small table near the back of the library.

"I'm so glad I found you! I didn't want you to think I'd forgotten. I'm going to have to cancel tonight. Maybe we can study tomorrow night? Something serious has come up. I don't know if you remember Helena Rodriguez, but she went missing in June last year when the W.A.S.P. murdered her family. We all thought she had died too, but she suddenly showed up tonight. She's in the hospital wing recovering, and I would like to be there when she wakes up," I quickly whispered.

"She escaped the W.A.S.P.?" Taylor asked.

"We're not sure what happened. She fainted upon her arrival."

"If she truly escaped the W.A.S.P., it's a miracle. Go back to the hospital wing. We can study tomorrow night."

I thanked her for being so understanding and headed back. On my way through the bookshelves, I distinctly heard Marley's voice and slowed my pace.

"I don't see why she had to stay in the hospital wing. Who knows if Lena is even going to wake up tonight? She should be helping us. Our Charms test is tomorrow."

"Even if Lena did wake up, what's Josefina going to do? She should've kept her promise to help us," Candi said.

"Besides, Lena is Juan's friend. He has obsessed over her every day since she disappeared. I can't believe she's alive. I thought Juan was just a crazy psychopath when he insisted that Lena was alive. I thought he needed to be committed to an institution," Bellony replied.

"Perhaps he should still be committed to one. There is no way he could have known she was alive. Pixie officials have been searching for months. How could he have known something when they didn't? He's not playing with a full deck of cards," Candi laughed.

"Why did Lena have to show up on the night we really needed Josefina? Couldn't she have stayed missing a few more days? We have the two hardest mid-terms, and she isn't helping us! I know who to blame if I fail them," Marley cried.

I felt anger boil in my blood as I stood behind the bookshelf. I felt strands of my hair rising from my shoulders. I had to breathe deeply to stop myself from levitating them. If only I could come around the corner and send the girls flying across the room. How could Josefina be so blind to how nasty they were?

"On another note, I wonder what Josefina got us for Christmas. It better be good," Candi said as I continued to listen.

"She needs to buy those new necklaces her dad created this season for us. It would be a shame if I had to wear old Martinez signature collection jewelry," Bellony said.

"Why else would we have Josefina as a friend if she didn't spoil us with her daddy's expensive jewelry on Christmas and birthdays," Marley snickered.

I felt sick. I couldn't stand to hear anymore. The girls weren't Josefina's friends. They were just using her for all kinds of reasons. Josefina was too kind-hearted to realize it. Why did I have to stumble upon this conversation? I couldn't tell her. She already thought I wasn't trying with them, but the reality was she didn't know them at all. I was afraid that she would come to their defense if I told her instead of believing me.

I left the library with a heavy heart and went back to the hospital wing. When I entered the nurse's office, I noticed that Josefina, Miguel, and Juan were smiling. Josefina jumped up from her chair and came toward me.

"Lena is awake, but Dr. Tweedle's with her at the moment. We might be allowed to see her when he is done."

"That's great!" I said, trying to look cheerful, but it was hard after what I had just overheard.

"Is something wrong?" she asked.

"No, I'm fine," I said, faking a smile.

Josefina kept casting glances at me while we waited. Why could Josefina read me so well but was completely clueless when it came to Marley, Candi, and Bellony?

We seemed to be waiting a long time before Dr. Tweedle finally emerged. His expression was grave, and I began to worry. "Good evening," he said, addressing us. "I'm afraid that Miss Rodriguez is not up for visitors this evening. She appears to be suffering memory loss. Whether it is short or long term, we cannot be certain. The W.A.S.P. has not been kind to her. At present, she doesn't seem to recall who anyone is nor where she is. I believe she should get some rest."

"But Dr. Tweedle, she must know who I am. I've known Lena my whole life," Juan cried.

"I'm sorry, Mr. Martinez. Miss Rodriquez is very confused right now. She has been through some very traumatic events. It's best if she is not disturbed. Nurse Adelina will take good care of her. With time, we are hoping her memory will return. For tonight, please return to your rooms. If anything changes, you'll be the first to know," Dr. Tweedle paused to look at me. "Jane, if you could please come to my office. I won't keep you very long," Dr. Tweedle said, walking toward the door.

I followed Dr. Tweedle down the grand staircase to the second floor. He turned into the west wing and opened the door to his office. He ushered me inside, and my knees gave out when I reached the sofa. Dr. Tweedle took a deep breath as he sat behind his desk.

"Even in her confused state, Miss Rodriguez was able to share some information about the W.A.S.P… Right now, she believes they have recaptured her. She doesn't remember who I am and has shown no response when I mentioned the Martinezes. She must have reached the school from a repressed memory. It seems like the W.A.S.P. has been torturing her for some time. It was lucky she managed to escape. We still don't understand how she escaped them or why the W.A.S.P. kept her alive. The only conclusion I could come to was that the W.A.S.P. thinks Miss Rodriguez is of an age to possibly know you. They were hoping she would have the information they needed."

"Dr. Tweedle," I said, alarmed. "Lena did know me. Do you think she told them?"

"It's hard to know what information Miss Rodriguez has shared. She's in such a confused state that I cannot be certain. Unfortunately, there's one phrase Miss Rodriguez has been repeating," Dr. Tweedle said, looking distraught.

"What is it?" I cried in fear.

"She keeps screaming, 'I don't know where she is.'"

16

Preparing for a Wedding

THE CLOTHES FELT soft in my hands as I folded them and placed them in my bag. Dr. Tweedle would be coming to retrieve me soon for Christmas break. The last week had been extremely difficult trying to concentrate on mid-terms when the news Dr. Tweedle had shared hung over my head.

Dr. Tweedle had spent the last week at Lena's bedside. It had taken a while to convince her that she was safe. After a few days, Dr. Tweedle allowed the Martinezes and me to see her. She showed no signs of recognition of our faces or our names. As bad as her memory loss was, Dr. Tweedle believed it might be a good thing. Maybe she wouldn't remember the pain she went through. Perhaps she had not told the W.A.S.P. anything about the pixie society or me. Her mind might have shut down under the torture the W.A.S.P. had subjected her to.

Juan insisted on visiting Lena every day in hopes of restoring her memory. However, it didn't seem like he was making any progress. He kept telling her that they had been friends their entire lives, but she couldn't remember anything from her past. Since Lena's parents had been murdered, the Martinezes offered to bring Lena to their house for Christmas. Dr. Tweedle was nervous about letting Lena leave the school, but she agreed to go with them in hopes that something would trigger her memory.

I finished packing my bag and checked the room one last time. Josefina and Miguel had already left for break, so I had no one to say goodbye to. Throwing my bag over my shoulder, I exited the room. Dr. Tweedle was already waiting for me at the bottom of the grand staircase.

"Do you have everything?" he asked me, his gaze wandering to the bag on my shoulder.

"Yes, Dr. Tweedle. We can head for the manor now," I replied as I stepped off the last step.

Dr. Tweedle pushed one of the doors open, allowing me to walk through. We crossed the grounds to the clouds. Dr. Tweedle held out his hand to me, and we stepped aboard the cloud that would take us to the ground.

"While you are at the manor this week, I want you to be very careful. Do not use any magic if it can be avoided. Until Lena regains her memory, we won't know how much information the W.A.S.P. knows about you. With the attack from a few weeks ago being so close to your home, it pains me to even let you return for Christmas," he said as we got into the carriage.

"I promise I'll use the utmost caution. Don't worry about me, Dr. Tweedle," I replied, even though I was scared about what the W.A.S.P. might know.

I felt like my world was being turned upside down as the *teleportation charm* settled over us. When the dust cleared, we were at the end of the manor's long driveway. Dr. Tweedle snapped the reigns, and the two horses moved through the black iron gate.

I clutched my bag to my chest as the manor rose before us. I hoped I'd be able to see Robert often over the next week. My heart pounded at the thought.

Dr. Tweedle pulled the horses to a stop at the foot of the stairs.

Taking a deep breath, he turned to look at me. "Jane, please be careful while you are here. It is important that you stay alert and watch for suspicious behavior. If Marie has a Christmas party, you never know who might be invited. Please control your magic and don't cast any charms," he seriously said.

I swallowed the lump in my throat and nodded.

"I will return to pick you up on New Year's Eve. Perhaps I'll be able to come earlier than I did last year, so you'll get to enjoy the celebration. I do not want you staying here longer than you have to," Dr. Tweedle said, patting my hand.

"Thank you," I replied as he went around the carriage to help me down.

"Be safe, Jane. I look forward to seeing you in a week."

"Have a wonderful Christmas," I replied as he boarded the carriage.

He tipped his hat to me and waved as he pulled away.

Sucking in a breath, I climbed the stairs to the front door. Within moments of my knock, Marie was flinging the door open. She looked down her nose at me as she scowled.

"Get in here and wash up at once. The dressmakers should be here any moment. As soon as you drop off… your things," she said, sneering at my small bag, "head straight to Emily's room."

I bowed my head to her and quickly walked up the stairs. I couldn't fathom how Mr. Doyle had gotten the dressmakers here the week of Christmas. He must be paying them an outrageous sum.

In the attic, I looked over my clothes and fixed my hair into place. I did one more check before heading down to her room. Emily would be so mad if I were late.

Emily was pacing when I entered the room. She glanced up, and when she realized it was only me, she pouted.

"Jane, it's about time you got here. The seamstresses will be here any minute. They are already late," she snapped.

I stood by the door, unsure of what to do with myself. Obviously, there was nothing I could do to make them arrive faster.

"Make me a cup of tea while I wait," Emily barked at me.

Scurrying around, I put on the teapot and waited for the water to boil. I wondered whether Emily would offer the seamstresses tea, so I added a few more cups to the tray along with the sugar bowl and cream.

I was on the stairs with the tea tray when I heard a knock on the front door. I saw Marie gliding to the door out of the corner of my eye.

"You've finally arrived," I heard Marie say, her voice drifting up the stairs. I entered Emily's room with the tea, placing the tray on the small coffee table in the sitting area.

"Are they here yet?" Emily asked nastily as if I had anything to do with their late arrival.

"Your mother is seeing them in now, ma'am," I replied as I retreated to the corner.

I could hear the seamstresses coming up the stairs with Marie.

"What a lovely home," one of them exclaimed in a strong English accent.

Marie didn't return a thank you to the compliment as she led them into Emily's room.

"Zis must be de bride," the other woman gushed in her French accent.

Emily took in both women. "I thought you were going to arrive an hour ago."

"We are so sorry, miss. We had a terrible time getting a carriage," the British woman replied.

"Let us begin and waste no further time," Emily demanded, causing the women to rifle through their bags. I knew then that Emily was not going to offer the women tea. No matter how esteemed these women were in Europe, Emily only saw them as servants whose only purpose was to meet her needs.

One of the women pulled out a few pieces of paper, while the other pulled out a large sheet of paper and placed it on an easel.

"How about you begin by giving us some details for your ideal wedding dress," the British woman said as she pushed a strand of her blonde hair from her eyes. She sat intently poised with her pencil over her paper.

"The dress needs to have short sleeves since the wedding is in June. I want a lot of lace and a soft pink sash around the waist. Other than the sash, the entire dress must be white. I don't want the skirts to be too full, but my hips should be accentuated. As for the train, I want the longest possible," Emily prattled, ticking off each detail on her fingers.

"Oh, and I want the sleeves to flair out at the shoulders." The seamstress's pencil flashed across the page. "Also, my waist needs to look extremely small," Emily commanded.

The other seamstress listened intently as she moved toward the easel. Her long dark hair fell over her right shoulder as she began sketching.

"This dress must be the height of fashion in Europe. I don't want to be seen in anything that resembles last year's design," Emily said, her voice haughty.

"No need to worry, miss. Your dress will be done in the latest fashions. We can also assure you that it will be one of a kind."

Emily had a smug look on her face as she watched the French seamstress sketch.

Within moments, she had drawn a dress that fit Emily's description. Emily rose from her chair and inspected the design.

"I want the sleeves to flair out more, and I hope the train is longer than this picture shows. The skirt should be fuller at the hips, and I want the bodice to come down in a V when it meets the skirt," Emily said, pointing to the offending areas.

The seamstress quickly fixed those aspects.

"Something is still not right," Emily complained. "Can you add more pleats to the back?"

Once the seamstress had made the changes, Emily scrutinized the drawing again.

"I want more lace," Emily stated with a roll of her eyes. "It could use more ruffles around the collar."

The seamstress quickly obliged Emily's demands. An hour must have gone by, and Emily still wasn't satisfied, but she agreed to move on to measurements.

"Pleaze step on ze platform so I can take ze mezzurments," the French seamstress crooned.

"Jane, get over here and help," Emily commanded.

I moved from my place and held the measuring tape. They took measurements around Emily's neck, bust, waist, and hips first. Then, across her shoulders and from her hips to the floor. I could tell that Emily was getting impatient even though the measurements had to be taken correctly.

I couldn't help but think how easy pixie clothes were. They expanded or contracted to fit the size of the wearer. There were no measurements involved since the fabric was magic. I wondered what these seamstresses would think of that?

Finally, Emily stepped down from the platform, and the seamstresses began collecting their things.

"We have enough of an idea of what you are looking for to begin buying material. Remember that changes can be made anytime," the British blonde said as they moved toward Emily's bedroom door.

"Ve vill be back soon to start on a esign," the French brunette added.

I followed them into the hallway and showed them down to the door. They bade me goodbye and hustled toward their waiting carriage. I wondered how many more changes Emily would make to the dress before everything was said and done. I returned to Emily's room to see if she or Marie needed anything else from me.

"Those seamstresses better make the dress exactly how you want it for your wedding. Drake better of hired the best. Hopefully, these women don't return with cheap materials. It was bad enough that they were late," Marie was saying.

"I'm sure Drake has hired the best, mother. My fiancé doesn't do anything unless it is the best," Emily said, scrutinizing her make-up in the mirror.

"That man should give you everything you want and nothing less. If he refuses you anything, persuade him until he gives it to you. You must gain control over him and not let him cater to that ridiculous mother of his. You need to become the center of his world."

"I know, mother," Emily replied, annoyed.

Marie stood from her seat and turned to leave the room. Her eyes raked over me, and she smiled cruelly. "Emily, perhaps Jane could begin addressing the invitation envelopes."

Emily shared the nasty smile. "What a wonderful idea, mother."

As Marie passed by, she whispered, "Every single envelope better be written out neatly, or I will break your fingers."

I watched as Emily pulled out multiple sheets of paper with a long list of names.

"Our guest list has over five hundred people. Here is the list of names and addresses. You need to write out all the envelopes for now. You can stuff them too when the invitations are ready," Emily cackled.

She slapped the list down on the coffee table. No wonder both Emily and Marie enjoyed the fact that I would have to write out the envelopes.

"The envelopes are in the office downstairs," Emily laughed, prancing out of the room.

When I knew she was out of hearing range, I sighed deeply

and picked up the list. I didn't think there would be this many people attending. I walked down the stairs and made a right to go to the office. Pushing open the door, I walked toward the oak desk in the middle of the room. Large piles of envelopes cluttered the desk. I pushed some of them to the side to clear a space where I placed the list.

Picking up a fountain pen, I grabbed an envelope and looked at the first name. Mr. Doyle's mother was at the top. As neatly as I could write, I marked down Mrs. Catherine Doyle on the envelope and the address. I wrote extremely slowly. Then, triple-checked that I didn't make any mistakes. This task was going to take me forever.

I was in the process of writing the fifth name when I heard the hinges of the office door creak. Looking up from the envelope, I saw Marie scowling at me.

"What are you doing in here?" she snapped.

"I'm writing out the invitation envelopes," I replied.

"Well, I suppose you can stay here. Don't touch anything unless you feel like cleaning it. Emily, Preston, and I have been invited out to dinner. I expect those envelopes to be finished by the time we return."

I nodded, not sure how I was going to accomplish that. I hoped they would be out for a long time. I resumed my writing as Marie left the office. I heard a commotion coming from the front entryway a few minutes later, and I knew the family was leaving. At least they wouldn't be around to bother me.

I felt the silence settle over the house the minute they were gone. My hand was already beginning to cramp, and I hadn't even made a dent in the list. For a moment, I wondered whether the *quick complete charm* would still allow me to write neatly. Then I remembered Dr. Tweedle's warning about magic. Trying to ignore the stack of envelopes and the multiple pages of names, I continued writing. I had to admit that this was one of the worst tasks Marie had ever issued me.

Addresses flashed across my eyes, and my hand responded accordingly. I was so consumed in my task that I didn't even hear the office door open. Robert's voice startled me, almost ruining the envelope I was working on.

"You didn't come for dinner. Since Marie is out of the house, I thought I would find you. I'm sorry I scared you," he quickly apologized when he noticed I had jumped.

"That's okay. Emily has me addressing her wedding invitations. They want me to finish them before they return."

Robert eyed the stack of envelopes. "Are you supposed to use all of these?"

"There are over five hundred guests on the list, so I'll be very close to using all of these."

Robert crossed the room and came to stand behind me. He glanced at the list and shook his head.

"Please let me help you with this, Jane."

"I can't. Marie and Emily want each envelope to be written out neatly. Marie threatened to break my fingers if anything was not legible."

"Don't worry. I'm capable of writing neatly. Even though I worked for Mr. Wicker, I still learned how to read and write. One of Mr. Wicker's cooks took pity on me, and he taught me. He was the only reason I didn't starve to death too. Let me help you. I don't think you'll finish before they come home."

I looked at the stack of envelopes, unsure of what to do. I trusted Robert, but I didn't want to get in trouble. I certainly didn't want to get him in trouble. I was about to object when Robert grabbed one of the pages of the list and a fountain pen off the desk. I watched him for a minute as he wrote and then turned it to face me. His elegant scrawl dashed across the page. I thought it looked better than mine.

"Does this prove I'm capable of helping you?" he asked with a raised eyebrow.

I moved over and passed him a page of the list. Robert grabbed a chair, placing it right next to mine. My heart rate sped up at the simple fact of having him so close to me.

"I'll mix the envelopes I address with the ones you address. Marie can't possibly look at all five hundred envelopes," Robert said.

"Marie is crazier than you think. Thank you for helping me, Robert. I just hope it doesn't result in punishment."

Robert flashed me one of his smiles, and I felt butterflies in my stomach.

"Marie is having another Christmas party this year. She told me I would be helping out again," Robert commented.

"I wonder how late we'll be up cleaning after this one."

"I don't care as long as there's mistletoe," he grinned.

I could feel myself blushing. He continued. "This year, I would very much like to kiss you beneath it."

Last year, Robert and I accidentally stood under the mistletoe while cleaning up after the Christmas party. He had only kissed my hand before disappearing out to the barn. My cheeks felt like they were on fire.

"I think I would like that very much too," I whispered.

Robert's huge smile flashed across his face. He looked so happy, and my heart felt like it was flying. We worked in silence for a while. However, I was finding it hard to concentrate when every so often, Robert's arm would graze mine as he reached for another envelope. Struggling to focus, I wrote slowly so that I wouldn't do anything wrong and that everything was legible.

With Robert helping me, it didn't take as long as I had thought. We each took one of the last two pages. As my hand began cramping, I was glad to see the end of this torture was in sight. Robert and I discussed Emily's dress fitting when Robert abruptly stopped talking. I glanced over at him to see that his skin had gone very pale, and sweat glistened on his forehead.

"Robert, what's wrong?" I asked, grabbing his arm. What had come over him? His skin looked waxy and white.

Robert took a deep breath and used the sleeve of his shirt to wipe the sweat from his brow. He turned to gaze into my eyes.

"Did you know that Mr. Wicker was invited?"

17
The Best Christmas Present

Mr. Wicker, the man who had tortured Robert for most of his life, was invited to Emily's wedding. My mind kept replaying that fact as I worked to clean the manor for the Christmas party that evening. I couldn't understand why he had been invited. Last year, Mr. Wicker had been a suitor of Emily's, and she had rejected his marriage proposal. Why would he be on the guest list when the woman he had intended to marry was being betrothed to someone else? Perhaps he was an acquaintance of Mr. Doyle's. I wondered if that meant he had been invited to the Christmas party this evening.

Poor Robert. He would have to encounter his old master on multiple occasions. According to Robert, Mr. Wicker had been worse than Marie. He had taken Robert in when Robert had been separated from his mother, forcing him to become his household slave. Robert had told me that he had been beaten many times for talking. Even though he'd been working for the manor for over a year, I knew Robert still feared Mr. Wicker and became distressed when he had to encounter him.

I pushed thoughts of Mr. Wicker from my mind as I scrubbed

the floor of the first-floor guest bathroom. I pushed hard on the brush, trying to force the bristles into the cracks in the tile. Since I arrived at the manor, I had not used magic, and I was severely missing the *quick complete charm*. Doing everything the normal way was incredibly tiresome, especially when Marie always gave me the most extensive list of chores.

I was in the middle of doing a final mopping of the floor when Marie barged in.

"Are you almost done in here?" she snapped.

"Yes, ma'am," I said, plunging the mop into the bucket of water.

"Good," she said as her eyes crawled over the bathroom, inspecting for the tiniest speck of dirt. "I want you to clean yourself up and report to Emily's room to help her prepare."

I bowed my head as she walked out, relieved she hadn't given me a long list of commands. I carried the dirty water out of the kitchen's back door and dumped it. Then, replacing the bucket and mop in their rightful places, I went to the attic to freshen up. I knew Emily wouldn't appreciate it if I came into her suite of rooms with dirt on my hands and face.

Moving quickly, I splashed water on my face and changed my dirty clothes. Collecting every strand of my blonde hair, I braided it down my back, so it would be out of the way when I served the guests this evening. Giving my cheeks a quick pinch for color, I exited the attic and mentally prepared myself to help Emily.

Emily was impatiently waiting in her bathroom when I arrived at her suite.

"Hurry up and get me out of these clothes! I need to bathe before the guests arrive."

I helped Emily out of her gown. She shed her undergarments, and without shame for her nakedness, she pranced toward the already drawn bath. Once her body became submerged in the water, she commanded me to wash her long black hair. Gently,

I worked the soap into her tresses, careful not to pull her hair or scrub her scalp too hard.

"Drake has sent me a letter telling me that he has a special surprise for me this evening," she bragged as I rinsed the soap from her hair. "I am just dying to see what it is!"

She leaned forward so I could begin scrubbing her back with the sponge.

"You don't have to scrub that hard! I am not as filthy as you," Emily barked.

I had hardly been scrubbing, so I knew she was just trying to find something to complain about. When I had finished, I handed her the sponge, so she could wash the rest of her body. I turned my back to her to give her privacy.

I heard the water trickling from the sponge as Emily finished. Awaiting her next set of instructions, I moved over to the tall cabinet in the bathroom and removed a fluffy white towel. Emily declared she was done, and when I turned around, she was already standing up out of the water. Adverting my eyes, I rushed over with the towel and draped it over the front of her shoulders as she stepped from the tub. Her eyes held a gleam of wicked amusement.

"Does my nakedness embarrass you? It's not as if you have never seen a female body before. You do have the same anatomy, right?" she cackled nastily.

I busied myself with cleaning up the water that had spilled around the tub and refused to answer her. Emily quickly patted her body dry and then threw the towel to the side as she boldly strolled out of the bathroom.

"Jane, get my undergarments out of my closet and pull out the green dress with the long sleeves," she called back to me.

When I entered Emily's room, she was standing openly in the center of the room, not attempting to cover herself. I dashed into her closet.

"Jane, I don't know what your problem is. I'm going to be a

married woman soon. You do know what happens to a woman on her wedding night, don't you?" Emily teased.

I could feel the blush coming to my cheeks, and I was glad to be deep inside Emily's closet where she couldn't see me. I had heard the whispered conversations among the servants about what happened between a man and a woman, but no one had ever thoroughly explained everything. Why was Emily talking about this? This was not a proper conversation for a lady. Perhaps Emily's wedding dress shouldn't be white after all.

I ignored Emily as I came out of the closet with the clothes. I handed her the undergarments and then prepared her dress so she could step into it. Emily took her time putting her underthings on, and she gave me an evil grin as she stepped into the dress.

As I began doing up the buttons down the back of the dress, Emily started to speak again.

"I could tell you what happens, but I'm not going to. I will let you find out for yourself, but I doubt you ever will. Who would even want to marry you?" Emily snickered.

My mind went to Robert, and I smiled behind Emily's back. She could degrade me all she wanted, but she knew nothing. My fingers nimbly fastened the remaining buttons on the dress. Emily walked toward her floor-length mirror and gazed at her reflection. I crossed the room and pulled out her vanity chair because I knew my next task would be her hair and make-up.

When Emily was done admiring herself in the mirror, she took a seat in front of me. Per Emily's instructions, I began creating a braid on each side of her head and merging them into a French braid down her back. She then instructed me to find her green beaded hair comb, and when I did, I placed it above where the two braids converged. Emily analyzed her hair in the mirror and then snapped at me to fetch another mirror so she could gaze upon the back of her head.

As she admired her hair, I was surprised she hadn't found anything wrong with it.

"I don't want a lot of make-up, Jane. Just some blush, but not too much. Do you understand?" Emily said slowly.

It didn't take long to do what Emily had asked. She stared at herself for a very long time, and I thought she was going to complain. Surprisingly, she got up from the vanity chair.

"Get down to the front door so you can greet the guests. I am finished with you," Emily commanded.

I couldn't believe my ears. Typically, Emily was challenging. I had expected to change her hair, make-up, and outfit at least a dozen times. This was the first time she hadn't thrown a fit.

Making my way down the stairs, I ran a hand over my head to push back any loose strands. Marie would be furious if I looked disheveled. I wondered how long I would have to wait before the first guests arrived.

I hadn't been standing at the door very long when the first knock came. Opening the door, I saw Mr. Doyle and his mother standing on the steps. Behind them in the turnaround was a shiny black automobile. I had heard about automobiles, but I had never seen one before. I struggled to contain my awe as I greeted the Doyles.

"Where is Emily?" Mr. Doyle asked. "I want to show her my new automobile."

"Oh, Drake, is that you?" I heard Emily yell from the top of the stairs.

She slowly made her way down the stairs, her exquisite green dress flowing behind her. Mr. Doyle watched every step she took, never taking his eyes off her. When she reached the bottom, he took her hand in his and brought it to his lips.

"Drake darling, you haven't forgotten about my surprise, have you?" Emily inquired.

"No, sweetheart, it's right outside," he said, sweeping his hand toward the open front door.

I noticed Mrs. Doyle rolling her eyes, so I stepped over and offered to take her coat. Emily squealed so loud when she saw the automobile.

"When we are married, you'll never have to ride in a carriage pulled by repugnant horses again," Drake told her.

Suddenly, Marie's voice permeated the hall. "Jane, don't tell me you left the door open. There is a horrible draft." She rounded the corner coming from the direction of the dining room, saw the Doyles, and then stopped.

"Good evening. Merry Christmas. It is so good to see you. Jane, show them in and close the door," Marie said as she strolled across the front hall.

"Mother, Drake has purchased an automobile," Emily gushed.

"Lovely," Marie said with a small smile as she joined the Doyle's. I quickly closed the door and took Mr. Doyle's coat.

"I see you have someone to answer the door this time," Mrs. Doyle remarked snidely.

"Yes, it appears so," Marie said, shooting an evil glance. "Why don't you come with me into the parlor for some hors d'oeuvres while we wait for the other guests?"

Emily looped her arm around Mr. Doyle's and followed her mother across the front hall to the parlor. My heart rate sped up as I realized Robert would be helping tonight. I couldn't wait until everyone arrived so I could move on to my other tasks and be with him. Standing by the door was nerve-wracking initially, but as soon as guests arrived, I became fairly busy greeting and taking coats.

After a while, Marie came out of the parlor and made her way through the mingling crowd to me.

"Most of my guests have arrived. Stay at this door for a few more minutes and then head to the kitchen to help serve drinks and hors d'oeuvres," she commanded me.

I nodded so she knew I understood, and then she disappeared through the crowd.

Several minutes went by, and I was just getting ready to head to the kitchen when another knock sounded at the door. I opened the door to find Mr. Wicker standing there. My heart lurched in my chest. I tried to put a smile on my face as I greeted him. He gave me a look and squinted at me. I hoped that my hands weren't shaking as I took his coat. He clutched the top of his ruby-encrusted cane as he wobbled away from me into the crowded room. I was glad he hadn't spoken to me.

Taking deep breaths to clear my head, I made my way to the kitchen. I collected a full tray of champagne glasses and circled through the front hall and ballroom. With a silent sorry to Dr. Tweedle, I used my magic to keep the tray from wobbling.

I crossed paths with Robert several times, and he would wink at me as I went by. I had gotten close enough to him one time to whisper Mr. Wicker's name, so he would be prepared. I saw him blanch, but he continued to keep his head up, focusing solely on his task. I couldn't believe how calm he looked. I knew what seeing Mr. Wicker would mean to him, and I was so proud of him for trying to overcome his fear. Robert was safe here. Mr. Wicker could never hurt him again.

After circling several times with champagne and hors d'oeuvres, it was time for dinner. Together with a few other servers, Robert and I helped Ellen serve the dinner. The Christmas ham smelled good, and the mashed potatoes looked so creamy. My stomach rumbled as I walked around the table, refilling glasses. I knew there would hardly be anything left over, but I hoped Ellen had put something aside in the kitchen.

As I circled the table, I noticed Marie was subtlety watching my every move. I straightened my posture and paid attention to how I poured from the water pitcher. I wanted Marie to believe my etiquette school was teaching me something. Hopefully, she didn't know much about etiquette training. I was afraid that it would be harder to fool her as my years went by at the Jelf Academy.

Every so often, I was glad to escape Marie's gaze as I ducked into the kitchen to refill the pitcher. The other guests acted as if I didn't even exist. Not even Emily or Preston glanced at me as I made my way around the table. Everyone was in deep conversation. I could tell that Emily wasn't too happy that Mrs. Doyle was sitting on the other side of Mr. Doyle. She kept trying to exclude her from the conversation, but Mrs. Doyle didn't notice because she kept adding her two cents to everything. I was trying hard not to laugh as I saw Emily's aspirated face.

Once dinner was complete, the guests moved back into the front hall and ballroom. Robert and I helped clear the table, and then we continued carrying around drinks. The music from the band leaked out into the front hall, and when I glanced into the ballroom, I saw that some guests were already beginning to dance. Dance cards flashed on all the women's wrists, and I wondered who Emily would allow to fill her card. The music was vivacious. I wished I could be dancing with Robert this Christmas. As I walked around the outside edge of the ballroom, I noticed Mr. Wicker approaching Emily. Stepping closer, I managed to overhear the conversation.

"No, Mr. Wicker, I do not wish to dance with you. My dance card is full," Emily was saying stiffly.

"There is no way your card can be full. The dancing is just beginning," he complained as spittle flew from the corners of his fat lips.

Emily retreated a step, a look of disgust on her face. "Mr. Wicker, how dare you! Are you calling me a liar and questioning the availability of my dance card? You insult me in my own house!" she said shrilly.

"You insult me by not dancing with me!" Mr. Wicker snarled. I noticed that some of the other guests started staring at them.

Suddenly, Mr. Doyle jumped into the conversation by sliding himself in between Emily and Mr. Wicker.

"Mr. Wicker, my man," he said jovially. "Are you harassing my future wife?"

"I was just asking for a spot on her dance card," Mr. Wicker huffed.

"And I told him it is full," Emily said sweetly.

"If the lady says her card is full, I think it would be best to find another partner. I've certainly filled several places on Miss Emily's card," Mr. Doyle said as he led Mr. Wicker away from Emily.

Emily stared after them with an evil smile on her face. I moved away from her before she could realize I was there. I couldn't believe Mr. Wicker still sought Emily out after her rude rejection last year. I had no idea why the man thought he would receive any other reaction from her.

The night flew by as dance after dance was played. I watched the couples twirling around on the floor. Robert and I continued offering refreshments to the winded guests. I could tell Robert was sending me messages with his eyes, and I tried to keep the blush from my face. Soon the crowd began to thin, and the band died down. I resumed my position at the front door to reissue coats and bid farewells.

"I am actually surprised by how wonderful your Christmas party was," Mrs. Doyle said, giving Marie a backhanded compliment.

Marie's eyes narrowed as she watched the Doyles exit the front door, and Mr. Doyle helped his mother into the new automobile.

When I had closed the door behind them, Marie mumbled to Emily about how much she hated Mrs. Doyle. With all the guests gone, I made my way to the kitchen to begin the cleanup. I could sense Marie on my heels. Before I reached the door to the dining room, I turned to face her.

"Jane, I want every room downstairs mopped and swept clean. I don't want to see a single speck of dirt tomorrow morning. Also, a good polish would do well to get the scuff marks up from dancing.

My floors should look like glass. If I cannot see my reflection in them, you will be severely punished.

"There is a stack of dishes on the kitchen counter that need to be taken care of, and I want everything in that kitchen to sparkle. I will inspect everything in the morning. Also, do not forget to clean the guest bathroom thoroughly," Marie commanded as she gripped the balustrade.

"Yes, ma'am," I replied, bowing my head.

Glad that she was going to bed, I quickly made my way to the kitchen to get started. My first order of business would be to take care of the dishes. Robert was already waiting for me, and he had begun shoveling leftover scraps into the garbage.

"Would you like to wash or dry?" he questioned, raising an eyebrow when he saw me enter.

"You can dry," I replied, taking my place in front of the sink. I began washing dish after dish, my hands starting to prune. Robert stood silently beside me as I handed the dishes to him. It was nice that we could work in such an easy silence, comfortable in the other's presence.

Once the dishes were finished, Robert and I worked at scrubbing down the kitchen, which didn't take long because Ellen always kept her workstation reasonably neat. I prepared the bucket and mop and quickly wiped down the kitchen floor before moving into the dining room. Robert helped me move the table and chairs and roll up the rug in the center of the floor. While I started in the dining room, Robert disappeared to find another mop and bucket.

I slid the mop over the floor, which was really not that dirty since I had mopped it before the party. Preston had actually behaved himself and hadn't thrown food on the floor. I was surprised he hadn't been disruptive since he acts that way on a day-to-day basis. Next year, he would be fifteen years old, and I could never get over how he acted.

Robert re-entered the dining room with another mop and bucket.

"I'll start in the ballroom, and we can meet in the middle of the front hall," he said, toting the mop and bucket of water across the dining room.

It wasn't long before I had finished the dining room floor and moved into the front hall. I moped to the guest bathroom and decided to finish that first. I had gotten a head start in the dining room, and the ballroom was a much larger area. By the time I finished in the bathroom, Robert and I could work on the front hall together. For a moment, I considered using the *quick complete charm* but decided against it. What if Robert caught me? Not that Robert would be a member of the W.A.S.P., but he didn't know who I truly was. Robert was special to me, and I cared about him so much. I would be hurt deeply if he rejected me in any way. I would never do anything to jeopardize our relationship, and I wasn't allowed to tell him what I was anyway. A part of me felt guilty that I wasn't being honest with him. Wasn't an omission just as bad as a lie?

Once I finished with the guest bathroom, I headed back into the front hall. I could see Robert was almost to the door of the ballroom. If we worked at the same pace, we would meet in the middle. My arm started to get tired, but I pushed myself to keep going. We still had to polish all the floors.

Robert smiled at me from across the floor, and I couldn't help the blush that spread across my face.

"How's the mopping going?" he asked.

"It's great," I replied. "This is the most fun I've had in years."

"Well, I'm honored that you have it with me," he said with a chuckle.

I looked down at my mop and bucket. I could feel the smile spreading across my face. Robert always made the sweetest comments.

It wasn't too long before we both reached the middle. I noticed the sweat across Robert's brow, and I hoped my face didn't look dirty. I quickly ran my sleeve over my forehead while Robert looked down to plunge his mop into the bucket.

"Step one is now complete," I said with a sigh. "Marie wants all the floors polished as well."

Robert let out a deep sigh and sat on the first step of the stairs. I joined him as we waited for the floor to dry.

"Did you see Mr. Wicker?" I asked.

"I did my best to avoid him. I can't wrap my head around the fact that he was here. If he is invited to the wedding, I should have expected to see him tonight."

"Emily refused to add him to her dance card. They were arguing before Mr. Doyle stepped in. That's why I don't understand how he was invited. Emily hates him," I said.

"Maybe he's friends of the Doyles, but I don't recall if they were ever invited to Mr. Wicker's house," Robert said with a pensive look.

"Every time Emily sees him, she goes out of her way to insult him. He was so disgusting and practically spitting on her when he talked," I replied.

"I don't blame Emily for rejecting that man. He makes my skin crawl. I'm so lucky to be away from him. He's evil."

When the floors were dry, Robert and I began polishing. He started in the ballroom and I in the dining room with the plan to meet in the middle. I was feeling exhausted by the time I had polished my way back to the stairs. The floors looked perfect to me, and I hoped Marie would not find anything to complain about. Practically throwing myself, I sat down next to Robert again.

"I'm glad it's finally over," Robert said, flexing his fingers.

I leaned back on the stairs and rested my head. I could feel my eyes beginning to droop. Every muscle in my body ached. Would I even be able to climb the stairs to the attic?

"Jane, are you alright?" I could hear the concern in Robert's voice.

"Yes, I'm just drained," I replied, sitting up.

"Well, I hope it's not too late for a mistletoe kiss," Robert said mischievously with a glance at the mistletoe that hung between the doorway to the ballroom and the front entryway.

I knew that my cheeks were red again. "It's never too late for a mistletoe kiss," I replied.

I let Robert take my hand and pull me over to stand beneath the mistletoe. My heart felt like it was going to pound out of my chest. He cupped my head with his hands, and I felt him rubbing my cheekbones with his thumbs. Slowly he bent his head down to mine. I closed my eyes, anticipating him to kiss my lips, but instead, he kissed both of my cheeks and then my forehead. His warm breath caressed my face.

"Jane, do you know how much you mean to me?" he asked, clutching my hands and resting his forehead against mine.

"You mean the world to me, Robert," I replied. I could feel my legs beginning to shake beneath me. I couldn't tell if it was because I was exhausted or because I had never seen Robert look so serious before.

"Jane, I have to tell you something."

"Yes, Robert?" I said, leaning back to look into his chocolate eyes.

"I love you," he whispered.

My heart exploded. Had I heard him correctly? Did he just tell me that he loved me? It had been years since I heard those three little words.

"I love you, Jane," he said louder. "I know I have nothing to offer you, and I understand if you don't feel the same, but I just had to tell you."

I thought my legs were going to go out beneath me. I was glad to be holding onto him. Robert loved me. I didn't think I could breathe.

"Are you alright?" he asked. Could he feel me trembling?

"Yes, Robert. I'm fine. I love you, too," I whispered.

Robert pulled me to him and gave me the kiss I had anticipated. His lips were soft and warm. It was the best kiss we ever shared. Robert held me so gently. I couldn't believe I was in his arms and that he had told me he loved me. This was more surreal than finding out a school for people like me existed.

Robert took a step back from me but still kept his hands on my arms. "Jane, I want to give you something."

Robert reached beneath the neckline of his shirt and extracted the chain which held his father's ring. Lifting it over his head, he held it in the palm of his hand.

"Your father's ring," I breathed. The ring was the only connection Robert had to his family. It had his family crest on the front. Robert's mother had given him the ring, and he had been wearing it the day he became separated from her. Robert never had a chance to find his parents because of Mr. Wicker. He had told me that he wasn't even sure where to begin looking because he couldn't remember anything from his childhood.

"This ring is all I have. I want you to have it as a promise. I promise to love you for the rest of my life. I promise to always be by your side, and I promise that we will have a life together someday. I know this isn't much, but all I have to give you is my heart."

"Your heart is all I could ever want, Robert," I whispered.

Robert undid the clasp on the chain and placed the ring around my neck.

"One day, Jane, I promise to give you the life you deserve," he said, kissing me again.

18
The New Year's Eve Party

My fingers caressed the chain around my neck as I tucked Robert's ring beneath my clothes. My head was still spinning. I could hardly believe Robert had given me his only family heirloom. My heart swelled as I closed my eyes to relive the best Christmas of my life. Robert loved me, and I loved him. For the first time, I had happy thoughts about my future. As long as I had Robert by my side, nothing else mattered. Is this how my mother had felt when she had fallen in love with my father?

My Christmas break had flown by, and I was in the middle of collecting my things. It was hard for me to comprehend that it was New Year's Eve already. Even though I couldn't wait to return to the academy, I didn't want to leave Robert. Leaving this time was extremely difficult.

I was also nervous about returning to the Jelf Academy. How was I even supposed to keep this a secret? I felt like Josefina would take one look at me and know that something was different. I couldn't tell anyone. Loving a human was forbidden. Would Josefina even understand?

I paused in my packing when I heard a commotion downstairs.

Looking through the attic window, I spotted Dr. Tweedle's carriage parked in the drive. I knew it wasn't that late, so I was shocked he had come for me already. Last year, he arrived at midnight. Quickly, I threw the rest of my belongings into my bag and hurried out of the attic.

"I still don't understand why you're here so early," Marie's shrill voice echoed up to the second-floor landing.

"I'm here to take Jane back to the Jelf Academy. Her holiday break is over," Dr. Tweedle replied calmly.

"You didn't come for her this early last year. It is only eight o'clock. How do you know that Jane is even finished with her chores?" Marie squawked.

"Madam, how do you know when I came for Jane last year? I believe you were not home. Besides, this house looks spectacular. I can't imagine what Jane would have to finish. Oh, there you are, Jane, dear," Dr. Tweedle said, spotting me at the top of the stairs.

Without saying a word, I continued down the rest of the stairs and stood at his side.

"It was lovely to see you again, madam," Dr. Tweedle said as he opened the front door. He put an arm around me and ushered me outside and down to the carriage. I caught the surprised look on Marie's face, and I hoped she would forget about this by next weekend.

Dr. Tweedle helped me into the carriage and hastily came around to the other side. He briskly cracked the whip, causing the horses to surge forward. When we reached the end of the driveway, Dr. Tweedle started to chuckle.

"Is that woman always so demanding? Every time I come to collect you, she's difficult."

"I'm sorry she makes it so awkward, Dr. Tweedle," I said. "She's just used to getting her way. I'm not at her beck and call every day when I'm at the academy."

"There have been a few disappearances over the last week, and the authorities are suspecting the W.A.S.P., but there hasn't been any evidence. I'm hoping it's just a misunderstanding, but it doesn't look good given the current circumstances. The sooner we get back to the academy, the safer we are," Dr. Tweedle said.

"Thank you for coming for me earlier than last year," I replied.

"You're welcome. This year, you'll be able to enjoy the New Year's Eve party."

"How was your holiday?" I asked.

"Mine was quite lovely. Thank you for asking. I hope yours was as well," Dr. Tweedle said as he pulled the horses to a stop on a secluded part of the road.

"My holiday was better than last year," I replied as I watched him pour the *teleportation charm* into his hand.

"Hold on, Jane," Dr. Tweedle said, tossing the dust into the air.

I clung to the side of the carriage as the familiar sensation of teleporting took over.

It wasn't long before we rode the cloud up to the Jelf Academy. It felt good to return, but Robert nagged at the back of my mind. I missed him already and wished he could be here with me.

Dr. Tweedle held the front door for me when we reached the castle. "The party begins at nine o'clock. You have some time to freshen up, unlike last year," he commented.

"Thank you so much, Dr. Tweedle," I said as I headed up to my room.

After climbing all the stairs to the fifth floor, I took a deep breath. Looking down, I made sure Robert's ring was hidden beneath my blouse, and then I laid my hand on the panel. When the door slid open, Coco, Josefina's cactus cat, leapt into my arms. Thankfully I reacted in time to catch her

"Hello, girl. Did you miss me?" I asked as I rubbed her head. Her dark gray fur felt so soft under my fingertips.

Looking up, I noticed Josefina was surrounded by Marley, Candi, and Bellony.

"Jane, I'm so glad you got back early this year!" Josefina said, noticing that I was standing in the doorway.

"Yes, I won't have to miss half the New Year's Eve party," I said, closing the door and crossing the room.

Marley, Candi, and Bellony didn't look too thrilled that I was here. I ignored them as I gently put Coco down on my bed and placed my bag on my desk. I began unpacking as the girls resumed their chatter.

"Girls," Josefina said, interrupting them. "I'm sure Jane would like to freshen up before the party. We'll see you downstairs in a half-hour." Josefina rose from her bed and ushered them all to the door. They looked surprised as they mumbled their goodbyes. Josefina closed the door behind them and turned to me with a massive smile on her face.

"Now, it's time for me to give you your Christmas present!" she exclaimed, reaching under her bed to pull out a box.

"Josefina, you didn't have to get me anything. I'm sorry that I didn't get you anything," I said sadly.

"Jane, it's okay that you didn't get me anything. I understand. I wanted to get you something because you're my best friend. It's just something little," she said, handing me the box.

"Thank you. You don't know how much this means to me," I said, taking the box and sitting on the edge of my bed.

I unwrapped the gift and lifted the lid. Inside was a beautiful purple dress with beaded white flowers around the collar and waist. It wasn't over the top, like a ball gown, but casual. Next to the dress was a small box. Slowly, I opened the box to find a fantastic amethyst necklace. The large amethyst in the middle was pear-shaped, and a spiral of silver was wrapped around it. Attached to the bottom of the spiral were three more amethysts in a marquis shape. The two smaller ones were on both sides of the larger one. The necklace was stunning.

"Thank you so much, Josefina. I don't even know what to say," I exclaimed as I touched the necklace.

"I didn't want the other girls to be around when you opened this. I only gave them jewelry. When I saw that dress, I thought you had to have it because it matches your eyes. You could wear it tonight to the party!" she said excitedly.

"Josefina, this is so nice of you," I said, tears welling in my eyes. Besides my school uniform, I didn't have nice clothes.

"Awe, Jane, don't cry," Josefina said, coming to my side. "We're going to have fun tonight. I bought you amethysts because of their calming power, plus they matched the dress," Josefina laughed.

"I don't know how I can ever repay you," I said, hugging her.

"Come on; the party is going to start soon. Get into that dress so I can do your hair," Josefina said, squeezing me back.

I raced off to the bathroom with the dress and the necklace. The fabric was so soft, and it felt incredible when I slipped it on. Since it was made out of pixie material, it fit perfectly. Slowly, I unclasped Robert's ring from my neck. I felt weird taking it off, but I wouldn't be able to wear it unnoticed with the dress. Putting on my new necklace, I clutched the ring in my fist. I needed to hide it before anyone saw it.

Calmly, I walked out of the bathroom, holding the outfit I had just taken off over my clenched hand.

"Let me put this away, and then you can start on my hair," I told Josefina as I walked toward my side of the room.

"Jane, that dress looks amazing on you," Josefina cried.

"Thank you," I replied, turning my back to her and subtly opening up my rock case. I slipped the ring into an empty compartment.

When I turned around, Josefina motioned for me to sit on the edge of her bed. She ran a brush through my long blonde hair and then braided it into a crown on the top of my head. Josefina was quick at braiding, so it didn't take long. When she was finished,

I looked in the mirror and complimented her on how beautiful my hair was.

"Are you ready to head down to the dining hall? It's a little after nine," she said, checking the clock.

"Sure," I said, looping my arm through hers. I wasn't sure if it was the calming effects of the new necklace, but I felt terrific.

"How was your Christmas holiday?" I asked on the way down.

"It was nice. I wish you could've come home with us. Lena is doing a little better. She still doesn't remember us. I think she is just taking our word for it."

"I hope her memory returns."

"She remembered she doesn't like broccoli. We're all hoping something will trigger her memory. Lena finally seems to realize she is safe now. Dr. Tweedle plans to test Lena on what she remembers from her pixie classes. Juan has offered to be her tutor. Hopefully, she remembers the lessons to catch up on her fourth year," Josefina said.

I was sure Dr. Tweedle was also trying to find out what she had told the W.A.S.P. Pixie lives, including mine, were at risk.

The dining hall was already full when Josefina and I arrived. We got in line at the buffet and filled our plates with appetizers.

"Miguel and Juan are sitting over there with Lena and Andrew," Josefina said, pointing in their direction.

"Jane, it's so good to see you," Miguel called when he spotted us.

"Hello," I said, nodding to Lena, Juan, and Andrew as I sat down.

"How was your Christmas?" Miguel asked. "Andrew was just telling us about his trip to Norway. His parents took him skiing."

"That sounds like it was more fun than I had," I commented.

"Well, if you have awful balance, trust me, it's not," Andrew laughed.

"How was Marie this Christmas?" Josefina asked.

"The same as always. I was cleaning again for another Christmas party. Emily was also measured for her wedding dress. Mr. Doyle had dress designers from Europe come to create the dress."

"Wow, that must have been expensive!" Josefina exclaimed.

"Mr. Doyle is wealthy. He will do just about anything to make Emily happy," I said.

"I wonder how long it took them to cross the Atlantic. Thankfully, we have the *teleportation charm*, so my parents and I could get to Norway in a few minutes," Andrew said.

"The abilities of pixie magic never cease to amaze me," I laughed.

"Yes, I don't know how humans do it. I couldn't be cramped on a boat for days or traveling in a carriage forever just to get somewhere," Andrew said, shaking his head.

I honestly didn't know anything about travel. I had never left the manor until the Jelf Academy.

"Speaking of ways to get around, Mr. Doyle also bought an automobile for Christmas," I said.

"Yes, he obviously has money," Juan commented. "I'm glad we don't have to rely on human forms of transportation. Once we teleport where we want, a horse and buggy will do just fine for the rest of the way."

I could see the confused look on Lena's face, and Juan leaned over to explain what we had been talking about.

All of a sudden, I heard a commotion behind me. Turning my head, I saw Marley, Candi, and Bellony approaching our table. On instinct, I slid down toward Miguel and Andrew so that the girls couldn't shove me out of the way. Without acknowledging anyone besides Josefina, they sat down. Miguel shook his head, but he continued to ask me about my Christmas.

"I'm going to assume it was awful," Miguel said with a frown.

"Yes. I was cleaning before and after the Christmas party. I was cleaning again last night into the early hours. I wonder if I'll even be able to make it to midnight," I joked.

"Why do you have to clean?" Andrew asked, a confused look on his face.

"I live with my stepmother. My father passed away when I was five, and ever since then, my stepmother has treated me like a servant. I have nowhere else to go, and I don't have the means to leave. Also, the house has so many memories of my father," I explained.

I could see the pity on Andrew's face, and I became slightly uncomfortable.

"It's fine," I said, trying to make it sound less terrible. "It's nothing that I can't handle."

"Jane," Josefina called down to me. "I almost forgot to ask you. Did you clean up all by yourself, or did your friend help you? His name's Robert, right?"

At the mention of Robert's name, I could feel the blush coming to my cheeks. I raised my glass of water to my lips in an attempt to put out the heat that had washed over my face. It had been a long time since I mentioned Robert to her. How had she remembered his name?

"Yes, Robert helped me," I choked out.

"Who is Robert?" Marley asked snidely.

"Robert is a friend of Jane's. He works at the manor where she lives," I heard Josefina explain, grateful that I didn't have to.

I caught the girls' devious smiles out of the corner of my eye. I could only imagine what they were thinking. Probably something along the lines of "Jane, the half-human, is friends with the human help." My cheeks burned even redder. I turned away from them and faced Miguel.

"Are you alright, Jane? You're flushed," he commented.

"I'm fine. Just feeling a little hot suddenly," I replied, taking another sip of my water.

Soon, my cup was empty, and I slowly stood from the table to get a refill. Before I could even move away, Betty Ann approached with Thomas on her arm.

"Jane, is that a new dress? How did you ever afford such a thing?" she asked loudly.

I noticed Marley, Candi, and Bellony hiding their faces behind their hands to conceal their laughter.

"What do you want, Betty Ann?" I asked.

"I wondered how a charity case could afford a dress like that. If you all don't know, Jane is a dirt-poor half-human who gets her books by borrowing money from the school. Perhaps she has resorted to stealing now," Betty Ann announced.

"Everyone here knows Jane's financial situation, and we don't care, so if you're thinking of trying to embarrass her, think again. Move along, Betty Ann. No one cares what you have to say. How dare you accuse her of being a thief! If I didn't know any better, I would say you're jealous of her," Miguel said, standing up.

Betty Ann laughed one of her false laughs. "Why would I be jealous of a half-human? That is absurd!" Betty Ann said, motioning with her hand that held her drink.

Juan jumped up in seconds. He grabbed Betty Ann's wrist and directed her cup away from me. "Don't even think about ruining another of Jane's dresses," he growled.

"Take your hand off of her," Thomas said, jumping in.

Juan let go of Betty Ann, but he kept a hostile eye trained on her.

"Let's go, Thomas," Betty Ann said, examining her wrist. She gave me a very nasty look before she walked away.

"Thank you, Juan," I said. I was grateful he had stopped her from carrying out her plan of coming over here.

"She ruined a dress of yours," I heard Lena whisper.

"What did you say, Lena?" Juan asked, kneeling next to her so that he could hear her better.

"Did that girl ruin a dress before?" she asked.

"Yes!" Juan said excitedly. "At the Harvest Festival, Betty Ann ruined Jane's dress with the punch. Do you remember? We helped Jane. You took her back to her room. Do you remember that?"

Lena scrunched her face up in contemplation. "I don't know. I'm trying to remember. I thought the exchange seemed familiar, but now I'm confused." Lena put her face in her hands. "Everything is so confusing."

"It's okay," Juan said, patting her shoulder. "I'm sure it will come back eventually."

"I'm sorry. I'm trying so hard, but I don't remember anything. I don't remember you or anyone at this table. All I remember is pain and somehow finding my way here. I'm sorry," Lena sobbed.

"Lena, I love you. I promise I will help you figure this out. I'll help you to remember," Juan said.

Lena looked taken aback. "How can you say you love me when I barely know you? I know you say we had a past together, but I don't remember one second of it! This holiday with your family has been very nice, but I need some time to think!" Lena rose from the table and ran from the dining hall.

Juan's face looked stricken as he watched her leave. I felt so bad for him. Lena had confessed to Josefina and me that she was in love with Juan. It was so terrible that she didn't remember. What had the W.A.S.P. done to her?

"I'm not giving up on her," Juan said through clenched teeth. "I'll just have to make her fall in love with me again. I'll do whatever it takes to restore her memory."

I patted Juan's shoulder, hoping against hope that Lena's memory wasn't lost forever.

19

Peer Pressure

Classes resumed with fervor, the teachers in a frenzy to teach us as much as possible. January flew by at an alarming rate, and soon I was beginning to see flyers posted for the Valentine's Day dance. I wasn't disappointed that I couldn't attend because I was looking forward to seeing Robert. I hardly ever found myself dreading my weekly return to the manor.

Since break ended, Josefina was always busy with the girls, claiming they needed to study every night. I highly doubted they were that committed. When Josefina wasn't around, I studied in my room or snuck out to attend to my dragon egg. Once in a while, Josefina would ask me to study with her and the girls. I had agreed to join them a few times, but they always glared at me as if I was interrupting something. It was always, so I just went back to finding excuses not to go.

In the past month, Dr. Tweedle had been working with Lena. She was catching onto her schoolwork rather quickly. Dr. Tweedle believed she would complete her fourth year on time, which was fantastic. She only had a memory of her school subjects. Lena also continued to distance herself from Juan. He remained persistent, but I saw his face fall every time she rejected his help or refused to spend time with him. Every day, I prayed to the pixie gods that she would have a breakthrough.

Once again, Lena had opted not to sit with us for breakfast. I noticed Juan's longing expression as he watched her across the dining hall.

"Stop staring at her," Josefina commanded. "You're going to scare her away."

"This is killing me," he sighed.

"Juan, you have to understand that Lena doesn't remember growing up with us. Your persistence is frustrating her. We've tried everything we can think of to trigger her memory. Give her some space," Josefina lectured.

Juan gave her a piercing look but nodded his head and turned away.

"I'm sure if she has questions, she'll come to you. Quit trying to shove memories down her throat."

"Okay. Stop preaching," Juan grumbled.

"Josefina has a point," Miguel added. "None of us want you to lose her."

"Don't lose hope, Juan. She might eventually remember something," I said.

Marley, Candi, and Bellony looked extremely bored by our conversation, so they tried changing the subject as soon as they got a chance. They were so self-centered and inconsiderate. Breakfast couldn't end soon enough. I needed to get away from those three.

When Miguel and I entered the Charms classroom, we noticed that Josefina stayed behind to finish her conversation. As soon as I entered, Mr. Withermyer's green eyes flicked to me and didn't leave me until I was seated.

Josefina skirted into the classroom right as the bell rang, causing Mr. Withermyer to shoot her a nasty look.

"As soon as Miss Martinez takes her seat, we can begin," he stated. Josefina's cheeks quickly turned red as she slid in beside me.

"Today, class, you will be creating a *love charm*. Don't get overly excited because we will not be testing them on each other. I will be collecting samples of your charms to analyze. You will be graded from the conclusions I draw. While I pass out the Bunsen burners, open your books to the *love charm*. Everything you will need should be in your pixie dust cases. You have until the end of class to finish your charm and turn in a vial."

Once the burners were handed out, Mr. Withermyer gave us the signal to begin.

According to the instructions, I had to grind down all the ingredients into a fine powder. The components had to be added to boiling water in the order specified. To finish the charm, a person's essence had to be added for it to work. This ingredient had to come from the person who wanted to use the charm to make someone fall in love with them. The mixture had to return to a boil again before it could be drained. After being drained, the dust had to dry completely before it was bottled.

Before I could even begin on the *love charm*, I needed to create a *fountain charm* for the water and a *fire charm* to light the burner. I searched through my pixie dust case for vials of previous charms and was relieved to find a *fountain charm*. I would only have to make a *fire charm*. I grabbed the rubies I needed, quickly made the *fire charm*, and then lit the burner. My *fountain charm* immediately turned to water when added to a pot. While the water started to boil, I began crushing the stones for the *love charm*. The *love charm* required: one cup of powdered jade, three-fourths cup of powdered sapphire, and one-fourth of a cup of powdered sugilite.

As soon as the water came to a boil, I added the jade first, then the sapphire, and finally the sugilite. I kept an eye on the clock, making sure the mixture boiled for precisely ten minutes. Out of the corner of my eye, I saw Betty Ann watching me. There were so many things to accomplish that I didn't care if she was trying to cheat off me.

When ten minutes had passed, I plucked a few strands of my hair and added them to the boiling water. Looking through my pixie dust case, I located a strainer. Carefully, I drained all the water until a beautiful mixture of green, blue, and purple dust remained. I spread the dust onto a thin towel for it to dry.

Glancing at the clock, I saw only four minutes were remaining. I lifted the ends of the towel and began patting the powder, hoping it would become reasonably dry in time. Plucking an empty vial from my case, I started filling it with my charm at the last minute. Once I had filled the vial, I wrote my name on a label along with the name of the charm. It wasn't long before Mr. Withermyer began walking around the room collecting the vials. His piercing green eyes glared into mine as he grabbed the charm off my desk.

The charm book stated that the *love charm* was supposed to be added to the food or drink of the person whom the charm was supposed to affect. I couldn't help but wonder how Mr. Withermyer would test them.

When the bell rang, I waved goodbye to Josefina and headed toward History of Pixies with Miguel.

"Making a *love charm* was intense. It's just like Mr. Withermyer to have us create two other charms before attempting the assignment," Miguel said in disgust.

Mr. Collyworth soon entered the classroom. I noticed the word Egypt glowing brightly on the board behind him.

"Good morning, class. Today we are going to be talking about Egypt. Egypt, located in northeast Africa, is one of the well-known ancient civilizations. Although many events happened prior to establishing the Old Kingdom era, that's where we will begin our lecture. One of the first rulers during this time was a pixie pharaoh named Djoser, who is known for creating the first step pyramid. The building of this pyramid took a long time, but not nearly as long as human historians claim. All the great pyramids in Egypt were actually built by pixie pharaohs.

"Now, since these pixie pharaohs had accomplished building these great structures, the Egyptian people believed them to be invincible, god-like beings," Mr. Collyworth explained.

Points of importance flashed on the board as he talked. I quickly wrote them down along with the additional details of the lecture.

Mr. Collyworth spent the rest of the lecture explaining Egyptian pixie culture. My hand was starting to cramp from the number of notes. I was relieved when the class had ended. Climbing to the third floor, I entered the west wing and went into the first door on the left. Taylor was already in the classroom, so I slid into my seat next to her.

"Hi, Jane. How are you today?" she asked me.

"I'm doing fine. How about you?"

"I'm hoping I did okay on my *love charm*. I wasn't expecting to make two other charms as well. Mr. Withermyer is unfair. From now on, I'm going to make charms in my room, so I have them ready in case something like that happens again," Taylor said.

"That's a great idea," I replied.

"Would you like to come by my room some evening this week to create charms together? You're so good at that class. It would be great to have the help," Taylor said.

"Sure, I'd love to help! Just let me know when you would like to. I'm available any time."

Before Mrs. Harris began class, Taylor and I agreed to meet that evening. I wrote down her room number on the corner of my notebook so I would remember.

It wasn't until class started that I noticed Josefina hadn't shown up for class. That wasn't like her. The longer the course went on without her appearance, the more I worried. Did she feel okay? Did something happen? All sorts of thoughts ran through my head as I tried hard to pay attention to the lecture.

When the bell rang, I quickly waved goodbye to Taylor and raced to my room, hoping to find Josefina. Urgently, I slapped my hand onto the door panel but was utterly stunned when the door swung open, revealing Josefina and Marley. It was shocking to see Marley by herself. She was never without the other two.

"Josefina, are you okay? You weren't in Zodiac Signs," I stammered.

"Yes, I'm fine. Marley just needed my help," Josefina said. "She has a Predicting the Future test after lunch."

"So, you missed class?" The question just popped out of my mouth before I could stop it. I couldn't understand why Josefina had skipped class to help Marley study. Why couldn't they have gone over Marley's notes during lunch?

"Zodiac Signs wasn't that important," Josefina said, sounding defensive. "Marley needed my help, and I'm a good friend. Why do you sound so appalled?"

I shook my head and crossed over to my bed. "I'm just surprised," I said.

I couldn't believe Josefina was potentially hurting her education and breaking the rules to help Marley. I had never seen her do anything like this before, and I couldn't understand why she was getting so defensive with me.

"I'll see you in the dining hall, Josefina," Marley said, throwing her bag over her shoulder and glaring at me before she walked out.

When she was gone, Josefina turned to me. "Why do I always feel like you're judging Marley? Now you're judging me for missing one class?" she said.

"I'm not judging anyone. I'm just surprised that you skipped. I thought something bad had happened." I tried to keep my voice at a normal level, but it was hard.

"One class isn't going to kill me, Jane. We don't have to follow all the rules."

"Josefina, I've never known you to do something like this," I explained. Why was she getting angry with me for being concerned about her?

"Marley needed my help, so she asked me to study with her. Skipping one class is hardly something to be so shocked about. Marley and the rest of the girls aren't bad people."

"I never said they were," I said, feeling frustrated. "I'm sorry. I was just surprised. I'm not judging anyone."

Josefina was making me really mad. How could she defend them so vehemently but couldn't see that they had judged me for being a half-human? I was almost on the verge of telling her about everything I'd overheard, but I stopped myself. I didn't feel like getting into it, especially in her current mood. She probably wouldn't believe me anyway. She would defend them, and I just wanted to get out of the room.

"I'll see you in the dining hall for lunch," I said, opening the door and leaving before she could say anything else. I didn't want to say anything I would regret, so it was easier to walk away.

During lunch, Josefina didn't try to continue our conversation. The girls surrounded her as usual. Everything seemed normal on the outside, but I could feel the tension. I wondered if Miguel could too. Did he know that his sister had skipped a class today? I had a feeling he wouldn't approve either. I couldn't comprehend why she didn't realize I was only concerned about her. There was plenty of time outside of class to study, so why hadn't Marley asked for help last night?

On the way to Magical Creatures, Miguel and I did most of the talking while Josefina stayed quiet. I was sure Miguel was mentally probing for an explanation, but I wasn't sure if she would give him one.

"Good afternoon, class. I hope everyone has had a good lunch," Mrs. Rowley stated. "If you look behind me in the fenced area, there is the animal we will be discussing today. Can any of you tell me what it is?"

Looking behind Mrs. Rowley, I saw a massive animal with the body of an ox, but the fur was puffy and brown like a bear. The head of the animal looked like a stag with many points on its antlers. There was a regal air about him that amazed me. I grabbed my book and began paging through it.

"Miss Barber," Mrs. Rowley said. "Do you know what kind of animal this is?"

Betty Ann rolled her eyes, sighing at being called on. "Is it a griffin?"

"Good guess, but no. A griffin has the body of a lion and the wings and head of an eagle."

As I paged through my book, I found a picture that looked like the animal in front of me. Quickly, I raised my hand, and Mrs. Rowley called on me.

"Is it a parander?" I asked.

"Good job, Jane! You are correct! This animal is a parander."

I noticed Betty Ann shoot me dirty looks for answering correctly.

"If the parander feels scared or threatened, he can change shape. Watch closely as I approach the fence," Mrs. Rowley said.

Slowly, Mrs. Rowley took a few steps toward the fence. The parander's head shot up from the grass it had been munching and stared right at her. Within seconds, it disappeared and, in its place, stood a tree whose branches looked just as numerous as the parander's antlers. I had never seen anything transform before my eyes like that. Mrs. Rowley walked back to her desk with a smile on her face.

"As you can all see, the parander has transformed into a tree since he felt threatened by my presence. Paranders can change into almost anything in nature. They tend to pick objects around them to blend in easily."

For the rest of the class, we observed the parander as Mrs. Rowley lectured about the species. For the last five minutes of class, we were allowed to tend to our dragon eggs. Mrs. Rowley told us that she had high hopes of them hatching very soon.

Once the class ended, I said goodbye to Miguel and Josefina and headed across the lawn to Earth Catastrophes. I tried to concentrate throughout Mr. Laruse's lecture but kept thinking about Josefina. I didn't want her to be mad at me. I decided I would apologize to her again when classes were over and explain to her why I was so concerned. My mind was so consumed with what I was planning to say, and I didn't realize Earth Catastrophes was over until Taylor tapped me on the shoulder.

"Ready for Predicting the Future?" she asked.

Coming out of my daze, I nodded and followed her into the school. Taylor and I entered the classroom and sat down on the pillows. Ms. Crescent was seated on her pillow at the bottom of the amphitheater. When the class was full, she opened her eyes and stood up. The large earrings in her ears jangled along with the many bracelets on her wrists.

"Today, I will show you the art of predicting the future using pyromancy. Can anyone tell me what that is?"

Taylor's hand shot up. "Pyromancy is the art of burning something and trying to see the future in the flames or the smoke."

"Correct. For this class, we will use a specific form of pyromancy called botanomancy. One by one, I'm going to call you into my office to perform a reading, so you can see how it's done. I will light this sage stick," Ms. Crescent said, picking up what looked like a bundle of herbs.

"While the sage burns, I will make predictions based on what I see in the smoke. When your reading is finished, you may leave. Tomorrow, it will be your turn to practice reading a partner's future using sage. I'll begin with Miss Barber."

I watched as Betty Ann rose from her seat with a smirk. I knew the only thing she was happy about was getting out of class early by going first. Ms. Crescent and Betty Ann disappeared behind the beaded curtain.

The rest of us waited for our turns, most hardly speaking. It wasn't long before it was my turn. As I got up, I whispered to Taylor and told her I would see her after dinner for charms practice. I parted the beaded curtain and entered Ms. Crescent's office.

"Come in, Jane. Have a seat," she said, motioning towards the pillow in front of her.

Slowly, I sat down on the orange pillow while Ms. Crescent took the lit sage stick and swirled it around my head, creating trails of smoke. Her green eyes followed the smoke, squinting into the hazy room.

"Interesting," she muttered as she continued swirling the stick. "I can tell you have secrets untold."

I could feel sweat breaking out on my face, and I knew it had nothing to do with the burning herb. What secrets was she talking about? Did she know what they were? I couldn't tell Robert I was a pixie. I couldn't tell anyone from the pixie world about Robert. Josefina couldn't know I didn't fancy her friends. Marie didn't know I was attending a magic school. I was keeping so many secrets from so many people. The fact that I had secrets was a bit of an understatement.

"I see trouble for you in the near future. Your secrets will cause problems if you don't handle them correctly. Be aware of your actions," Ms. Crescent said as she snuffed out the sage, the scent lingering.

Once Ms. Crescent indicated that I could leave, I rose from the pillow and exited the office. What had she meant? Would problems occur if I kept my secrets or if I told them? Ms. Crescent's predictions were always unclear. Josefina already seemed like she was mad at me. I had to stop that argument before it became worse. I hurried up to my room and waited for Josefina.

I sat on my bed for what seemed like a long time. As I thought through what I would say, the door swung open. Her brown eyes stared into mine, and before I could say anything, she began speaking.

"Jane, I'm so sorry for this afternoon. I didn't mean to get so mad at you. I know you were only concerned about my well-being." She crossed the room and sat down next to me.

"I'm sorry for making you think I was judging you. I just thought something bad happened," I replied.

"I'm the one who should be sorry," she said, putting her arm around me. "After dinner, would you like to study with the girls and me?"

"I can't go tonight," I replied, almost feeling sorry. "I promised Taylor that I would help with charms after dinner."

Josefina looked a little sad but nodded her head. "Yes, I should do that too after today's class. Perhaps you can help me with charms another evening this week."

"Sure. I would love to help you!" I replied.

Josefina seemed to brighten, but I hoped she wasn't still mad at me because once again, I had an excuse to escape the girls' company. I didn't want her to think I had done it on purpose. I was willing to do anything to stop Ms. Crescent's prediction from coming true, even if it meant spending time with Josefina and the girls.

20

THISTLE

EVEN THOUGH I felt guilty about studying with Taylor, I had a great time making charms with her. We had spent the evening replenishing our stock of first-year charms. Taylor joked that she would be fine as long as we didn't test the charms on each other. Additionally, I helped her understand the confusing instructions, especially the second-year charms we had just learned. Even though Taylor was great at memorizing facts, she seemed to mentally freeze up when it came to the physical application of what we had learned. I explained some of the techniques I had found useful when creating charms, and she seemed to be catching on fast.

∽

We had been up so late that I was still feeling the effects as I tried to concentrate on Mr. Withermyer's lecture the next morning. He was discussing how love charms should not be used lightly, even though the effects of the charm eventually wear off. The way he talked about *love charms* made me think that he hated them. The distaste was evident in his voice. It seemed if he could remove *love charms* from the curriculum, he would.

His face appeared sterner than usual for the entire lecture, and his chiseled jaw clenched tightly. I wondered what had happened to him to make him talk about *love charms* as if they were poison. However, he had a point. Who would want to fall in love with someone against their will?

Still exhausted, I found it even harder to stay awake in History of Pixies. Even though I found the topic of Egyptian pixies interesting, Mr. Collyworth's slow droning voice was putting me to sleep. During his lecture, I felt my head bobbing toward my desk. I hoped no one, especially Mr. Collyworth noticed.

It was a relief when History of Pixies ended, if only because I got to move around and try to shake the feeling of exhaustion. When I reached Zodiac Signs, I was glad to see Josefina in class. Thankfully Marley hadn't talked her into skipping again. I slid into my seat between Josefina and Taylor, praying that Mrs. Harris's lecture would be better than Mr. Collyworth's.

"Today, we will analyze our zodiac signs," Mrs. Harris said as she walked around the circle of desks. "I want you to read about the traits of your zodiac sign. I will hand out a chart that you will use to write an essay. As you go through the traits, write the ones that apply to you in the left column. Place all the traits you disagree with on the right." Mrs. Harris began passing out the forms.

"Once you have analyzed your zodiac sign completely, you will have your list of traits. From your results, I want you to write an essay on whether you believe your zodiac sign is right for you. Be completely honest when deciding what column to put a trait in. Next week, I will collect the essays and discuss your findings. During today's class, you can begin categorizing the traits for your sign."

I suppressed a yawn as I opened my book. At least today's class would be interactive instead of a lecture. The description of the Pisces sign began on page fifty-two. I pulled the form closer and started reading.

For the rest of the class, I began writing down traits. Written in the left column: compassionate, kind, imaginative, sensitive, and selfless. On the opposite side: gullible, laziness, and unrealistic. Overall, I felt like my personality did match what Pisces stood for. By the time I had reached the end of the chapter, the bell had rung. Quickly I jotted down a few final traits before packing my book away.

"Do you feel like your sign matches you?" I asked Josefina as we headed up to our room.

"Yes, I believe a decent amount matched how I feel about myself. I don't think I'm devious, but I'm bound to disagree on a few. Everyone is different," she replied.

"I know what you mean. There were a few that don't describe me. Lazy was one of them."

"You are far from lazy. With all that work you do for Marie, there's no possible way you could be lazy," Josefina said, shaking her head.

"You're not devious at all. I guess there are just some outliers," I stated.

I was happy Josefina didn't seem mad at me anymore. She had been asleep when I returned from studying, but she was her usual talkative self this morning.

When we reached our room, I dumped my bag on the floor and fell onto my bed. It felt so good to lie down. It would have been so easy to fall asleep during lunch. I let out a deep sigh and relaxed on the pillow.

"You got back late last night," Josefina commented.

"Yes, I'm tired. I was showing Taylor how to create charms. We created ones we thought we might need in the future. I was glad I could help her. There were a few she was having trouble with."

"When do you want to help me with charms?" Josefina asked.

"We could do it tonight. I don't have anything planned," I offered.

Josefina looked undecided, and it took her a while to finally reply. "Okay, I need to see if the girls need me for anything."

I closed my eyes and tried to leave my face expressionless. Why did it seem like Josefina revolved around the whims of those three girls? Did she ever do what she needed or wanted to do anymore? I wished I could talk to her about my feelings, but we had just made up. I didn't want her to be mad again. I hated that it felt like we were drifting apart. I missed my best friend even though she was right next to me.

I stayed on my bed for a few moments longer until Josefina coaxed me to get up. Stretching my hands toward the ceiling, I followed Josefina into the hallway. I hoped the dining hall was serving something good for lunch. My stomach rumbled.

We bumped into Miguel on the way downstairs. "Thank the gods it's lunchtime. I was dying to get out of Earth Catastrophes today. The lesson was so dull," he said.

"Great. Sounds like something to look forward to," I sighed. I was already exhausted. I couldn't imagine sitting through a dull lesson.

Once we reached the dining hall, I could see some kind of noodle, and the smell of garlic permeated the air. It smelled delicious. When I reached the buffet table, I filled my plate with buttery noodles. There was an assortment of bread at the end of the table, so I added a roll to my dish.

Josefina, Miguel, and I sat at our regular table with Juan. Lena was still choosing to sit across the room with Rosie, a girl with chestnut red hair and freckles. I noticed Juan watching her as she laughed at something Rosie had said. I knew how he felt. Being separated from Robert during the week was hard. I hoped that Lena would at least talk to Juan even if she didn't regain her memory. Miguel seemed to notice how sad Juan was, but Josefina was waving at the three girls who had just entered. Miguel shook his head when he realized what she was focused on. We scooted down the table away from her without saying a word. Soon those spaces would be filled, and Josefina wouldn't even notice. A part of me was glad I wasn't the only one who noticed Josefina's distance.

"What does Mr. Laruse talk about in Earth Catastrophes?" I asked Miguel, ignoring that Marley, Candi, and Bellony had joined the table.

"He lectures about earthquakes, which he has no way of demonstrating because he can't cause an earthquake. We aren't even on the ground," Miguel complained.

"I can hardly wait. He is late for his classes, too," I said.

"I don't know where he is before each class, but he always looks distracted," Miguel commented.

"Are you talking about Mr. Laruse?" Andrew asked as he sat down with his lunch.

"How did you know?" I chuckled, picking up my fork to twirl the noodles around it.

"Mr. Laruse always seems flustered and confused," Andrew said.

"On the first day of school, he thought my class was the first-year class," I replied. "He was wondering why we looked so familiar."

"Mr. Laruse is crazy," Marley said, interrupting me and leaning down the table. "Just look how his hair sticks out on both sides of his head."

"His class is probably the second stupidest class in this whole school. He doesn't even know what he is lecturing about," Candi said with a nasty laugh.

Miguel, Andrew, and I grew silent. Marley and Bellony joined in with Candi's laughter. Then, they continued discussing which teachers they thought were ridiculous. They seemed to have something nasty to say about all of them. Miguel angled his body away from them and continued eating his lunch. I finished up with mine, and when Miguel got up with his empty plate, I followed.

When we were away from the table, Miguel spoke. "I wish those girls would eat somewhere else. I tried talking to Josefina about them, but she won't listen to me. I told her about everything I observed, but she yelled at me and told me to stop being rude. I know she skipped class yesterday. I know those girls are a bad influence on her. I don't understand why she can't see it," he whispered.

"You're not the only one who sees their influence on her. I feel like I'm losing Josefina. I don't know how to tell her because she becomes so defensive," I admitted.

"I know Josefina likes those girls because they were the only ones who talked to her when we were children. When our father discovered the gem mine, we had more money than ever before. We moved to a better neighborhood where most of our neighbors believed we didn't belong there. It never bothered me when the neighborhood children didn't talk to me, but it was different for Josefina. As I am sure you know, Josefina loves being social. When the girls finally accepted her, she was over the moon.

"I could tell they only wanted to be friends with Josefina, so she would give them presents and do things for them. I was so happy when we met you. I thought she would finally realize what a true friend was like. She would see that the girls were only using her. Now I don't know if she ever will," Miguel sighed.

I opened my mouth, almost telling him what I had overheard the girls saying about me, but I changed my mind. Miguel had a stronger bond with Josefina than anything I had ever seen before. What if he told her what I said or what if she read his mind? I knew the twins could block thoughts from each other, but I wasn't entirely sure how their connection worked. I didn't want her to find out, especially from her brother.

"Miguel, I understand how you feel, but I don't want Josefina to be mad at me," was what I said instead.

He nodded his head, and then I watched as he glanced at the clock in the dining hall. "We better get ready for Magical Creatures," he said.

I agreed and headed up to my room to pack my bag for the

second half of the day. Josefina was still talking to the girls when I left the dining hall. I hoped she wouldn't be late or conned into skipping class. As I walked to Magical Creatures, I didn't see Josefina. It concerned me, but any decision she made was her own. I couldn't worry whether she got to class or not.

Wrapping my coat tighter around me, I hurried across the lawn. Mrs. Rowley had a giant smile, and I could tell she had an announcement. I felt myself beginning to smile too. I slid into my seat next to Miguel, glad that the outdoor classroom was magically heated. Mrs. Rowley was about to start class when I noticed Josefina racing toward the classroom. Mrs. Rowley glanced at her as she took her seat but then looked around the classroom.

"I have some fascinating news today," she began. "This morning, several of the dragon eggs have hatched!"

I felt a lump rising in my throat and a panic flutter in my chest. Had my egg hatched without me? I thought of my dragon all alone. I had spent so much time outside of class with my egg that I hadn't anticipated it to hatch without being there.

"For today's class, those of you whose dragon has hatched can begin taking care of them. For those who still have an egg, I would like you to continue paying close attention and note any changes. I will begin calling the names of the students whose dragons have hatched. Once I have called your name, you can come with me to meet your dragons."

My stomach was a bundle of knots. Please, I prayed, don't let my dragon have hatched without me. I would feel terrible.

Mrs. Rowley began calling the names. "Miss Barber, Mr. Nickles, Mr. Foster, Miss Swan, Miss Martinez, Mr. Martinez…"

The twins rose from their seats, excitement in their eyes. Mrs. Rowley finished calling out the names, and I breathed a sigh of relief. Collecting my journal, I went to the nest. Kneeling in a light layer of snow, I inspected my egg. Nothing seemed out of the ordinary. I placed my hands on the purple shell and concentrated on sending heat to my hands.

Time was ticking by, and the class was more than half over. I began to feel discouraged. Unless my dragon waited until this time tomorrow, I wouldn't be here. My heart began to hurt. I had taken care of the dragon egg the best I knew how.

I sighed deeply, and as I packed away my journal, I swore I saw my egg twitch. Had I imagined it? Had I only seen what I wanted to see? I paused and turned my full attention to the egg. Just as I was about to give up, the egg twitched again. Quickly, I raced across the field to find Mrs. Rowley.

"Mrs. Rowley! Mrs. Rowley, please come quick! I think my egg is hatching!" I yelled as I neared her.

Mrs. Rowley hastily responded to my distress. She followed me back to the egg. I threw myself down in the snow and watched anxiously. It wasn't long before Mrs. Rowley was beside me. Soon, I realized the entire class surrounded my egg.

"Students, although I would like you to be able to see, please take a step back from Jane's egg. I was hoping a dragon would hatch during class," Mrs. Rowley said excitedly.

Mrs. Rowley didn't ask me to move either, so I stayed on the ground next to my egg. When my egg shook again, she didn't look alarmed, so I assumed this was normal. Suddenly, a hairline crack began near the top of the egg and spider-webbed outward. I watched in amazement as a tiny claw broke through one of the cracks. The dragon inside pushed through the shell slowly until its head popped through the top. Mrs. Rowley smiled as she watched the dragon fully emerge.

The dragon was beautiful. Its scales were many shades of purple. They were lighter around the head and chest but darker along the back and wings. On the back of the dragon's head were thin purple spikes that stuck out in every direction. Toward the front of the head were two thicker horns that arched backward away from the face. The dragon's pink tongue lolled out of its mouth in exhaustion as it fought to tip the remaining eggshell over.

It didn't take the dragon long to roll over, and soon it was slowly crawling from the shell that held it captive for so many months. It turned, and instantly its eyes connected with mine. I couldn't describe the feeling, but it seemed like the dragon was looking into my soul with eyes about the same color as mine. I was the first thing my dragon saw as it came into the world. The dragon appeared to smile at me and began shuffling toward me.

"Jane, put on your protective gloves," Mrs. Rowley instructed. "Baby dragons can be very unpredictable."

Quickly, I followed her instructions and got them on just as my dragon reached me. The dragon seemed to throw itself in my lap and touched its forehead to my leg. Slowly, per Mrs. Rowley's instructions, I allowed the dragon to smell my hand and then petted its back.

After a few moments, Mrs. Rowley asked to see the dragon. She thoroughly inspected the dragon. "It appears this dragon is female. Excellent job taking good care of this dragon while she was in her egg."

She passed my dragon back to me. I looked upon her with wonder. Carefully, I ran my gloved hand over her purple scales. She flexed her tiny, leathery wings and appeared to yawn. She lay down next to me and put her little spiked head on my legs. My dragon was small, about the size of a puppy. I watched as she lifted her thin purple tail and curled it around her body. Her tail had an arrow-shaped barb at the end, which rested near her nose. She sighed deeply, smoke rising from her nostrils in spirals, and closed her violet eyes.

I couldn't stop staring at her. Today, I witnessed one of the most amazing things. Silently, I thanked the gods. I couldn't describe how I was feeling. In my wildest dreams, I would never have imagined that animals like dragons lived in the same world I did. Every day of my life at the Jelf Academy seemed like the perfect dream. I was always afraid I would wake up in the manor's attic, and none of it would be real.

My dragon was breathing deeply now, and I knew she had fallen asleep. The bell rang for class to end, and I was unsure of what to do. Mrs. Rowley came back over to me, and when she saw my dragon was sleeping, she chuckled.

"You can pick her up slowly. She might not even wake up. Your dragon has had a big day today. We can set her up with a nest in the heated barn if you come with me. Don't worry about being late for your next class. I'll write you a tardy excuse. It's not every day you get to be here when a dragon hatches," Mrs. Rowley said with a smile.

Cautiously, I slipped my arm underneath my dragon's back and scooped her into my arms. I watched as she yawned and blew more smoke spirals, never opening her eyes. As I followed Mrs. Rowley across the field, I gazed down at my little dragon that no one else had wanted. Looking at her tiny face as she slept, I couldn't help but think the spikes on her head reminded me of a purple flower I had seen in the woods near the manor. The flower was beautiful and resilient, but most people considered it a weed. *Thistle*, I thought, holding my dragon closer. I will call her Thistle.

21

Discovered

By the end of the week, my heart was torn in two. On the one hand, I didn't want to leave the Jelf Academy because of Thistle. Over the last week and a half, I had become extremely close to her. Now that the dragons had hatched, we spent every day in Magical Creatures class learning how to care for them. Baby dragons spooked easily, so Mrs. Rowley showed us how to calm them down if it would ever happen. Thistle was usually excellent and seemed to trust me more than some of the other dragons trusted their students. It always felt like Thistle was happy to see me and eager for my approval. There was something so special about Thistle, and it hurt to be away from her, so I continued to sneak down to the barn to see her.

On the other hand, I ached to see Robert. This weekend was Valentine's Day, and all I wanted to do was get back to the manor to be with him.

As usual, Josefina was in a mood when it came to the dance. She couldn't stop commenting on how she didn't want to wait until next year. Josefina didn't understand why I wasn't excited about the dance, but I didn't feel like discussing a dance we couldn't even attend.

My bag was packed and ready to go when the time came for me to meet Dr. Tweedle. As we walked across the lawn, I glanced toward the Magical Creatures classroom. I hoped Thistle would understand why I had to leave her for another weekend. Dr. Tweedle followed my gaze and smiled.

"Mrs. Rowley has told me your dragon has taken a liking to you."

"Yes. Thistle always loves to see me. I like taking care of her," I replied.

"Oh, so you gave her a name," Dr. Tweedle said sadly.

"She is my dragon, after all. I had to call her something," I said.

"I just don't want you to get hurt, Jane. In a few months, those dragons will be able to survive on their own. They will be released into the world when they are ready."

I felt my heart rise into my throat. When we first received our egg, Mrs. Rowley had said something about that, but I hadn't thought about it since. How could I possibly let Thistle go?

"Yes, I know," I mumbled.

I stayed quiet the entire ride to the ground, even after I boarded the carriage.

Before I knew it, Dr. Tweedle had cast the *teleportation charm*, and we were riding up the manor's driveway. I had to get my mind off Thistle and focus on whatever Marie and Emily wanted me to do. Dr. Tweedle slowed the two white horses at the steps that led to the front door. I tried to hide my feelings as I smiled at Dr. Tweedle to say goodbye, but I had a feeling he could see right through me.

The house was unusually quiet when I entered. Typically, Marie would be waiting with a list of chores to thrust on me upon my arrival. Unsure of what to do, I decided to head to the attic. I was thankful I had a few moments of peace before I was forced to hurry around. Taking a deep breath, I placed my bag down on the thin mattress.

Knowing I couldn't stay up here for very long, I fixed the loose strands of hair coming out of my braid. Marie would be wondering where I was since she hadn't seen me arrive. Going downstairs to the kitchen to check with Ellen seemed like a good idea. I figured I would probably be needed to serve dinner soon.

As I left the attic, I wondered what torture Marie would subject me to this weekend. My only hope was that it included Robert.

I was on my way past Marie's room when her door banged open. The noise of it stopped me dead in my tracks. She looked just as startled to see me, her cold eyes roving down my body.

"What are you doing sneaking around?" she barked harshly.

"I wasn't sneaking around, ma'am. I…"

She cut me off. "When did you get back here?"

"Just now, ma'am. I was just heading to the kitchen," I stammered.

"I didn't see you arrive. You need to come straight to me when you get back from that silly school. Where the hell have you been?" Her gray eyes looked hard as stone.

"I just dropped off my bag in the attic, ma'am. Dr. Tweedle brought me back only a few moments ago," I replied.

Marie continued to glare at me as if I were lying.

Finally, she crossed her arms and yelled, "Get down to the kitchen and help Ellen! After dinner, I have a task for you to do."

She shooed me down the stairs as if I wasn't moving fast enough. I could have been in the kitchen already helping if she hadn't stopped me, but I wasn't going to point it out to her.

As soon as I entered the kitchen, Ellen put me straight to work peeling potatoes. I hunched over the sink to start rinsing and slicing potatoes before adding them to a frying pan. Ellen also instructed me to cut the kernels off of cobs since Marie wouldn't be caught dead eating the corn right off the cob. While I worked on the corn, Ellen basted the ham already cooking in the oven.

With the corn completely stripped from the cobs, I stacked the dishes up and went into the dining room to set the table. It appeared to be a quiet night since only Marie, Emily, and Preston were having dinner. I laid out the plates and the silverware and then went back into the kitchen to get the cups. When I had everything placed on the table, I double-checked that all the utensils were in the right places. I didn't want Marie to find anything to complain about since she was already in a foul mood. Once the table looked perfect, I returned to the kitchen to fry the potatoes.

The potatoes and ham were almost done when I heard the family enter the dining room. I turned down the heat on the potatoes and grabbed the water pitcher. As I walked around the table, I filled everyone's glass. Preston was slumped in his seat, his face very close to the table.

"I'm hungry! Where is the food!" he complained, lifting his fork and knife to bang on his plate.

"Hurry up with the food, Jane," she hissed. "Can't you see that Preston is starving?"

I raced back into the kitchen and poured the corn into a bowl. Then, I swept the fried potatoes from the pan and onto a platter.

"Is the ham almost done?" I asked Ellen. "Preston is hungry."

"Is that why there's commotion coming from the dining room?" she asked, rolling her eyes. She hurriedly whipped the ham from the oven, letting out a shriek as she placed it on the stove. A few of her fingers turned bright red.

"Jane, get this ham into the dining room," she yelled, rushing to the sink and sticking her fingers under a cold stream of water.

While her back was turned, I slightly levitated the ham onto a platter and carried it to the dining room table. Preston stopped banging his utensils as soon as he saw the food. Greedily, he stood up from his seat and tore a chunk out of the side of the ham, throwing it onto his plate. Before I would be subjected to watching him dig into it, I went back into the kitchen to retrieve the potatoes and corn.

Preston was chewing with his mouth open when I returned with the side dishes. As soon as he saw me, Preston dove for the potatoes and piled them on his plate. Then, he grabbed his cup of water and drained it. Knowing that he would be demanding more, I went to get the pitcher.

"This potato is too burnt," Preston whined, throwing a slightly browned potato over his shoulder onto the floor.

I could figure out the first thing on my list of chores: cleaning the dining room. I stood in the corner as I watched Preston eat. Marie and Emily acted as if nothing was amiss while discussing some details about Emily's wedding. How could they just sit there while Preston ate sloppily and threw his food everywhere? I was utterly disgusted. He would be turning fifteen this year at the end of July. How long would he keep acting like this?

When dinner was over, Marie commanded me to come to the office after I finished cleaning. I got to work clearing the table, washing the dishes, and cleaning the floor. I tried to do it as quickly as possible without using the *quick complete charm*. I wasn't sure what Marie had planned, and I didn't want to keep her waiting.

Leaving the dining room, I crossed the front entryway past the stairs. The hallway was dimly lit, so I felt my way along the wall to the door. I knocked and waited for Marie to allow me to enter. Her sharp voice penetrated through the door, and I pushed it open.

"Are your hands clean?" Marie barked without looking up from the desk.

Quickly I examined my hands before confirming they were.

"Good. I don't want any of your filth to ruin these invitations. For the remainder of the evening, you will place Emily's wedding invitations in the envelopes you addressed a while ago. Each invitation must be placed in the envelope correctly. Don't just shove them in. That will crinkle the invitation. Along with each invitation, you must include a response card. Do you understand?" Marie said.

"Yes, ma'am," I said, glancing at the stack of invitations and response cards.

"So, you know how many things go in each envelope?" she asked condescendingly.

I nodded, hoping she would just let me get started.

"How many, Jane?" she probed again.

"Two, ma'am," I muttered.

"That's right. This one," she slowly lifted the invitation, "and this one," she said, raising the response card as if I had told her I hadn't understood instead of saying yes. "Don't mess them up!"

Marie rose from the desk and headed for the office door.

"Do the work here, but don't touch anything other than the invitations and envelopes. Tomorrow, you need to be up early. You'll be out in the barn, mucking out the stables," she said with an evil laugh.

I tried to keep my face expressionless. Marie thought she was punishing me by sending me outside, but she had no idea how excited I was.

The following day, I awoke well before dawn. My back muscles ached from being hunched over in the office chair all night. My mattress hadn't helped any either. It had taken me over four hours to stuff the envelopes. I hadn't returned to the attic until very late, but none of that mattered now. I was going to see Robert today!

I pulled out my mother's mirror and inspected my face for dirt. I knew I would probably become dirty over the course of the day, but Robert didn't need to see me that way first thing in the morning. I scrubbed at my face and then began straightening up my hair. After braiding my hair, I swirled it into a bun and pinned it so that it would be entirely out of the way. Since I would be in the stables all day, I didn't want my hair to fall on my face.

Although I was excited, I tried not to run down the stairs. If I looked the least bit happy, Marie would never let me work outside again. Since the land sloped off, I slowed my pace so I wouldn't fall. The barn loomed before me with its cracked red paint as I came toward it. My fingers reached for the door handles, which were cold to the touch. Slowly, I pulled the door open and peeked inside.

"Robert, I'm here," I called, not wanting to catch him in an indecent predicament.

In the dim light, I saw his head lean down from the loft.

"I'll be right down," he said excitedly. "You're here early."

Within a few minutes, Robert was climbing down the loft ladder and greeted me with a huge hug and kiss. It felt so good to be with him again, instantly making me forget everything wrong in my life. I snuggled my head into his shoulder, breathing in the smell of dry hay. Robert's hand moved in comforting circles on my back. I would have loved to stay holding each other, but we had a job to do.

Robert pushed both barn doors open and locked them into place to let the light in. The horses huffed as the sunrise flooded into the barn. Robert went about collecting the mucking tools and handed me a shovel. I opened the first stall and grabbed the horse's bridle. The horse lumbered behind me as I led him into another stall. Once he was situated, Robert and I began shoveling.

We filled up a wheel barrel with the muck and dirty hay, which Robert offered to take to the field to be used as fertilizer. It could be quite heavy when the wheel barrel was full, and forever the gentleman, Robert, refused to let me push it. While Robert left with the first wheel barrel, I grabbed the other one and began filling it. It took a while, but Robert was back before I had the second barrel full.

"I know this work is awful, but I'm glad you're here. I've been dying to see you," he said as he shoveled beside me.

"I couldn't wait to see you, too. I tried not to look overly happy when Marie told me I would be helping you last night."

"It's so hard to spend time with you. The weekends are too short," Robert complained.

"Yes, and the weeks are too long," I added, refraining from complaining too much. Even though I missed Robert incredibly, he didn't understand that the Jelf Academy was my salvation.

"What did Marie have you do last night?" Robert asked as he dumped another shovel full.

"Emily's invitations needed put into envelopes. I had to stuff over five hundred envelopes."

"My hand hurt for days after helping you address all those envelopes. I can only imagine what it was like to put the invitations inside them."

"I have so many paper cuts," I said, holding out my hands.

Robert gripped the second wheel barrel and moved to leave the barn. The first stall was done, so I laid down fresh hay and moved the horse back into it.

I thought we were moving along at a decent pace. Plus, the task wasn't that bad because I had Robert to talk to. Marie wasn't breathing down my neck and throwing nasty comments at me. Emily wasn't prancing around me, demanding outfits and hairstyles. Preston wasn't making a never-ending mess. Though the barn smelled, and my arms felt like they would fall off, this was one of my best days at the manor. I would take a day shoveling manure with Robert over any other chore.

Robert and I had just finished up with the next stall, and the wheel barrel was packed again. Robert left the barn while I began adding fresh hay to the stall. Soon, I was running out of hay and would need to go up to the loft for more. I stood there, staring at the loft, debating what to do. A bale of hay was heavy, and there was no way I would be able to lift one and carry it down the loft ladder by myself. The only way I would be able to get a bale of hay was to do it with magic.

Turning around, I glanced at the barn doors behind me. Robert was nowhere in sight since he'd just left with the wheel barrel. I had been timing him and knew it took him a while to push the wheel barrel out to the field and back. I would have plenty of time to levitate a bale of hay from the loft. Concentrating on one of the hay bales, I imagined it floating up. I watched as it lifted into the air. Coaxing it over the ledge, I began lowering the bale when a voice suddenly startled me.

"What the hell?"

I turned suddenly to see Robert standing in the doorway. Losing all my concentration, the hay bale crashed to the floor with a bang.

22

LOVE IS ALL THAT MATTERS

"Jane, what's going on?" Robert asked quizzically. He refused to move from the doorway.

"What do you mean?" I asked, hoping I could convince him that he had imagined it. Maybe, if I played stupid, he would start believing that his eyes were playing tricks on him.

"You know exactly what I'm talking about," Robert stated as he shoved a hand through his shoulder-length auburn hair.

I tried looking confused. "No, Robert, I don't," I stammered.

"I watched as that hay bale levitated up from the loft, and it was halfway down before it crashed to the ground."

He pointed to the large hay bale that had landed a few inches away from my feet. I glanced at it and then back at him, trying to keep the confused look on my face.

"You were watching it the entire time," Robert finally said as he entered the barn. "I know you saw it too. What is going on?"

"Robert, I..." I started to say, looking down at the ground.

What was I supposed to say? It didn't seem like I would be able to convince him otherwise.

"Jane, what just happened? I watched you watching that hay

bale as it moved up and out of the loft. I know you saw it, too. Why are you pretending you didn't?"

Robert was in front of me in two steps. His right hand lifted my chin, forcing me to look him in the eyes.

"That hay bale was floating in mid-air. The moment you turned, it fell to the floor...." He said slowly.

I could almost see his mind working behind his eyes. I wasn't sure if it was the look on my face, but he seemed to put two and two together. Quickly, he dropped my chin and took a few steps away from me. The look in his eyes sent chills down my spine.

"Robert, let me explain."

"What are you?" he asked, keeping his distance from me.

"Robert, I'm still the same girl you fell in love with. I've wanted to tell you, but I haven't because I'm not allowed to. Please let me explain," I pleaded.

He looked at me with weary eyes but backed toward the hay bale, taking a seat. "What are you talking about? What do you mean when you say you weren't allowed to tell me?"

"Pixie society does not want humans to know anything about us."

"What?"

"Just please let me tell you everything," I said, feeling alarmed. It was hard to focus, my mind in a panic.

Robert looked so confused. He repositioned himself on the hay bale, his eyebrows furrowed.

"I am a pixie. Well, technically, half pixie. My mother was a pixie, but my father was human." I took a deep breath and watched his reaction.

Robert squinted at me. "What exactly does that mean?"

"Well, I can move things with my mind. That's what I was doing with the hay bale. I thought you would be gone for a longer time."

"Are Marie and her children pixies too?" Robert asked, looking nervous.

"No. I'm the only one."

"Then how do you know anything about a pixie society?"

"Robert, the Jelf Academy isn't a school for etiquette but for pixies. People who are just like me. I had no idea there were others like me until last year when I met Dr. Tweedle, the headmaster."

"Who else knows about you?" Robert asked.

"Marie knows I can move things with my mind. She caught me doing it when I was young. All my life, she has constantly threatened to throw me out into the street if anyone sees me using magic. She doesn't know I'm a pixie and that there are others like me. Marie has no idea the Jelf Academy teaches me more about magic. Dr. Tweedle made her believe I was attending an etiquette school."

"I don't understand why you have to hide who you are. Why couldn't you tell me?" Robert asked, still looking confused.

"Pixies have to stay hidden because it could become perilous for us if humans knew we existed. A group called the World Association for the Slaying of Pixies, also known as W.A.S.P. This group consists of humans who hate pixies. Their main purpose is to capture and kill any pixie they find."

Robert looked stunned and even more confused.

"So, let me get this straight. You're not a human but a mythical creature who looks nothing like what I would imagine a pixie to look like. You attend a school to learn magic, and a group of these humans, kill people like you." He sounded skeptical as he ticked off his statements on his fingers.

"You sound like you don't believe me."

Robert shook his head and ran his hands through his hair again.

"I watched that bale float out of the loft. I just can't even believe it."

I glanced at the open barn doors behind me to make sure no one was around. Then, I turned back to Robert and concentrated on the hay bale he was sitting on. Within moments, it began rising from the ground. Robert yelled in surprise as his feet lifted off the floor.

"Okay, Jane, I believe you!" he practically yelled as he clung to the hay bale beneath him.

"Keep your voice down," I hissed as I gently began lowering him. Robert jumped off it as soon as it was close enough to the ground.

"So, can you move and lift anything no matter how heavy it is?" he asked in awe.

"The heavier something is, the more concentration it takes, but I haven't had any trouble with lifting or moving things."

"You seem skilled already, so why do you have to attend a school anyway?"

"Pixies can do other things besides move objects. At the Jelf Academy, I'm learning how to create charms and predict the future. I'm also learning about my people's history."

"Charms and predicting the future?" Robert questioned. "I can't even begin to imagine what that all entails. You said your mother was a pixie, but your father wasn't?" He took my hand and led me to the hay bale, where we both sat down.

"Yes. My mother broke one of the biggest pixie laws when she married my father. Not only is it against the law to tell humans what we are, but it's also the same with marriage."

I looked at Robert and caught the scowl on his face. I slipped my hand out of his and scooted away from him.

"I understand if your feelings for me have changed. I would understand if you think I'm abnormal and want nothing to do with me," I said as my hands rose to my throat and pulled his ring out from under my blouse.

Robert quickly grabbed my hands and shifted closer to me. "Jane, how could you think such a thing? I love you, and nothing will ever change that. Sure, I'm a bit shocked. My mind is still trying to wrap around the fact that people like you exist, and there is magic in the world, but it could never change how I feel about you."

"Are you sure?" I asked, not believing my ears.

Robert leaned forward and kissed me. His lips were soft and warm, and I leaned into him.

"Jane," he whispered. "Never believe for a second that I could stop loving you. I wish you would have trusted me enough to tell me everything about you," he said, tucking a strand of my hair behind my ear.

"I told you I wanted to, but I'm not allowed. I would be in danger if someone in the W.A.S.P. found out about me."

"You don't think I would tell anyone, do you? I would never hurt you or put you in danger," Robert said, pulling me closer.

"My mother was a very talented and powerful pixie. Before she met my father, she was dedicated to hiding pixies. The W.A.S.P. believed my mother would cause their downfall. Not long after I was born, they killed my mother. One of my father's staff caught her doing magic, and he told other people. That was how the W.A.S.P. found her. They murdered her, leaving her body behind this barn." I could feel the tears running down my face, and Robert gently brushed them away with his fingertips.

"The W.A.S.P. recently learned that my mother had a child, and they believe I'll be more powerful than her. The society is currently hunting me, fearing that I might be the one to destroy them."

I saw the fear in Robert's eyes.

"We have to run away then! We need to get you into hiding!" he said shrilly, jumping to his feet.

"Robert, calm down. The W.A.S.P. doesn't know anything about me, and they have no idea I'm here. They think I'm with a pixie family, not a human one. I don't even think they know if I'm male or female. Besides, I need to stay here and continue attending the Jelf Academy. Don't you think it would be best if I knew how to properly protect myself? I just have to be careful when I'm using magic."

Robert didn't look convinced. "I just can't comprehend any of this," he said, pacing in front of me. He took a deep breath and huffed the air out harshly between his lips. "I just can't swallow the fact that this is real."

"I know how you feel. I had a hard time believing everything, too," I rose from the hay bale and touched his arm.

"We better get back to work before Marie becomes suspicious," I said.

"Wait! Do you expect me to just return to work? I want to know everything!"

"I can talk as we work," I said, mentally picking up a shovel and levitating it into his hand. The surprise on his face made me smile.

"You shouldn't be doing magic," he scolded.

"It's just you and me in this barn, and you already said you wouldn't tell anyone. I don't think I have anything to worry about."

He scowled at me but took the shovel, moving into the fourth stall.

"Last year, not long after you arrived at the manor, I met Dr. Tweedle in the woods on the property. It was quite a shock. This strange man knew my name, my mother's name, and that I had peculiar abilities. Dr. Tweedle told me he was the headmaster of a school called the Jelf Academy, and I that was destined to go there because my mother had when she was my age. He handed me an acceptance letter and a list of school supplies. However, there was one condition. Since the pixie government doubted my talent because I'm half-human, I had to prove my ability to continue my academy education.

"When I told Dr. Tweedle that Marie would never let me go, he went to the manor to talk to her. During their meeting, he put something in Marie's tea to convince her the Jelf Academy was an etiquette school and that I needed to attend."

I paused my story as Robert left the barn to dump the manure in the field. I couldn't digest the fact that he had caught me doing magic. I couldn't help feeling relieved about it, even though I was breaking another law. Now I wouldn't have to lie to Robert anymore. I would never have to feel guilty about keeping secrets from the man I loved.

Ms. Crescent's prediction from two weeks ago nagged at the back of my mind, but I quickly pushed the thought away. Now that Robert had caught me, telling him the truth seemed right. I wished I had told him sooner. He didn't care that I was a pixie. He didn't care that I was different! Robert now knew the truth, and he loved me anyway.

When Robert returned, I told him about my first trip to Jewel Caverns and my delight at meeting other pixies. I explained my first-year classes and what the teachers were like. Robert listened intently as we shoveled out the next stall. I talked about everything I could remember from my first year at the academy. Before I knew it, we were finished cleaning out the stalls. It had to be getting close to dinner time, which meant I needed to go back to the manor.

"I promise to sneak back out here after dinner when everyone has retired to their rooms," I said as I kissed Robert goodbye. "I have so much more to tell you!"

"Good. I can't wait to hear more," he said excitedly.

My fingers slipped out of his as I left the barn and headed back to the manor in the fading light. Trying not to trip, I climbed the hill and quickly walked in the front door. Knowing Marie would be furious if I entered the dining room covered in grime, I darted up to the attic.

I hurriedly filled my washtub and heated the water to a pleasant temperature. Tentatively, I lowered a foot into the water and then slipped my whole body into the tiny metal tub. It felt fantastic to scrub the dirt from my skin. Sighing, I rapidly washed my hair and stepped from the tub. After combing my wet hair, I twisted it into a braid down my back.

I made it to the kitchen in time to help Ellen finish cooking. Briskly, I set the table, surprised that for the second evening in a row, only the family was having dinner. Typically, Mr. Doyle called upon Emily every weekend. I wondered why he hadn't come to visit.

Throughout dinner, all I could think about was Robert. I still had much to tell him about. I hadn't even mentioned Thistle. I could only imagine his expression when I told him dragons existed.

My excitement buoyed me through dinner service and, even afterward, while completing the chores Marie assigned. As I cleaned up, I decided to show Robert some other magical things I could do. My pixie dust case was in the attic, and inside were several samples of charms Taylor and I had created. I could show him a few of those.

It was late when I finished Marie's tasks, but I was sure Robert would be waiting for me. I crept up the main staircase, pausing briefly outside Marie and Emily's rooms. No light shone from under the doors, and both rooms were silent. Assuming they were both asleep, I climbed to the attic to retrieve my case.

*

"I almost thought you weren't coming," Robert said sleepily when I finally made it to the barn. He was in the loft, lounging on a clean spread of hay.

"I'm sorry, Marie had a few things for me to do," I said, climbing the ladder.

"It's okay," Robert said, sitting up and patting the hay beside him.

I sat down next to him and plucked the case from my pocket. Robert watched in amazement as I expanded the case to its regular size.

"What's that?" he asked, examining the box.

"This is my pixie dust case, which holds all the ingredients I need to make charms. It also contains storage compartments where I can store completed charms or anything else I want."

Dragon Scales

Using the pointer finger of my right hand, I opened the box and found the compartment with the completed charms. Robert leaned closer to look at the labeled vials as I pulled them from the box. He picked up a vial full of ruby red dust, but I quickly grabbed it off of him.

"Sorry, this is a *fire charm*, and it's very volatile. This whole barn could go up in flames from just a pinch of this powder," I said, placing the vial back in the box.

Standing up, I crossed to the side of the loft where Robert kept empty buckets. I grabbed two of them and brought them over. Picking up the vial containing the blue and white dust, I turned to him.

"This is called a *fountain charm*," I said, upending the vial into one of the buckets.

Robert was speechless as pixie dust turned into water right before his eyes. He blinked several times and then dipped his hand into the bucket. Robert stared at his glistening wet fingers and shook his head.

"It's right in front of my eyes, and I still can't wrap my mind around this," Robert said, wiping his hand on his pants. I smiled at his reaction as I took the bucket of water and poured half of it into the other bucket.

"Prepare yourself for my next trick," I said, feeling like a magician.

I placed one bucket in front of Robert, grabbed the other one along with my vial of the *calling charm*, and headed toward the ladder.

"Where are you going?" Robert asked, leaning over the loft edge as he watched me climb down the ladder.

"You'll see. Just watch the bucket of water," I called up to him.

I moved where Robert couldn't see me, but not far enough to be submerged in darkness. The light from the lantern upstairs still allowed me to see and would be crucial when I cast the *calling charm*. Placing the bucket of water on the floor, I found some dry hay and moved it toward the bucket so I would have something to sit on.

Uncorking the charm, I poured it into the water and concentrated on Robert. Closing my eyes, I envisioned him sitting up in the loft, picturing his auburn hair and soft brown eyes. I knew the charm had worked when I heard Robert's startled gasp.

"Jane, I can see your face in the water!"

Opening my eyes, I peered into the bucket in front of me. Robert's face held the look of surprise and awe I had been expecting.

"This is one of the ways pixies can communicate with each other," I said.

"How did you do that?" he asked.

"When I cast the *calling charm*, I just have to concentrate on the person I'm trying to contact and their location. If I can picture them in my mind, the charm will work."

"So, you could do this from anywhere?" Robert said, leaning farther over the bucket.

"Yes, I just need this charm and some water. The *calling charm* allows me to see and speak with you. However, the person you are contacting must have a container of water nearby, or the charm won't work. We have another charm called the *See All Charm* that would allow me to see you, but you wouldn't be able to see me."

"Jane, I've just had the most brilliant idea," Robert practically shouted, startling me. "All I need is a bucket full of water, and you could talk to me, right?"

"Yes," I replied hesitantly.

"You could use the *calling charm*, and I could talk to you while you're away! I wouldn't have to miss you during the week!" He sounded thrilled.

I could feel my excitement blossoming as I considered the possibility, but a trickle of fear overshadowed my mind. "Robert, what if someone caught me? I would be in so much trouble."

"Are you telling me that you are never alone?"

"Well, Josefina is spending more time with those girls I told you about. They normally go to the library to study...."

"That would be the perfect time to talk to me!"

"I'll think about it. Hold on. I'm on my way back up."

Picking up the bucket of water, I went to the doors of the barn and dumped the water to break the charm. Gripping the handles of the ladder, I climbed back into the loft.

"That was amazing," Robert said. "Tell me more about the wonderful pixie world!"

I sat down beside Robert, and he wrapped his arms around me.

"I started a new class at the Jelf Academy this year. It's called Magical Creatures, and we get to learn about all types of magical animals. There is a pen in the outdoor classroom where Mrs. Rowley brings different animals to the school, so we can study them."

Robert gave a slight chuckle in my ear. "So, you've gotten to see unicorns and dragons, huh?"

"Well, unicorns are very rare and are hardly ever seen, but dragons, on the other hand," I said, a smile creeping onto my face.

"Wait, you've seen a dragon? They actually exist?" Robert sounded startled.

"To be honest, I've raised a dragon from an egg. She just hatched two weeks ago." I craned my neck to look up at Robert's face.

"Just when I think you can't surprise me more than you already have, you proceed to tell me you've raised a dragon!"

"Every day at the Jelf Academy is a surprise to me. Sometimes it's hard being the only one who didn't grow up in the pixie world. You wouldn't believe how nice it is to tell you everything I've experienced. No one else has understood how mystified I am by everything."

"I'm so happy you aren't attending a school for etiquette. I thought Marie was sending you away to become a better slave for her. Now I see why you love the Jelf Academy. It's incredible to know magic and creatures like dragons exist."

"You don't know how much I wish you were a pixie. I'd love for you to see the Jelf Academy and Jewel Caverns. Then you could come to school with me and meet my friends."

Robert began stroking my hair. "I'm glad you're happy there. As long as you're happy, I'm happy too. I just feel bad that you're breaking pixie rules. I wouldn't want your happiness in the pixie world to be ruined because of me," he said, sounding sad.

"No, Robert. Please don't feel bad. You're the one thing that makes me happier than the pixie world. I love you. I never want to lose you, not for all the magic in the world. I don't care that I'm breaking the rules by loving you. I would do it again in a heartbeat. I just wish I had told you the truth sooner. I was afraid you wouldn't love me anymore," I said, resting my head on his shoulder.

His hands caressed my back and neck as he held me close.

"Jane, you never have to be afraid to tell me anything. I love you."

It felt splendid to relax against Robert completely and be held by him. I continued to talk about other aspects of the pixie world and told him all about Thistle. I felt like a huge weight had been lifted from my chest. I stayed in the barn talking to him for a long time before deciding it was time to return to the manor. It was painful to disentangle myself from his arms and leave the warmth of his side.

I exited into the cold night and began my way up the hill. When I was halfway to the manor's front door, a chill I hadn't felt in a while slid down my spine. It felt like someone was lurking in the dark shadows watching me. Glancing around, my heart rate began to quicken. My mouth felt dry, and I couldn't get enough air. Breaking into a sprint, I rushed toward the house, fear clawing at my insides. My fingers fumbled with the door handle, but I finally managed to pull it open. As quickly and quietly as possible, I climbed the stairs to the second floor. Every creak of the stairs threw me into an even deeper panic. It wasn't until I was finally back in the attic with the door closed that I allowed myself to breathe.

23

Birthdays Are Anything but Happy

"Wake up, Jane," a soft voice called to me.

I twisted under the blanket that was pulled up to my chin. I felt so tired, and I didn't want to open my eyes. A few moments later, I felt a hand on my shoulder gently shaking me. I stretched my limbs and angled myself toward the source of the touch.

"Happy birthday!" Josefina said when I opened my eyes. A smile crept over my face, and I pushed the blanket off my chest.

"I can't believe you remembered!" I replied excitedly.

"I wouldn't forget my best friend's birthday," Josefina said, sitting on my bed to hug me.

"Thank you, Josefina." I crawled out of bed and stretched my hands to the ceiling. February twenty-fourth had arrived along with my eighteenth birthday. I gazed at my reflection in the bathroom mirror. How was it possible that I was eighteen years old? My violet eyes searched my face as if they would find something different. According to society, I had passed into adulthood in the breath of a day.

I ran a brush through my blonde hair and then began French braiding. I didn't know why I was excited about my birthday. For the majority of my life, my birthday was never recognized. The day was never one to illicit exuberance. Last year was the first time my birthday could have been special, but with the announcement of pixie deaths at the hands of the W.A.S.P., there was hardly any reason to celebrate.

Finishing up in the bathroom, I quickly dressed in a purple uniform and organized my schoolbooks for the day. I hoped today would go smoothly.

When Josefina was ready, we headed down to breakfast.

"Happy birthday, Jane," Miguel and Andrew said at the same time as I approached the table.

"Thank you," I said, beaming.

"Josefina reminded me," Miguel said.

Josefina lightly slapped him on the arm. "You aren't supposed to tell her that!"

I couldn't help but laugh, causing Miguel and Josefina to start to chuckle.

"What is so funny this morning?" Marley asked as she, Bellony, and Candi approached the table.

My good mood almost faded.

"Nothing. Today is Jane's birthday," Josefina announced. Instantly, a part of me wished she hadn't.

"Oh, happy birthday," Marley said, but her voice dripped with sarcasm.

The three girls appeared to have fake smiles plastered on their faces as they slid into seats next to Josefina. I watched them warily as I picked up my fork and speared a bite of waffle. I decided to ignore them and not let them dampen my mood.

As the bell rang to signal the end of breakfast, I swung my

bag onto my shoulder. My first obstacle of the day was Charms. Mr. Withermyer's class would most likely be challenging, but I wouldn't let him ruin my birthday.

Those haunting green eyes found me the moment I walked into the Charms classroom. Trying not to appear intimidated, I slid into my seat and pulled my Charms book from my bag.

"Pull out your books and turn to page 210," Mr. Withermyer commanded as he rose from his desk.

There was a rustling of pages as all the students began flipping through their books. Once I found that page, I read the title and the description of the charm. The *undoing charm* could eliminate the effects of any charm. For example, if a pixie had a *confusion charm* cast upon them, the *undoing charm* would dispel the disorientation. Glancing at the ingredients, I was surprised to find there were only two. Overall, the charm didn't appear too complicated. However, knowing Mr. Withermyer, there had to be a twist.

"I'm only giving you twenty minutes to complete the *undoing charm*. When the twenty minutes are up, you'll come to the front of the classroom one at a time. I will place a *confusion charm* of my own creation on each of you. If your *undoing charm* is completed correctly, it will be able to remove my charm, and you will pass this assignment. If it does not, you will fail. Your time begins now."

I jumped into action and fished the sandstone and basalt from my pixie dust case. My pulse quickened as I began, and I could feel heat flush to my face. Mr. Withermyer would be casting a charm on me. I was anticipating it to be stronger than anything my peers would create. I remembered last year when we had to test our *confusion charms* on our classmates. When Betty Ann had cast her charm on me, I'd been able to fight the effects of her charm. Dr. Tweedle had told me only very talented pixies could fight the effects of a charm. He even confessed to having trouble mentally combating charms on occasion. Dr. Tweedle concluded that Betty Ann's charm must have been insufficient or not appropriately prepared.

I hadn't said anything then, but Dr. Tweedle didn't know Betty Ann had copied my charm exactly. When I had cast mine on Taylor, she became completely confused and was sent to the hospital wing. Dr. Tweedle assured me it wasn't my fault. When he had analyzed my charm, he said I created it correctly. I wondered if I'd be able to fight Mr. Withermyer's charm.

The twenty minutes went by quickly, and before I knew it, Mr. Withermyer told us to put down our materials. I followed the instructions entirely and hoped I had done it right. I didn't want to be confused by Mr. Withermyer longer than I had to.

Mr. Withermyer began calling up students. The moment he sprinkled his charm on them, they instantly became confused. Watching my classmates lose their minds so easily was unsettling. Mr. Withermyer's charm was obviously powerful. For students whose charm worked, Mr. Withermyer informed them they had passed when they returned to normal. For those whose charm didn't work, Mr. Withermyer used his *undoing charm* and announced their failure.

My palms were sweating by the time Mr. Withermyer called on me. I prayed I wouldn't drop my charm as I made my way to the front of the class. I noticed Betty Ann's sly smile, and I could tell she was anxious to watch my turn. She would be pleased to see me fail.

I took a deep breath and handed Mr. Withermyer my charm, resisting the urge to wipe my sweaty hands on my skirt. His green eyes flashed, and I saw anticipation in them. I could tell he was just itching to make me look incompetent. Mr. Withermyer grabbed for his *confusion charm*, and before I knew it, he had sprinkled the light green dust over me. My mind began to cloud at a rate I had never experienced. My first instinct was to fight it, forcing my mind to throw up a barrier to push the haze away. This had been easier when it had been Betty Ann's because Mr. Withermyer's was stronger. Repeating facts in my head, I pushed against the charm.

It felt like I had been standing at the front of the room for a while before hearing Mr. Withermyer's voice.

"What is your name?" he asked haughtily, already expecting me to be confused. His slight smile seemed to convey that he had finally accomplished a demonstration of my failure. Seeing his cocky assumption only made me determined to push the haze from my mind completely.

"My name is Jane Fitzgerald," I said clearly.

The frown on his face had been instantaneous. I was the only student to answer his question correctly. Mr. Withermyer prowled in front of me, trying to hide his shock. I noticed most of the students were staring at me in awe. Everyone who had gone before me succumbed to Mr. Withermyer's charm. Mr. Withermyer looked at a loss for words as he clutched at his temples with one hand over his forehead. Finally, he approached me.

"I don't know what you're playing at, Miss Fitzgerald, but if you think you can get away with casting a *shield charm* on yourself before coming up here for this exercise, think again! You have automatically failed this assignment since you've made it impossible for me to test your *undoing charm*. I hope this stunt was worth it. Now gather your things and go to Dr. Tweedle's office."

"Mr. Withermyer, I didn't do anything. I don't even know how to make a *shield charm*," I said, flabbergasted.

"I don't have time for your sorry lies. You are dismissed," Mr. Withermyer replied, turning away from me and calling the next student.

My blood was pounding in my ears as I collected my books. This was ridiculous and unfair. I hadn't cast a *shield charm*. We hadn't even learned how to make them. Mr. Withermyer was angry that I had been able to resist his charm. I hadn't intended to make him look like a fool. I was just naturally doing what my instincts told me to do.

I exited the Charms classroom and darted across the hall to

Dr. Tweedle's office. I was sure Mr. Withermyer would be in the process of sending a note along to tell Dr. Tweedle I had cheated. Letting out a harsh breath, I knocked on the door.

"Come in, Jane," Dr. Tweedle called.

Pushing in the door, I entered the light blue office. Dr. Tweedle was seated behind his desk, and he gestured for me to sit on the sofa. I dropped my bag to the floor and lowered myself onto the soft cushions.

"So, Jane. Would you like to tell me why you're here?" Dr. Tweedle asked as he crossed his hands and placed them on the desk.

"Mr. Withermyer accused me of cheating in Charms," I said.

"And did you?" Dr. Tweedle asked, leaning forward.

"No, of course not. I would never...." I stopped mid sentence as a note flew into the office and landed on his desk.

Dr. Tweedle grabbed the note, and I watched as he read it. When he finished, he laid the message down and looked at me.

"Why don't you tell me what happened," he said.

"Today in Charms class, we were instructed to create the *undoing charm*. Mr. Withermyer told us he would test our charm by casting a *confusion charm* upon each student. If our *undoing charm* worked, we would pass the assignment. When Mr. Withermyer placed his *confusion charm* on me, I couldn't ignore my instincts. I mentally fought the charm. I didn't mean to fight it, but I couldn't help but put up a mental barrier when my mind fogged over. When I didn't become confused, Mr. Withermyer became very angry. He told me I automatically failed since he could not test my *undoing charm*. He also accused me of casting a *shield charm* on myself before my turn. He thinks I did this on purpose to make him look like a fool, but I swear to you, Dr. Tweedle, I don't even know what a *shield charm* is or how to make one. We haven't learned that one yet," I said desperately, hoping he'd believe me.

"So, you've never learned the *shield charm* in class or even read ahead in your book? Never attempted to make one on your own?" Dr. Tweedle questioned.

"No, sir, I have not."

"Jane, are you telling me you mentally blocked the charm of a professor who has years of experience in his field?"

"Yes, sir. I know that's what happened. If you don't believe me, allow me to demonstrate it. I promise you I did not cheat."

"What you're claiming is very interesting. It's unbelievable that a student in their second year could accomplish such a thing. Fighting off a charm without using a *shield charm* is remarkable. Normally it takes years of mental training and concentration to create such a barrier in your mind."

"I'll demonstrate it if you would like," I said again.

"No, Jane. That won't be necessary. As I recall, we had a similar conversation last year about combatting charms. Back then, I hadn't believed you'd done it. Now that you're telling me this again, I believe you. I'll talk with Mr. Withermyer, and I'll personally test your *undoing charm*. You shouldn't be punished for accomplishing something beyond your years of study. I'll also send a note to Mr. Collyworth to explain why you weren't in History of Pixies today," Dr. Tweedle stated.

"Thank you so much. I appreciate it, and I'm glad you believe me," I said, standing from the sofa.

"You are very talented, Jane. I'm sure you'll receive exciting opportunities in the future." Dr. Tweedle smiled up at me.

I left the office and headed for the Zodiac Signs classroom. It was seven minutes before ten o'clock, and the bell hadn't rung yet, so I was early. I took my time climbing to the third floor. I waited in the hallway as students from the previous class streamed out. Marley was one of the last students out of the classroom, and when she saw me, she shot me a nasty glare before prancing away down the hall.

I entered the classroom, wondering why she had looked at me

that way. I had never done anything to her or her friends. Did she hate me because I was half-human or friends with Josefina? Perhaps it was both reasons. My thoughts turned from Marley when Taylor walked into the room.

"Hi, Jane. Happy birthday!" Taylor said.

"Thank you, Taylor. How did you know it was my birthday?"

"I remembered from the beginning of the year when we did that exercise on our zodiac signs."

"Oh, I remember. Your birthday is June twenty-sixth, isn't it?"

"It is!" Taylor looked thrilled that I remembered. "How is your day going? I just got out of Charms," she said with a frown.

"Oh, gods! Are you okay? Did Mr. Withermyer cast a *confusion charm* on you?"

"No, actually, he didn't. He remembered my reaction from last year, so he used a *quick complete charm* instead. I was still very nervous," Taylor said, color coming to her cheeks.

"At least he isn't completely evil. He did send me to Dr. Tweedle's office today, though," I replied.

Taylor was just about to ask why when Josefina burst into the classroom.

"Jane, what happened? Why did Mr. Withermyer dismiss you from class today? I didn't understand what he was accusing you of."

"When he cast the *confusion charm*, my instincts told me to fight it just like I did last year when Betty Ann cast it on me. When I didn't become confused, Mr. Withermyer thought I had cast a *shield charm* on myself prior to being called to the front of the room. He thought I was trying to make him look stupid, so he sent me to Dr. Tweedle's office."

"What did Dr. Tweedle say?" Josefina asked, leaning on her desk, staring at me with wide eyes.

"I explained what happened, and Dr. Tweedle believed me. He said it was possible to fight off the effects of charms. He seemed very impressed that I had because he said it normally takes a lot of mental training. I'm not sure how I managed it myself."

"At least Dr. Tweedle believed you," Taylor said.

"Dr. Tweedle said he would talk to Mr. Withermyer. He's also going to test my *undoing charm*, so I won't have to fail the assignment."

"That's great!" Josefina said, looking relieved.

Our conversation ceased when Mrs. Harris called the class to attention. She began by explaining that the movement of the stars could increase or decrease the chances of compatibility when two people meet for the first time.

"So, the expression 'the stars were aligned' is actually true. When different zodiac signs rise and fall in the sky, it influences our first impressions of new people we meet," Mrs. Harris explained.

She walked around the circle of desks and passed out the assignment. For today's class, she wanted us to read a chapter in the book and answer questions on the text. As I began reading the chapter, I scanned the list of questions to understand what I was looking for.

I became so consumed in the chapter that class flew by in the blink of an eye. I collected my supplies and followed Josefina up to our room.

"I have to run down to Marley's room," Josefina said as she dropped her bag and turned to leave. "She stopped me in the hall before Zodiac Signs and asked for my help."

"Okay," I said, taking a seat at my desk. "I'll see you later at lunch."

Josefina left the room, and I pulled my Zodiac book closer, opening it to where I had left off. I only had a few questions left on the assignment, and I was determined to finish it before lunch. The last few questions weren't hard to find, and I double-checked all of my answers to make sure I had written everything correctly.

By the time I left my room for lunch, the halls were quiet. All of the students were probably in the dining hall by now. I made my way down three flights of stairs, but I paused when I got to the second floor. I could distinctly hear loud voices coming from Dr. Tweedle's office, and my heart jumped into my throat when I heard my name. Dr. Tweedle had to be having a discussion with Mr. Withermyer about what had happened earlier.

"You need to stop doing this, Phillip. You find fault with everything she does," Dr. Tweedle's voice thundered.

"She was trying to make me look like a fool!"

"Jane is guilty of no such thing! She explained to me what had happened, and I believed her. What she has accomplished today is commendable, and instead of praising her for it, you punished her instead. Being able to combat a charm mentally takes talent. You, of all people, should know what it's like to excel at something beyond your education. Did I punish you for it?"

"No, sir," Mr. Withermyer answered.

"Then you need to stop punishing Jane. She is very talented, and it's a shame she wasn't raised in the pixie world. Jane is so gifted; if she had started at a younger age, she could be further in her education by now. You need to put your personal issues aside. The past is in the past."

I couldn't tell if Mr. Withermyer had responded, and sensing their conversation was probably drawing to a close, I ran for the stairs, hurrying to the first floor. My heart was thundering in my chest. Once again, I had overheard Dr. Tweedle and Mr. Withermyer discussing me. I knew the personal issue had something to do with my mother, but I didn't understand how. Mr. Withermyer was younger than my mother, so how had he known her?

During lunch, I remained quieter than usual, my mind still spinning with what I had overheard. Miguel and Andrew were the only ones who noticed, and when they asked me about it, I pretended I had been thinking about classwork. As usual, Josefina focused on the three girls, so she was oblivious. Knowing that Magical Creatures was the next class, I pushed thoughts of Mr. Withermyer to the back of my mind. I'd get to see Thistle soon, and that was what mattered. Seeing her would make my birthday so much better.

I couldn't get to the Magical Creatures classroom fast enough. When the class began, Mrs. Rowley told us to check on our dragons, but she also had an announcement, so we needed to return to our seats in five minutes. Quickly, I made my way to the dragon enclosure, eager to spend as much time as possible with Thistle.

"Hey, Thistle, girl," I said when I reached her stall.

Thistle had grown so big over the last month. She was now the size of a pony. Her purple scales glistened, and she flapped her wings in excitement. I crossed her stall and threw my arms around her neck. Her little pink tongue darted out and touched my cheek. This was how Thistle always greeted me, especially when I would sneak out at night to see her. I patted her nose, and she rubbed it against my hand.

"Did you know it's my birthday, Thistle?" I whispered to her. "You are definitely the highlight of my day."

I checked Thistle's trough, and when I saw it was low, I grabbed a bucket. I dumped a whole bucket of water into it and rubbed her head again.

"I'll be right back. Mrs. Rowley has an announcement," I whispered as I left the stall and walked back to my seat.

When everyone had returned, Mrs. Rowley stood from her desk, clearing her throat.

"Class, as you know, your dragons are now a month old and growing like weeds. This morning, I invited a dragon expert to have a look at them. After examining their wings, he believes they should be ready to fly. Usually, when dragons are a month old, they are ready to leave the nest and fend for themselves. The dragon expert believes it's time to release the dragons into the wild before they become too dependent on us. For today's class, we'll let your dragons fly for the first time and release them into the wild."

My heart dove into the pit of my stomach. Did Mrs. Rowley just say we would be releasing our dragons? Heat flushed my face, and I felt faint. She couldn't have meant today. I had to have misunderstood her. I couldn't lose Thistle today. Hot emotion hit me square in the chest, and I had to take a deep, shaky breath to keep from crying out. This was not happening.

Mrs. Rowley must have instructed the class to head over to the dragon enclosure, but I hadn't heard her. My grief was drowning out everything around me. My legs felt leaden as I followed my classmates across the field. No one else appeared as distraught by the news as I was. I knew from the beginning that I would have to give Thistle up, but I didn't think it would be so soon after she hatched.

"What I want each of you to do is enter your dragon's stall, loop a lasso around their necks, and bring them out into the open field. Once everyone has their dragons outside, I will tell you when to remove the lasso," Mrs. Rowley instructed.

It was so hard opening Thistle's pen when I knew it would be for the last time. Thistle came bounding to me again with that same excited look. Her pink tongue darted out and found my hands holding the lasso. My shoulders sagged, and tears sprung to my eyes. I patted her nose and took a shaky breath. Her violet eyes met mine, and I could have sworn I saw a look of confusion on her face.

"Hey, little girl," I said as I held up the lasso. "Everything is going to be okay."

I threw my arms around her neck and pressed my face into her cool scales. Tears came to my eyes, and I felt them slide down my cheeks. Thistle had been such a comfort to me even when she was still in her egg. I had taken care of her. It didn't seem right to be letting her go. I loved Thistle, and I had a feeling she loved me too.

Slowly, I backed away from her, my heart breaking with every step. Using my coat sleeve, I wiped at my face to clear away the tears. I slipped the lasso over Thistle's head and rubbed the bridge of her nose between her eyes.

"You are going to grow up to be such a great dragon. Please don't forget me," I choked out.

The tears began to flow again. I quickly ducked my head, wiping my face again. Haltingly, I led Thistle from her stall and joined the group of other dragons. I felt like I couldn't breathe. Was it possible for your heart to actually break in your chest?

"Now that everyone has their dragon, spread out in the field to give them room," Mrs. Rowley said.

A giant red dragon reared up on its hind legs and flapped its wings several times. It looked like it was ready to break loose from the lasso. When I saw that Betty Ann was struggling to hold him, I could understand why. Thistle clung to my side as I led her away from the crowded area.

When the dragons were spread out far enough, Mrs. Rowley addressed us again.

"Alright, class. Now you may release your dragons."

With a heavy heart, I removed the lasso from around Thistle's neck. I could hear the flutter of wings, and I looked up. The giant red dragon was the first to burst away. His strong wings beat against the air, and soon he was high up in the clouds. Other dragons were taking off to the sky, and with a queasy stomach, I turned to find Thistle still standing behind me. When my eyes met hers, she moved closer to me, resting her head on my shoulder. She didn't move.

We watched all the other dragons leap into the air, becoming green, blue, red, and orange flashes. I couldn't believe she hadn't left me yet. I knew it was only a matter of time as she watched the others soaring away. I stood very still, waiting for the moment when her head would leave my shoulder. Soon, all the other dragons became colorful specks far up in the sky, but Thistle remained. I was happy she was still beside me, but I also wondered if something was wrong with her.

Turning to her, I patted her snout. "What's wrong, Thistle? Don't you want to fly?" My voice cracked as I said the words, and I could feel my tears resurfacing.

I saw Mrs. Rowley making her way across the field, followed by the other students.

"Miss Fitzgerald, why haven't you let that dragon go?" Mrs. Rowley huffed out as she came closer.

"I did, ma'am," I said, holding out the lasso for her to see. "She doesn't want to fly."

Mrs. Rowley looked very puzzled. Once she reached us, she looked Thistle over.

"Nothing appears to be wrong with her. The dragon expert looked over them all and declared each one fit to fly. Everyone, just stay right here. I'm going to send a message to Dr. Tweedle." Mrs. Rowley walked to the classroom and stopped at her desk. I stood rooted next to Thistle.

The other students seemed surprised to see that Thistle hadn't flown away with the other dragons. She stayed next to me, her head remaining on my shoulder. A harsh laugh sounded, and the students parted as Betty Ann came forward.

"I knew your dragon didn't have a chance in hell when you picked that egg. I'm honestly surprised it hatched and was able to live this long. You honestly didn't expect that tiny runt to have wings strong enough to fly, did you? Maybe you should do it a favor and kill it now because that dragon is as good as dead out in the wild."

"Betty Ann, yes, my dragon is smaller than most others, and you had one of the largest dragons. As I recall, he was the first to take flight, though I don't know if it was because of the strength of his wings. I can think of many reasons he'd be so eager to get away from you," I replied. Thistle shifted her position and had somehow angled herself between Betty Ann and me.

Betty Ann stood there as what I said began to sink in. It appeared she couldn't come up with a remark, so she stalked away. Thistle's eyes never left sight of Betty Ann. My dragon seemed like she was ready to attack if Betty Ann would've harmed me.

The bell rang, signaling the end of Magical Creatures. The other students began clearing out, but I remained, unsure of what to do. What would happen to Thistle? Every time I shifted my weight, Thistle would adjust her position. When I took a few steps forward, she followed me.

Mrs. Rowley joined me again. "I don't know what to do. I've never had this happen before. Dr. Tweedle is on his way down to assess the situation," Mrs. Rowley told me.

I continued to pat Thistle as we waited for Dr. Tweedle. I was glad Mrs. Rowley hadn't told me to go to my next class. I was sure it would've been impossible. I was confident Thistle would follow me.

Dr. Tweedle exited the academy's front door, and I watched as he walked toward us, his long coat blowing in the icy air. He entered the pen and shook his head as he came toward me.

"What is it this time, Miss Fitzgerald?" he asked as he pushed his round glasses up the bridge of his nose.

"Thistle doesn't want to fly away," I said.

"Ah, yes. This must be the famous Thistle you told me about," he said with a wink. "She seems attached to you."

Thistle had placed herself between Dr. Tweedle and me during this exchange, and she was eyeing him warily. Dr. Tweedle extended his hand out to allow her to sniff him. When Thistle seemed to approve, he petted her slightly on the nose.

"In all my years of teaching at the Jelf Academy, I've never seen a dragon become so attached and protective of a pixie," Dr. Tweedle said. "I'm honestly at a loss."

Thistle shimmied back to my side and attempted to lick my

face. I couldn't suppress the giggle that escaped my lips as I put my hand up to block her tongue. A huge smile spread across Dr. Tweedle's face as he watched Thistle.

"Dragons are brilliant creatures," Dr. Tweedle mused. "That's how they've managed to stay hidden from humans. I've never seen a dragon forced into something they didn't want to do. The fact that Thistle is still here is because she wants to be. If Thistle continues to have this attachment to you, would you take care of her, Jane?"

"Yes. I love Thistle and would do anything to care for her," I replied, looking up at him.

"Then it seems my hands are tied. I'll speak with Mrs. Rowley about keeping Thistle's stall open for her to stay. It seems like this dragon is yours for as long as she wants it to remain that way," Dr. Tweedle said.

The meaning of his words hit me full force. Thistle wasn't going to be forced to leave!

"Thank you so much, Dr. Tweedle," I said excitedly, wrapping my arms around Thistle's neck.

"Happy birthday, Jane,'" he whispered, winking at me before walking away.

Without a doubt, today was the best birthday of my life.

24

A Fateful Mistake

THE DAY FOLLOWING my birthday was one of the happiest I had ever known. Dr. Tweedle told me I could take care of Thistle every night after dinner, So I didn't need to sneak out to see her. He also said that Mrs. Rowley would look after her while I was at the manor. I had been so ecstatic about keeping my dragon that, against my better judgement, I used the *calling charm* to contact Robert.

I had locked myself in the bathroom when Josefina was studying in the library. He was so happy for me when I told him about Thistle. After our conversation, Robert made me promise to call him later if I had the opportunity. I knew I shouldn't, but I loved being able to talk to him while I was at the academy. For the first time in my life, I felt like everything was going great for me.

I fought the urge to skip as I brought my tray to the lunch table. Miguel and Andrew looked up as I sat down beside them.

"You seem happy today," Miguel commented as he dipped his spoon into his soup.

"I am happy," I said. "It's because Thistle stayed."

"I didn't name my dragon," Andrew stated. "I didn't want to become too attached since we would have to release them."

"I couldn't help becoming attached to Thistle from the moment I picked her egg. I felt like she needed me." I couldn't keep the smile off my face as I talked about her.

"It's wonderful seeing a big smile on your face every day," Miguel said. "It's just a shame that someone else hasn't cared to notice." Miguel inclined his head toward the other end of the table.

Josefina was fully immersed in conversation with the girls.

"Miguel, it's okay. The girls were Josefina's friends long before I was."

"It's not just that she ignores you. Ever since they started the Jelf Academy, my mental connection with her hasn't been strong. It feels like she has a barrier around her mind and is hiding something from me. Every time I mention those three, she becomes defensive. My sister has never been like this. Maybe you could talk to her for me since she's constantly tuning me out?" Miguel asked.

"I don't know, Miguel. I don't think she would listen."

"I know Josefina values your opinion and friendship. Besides, you're her roommate, so you'll have time alone with her. Could you please just try?"

I sighed deeply before responding. "I can't make any promises, but I'll try. It might take me a while to bring up the topic."

"Okay. Thanks, Jane. I really appreciate it."

Once I finished my potato soup, I crossed the dining hall to place my dirty dishes in a bin. When I turned around, Betty Ann and Thomas were behind me.

"Oh, look, Tom. It's the dragon whisperer," Betty Ann sneered, making Thomas chuckle.

"Why did Dr. Tweedle let you keep that filthy animal? This school is becoming ridiculous. They allow disgusting humans and half leprechauns," Betty Ann's glare shifted across the room to Izzy, Candi's roommate. "Now, Dr. Tweedle is allowing a dragon to stay because he favors you. I'm appalled to even go to this school. What's the crazy headmaster going to let in next?"

"Dr. Tweedle is not crazy. You're just jealous that he let her stay," I replied.

"Jealous of you? Ugh, of course not! If another pixie school existed in this area, I'd be begging my father to go there instead."

"I'm sure if most of the students here knew your opinion, they would wish so too because I can't imagine anyone would miss you. Now, if you'll excuse me," I said, walking past her and out of the dining hall.

I climbed the stairs to the fifth floor to my room. Once inside, I laughed, recalling Betty Ann's face. Did she honestly think I cared when she tried to insult me?

∽

The icy February air cut through my coat, and light snow began to fall. I shivered slightly as I slid into my seat in the Magical Creatures classroom. Now that our dragon project was over, Mrs. Rowley had collected our journals. I wondered if there would be a new creature for us to see today.

It wasn't long before Miguel sat at the desk beside me. Once again, Josefina wasn't with him. It had become a habit of hers to either be late to class or arrive right at the bell. It was disheartening to see how much my best friend had changed. I just wanted the old Josefina back.

As the bell rang, Josefina slid into her seat and cast me a sideways grin as if I had been a co-conspirator in her tardiness. Thankfully, I didn't have to fake being amused because Mrs. Rowley began talking.

"We're going to begin talking about dangerous creatures today. There won't be animals inside the fence, so we'll just reference the pictures in your books. This will be the topic for the next few weeks. Then, you will choose one to write a report on. We'll begin on page 251."

At the top of the page was a picture of an animal with three heads; one looked like a lion, one a goat, and the other a dragon. The body was mainly lion-like, but it had wings and a tail that looked like a snake's head. The word chimera was in bold letters.

"You should all be looking at the chimera. As you can see, this creature is a combination of several. All three of its heads breathe fire. Their population is the highest in Greece and the Mediterranean, but they've been spotted in other locations. Ancient Greek pixies believed that when a chimera was seen, it was an omen for a natural disaster.

"This animal is very dangerous and hard to escape. According to ancient texts, a pixie named Bellerophon managed to defeat one of these beasts. Whether this story is only a myth or not, no one knows," Mrs. Rowley said.

Turning the page, I saw an ugly thing with large, pointed ears, giant bat wings, and a hooked nose.

"This humanoid creature is called an imp. They're mischievous, wild, and uncontrollable. They've been known to steal babies, so protection charms can be used to keep them away from newborns. Imps love playing pranks, most of which are harmful, such as leading travelers in the wrong direction. If an imp has targeted you, charms can be used to trap the imp inside of an object."

Before the bell rang, Mrs. Rowley had gone over several more dangerous beasts. While I waited for Earth Catastrophes to begin, I looked at the horrifying creatures we would be discussing tomorrow. I shuddered, imagining coming across any of them.

"What are you reading?" Taylor asked, sitting beside me.

"The assignment for Magical Creatures," I replied.

"I've already finished those pages," Taylor said.

"I knew you would be ahead," I said, marking my place and sliding the book back into my bag.

"I wouldn't want to see any of those creatures in person," Taylor laughed.

The bell rang, and as usual, Mr. Laruse was absent. After ten minutes, I was beginning to wonder. He was never this late. Unsure of what else to do, I pulled out the Earth Catastrophes book and turned to where we had left off.

Mr. Laruse ended up being twenty minutes late. He dashed across the lawn, his tufts of hair blowing in the wind.

"I'm so sorry. Please open your books," he shouted before reaching his desk.

I turned back a few pages as Mr. Laruse began. When the bell rang, Mr. Laruse looked startled, but I couldn't help feeling relieved.

"That was the latest he's ever arrived," Taylor whispered while we walked back into the school.

We entered the front doors, and warm air washed over us.

"I'm curious about what Ms. Crescent will teach us today," I said with a sigh.

"Anything has to be better than our previous lecture," Taylor said with a laugh, and I nodded in agreement.

The lights were dim when we entered Predicting the Future. I saw Ms. Crescent had placed small, short tables between each seat. On the tables were two cups, a teapot, and a box.

"Today, we'll be reading tea leaves. On the tables, you will find a teapot full of boiled water, two cups, and tea leaves. A thing to remember when reading tea leaves: use a light-colored cup to see the images better. You'll start by placing the leaves in the bottom of the cup, followed by the boiling water. You must drink the entire cup of tea. Once all the tea is gone, interpret the shape of the leaves left in the bottom of the cup to make a prediction. You may work with the person sharing the table with you."

Taylor and I both began to prepare our tea. Steam rose from my cup, and I lifted it to my lips to blow on it. My first sip was scalding hot, and the taste was horrible. Taylor took a drink, too, and her facial expression mimed what I was thinking.

"This tea is awful," she whispered across the table.

When the tea finally cooled off, I downed it in one gulp. Taylor followed my lead, sticking her tongue out after she had finished. I placed the cup back on the saucer and gazed into it. It was hard to make out anything besides black clumps.

"This task would be easier if she didn't keep the lights so low," I whispered.

"I can't figure mine out," Taylor said, twisting her cup in her hand.

I squinted into my cup. "I think mine might look like bones. Do you want to trade and tell me what you think?"

We exchanged cups. "Yes, yours could be bones. What do you think mine is?"

"Maybe it's an open book," I replied.

I handed back her cup and picked up mine.

"So, if yours is bones, and mine is a book, what does it mean?" Taylor asked, grabbing her Predicting the Future book. I watched as she flipped through the symbols.

"Bones are supposed to mean a disagreement between friends," Taylor said with a frown.

"Well, that sounds great," I replied sarcastically. Maybe I couldn't keep my promise to Miguel.

"An open book means I'll learn something new," Taylor said. "These symbol descriptions are very vague."

"Perhaps I should disagree with you about your interpretation, so my prediction can be over with," I said with a chuckle.

Taylor laughed. "Nice try."

The bell rang, and I packed up my supplies. Taylor and I walked to the fifth floor together and parted when I reached my room. I pulled out my assignments due tomorrow and sat at my desk. There was a Charms test I needed to study for, a history worksheet, and the Magical Creatures reading.

I was just finishing up with history when Josefina came in.

"Are you ready to go to dinner?" she asked.

When I finished my last sentence, I put my work away, and we left the room together.

"Guess what happened during my Earth Catastrophes class! Mr. Laruse showed up twenty minutes late!" I said as we walked down the stairs

Josefina and I talked about our day and the classes we didn't have together. It was nice and almost reminded me of old times until the girls showed up. They stole Josefina's attention, and I faded into the background. Thankfully, Miguel and Andrew were already at the table.

"We finished the History assignment already," Miguel huffed, putting down his plate.

"We were so determined to complete it before dinner," Andrew added. "At least ancient Greek pixies are interesting."

"If you say so," Marley sneered, jumping into the conversation. I hadn't even known she was paying attention.

"Marley, we weren't asking your opinion," Miguel said. "I don't know why you felt obligated to give one."

Marley, Candi, Bellony, and Josefina gave Miguel the nastiest look. From the scowl on Josefina's face, I could tell she was arguing with Miguel.

"Josefina, you're going to meet us in the library again tonight, right?" Bellony asked, breaking her connection with Miguel.

It took her a moment to comprehend what Bellony had said.

"Yes, that's fine," she finally replied.

I was disappointed that Josefina was going to the library again. I thought we could study for Charms. Instead, after dinner, I found myself wandering out to the barn.

The sun had almost set as I let myself in. Thankfully, the stalls were lit by goblin fire. When I opened Thistle's pen, she came running toward me. Her tongue darted out, licking my cheek.

Breaking away, I went to collect water for her before going to the icebox to retrieve a leg of lamb. Mrs. Rowley had told me she would keep the icebox stocked with food for Thistle. I laid the lamb in front of her, and smoke floated up from her nostrils. I took several steps away before fire burst from her mouth.

While Thistle devoured her meal, I talked about my classes. I told her about my tea leaf prediction. She just snorted and licked her lips, which made me laugh. Sometimes I swore she understood me. I spent over an hour with Thistle but soon realized I should head back. I really needed to focus on Charms tonight.

Darkness shrouded the school as I crossed the lawn. The air was crisp, and the stars sparkled brightly. I quickly hurried to my room, which was dark and empty when I entered. Crossing to my desk, I turned up the goblin fire lamp and pulled out my Charms book. Mr. Withermyer's tests were always random, so I wanted to look over everything.

When my eyes grew heavy, and I couldn't look at my notes anymore, I rose from my bed and put my Charms book away. Josefina would be at the library for a while, and no one else could enter our room. Should I take the chance and call Robert? Technically, it was a perfect time.

Before I could talk myself out of it, I grabbed a vial of the *calling charm* and headed into the bathroom. I placed the stopper in the tub and turned on the tap. When it had filled enough, I sat on the edge of the tub, thought about Robert, and upended the vial.

The water began to ripple, and soon I saw the barn's ceiling.

"Robert, are you there?" I whispered, not knowing if he was alone.

It wasn't long before Robert's smiling face appeared. I couldn't stop the instant smile that came to my face.

"Jane, you managed to call me again!" he exclaimed.

"I promised I would try," I replied.

"How have you been?"

"I just came back from seeing Thistle and studying for Charms."

"I'm guessing Josefina is out again," Robert commented.

"Yes, but it allows me to talk to you," I replied with a shrug.

Robert's smile became more prominent. "I just finished my chores. I was lying here, thinking about you, when I heard your voice. I thought I had nodded off to sleep."

"I hope you weren't overworked," I said.

"Not any harder than usual. Working for Marie is heaven compared to Mr. Wicker. He would rarely let me sleep."

"I know what that's like."

"Don't worry. I'll help you if I can," he said with a smirk. He pushed his hair away from his face and winked.

I wasn't even going to argue anymore. As long as Marie didn't find out, I couldn't stop him.

"I'm sure you will. Has anything else happened at the manor?"

"No. I'm sure you have more exciting news," Robert said.

"I learned about some dangerous creatures in Magical Creatures class."

"What types of animals?" Robert questioned, leaning close to the bucket.

I described the creatures we discussed, and Robert's face paled.

"You weren't around them, were you?"

"No, Mrs. Rowley isn't going to bring in the animals from this section."

"Good. I worry enough, ever since you told me about the W.A.S.P."

"Robert, don't worry about them while I'm at school. This is the safest place I can be."

"I just miss you so much," Robert said. "I love you, and it's so frustrating to see you but not hold you in my arms."

"I love you too. I hope I get to work with you this weekend."

"I'm just happy I can talk to you and see you while you're away."

Robert stared into my eyes, and I felt myself starting to blush. If only I could reach into the water and touch his face.

"You are so beautiful. I could stare at you all night," Robert said.

"Oh, stop it!" I replied, turning slightly away from the tub.

"I mean it, Jane. You are the most beautiful girl I've ever seen. I know it's getting late, so I'll let you go for the evening," he said with a sad smile.

"Good night, Robert," I said, pressing my fingers to my lips and blowing him a kiss.

It was painful to pull the plug on the tub and watch Robert's face disappear with the water. The weekend was only a few days away, so we wouldn't be apart much longer. Standing from the edge of the tub, I ran my hands over my skirt and opened the bathroom door.

My heart stopped when I saw Josefina sitting on the edge of her bed.

"Josefina," I exclaimed, my voice cracking. "I didn't even hear you come in."

Josefina narrowed her eyes as she stood up.

"Who were you just talking to in the bathroom, and what is around your neck?"

25

Disagreement and Deception

My hand shot up to cover Robert's ring.

"Josefina, please sit down and let me explain," I stammered, angling myself around her and going to my side of the room.

"What's going on, Jane? I heard you talking to someone in the bathroom, which is odd. Who were you talking to?"

"Josefina, I've wanted to tell you, but you've been preoccupied lately. Robert and I are in love. We've been for a while."

"Robert, as in the boy who works at the manor with you?" Josefina practically shouted.

"Yes, he gave me this ring," I replied. My fingers absentmindedly caressed the metal.

"How long has this been going on?" Josefina asked.

"I've liked Robert for a very long time, but he didn't confess his feelings for me until last year. I tried to deny my feelings, but I couldn't. He gave me his ring for Christmas."

"When were you going to tell me?" Josefina asked.

"I wanted to, but we're hardly alone anymore. I never had a good opportunity, and I was afraid of what you would think," I said, looking down at my feet.

Josefina looked nervous. "Robert is a human. You know a relationship with him is against the law."

"I know, but I love Robert. He makes me the happiest I've been in a while."

Josefina began pacing the room. She raised her hands to her temples and rubbed in slow circles.

"I can't believe you're telling me this! You're not allowed to love him! There are plenty of pixie boys at this school. Why can't you fall in love with one of them?" she cried.

"That's not how love works," I retorted angrily. "I can't make myself love someone just because they're a pixie. Robert has been there through the hard times I've had at the manor. He knows what Marie is like."

"How does this explain who you were talking to in the bathroom…." Josefina stopped pacing, and all the color drained from her face. "Oh, my gods. He knows! You told him what you are! How could you, Jane?"

"I didn't plan on telling him anything!"

"How long has he known?" she seethed.

"He found out recently. It was an accident."

"You know how dangerous it is. How could you tell him?"

Josefina's face had gone from pale to bright red.

"Josefina, just listen to me." I had to refrain from screaming. "I was never going to tell him. He found out by accident."

"Dr. Tweedle told you not to use magic at the manor! The W.A.S.P. is trying to find and kill you! Why would you do something so stupid?"

"I was alone. I didn't think anything bad would happen," I replied, frustrated.

"So, Robert caught you, and now he knows," Josefina moaned,

putting her face in her hands. "This is very bad, Jane. This could put the whole pixie world in danger."

"Robert isn't going to tell anyone."

"How do you know that? How do you know he isn't a member of the W.A.S.P.?" Josefina asked hysterically.

"He's not! I'm pretty sure I'd be dead right now if that were the case. Robert would never hurt me. It's insulting that you would even assume that!"

"Pixie laws are in place for a reason. Telling humans about what we are can harm us. Loving humans can harm us!"

"Robert would never harm me or anyone else. He's accepted me for who I am. His love for me didn't change. I was so afraid he would think I was an abomination," I said.

"So, you would've never told him if he hadn't caught you?"

"Yes, Josefina!"

"Were you planning on hiding your magic from him forever?" Josefina questioned.

"Yes. After I finish the Jelf Academy, if I had to leave the pixie world for good, I would do it for him," I responded without hesitation.

"You would just disappear?"

"My mother did because she loved my father."

"Why is this something you would even consider? How could you just leave the pixie world?"

"I would do anything for Robert. I'm not saying I would want to leave, but if I had to choose between living in the pixie world or being with Robert, I would choose him."

"You're so talented. Why would you just throw it all away?" Josefina asked, shaking her head.

"I love Robert more than I love my magic. If being with him means I can't be a part of the pixie world, I would accept it. It's how my mother must have felt about my father. I now know what it feels like to love someone so much that you can't live without them. No matter the consequences."

"I just can't make sense of what you're saying. Why is this the first time I'm hearing about your feeling for Robert?" she wailed.

"I said I wanted to tell you. Every night you're at the library, and if you're not there, the girls are in our room. Besides, I was afraid to tell you. I didn't want you to react this way. Being a human doesn't make a person evil. Everyone seems to forget I'm half-human. I'm sorry he found out what I am, but I can't be sorry for loving him. Why can't you be happy for me?" I asked her.

"Jane, I don't care if you're in love with Robert. I'll admit that I'm shocked by all of this, but that's not why I'm upset. I'm upset because you're supposed to be my best friend, and you couldn't even tell me," Josefina said, throwing herself on her bed. She turned her back to me, refusing to say anything else.

Josefina was still cold toward me the following day, even though I tried to apologize again. She warmed up a little by lunch and walked with Miguel and me to Magical Creatures, but she was still distant. After classes, I prepared to explain myself again. I felt so guilty. Maybe I should have tried harder. Last year, I shared everything with Josefina. However, I couldn't help but feel like our relationship had changed. I didn't feel like her best friend anymore.

I began my homework while I waited. I was so immersed in my reading that I was surprised to see it was time for dinner when I finally glanced at the clock. I supposed Josefina was so mad she decided not to come back to our room.

Closing the Earth Catastrophes book, I placed it on the shelf above the desk. Standing, I took a deep breath and prepared to head downstairs. I was about to open the door when it suddenly slid open. Josefina stepped in, and I took a step back. Her eyes met mine, and she sighed deeply.

"Jane, can I please talk to you?" she asked. She crossed the room and dropped her bag on the floor. "I'm sorry I was so mad earlier."

"No. You have every right to be. I should have told you about Robert," I began, but Josefina raised her hand to stop me.

"I'm sure you wanted to tell me, and you were right when you said I've been preoccupied. I'm sorry. I'll try to be better at splitting my time. I meant it when I said you're my best friend."

"So, you forgive me?" I asked, hoping she would talk to me again.

"Yes, Jane. I'm very sorry too. Are you ready for dinner? I'm starving," she replied.

Josefina was her usual talkative self on the way down. She talked a mile a minute about our classes. It was almost like my best friend had returned. Josefina sat next to me and even asked the girls to sit on the other side of the table. They looked confused but sat without complaining. I thought it was odd, but I was happy Josefina was acting like my friend again.

I laughed over something Josefina said and reached for my glass. I had almost brought the cup to my lips when Andrew suddenly jumped up and grabbed the cup out of my hand.

"Don't drink that!" he cried. I stared at him as he grabbed Miguel's cup, too.

"What are you doing?" Miguel asked, giving his roommate an odd look.

"I swear I saw Josefina put something in your cups when you weren't paying attention," Andrew replied.

"What are you talking about?" Josefina asked.

"Why would she put something in our drinks?" Miguel said with a chuckle.

"I don't know, but I swear that's what I saw," Andrew replied.

"You must be seeing things," Josefina laughed, returning to her food, but something in her tone had me grabbing for the cup Andrew had taken.

At first glance, my water appeared normal, but then I noticed a slight sparkle on the surface. I felt heat flush to my face at the realization Josefina had put something in my drink. Andrew quickly snatched the cup back before anyone could say anything. He rushed away and dumped out the liquid. Miguel just laughed and went to get another beverage. I couldn't help but feel troubled.

When we finished dinner, I grabbed Josefina's arm.

"Can I talk to you?" I asked. "Do you mind if we go up to our room for a moment?"

Josefina agreed with a quizzical look, and she led the way back up to the fifth floor. Once we were inside, I turned to face her.

"What did you put in my water?"

"Nothing. Andrew must've been joking around."

"Josefina, just tell the truth. I could tell the cup had been tampered with when I looked into it," I sighed.

Josefina sat down on her bed and looked at the floor.

"It was just a little charm," she said with a sigh.

"Why would you put a charm in our drinks?" I said, feeling angry.

Josefina sat on her bed and refused to say. She wasn't looking at me, and her gaze remained on the floor. This only irritated me.

"What charm did you put in my drink, Josefina?" I asked again.

Something in Josefina seemed to have snapped. She jumped up from her bed.

"It was a *love charm*, okay."

"Why would you put a *love charm* in my cup?" Anger bubbled up in my chest.

Josefina began pacing the room. "I was trying to make you fall in love with Miguel," she finally admitted in a whisper.

"Why would you do that?"

"Last night, you said you would disappear forever to be with Robert. How could you just forget who you are? I thought if you fell in love with Miguel, you would forget about Robert. Then you wouldn't be breaking any pixie laws. You wouldn't have to give up the pixie world. If you loved my brother, we could truly be sisters." Tears started to stream down Josefina's face.

"Why would you try to do this?" I yelled.

"I don't want to lose you, Jane. I'm afraid of what will happen. Nothing good ever comes from letting humans into our world."

"That's not your decision to make! I love Robert, and nothing will change that. I do love Miguel, but not how you want me to. Miguel is like a brother to me. How could you manipulate me like that? You lied last night when you told me it didn't matter if I loved Robert. You said you were upset that I hadn't told you." Tears of frustration burned under my eyelids, and my heart felt like it had been stabbed.

"I'm sorry, Jane. I just thought it would change your mind."

I shook my head and backed further away. "Friends don't do things like that! Do you even care how I feel? Do you care how Miguel feels? What was your plan anyway? You know *love charms* don't last. Would you sneak a *love charm* into our food every day? Magic shouldn't be used that way. Best friends don't manipulate each other! Best friends are supposed to listen and care about one another's feelings!

"I told you last night about how much Robert means to me. I know I didn't tell you right away, but I still shared something very important. Didn't you care at all?"

"Yes, I do care. I care about your safety. I care that you're breaking the law. I don't want you to get hurt," Josefina sobbed.

"It's not up to you to tell me who I can love and who I should love. I can't believe you would betray me this way," I shuddered. This wasn't happening. I had to be dreaming, or my mind wasn't functioning properly.

"I'm so sorry, Jane. I didn't mean it. Please forgive me. I never meant to hurt you. I care about you and want to protect you. When I was talking to the girls, it seemed like a good idea."

"What?" I couldn't stop my voice from rising. "You told the girls about Robert?" All I could see was the color red.

"No, I didn't tell them about Robert," Josefina said, sounding defensive. "All I said was you had a problem I wished I could fix. They told me to use a charm."

"I don't have a problem! Why would you listen to them anyway? Why would you even talk to them about me? I guess that was why they were so accommodating to let you sit next to me at dinner," I said, feeling even angrier that Marley, Candi, and Bellony knew any details about my personal life.

"Because they are my friends," Josefina replied.

"Do you think so?" I felt so angry; I didn't care anymore.

"Yes, Jane. They're my friends. I've known them since I was eight."

"Do you really know them, Josefina" I pushed.

She looked taken aback by my question but then vigorously shook her head. "Of course, I know them."

"Then I'm sure you know everything they've said about me."

"What are you talking about?"

"I overheard them months ago. They were talking about my parents and my father being human. Oh, and I clearly recall their comment about my blood being filthy and tainted!"

"That doesn't sound like them," Josefina huffed.

"Are you accusing me of lying?"

"I'm saying my friends wouldn't say those things. Before my father discovered the gem mine, my family didn't have a lot of money. Marley, Candi, and Bellony were the only ones who talked to me when we moved to our new neighborhood. They didn't care that I used to be poor," Josefina said.

"I'm sure they cared about the gem mine your father found, though."

"What does that mean?"

"It means I heard them saying they're your friends because

of the jewelry you give them for Christmas. They're using you, Josefina," I said pointedly.

"Okay, and when did you 'supposedly' hear this?" she asked, forming air quotes as she said supposedly.

"Before Christmas. I didn't tell you because I didn't want you to be mad. You're always so defensive when it comes to them. Can you honestly tell me you're not aware of how condescending they are? You never noticed when they physically pushed me down the bench in the dining hall?"

"I know you don't like them, but you didn't even give them a chance. You're just finding things to complain about," Josefina said, crossing her arms over her chest.

"Are you serious? I have given the girls plenty of chances, and they've been subtly nasty. How can you not see it? I'm telling you what they've done, and you're not even listening. Instead, you're defending them and calling me a liar!"

I felt tears coming to my eyes. Josefina had betrayed me in an unimaginable way. Now she was digging the knife in deeper.

"I didn't call you a liar," Josefina said.

"By defending them, you're implying I'm making it up. Why can't you see they're using you? You help them with their schoolwork. They convinced you to miss class. Can you remember the last time they helped you? Do they care about what you have to say or how you feel? I'm not the only one who sees how they take advantage of you. You tell me all the time that I'm your best friend. Then why aren't you listening to me?"

"I am listening, but the girls are my friends, too. I don't think they're using me. I'm allowed to have other friends besides you," Josefina snipped.

"Yes, Josefina. You can have other friends. I'm sure they're the type of friends you don't try to manipulate with your magic. I can't even look at you right now," I raged as I left the room, slamming the door behind me.

26

A Disturbing Discovery

"Have you finished buttoning it yet?" Emily screeched as the blonde seamstress worked on the buttons of the wedding dress. My arms were starting to hurt from holding up the train of Emily's gown.

The blonde seamstress paused and bit her lip.

"I'm afraid I need to add more material. The last few buttons won't come together."

"What do you mean they won't come together? Are you telling me my dress doesn't fit?" Emily fumed.

"Madame, diz iz somezing that can easily be fixed," the French seamstress said as she circled Emily.

"My wedding is in two months! My dress should be perfect!" Emily huffed.

"It will be okay, miss. That is why we have fittings," the English girl said with a smile, reaching for her measuring tape.

"You probably measured wrong the first time," Emily muttered under her breath.

The spring sunshine was coming in through the window, and I could see buds blooming on the trees. It was the middle of April, and I hadn't talked to Josefina in over a month. Though we still shared a room, we avoided each other as much as possible. Josefina started staying later at the library with the girls, so I usually was asleep by the time she came back.

Miguel hadn't communicated much with his sister. For the past month, I sat as far from Josefina as possible in the dining hall, on the other side of Miguel, Andrew, and Juan.

I also decided to study with Taylor more often to take my mind off it. Taylor noticed the shift in my friendship, but she never asked about it. It was nice that she hadn't pried, but I needed to talk about it, so I explained what Josefina had done. Taylor didn't give her opinion and just listened. I was glad she didn't say anything negative. Even though Josefina had betrayed me, I still cared about her. I just wanted my old friend back, and tears came to my eyes every time I thought about it. I didn't know when I would be able to forgive her.

"Jane, quit lowering my train! Hold it up!" Emily's sharp voice brought me out of my reflection. I hefted the train back up, feeling the burn in my arms.

The seamstresses continued measuring and writing down the adjustments they needed to make. Marie stood in the corner, a look of distaste on her face. Hopefully, these women would be able to give Emily everything she wanted. Knowing Emily, she would probably change something about the dress at the last minute to make their lives difficult.

Thankfully, the seamstresses instructed me to lower the train, and I was able to step away. Her train was extremely long. I wondered who would take care of it on the wedding day. I hoped she wouldn't reserve that special honor for me.

The blonde seamstress began unbuttoning the back of the dress while the brunette continued making notes in her book. When the dress was pulled down to her ankles, Emily stepped out of it and grabbed for her robe on the settee. Flinging it over her shoulders, she spun around to glare at the women.

"My wedding dress better be perfect by next month, or I won't recommend your business to anyone!" Emily cried.

The seamstresses bobbed their heads and proceeded to collect the dress in a garment bag. When they had finished, they briefly discussed when they would be back before I showed them to the door. I watched as they loaded the dress into their carriage. They looked relieved to be leaving.

"Jane," I heard Emily calling as soon as I stepped back into the house. With a small roll of my eyes, I rushed back up to her room. Emily and Marie were lounging on the settee when I reentered.

"Go into my closet and find my midnight blue dress," Emily commanded without looking up at me.

"I'm beginning to feel disappointed with these dress designers," Marie said. "The dress should have fit you."

"Didn't they measure properly when they were here in December? How incompetent!" Emily said.

"I would have a word with Drake. They better give you what you want. If they don't, he shouldn't pay them a dime!"

I found the dress Emily had requested and brought it out of the closet. Marie stood up from the couch and moved toward the door.

"Emily, get ready. We will be heading to the Doyles' mansion soon. Jane, Emily will tell you what needs to be done tonight," Marie said, turning her steel-gray eyes on me.

Emily slowly pulled herself up from the sofa. She shrugged the robe from her shoulders and let it drop to the floor in a heap. My fingers nimbly worked on unbuttoning the blue dress, and then I held it open for her to step into. Pulling the dress up to her shoulders, I tilted the material forward so that Emily could slip her arms into the gauzy sleeves. I began to button the dress and noticed that the buttons were harder to pull together when I got halfway up.

"What are you doing?" Emily asked since it was taking me longer than usual.

"I'm almost done," I replied. "I just have to pinch the fabric for these last few."

I thanked the gods when I finally managed to do up the remaining buttons. I knew if I hadn't been able to finish buttoning, Emily would've killed me.

"Finally," Emily sighed, "I don't know what was taking you so long."

She strode over to her vanity and examined her hair, which looked perfect. She had requested me to do it before the seamstresses arrived.

"This will have to do," she muttered snidely as she turned in the chair to face me. "While I am at the Doyle's, I have a task for you to accomplish. I have received responses for my wedding in the mail, and there are too many for me to sort through. You need to open all the envelopes and record who is coming to my wedding and who is not. This is very important, so don't mess this up. The stack of envelopes is in my mother's office. You may get started now," she said as she brushed me out of her way.

I was glad the family would be gone for the evening again. Perhaps once Emily was married, she would have her mother and brother for dinner all the time. Marie could continue to leave me alone. June couldn't arrive fast enough.

Slowly, I headed down the main staircase. The family was in the front entryway waiting on the carriage. Preston was running in circles around Marie and Emily. Marie stood perfectly still, her spine like steel. She looked mildly annoyed by Preston, but she didn't open her mouth to reprimand him. Emily's foot tapped on the tile floor impatiently. Marie turned and looked at me when I reached the last step.

"Jane, after you are done with Emily's task, I want you to

clean this house," she harped before turning around and opening the front door.

The carriage stood waiting while they all climbed inside. I closed the door behind them and then headed to the office. Light from the window illuminated the large stack of envelopes on the desk. I sighed as I estimated the stack to be around two hundred. Knowing Emily, she had probably been receiving responses for weeks and let them pile up. Apparently, Emily was above opening an envelope addressed to her.

I went around the room, lighting the lamps. By the look of the sky, I anticipated the sun going down before I would finish the response cards. Pulling the chair out, I took a seat behind the desk and stared at the envelopes for a moment. I opened one of the desk drawers, pulling out two pieces of paper and a letter opener. On the top of one, I wrote the word accepted, and on the other, I wrote declined. Taking a deep breath, I grabbed the first of many creamy white envelopes.

The process was extremely slow. My back was beginning to hurt from leaning over the desk. No matter how many envelopes I grabbed, the pile never seemed to dwindle. The list of people who had accepted kept getting longer and longer. I paused when the next envelope I had pulled out had Mr. Wicker's name. He had accepted the invitation to the wedding. I shuddered for Robert's sake, but I wasn't surprised he was attending. He had made an appearance at all the other functions. Why would the wedding be any different? All I could do was warn Robert and hope he'd be able to avoid Mr. Wicker. With over five hundred people invited, that should be possible.

Soon, the sun began to set, and darkness settled over the room. The pile of envelopes finally appeared to be growing smaller. How was I going to have time to clean? The *quick complete charm* seemed to be my only option. It would be impossible to complete the response cards and clean the house before Marie returned.

My hand was aching, and my back was stiff by the time I sliced open the last envelope. Once I wrote the last name on the accepted sheet, I stood up from the desk, reaching my arms to the ceiling to stretch out my back. Cracking my knuckles, I left the office and headed to the kitchen.

The house's silence was welcoming. I dashed a pinch of the *quick complete charm* over my head and instantly felt full of invigorating energy. I leapt into motion, and it wasn't long before the kitchen and the dining room were spotless. I hadn't used this charm in so long, and it felt wonderful. Finally, I could get all my work done in a short amount of time.

Once the downstairs was complete, I headed upstairs. Taking a smaller amount of the *quick complete charm*, I sprinkled it over my head and began work on Marie's room.

I was so consumed with my task that I almost didn't hear the soft chuckle. My heart slammed hard against my rib cage. Sweat instantly sprung to my brow, and I was afraid to turn around.

"So, this is how you always get things done so fast," the familiar voice said, slowing my heart rate.

I turned to see Robert leaning against the doorframe of Emily's room. His arms crossed over his chest, and his head quirked to the side. The slight smile on his lips made him look extremely handsome. I wanted to wrap my arms around him.

"Robert," I gasped. "Don't startle me like that!"

"Jane, you're not supposed to be doing magic here, remember?" he said, a frown forming on his perfect mouth.

The *quick complete charm* had not finished its course, so I continued cleaning as I spoke.

"I know, but I had a lot to accomplish. Emily instructed me to open her response cards, and Marie commanded me to clean afterward. I wouldn't have had time to clean everything before they came home, so I needed to use the charm. Besides, I made sure no one was around."

Robert watched in amazement as I finished with Emily's room and the charm began to wear off.

"I could have been anyone," Robert said when I finished moving. "You need to be more careful."

"I know," I said, feeling the adrenaline subside.

"You don't have to risk your magic. I told you I would always help you," he replied, stepping forward to embrace me. I leaned into his strong arms and rested my head on his shoulder.

"We would still be working downstairs. At least that part of the house is complete. All I have left is Emily's bathroom and Preston's room," I murmured into his chest.

I could feel his laugh bubbling up. "Yes, that's true, but please let me help you with the rest. We don't know when Marie will be home. Let's not risk her catching you running around like this."

"Alright," I agreed. "I would become homeless if she caught me."

Robert released me, and we both started scrubbing Emily's bathroom.

"Mr. Wicker has responded to Emily's wedding invitation. He is attending," I told Robert.

"I figured as much," Robert replied as he rinsed out the tub.

"I'm sure it will be possible to avoid him."

"I was planning on doing my best to stay away from him. Let's hope I can manage."

We had everything back into place and looking pristine in no time at all. I was glad Robert had come to find me. He always seemed to know when I needed him.

"So, did you talk to Josefina at all?" Robert asked. I had explained to him what had happened between Josefina and me. Robert had seemed perturbed about what she had tried to do.

"No, I didn't. I'm not sure I want to. It's hard because I believed she was my best friend, and I still care about her." I could feel tears starting to form.

Robert shook his head as we left Emily's room and headed

down the hall toward Preston's. "I'm sorry, Jane. I didn't mean to upset you."

"It's not your fault. I think about it every day."

We arrived at Preston's door, and I placed my hand on the knob. Marie hadn't requested me to clean in here for a while, so I wasn't sure what type of mess I would find. The door opened with a twist of the knob, and we stepped inside. A disgusting smell infiltrated my nose. Glancing around the room, I saw that the bed was unmade, and a large pile of clothes had been strewn on the floor.

"What's that smell?" I said, raising my hand to my nose.

"I have no idea," Robert said, looking a little green.

"So, we agree a fourteen-year-old boy's bedroom shouldn't smell this way," I said, moving to the bed and pulling up the covers.

"No," Robert replied as he picked up the clothes. "I'll run these down to the laundry."

Robert left the room, and I continued making the bed. Lifting the collar of my dress, I placed it over my nose to try and shield myself from the smell. After the bed was made, I dusted off the end tables and the ledge of the fireplace. Looking around the room, I couldn't place what was causing the smell. Perhaps it was something in the bathroom.

When I entered the bathroom, the smell seemed to lessen, which I thought was odd. I had thought for sure that the smell would be coming from here. Confused, I reentered the bedroom, the scent growing more potent. Robert came back and let out a cough.

"It smells like something died in here," Robert complained.

I moved to the windows and pried them open. The fresh air came into the room, making the smell a tad more bearable, but it didn't eradicate it. I began picking up the blue rugs on the floor, and Robert moved to help me. As he lifted the one near the closet, I heard him gag.

"The smell is stronger over here," he said, dropping the rug.

I watched as he examined the floor. "Jane, doesn't this look like a loose floorboard?"

I crossed the room, the smell intensifying with every step. Pressing my sleeve to my nose, I looked to where Robert was pointing. He knelt and touched the floorboard. Once he managed to get a few fingers underneath, he began prying the board up. When Robert finally removed it, I almost retched at what I saw underneath.

Several mice and rats lay dead beneath the floor. Each one looked as if they had suffered some form of torture. I recalled the time Preston had dangled a dead rat in my face. I also believed he had placed a deer's heart in my bed. I took a step away from the rat grave. Why would Preston do this? I put my hand over my mouth and looked away.

"Jane," Robert stated calmly, although he was obviously shaken. "Finish the bathroom, and I'll take care of this."

Feeling sick, I backed up into the bathroom. I tried to focus on cleaning, but I began to gag as images of the twisted rat bodies forced their way across my mind. I tried breathing deeply to fight off the feeling of nausea. I didn't need to become sick on top of everything else.

It wasn't long before I was done in the bathroom. When I stepped back into Preston's room, Robert had finished cleaning the floor. With the windows opened, the smell was finally beginning to fade.

"The bathroom is finished," I said, my voice feeling small.

Robert began laying the blue carpet back down. "Let's get out of here," he said.

I slammed the window closed. Grabbing Robert's hand, I led him up to the attic. He looked confused but followed me anyway. I crossed to the mattress and sat down. Robert lowered himself down beside me and wrapped an arm around my shoulder.

"What was that?" I asked, aghast.

Robert shook his head and pulled me tighter to him.

"I have no idea," he murmured.

I snuggled my head into his chest, feeling overwhelmed.

"This isn't the first time he's had a dead animal in his room," I whispered.

I could feel Robert's body shudder against my side. He began stroking my hair and running his hand along my back.

"I don't understand why someone would torture a helpless animal," Robert finally said, his voice cracking.

"I don't know where Preston got the idea to do such a thing. I feel so sick," I replied.

Robert wrapped both of his arms around me and held me tightly.

"So, this is your attic?" he whispered in my ear as he gazed around the room.

The sheets over the old furniture looked like ghosts, and I noticed spider webs in the rafters.

"Sorry. I didn't have time to clean," I sighed, slightly embarrassed.

Robert's laugh rumbled through me. "Jane, I live in a barn," he said, burying his face into my hair. "Why are you worried about the state of this attic? Sure, it's a tad dusty up here, but at least it doesn't smell like horses."

He leaned further back on the mattress, pulling my body with his. I rearranged myself to lay next to him, and I rested my head in the crook of his shoulder. It was comforting to be held like this.

"I must say, this lumpy mattress is more comfortable than a pile of hay," Robert mused as he traced a finger across my brow and down my cheek.

"Yes, I suppose it is," I whispered into his chest.

Robert's finger landed beneath my chin, and he tilted my face upward. He then leaned toward me and kissed my lips. My whole body started to shiver, and I leaned into him, pressing my mouth against his. Robert cradled my head with his hands as he shifted position and propped himself up on his elbow. It was easier to kiss him this way, and I didn't have to stretch my neck to reach him. Robert continued to kiss me and run his hand through my hair.

Suddenly, I heard noises coming from outside, causing Robert to push himself away from me. I crawled toward the circular window and peered out.

"Oh no, they're back," I gasped. I watched as they exited the carriage and walked up the stairs to the front door. "I don't know how to get you out of here! You obviously can't leave through the front door!"

Robert looked alarmed but determined. He began pacing the attic floor. If Marie found him up here, there was no telling what kind of trouble we would be in. Swiftly, Robert grabbed several sheets from the old furniture. I watched as he began tying the ends together.

"I will have to go out the window," Robert said, surprisingly calm. "Do you think you could use your magic to help hold my weight as I climb down?"

I nodded as I began gathering more sheets. He quickly showed me how to tie sturdy knots that wouldn't come loose. When our escape ladder appeared to be long enough, I rushed to one of the windows facing the back of the house. Robert and I lowered the sheets, and I was relieved they were long enough to reach the ground. He handed me the end before grasping a section of the sheet and positioning himself out the opened window.

"I trust you won't drop me, Jane," he said as he paused in the window. He stole a quick kiss and then began lowering himself. "I love you," he said with a massive grin on his face, looking as if he were having the best adventure of his life.

I focused all my concentration on the rope and held on for dear life. It wasn't too difficult to support Robert's weight. I felt as if my powers had surged because it was so important to keep Robert safe. For his entire climb to the ground, I held my breath.

I would die if anything happened to Robert. When he reached the bottom, he raised his hand to wave up at me, and I released the breath I had been holding.

I was in the middle of pulling the sheets back up when I heard noises outside the attic door. Adrenaline soared through my veins as I pulled the sheets through the window as fast as possible. When I pulled the last of our sheet ladder through the window, my heart was in my throat. I dumped it on the floor behind some furniture and flung myself down onto the mattress. My breathing was rapid, so I needed to focus on slowing it down. I wanted to appear asleep.

No more than a second later, the attic door burst open. I laid very still and attempted shallow sleeplike breaths. I tried to relax my face and not squeeze my eyes closed too tight.

"Jane!" Marie snapped.

Slowly, I rubbed my eyes and rolled over to face her as if I had just woken up.

"I trust that you have completed Emily's task and cleaning this house!" she barked.

I sat up on the mattress. "Yes, ma'am," I replied.

Her cold gray eyes panned over the attic suspiciously. I hoped she wouldn't notice that several pieces of furniture were missing their covers. I tried not to look nervous, gazing up at her, anticipating her next command. When she seemed satisfied, she turned her stare back on me.

"Very well, I shall be inspecting the house. If I find anything out of place, I'll be back up here," she snapped. Then she turned and walked out of the attic, slamming the door behind her.

I curled up tight on the mattress and breathed a sigh of relief.

27

CODE RED

AFTER JAMMING MY Charms book into my bag, I left my room and walked down to the second floor's west wing. This morning I had left breakfast early. Another week had gone by without any words between Josefina and me. We simply passed like two ships in the night, neither taking note of the other's presence.

Whenever I contemplated talking to her, I would see her laughing with the girls and change my mind. She didn't appear to feel remorse for what she had done, and the girls remained at the center of her world. Obviously, she didn't notice how rude they could be or that they only cared about themselves. I tried to stop caring, but it was almost impossible. I was mad at myself for feeling this way because Josefina didn't appear to have similar feelings.

I entered the Charms classroom and just focused on getting to my seat. Mr. Withermyer was standing beside the blackboard, so I hoped today would be a note-taking day. When Josefina finally came in, she chose a seat far away from me, as she had been doing for the last month.

"Today, we will be taking notes on the properties of the *growing charm* used to grow plants. However, we aren't going to spend too much time on this charm. We will discuss it today and perhaps tomorrow," Mr. Withermyer said as the words *Growing Charm* flashed across the blackboard.

I sighed, thanking the gods that we weren't making a charm today. I placed my notebook in front of me and began taking down the notes that Mr. Withermyer was projecting on the board.

"This is an effortless charm with only one ingredient: moss agate. We teach this charm in the second year because its use is a manipulation of nature. It's a good introduction to transfiguration, a class you will all begin next year," Mr. Withermyer said when a letter zipped into the room landed on his desk.

Mr. Withermyer held up a finger as he walked over to his desk to pick up the letter. I watched his face as he read it, concern and worry darkening his expression. Slowly, he placed it back on his desk and somberly walked to the middle of the room.

"The letter was from Dr. Tweedle. He has requested that all students proceed to the dining hall for an announcement. Calmly rise from your seats and follow me. Please do not talk," Mr. Withermyer instructed as he swept from the room.

Fear reflected in my classmates' eyes. What did Dr. Tweedle have to tell us now? Had the W.A.S.P. attacked again? How many were dead? For a brief moment, I caught Josefina's eye. She looked just as scared as I felt, but she quickly looked away from me and down at the floor.

Other classes were also congregating toward the dining hall, and the students politely merged on the staircase. Josefina rushed ahead when she spotted Marley in the crowd. I didn't try to follow and was swept along with the crowd. When I entered the dining hall, I took the first seat I could find.

Dr. Tweedle stood behind the podium, looking flustered. I could feel my nerves tingling with anxiety. When every student had filed in, Dr. Tweedle cleared his throat.

"This morning, I received news that our pixie secretary of defense, Edmond O'Donoghue, has been captured by the W.A.S.P." Loud gasps echoed throughout the dining hall.

"This is the first time a government official has ever been taken, and we don't believe it was a coincidence. We have concluded that the W.A.S.P. knew Mr. O'Donoghue was involved in government affairs. Pixie officials are declaring a code red. All morning, I've received letters from parents demanding that their children be sent home. I have no other choice but to close the school for a week, perhaps longer. Carriages will be arriving in a half hour to take each of you home. I suggest you pack your belongings and prepare to leave. Letters will be sent out to inform you when the school will reopen. You are all dismissed to begin preparations for your departure."

Most of the students quickly left the dining hall, but I felt glued to my seat. Dr. Tweedle was closing the academy? I didn't move until I noticed Dr. Tweedle crossing the dining hall in my direction.

"I'll collect my belongings, and we can leave for the manor," I said.

"Jane, I'm not taking you to the manor," Dr. Tweedle replied.

"But you're closing the school and sending everyone home," I said, confused.

"You will remain here this week," Dr. Tweedle stated.

"Sir, I don't understand. All the other students are going home. Isn't it dangerous?"

"Actually, the Jelf Academy is one of the safest places for a pixie to be. Explaining that to hundreds of worried parents wouldn't be ideal at the moment. I understand that families want to be together in times of crisis, so I believed the best option would be to close the school. On the other hand, you would not be safer at the manor, so I'm keeping you here. Besides, how would we explain to Marie why I brought you back?"

"Dr. Tweedle, what am I supposed to do if there aren't any classes?" I asked.

"You could study and spend more time with your dragon. Just look at this week as a well-deserved holiday," Dr. Tweedle said, winking at me as he walked away.

I sat back down, allowing what Dr. Tweedle said to sink in. The pixie society was under a code red. I didn't know what to feel.

Unsure of what to do, I headed back to my room. Getting rid of my bag of books would be my first priority. When I entered the room, Josefina was still in the middle of packing her things. She didn't say a word to me when I entered. Instead, she refused to look at me and focused on collecting her belongings. I placed my bag on my desk and began unloading my books. Some subconscious part of me kept glancing at Josefina. I wanted to tell her to be safe, but she didn't glance at me. Feeling discouraged, I settled down at my desk. When I heard the door open, I couldn't help but look at her. Josefina had grabbed her bag and was starting to leave when she met my eyes. She opened her mouth as if she were about to say something and then suddenly snapped it shut as if she had thought better of it. Quietly, she exited the room, closing the door behind her.

I closed my eyes and told myself not to cry. Taking a deep breath, I glanced over to my schoolbooks and grabbed the Magical Creatures one. Flipping to the chapter where we had left off, I began to read. I tried multiple times to concentrate on the words, but they all seemed to blur together. My mind kept going back to the W.A.S.P. and Josefina. I couldn't stay focused, so I gave up and closed the book.

I leaned back on my desk chair and looked around the room. What could I do? My mind began making a list of possible activities. I could go to the library, but my mind couldn't focus on the books in front of me. Perhaps visiting Thistle was my best option. Now feeling like I had a purpose, I left my room and began climbing down the stairs.

The school was disturbingly quiet. I had never seen the building so still. It was eerie but exciting to be the only one here. I had the entire castle to myself for a week, possibly longer. I strolled out the front door into the brisk April air. The sun was shining brightly, so it was the perfect temperature.

The barn was colder than outside. I shivered as I walked down the row of stalls. Thistle's purple head was peeking out of her stall. When I reached it, I saw that she had been up on her hind legs. In the last month, she had grown to the size of a stallion. The doors on the stalls were tall because of the different creatures Mrs. Rowley would bring in for class, so it amazed me to see Thistle was able to see over them. I opened the door and stepped inside. Thistle began licking me and hopping around her pen.

"Okay, girl," I said, raising my hands in front of my face. "You need to calm down."

Thistle's tail moved back and forth several times, but she sat down on her haunches. I petted the tip of her nose, and she licked my hands. Moving around her, I checked her water supply, which didn't need refilling.

"Dr. Tweedle closed the school this week," I told her. "I'm the only one who gets to stay here."

Thistle gazed at me intently with her large purple irises.

"The W.A.S.P. has infiltrated the pixie government," I whispered. "I'm terrified."

Thistle snorted two smoke rings and nuzzled her head on my shoulder. I ran my hands down her snout, causing her to sigh deeply and release more smoke.

Suddenly, I heard a noise in the hallway. My body stiffened out of instinct. Sensing my nervousness, Thistle lifted her head from my shoulder and growled softly. I crept to the door and peered out. When my eyes landed on Mrs. Rowley, I let out a chuckle and a sigh of relief.

"Hello, Jane. Dr. Tweedle told me I might find you here," Mrs. Rowley said.

"Yes, I'm just checking on Thistle," I replied.

"This dragon is extraordinary. They're normally such independent creatures, so, amazingly, she has become so attached to you," Mrs. Rowley said, walking into the pen and extending her hand for Thistle to sniff.

Thistle licked Mrs. Rowley, and she laughed.

"Dragons are such intelligent creatures, and I've always wondered if they could be trained. Would you like to try?" Mrs. Rowley asked.

"Sure. I already feel like Thistle understands me," I replied.

Mrs. Rowley smiled widely. "Let me find some treats for her," she said as she disappeared in the direction of the icebox.

It wasn't long before Mrs. Rowley returned with a bucket full of chicken pieces.

"I've trained many animals, but I've never had the opportunity to train a dragon before. Every year we raise the dragons and release them when the time comes. We never had a dragon that decided to stay."

"So, you've never had any dragons become attached to their students?" I asked, amazed.

"Yes, in all the years I have been teaching at this school, this has never happened before. I have read your dragon journal multiple times, trying to figure out what you've done differently."

"Well, Mrs. Rowley. To be completely honest, I used to sneak out here at night to take care of Thistle's egg. I talked to her and added heat to her egg while I sat out here. I hope you aren't mad," I said, looking at the floor.

Mrs. Rowley looked me over but then smiled. "You probably shouldn't have been sneaking out here, but the fact you spent more time with your dragon is interesting. Did you do anything else?"

"Once Thistle was born, I named her. I also continued to come down to see her," I admitted. "From the moment I picked up her egg, I felt connected to her."

"Hmm, that's very interesting," Mrs. Rowley said, patting Thistle's nose. "Let's see if Thistle can understand commands. Jane, why don't you pick up a piece of chicken and command her to sit? You should put on your protective gloves, too."

I slipped on my gloves and then bent down for a sliver of chicken. I held it up to get Thistle's attention. As her purple eyes followed the chicken, she licked her lips. I held the chicken as high as possible, per Mrs. Rowley's instruction, and commanded Thistle to sit. She cocked her head to the side, looking confused. Again, I reached as high as I could and issued the command. As Thistle took a couple of steps forward, Mrs. Rowley instructed me to step back with the chicken and verbally command no.

Thistle cocked her head to the side again and then sat down on her haunches. Mrs. Rowley instructed me to praise her and give her the chicken. Thistle breathed a small fire on the chicken before she ate it. When she finished, I picked up another piece and gave the command again. Thistle still looked confused, but she sat faster than the first time. We continued with the sit command until Thistle understood what we expected of her. It was exciting, and I felt proud every time Thistle completed the command correctly.

When the bucket was empty, Mrs. Rowley went to retrieve more so we could focus on another trick. I patted Thistle's side, and she rubbed her nose into my neck, making me laugh. I was surprised by how quickly Thistle was learning, and it was so much fun to teach her. Mrs. Rowley seemed pleased that Thistle was responding.

"Here is another bucket with salmon," Mrs. Rowley said, placing it down.

"Mrs. Rowley, if Dr. Tweedle closed the school for this week, aren't you able to go home?" I asked as I leaned down to pick up some salmon.

"The Jelf Academy is my home. All teachers have living quarters on the premises, so we have somewhere to stay. On the weekends, some teachers may leave to visit family members. Mrs. Harris, for instance, has left to be with her husband. She doesn't stay at the school all the time," Mrs. Rowley explained.

"If you don't mind me asking, don't you want to spend time with your family or husband?" I asked.

"My husband passed away almost ten years ago with pneumonia. Ever since then, I have made the Jelf Academy my permanent home. Though we wanted to, my husband and I didn't have children. I guess that's why I decided to become a teacher," Mrs. Rowley said.

"I'm sorry to hear that," I replied.

"It's okay, Jane. I've accepted the path my life took a long time ago. Now, let's teach Thistle to lie down," Mrs. Rowley suggested.

We spent the rest of the afternoon teaching different commands to Thistle. We switched between the tasks to make sure Thistle had understood. At one point, Thistle had gotten a little overzealous and seared a hole in one of my gloves. At least they had done their job and protected me from getting burned.

"Perhaps we can talk to Dr. Tweedle about a glove replacement," Mrs. Rowley said as we walked back up to the school.

I thanked Mrs. Rowley for helping me with Thistle. She offered to help with training for the rest of the week if I would like. I quickly agreed since I wasn't sure what else to do besides spend more time with Thistle.

I climbed to the fifth floor and entered my room. I had an hour before dinner, so I decided to take a quick bath. What would it be like to eat dinner by myself? I couldn't help but feel sad about it.

After scrubbing my skin and washing my hair, I climbed out of the tub and stared at my clothes. There wasn't much in my closet. Just the dress Josefina had given me. I decided to wear it instead of a uniform. I concentrated on drying my hair, and once it was dry enough, I braided it. After finishing with my hair, I opened my pixie dust case and found the compartment where I had stored the necklace that matched the dress. I took off Robert's ring, exchanging it for the necklace. A calming feeling washed over me once I had clasped the amethysts around my neck.

When it was time for dinner, I descended the stairs and walked into the dining hall. It was odd to see the empty room and even stranger that the buffet was not set up. Dr. Tweedle was standing near the podium, and he turned to me as I entered.

"You look lovely, Jane," he said, coming toward me.

I could feel myself blushing as I thanked him for the compliment.

"You look so much like your mother," he said, looking me over. "I wondered if you would accept an invitation to join my colleagues and me in the teacher's lounge for dinner this evening," Dr. Tweedle asked.

"Yes, I would love to," I replied.

Dr. Tweedle extended his arm to me. I slipped my arm through his, and he led me out of the dining hall into the west wing. We walked past the History of Pixies classroom and Mr. Collyworth's office, reaching the end of the hallway. Dr. Tweedle held open the last door on the left, and I walked inside.

The teacher's lounge had a long table on the left side of the room and a cluster of sofas on the other side. The walls were a pale yellow with a strip of sage green wallpaper embossed with a flower pattern in the middle of the wall. The floor was a light wood, and there were green accent rugs in the area with the sofas.

Almost all the teachers were seated when Dr. Tweedle and I entered the room. Mr. Withermyer jumped out of his seat, and Mr. Collyworth began to rise as well. Mr. Withermyer's green eyes locked with mine, and a flush came to my cheeks. Both gentlemen remained standing as Dr. Tweedle and I approached. I noticed Mr. Laruse and Miss Pierce were not among the party.

"Miss Fitzgerald will be joining us this evening for dinner and every evening this week if she should so choose. You may sit in Mrs. Harris' seat since she won't be present," Dr. Tweedle said as he pulled out the seat next to Mr. Withermyer. I swallowed the lump in my throat and was about to take a seat when Miss Pierce entered the room, followed by Mr. Laruse.

"So sorry to be late," Mr. Laruse intoned as he went around to the other side of the table. "Oh, hello, Jane. Good to see you," he added, sitting next to Ms. Crescent at the other end of the table.

I finally sat down, and Dr. Tweedle sat down next to me at the head of the table. Mr. Withermyer and Mr. Collyworth resumed their seats, and the dinner began. I was happy that Mrs. Rowley was seated across from me. Dr. Tweedle began passing around bowls containing mashed potatoes and corn. He handed them to me, and it was apparent I would have to pass them to Mr. Withermyer. Feeling nervous, I turned toward him. He gave me a fleeting glance as he took the bowl and mumbled a thank you.

"Jane and I were able to teach her dragon a few tricks today," Mrs. Rowley stated, making me feel instantly comfortable.

"Is that so?" Dr. Tweedle asked with surprise.

"Yes. Thistle is very smart. We were surprised by how quickly she learned," I replied.

"So, Thistle is the name of this dragon I've heard about," Mr. Collyworth said, spooning mashed potatoes onto his plate. "Throughout history, I've heard of pixies who had formed bonds with dragons, but I haven't heard of anything like that occurring recently. I had always wondered if those stories were myths."

"I've never seen a student whose dragon became attached. Jane has told me she spent extra time with the dragon while it was inside the egg and after it had hatched," Mrs. Rowley stated, making me blush.

"From the moment I touched her egg, I knew there was something special about Thistle," I replied.

"It was fate," Ms. Crescent cried from the other end of the table in her dramatic voice.

"How is Jane able to keep this dragon?" Mr. Laruse inquired

as he pierced a piece of turkey from the platter and then passed it down the table.

"I was wondering the same thing," Mr. Withermyer added. I could almost feel his cold stare.

"Dragons are very intelligent creatures. It isn't Jane's choice to keep the dragon here. Thistle is choosing to stay. She may leave at any time she wishes, but that's up to the dragon. If we force her to leave, she might become violent. Thistle seems attached to Jane, and since we have room for her, there is no reason she can't stay," Dr. Tweedle answered.

I knew Mr. Withermyer believed Dr. Tweedle was giving me special treatment. Thankfully, Mr. Withermyer didn't say anything more on the subject.

"While we were training Thistle, Jane's gloves became damaged. She's going to need a new pair," Mrs. Rowley said, looking in Dr. Tweedle's direction.

"Maybe I can schedule a trip to Jewel Caverns toward the end of the week," Dr. Tweedle said, smiling at me.

"Oliver, is it safe? With the W.A.S.P. at large, maybe it isn't smart to go anywhere," Mr. Collyworth said with concern.

"I was planning to teleport from the academy to Jewel Caverns. The Caverns are the second safest place I can think of. The entrance is hidden in the mountains and protected by charms. Nonetheless, I'll wait for more news before planning the trip," Dr. Tweedle replied.

Mr. Collyworth looked satisfied by Dr. Tweedle's answer and continued eating.

"Jane, why have you decided to stay at the Jelf Academy this week?" Mr. Laruse asked.

I was surprised by his question. Didn't all the teachers know my stepmother was human? Seeing how Mr. Laruse could hardly remember what time his classes were, I guessed I shouldn't be so shocked if he hadn't remembered.

"Dr. Tweedle didn't believe it was safe for me to return to the manor. My stepmother and her family are humans."

"Oh, how horrible!" Mr. Laruse cried. "That's certainly unsafe! I wouldn't want to be anywhere near humans."

"Not all humans are terrible, and not all are members of the W.A.S.P. My father was human, and he was one of the most wonderful people I've ever known," I replied.

Out of the corner of my eye, I noticed Mr. Withermyer become tense. His green eyes subtly studied my profile. I reached forward to grab my cup of water, suddenly feeling uncomfortable.

"Perhaps we shouldn't be so stereotypical," Mrs. Rowley announced. "We just need to be careful, Jane."

I was grateful she had spoken up, which had lessened the tension, but I could tell Mr. Withermyer was still on edge. How could he become so irritated at the mention of humans, namely my father?

Mrs. Rowley managed to steer the conversation toward academics, and I just listened for the remainder of the meal. I was relieved the topic of humans had ended. Everyone always seemed to forget I was half-human. How could I not be offended by the terrible things said about the other half of myself? My father and Robert were perfect examples of how wonderful humans could be. Surely not all humans could be evil.

When the dinner was over, and the table had been cleared, Mr. Laruse stood from his seat.

"Would anyone like to play a game?" he asked, looking around the table excitedly. "We could play Dyfalu Llun, where we form teams, and we have to guess what someone is trying to draw."

Most everyone at the table seemed to agree it was a splendid idea.

"Jane, would you like to stay and play?" Dr. Tweedle asked as Mr. Laruse went to the cabinet and pulled out a stack of cards.

Not knowing what else to do for the rest of the evening, I agreed.

"I might turn in for the evening," Mr. Withermyer announced, standing from his seat.

"Awe, come on, Phillip. Stay to play the game! The teams will be uneven if you don't," Dr. Tweedle pleaded.

Mr. Withermyer looked slightly annoyed, but he sat back down.

"We can just split the table to make the teams. Philip, Jane, Abigail, and I can be on a team," Dr. Tweedle said. It took me a moment to realize he meant Mrs. Rowley.

Mr. Laruse laid the cards on the table along with a funny-looking quill.

"Jane, since you've probably never played Dyfalu Llun before, I'll explain it," Dr. Tweedle said. "On each person's turn, they will draw a card. Don't let anyone see the word on the card, but there will also be a category: a person, place, thing, or animal. You'll tell everyone the category and then proceed to draw the word in the air with the quill. The drawing dust in the quill will allow you to create a picture in the air. This way, everyone at the table will see what you are drawing. If someone on your team guesses correctly, your team gets the point. However, the other team can steal a point if they guess the right answer. I'll go first so you can understand how the game is played. It's straightforward," Dr. Tweedle said as he picked up a card and the quill.

It took him a moment before he announced the category was a thing. Then, he lifted the quill in the air in front of him and began to draw. It wasn't long before Mrs. Rowley guessed he was drawing a picture of a boat, giving our team a point.

Mr. Laruse's turn was next: the category a place. His picture wasn't nearly as good as Dr. Tweedle's, and it took a long time to guess he was drawing a school. I didn't know why, but I was nervous when it came time for me to draw. When I pulled my card, the word was a dog. I began drawing in the air in front of me. I started with the nose and then the mouth and eyes. I added floppy ears when Mr. Withermyer spoke.

"It's a dog," he said, sounding bored.

"That's correct," I said, passing the quill to the next person. My drawing dissolved into the air.

The game continued, and soon the majority of the table was laughing over each other's attempts at drawing. What I had thought was going to be a lonely night was actually turning out to be quite enjoyable. I was surprised to find that I didn't feel uncomfortable being the only student in a room full of teachers.

Mr. Withermyer picked up the quill and drew the top card from the deck.

"The category is animals," Mr. Withermyer said with a sigh.

He lifted the quill and began to draw. He drew three circles; the first one had horns, the second had wavy lines, and the last one had a triangle on top. He was in the middle of drawing faces on the circles when I spoke up.

"Is it a chimera?" I asked.

Mr. Withermyer paused in drawing and looked at me with shock. "Yes, that's what I was attempting to draw."

"You're good at this. How did you even guess that?" Mr. Laruse asked, laughing.

The other teachers also began chuckling as they looked at Mr. Withermyer's drawing. What he had drawn didn't look like an animal.

"I don't know," I replied, blushing. "Lucky guess."

Dr. Tweedle added another point to our team, and Mr. Withermyer passed the quill to Mr. Collyworth. While Mr. Collyworth began drawing, I noticed Mr. Withermyer glancing at me out of the corner of his eye. I wondered why he was looking at me so quizzically. Did he think I had seen his card as he lifted it from the deck? I don't know what made me think of a chimera. I certainly hadn't cheated.

I concentrated on what Mr. Collyworth was drawing, but I couldn't figure it out. Finally, Miss Pierce guessed an inn. We continued playing the game, and I discovered I was decent at drawing. I was even more shocked when Mr. Withermyer guessed most of my pictures correctly. Perhaps he was the one glancing at my cards. We played late into the evening until Mr. Collyworth announced he was tired. Dr. Tweedle and Ms. Crescent agreed, and the points were tallied. My team won by six points.

"Jane, you're excellent at playing Dyfalu Llun. Maybe we should play again sometime," Mr. Laruse said, rising from his seat.

"Thank you so much for inviting me to dinner," I replied.

"You are welcome to join us again tomorrow. It seems cruel for you to eat dinner alone," Dr. Tweedle said.

"Thank you. I would like that very much," I answered.

Everyone began to file out of the teacher's lounge, and I headed for the staircase. Perhaps being the only student at the school for the week wouldn't be so bad after all.

28

A Special Day

For the next few days, I would wake up, have a light breakfast, and then head outside to meet Mrs. Rowley to train Thistle. Mrs. Rowley even let me borrow a pair of protective gloves, but they were starting to rip. After training with Thistle, I would return to the castle and study for a while in the library. Before dinner, I would return to my room to take a bath and then meet Dr. Tweedle outside the teacher's lounge. Eating with the teachers became more comfortable as the week went on. I was even getting used to sitting next to Mr. Withermyer. I learned to ignore that he glanced at me when he thought I wasn't looking.

We didn't play a game every evening, but Mr. Laruse did insist on a rematch of Dyfalu Llun one night. We resumed the same teams, and once again, I was surprised by Mr. Withermyer's ability to guess what I was drawing. Mr. Laruse was disappointed about his second loss and vowed to play again at another time.

In the evenings, when dinner ended early, I explored the castle. I secretly discovered where all the teacher's personal quarters were located and that the castle had nine floors. Floors four through eight consisted of student dormitories, and I was surprised to find the ninth floor was a large open area with a swimming pool, which no one had ever mentioned before. The walls and ceiling surrounding the pool were glass, and I could see the stars beginning to come out as night fell. The room was also heated. I imagined the water was wonderful to swim in. Perhaps only the teachers utilized the pool, making it off-limits to students. However, I hadn't seen any signs or restrictions to bar students from the ninth floor.

Exploring the school at night was exciting and fun. There were so many places I had never been to before. Some, like the pool, I wasn't sure I was allowed in.

We still hadn't received any news about the W.A.S.P. The government was still declaring a code red, but no other pixie officials had been taken. Hopefully, the W.A.S.P. wasn't as knowledgeable as they appeared. Dr. Tweedle made plans to take me to the Jewel Caverns on Thursday. He hoped to hear more before we visited the caverns, convinced that traveling would be safe regardless.

When Thursday morning came, I awoke early. As the clock struck eight, I went down to the great hall to meet Dr. Tweedle.

"Good morning, Jane," he said as I walked down the last of the stairs.

"Good morning. How are you?" I asked him.

"I'm doing splendidly. I hope you are as well."

"Yes. Thank you so much for taking me to Jewel Caverns. I appreciate replacing my gloves."

"No need to thank me, Jane. I thought you could use a day of fun anyway."

He held his arm to me. I slipped my hand through his, and together we exited the large front doors before crossing the lawn toward the cloud.

It was such a beautiful day. The sun shone brightly, and it was already starting to feel warm. I looked toward the barn, suddenly feeling sad about not visiting Thistle today.

"Dr. Tweedle," I said, the thought just crossing my mind.

"Who will take care of Thistle during the summer when I have to return to the manor?"

"Well, I could take care of her. I'm sure Mrs. Rowley would be delighted to help as well. I think she has grown just as fond of Thistle as you have," Dr. Tweedle replied.

"I hope Thistle won't leave when I'm gone."

"She stays on the weekends when you are gone," Dr. Tweedle noted.

"Yes, I know, but I'll be gone for three months."

Dr. Tweedle paused to think about what I said. "It will seem like a long time, but Thistle appears comfortable here. All we can do is hope she will understand."

I nodded but still felt worried. I had to find a way to make her understand I would be coming back. Thistle was so important to me, and I couldn't lose her.

Dr. Tweedle and I boarded the cloud and rode it to the ground. Many different flowers were blooming across the meadow, which made me smile. Once we reached the carriage, Dr. Tweedle helped me to board. He already had the *teleportation charm* in his hand. I clung to the carriage as Dr. Tweedle climbed aboard and sprinkled the charm over us.

When the dust cleared, we were in the mountains outside of the Jewel Caverns. Dr. Tweedle leapt out of the carriage to find the hidden lever that opened the cave in the mountain. Once the entrance opened, Dr. Tweedle steered the horses inside the cave. When we were far enough inside, the door slid shut behind us, plunging us into darkness.

The absence of light didn't last long before the sprites came out to light the way. Each one cast off a different color. I couldn't help but smile as I watched them zoom ahead of us. Soon the tunnel widened, and the carriage burst into the large cavern.

With the activity in the cavern, you wouldn't know the government had issued a code red. Pixies filled the street, entering and exiting the shops as if nothing had happened. It was a flurry of activity. Dr. Tweedle snapped the horses into motion, making them trot down the road that spiraled to the bottom.

Dr. Tweedle steered the horses all the way to the bottom of the cavern where the shop called Creature Features was located. He parked the carriage and helped me out. The smell of animals infiltrated my nostrils once Dr. Tweedle opened the door.

Pete, the store owner, stepped out from behind the counter and stared at us with his one blue eye.

"Dr. Oliver, have you finally come to purchase one of my animals?" Pete asked as he walked toward us to shake Dr. Tweedle's hand.

"I'm sorry, Pete. Not today. We are here to replace a set of protective gloves," Dr. Tweedle replied.

"Are you sure? I just received some new gwilingis yesterday. I also have some firebirds here if that interests you. Their feathers are beautiful and great for lighting up a room. If you're not interested in those options, I have lightning birds that are great for sport hunting and delivering messages. They can also fly in any storm. However, I wouldn't recommend getting a minka bird. They're tough to train, and many people believe they bring death. I think that's a myth, though," Pete said with a shrug.

"I'm going to have to pass on the birds or any other animal for that matter. We're just here for the gloves," Dr. Tweedle stated.

Pete looked a little disappointed but finally nodded. "I swear I'll sell you an animal one of these days, Dr. Oliver," Pete said with a laugh, resuming his post behind the counter.

Dr. Tweedle followed me over to the gloves, and I picked a similar pair to my old ones. We quickly paid for them and left Creature Features for some fresh air.

"Will we be heading back to the Jelf Academy now?" I asked, climbing into the carriage.

"How would you like to stay longer and have some fun?" Dr. Tweedle asked, turning the horses around.

"What are we going to do?"

"Do you need anything refilled in your pixie dust case? Let's make a stop at Jewels and Powders."

Dr. Tweedle yanked the horses to a stop outside of the store and went inside. Jewels and Powders was surprisingly full. Dr. Tweedle purchased more astrological gemstones and a few other minerals to refill my case. I thanked him profusely for spending the money to help me. Dr. Tweedle just shrugged it off with a smile.

"Would you like to continue?" he asked when we got back into the carriage.

"What do you have in mind now?" I questioned.

"You'll see," he replied with a wink as he forced the horses into motion.

I couldn't help being confused when Dr. Tweedle parked the carriage outside Mr. Murray's Clothing Store.

"What are we doing here, Dr. Tweedle?" I asked.

"Jane, over the past week, I've noticed you don't own many clothes besides your uniforms. I thought perhaps I could get you a few new dresses today," Dr. Tweedle said with a smile.

"Oh, no, Dr. Tweedle, that is too kind. I couldn't possibly accept such a generous offer," I replied, placing a hand over my chest and taking a step backward.

"Please, Jane. Let me help you. Just humor an old man. I have no children or grandchildren of my own. Nothing would warm my heart more than to buy you a few things. I know how difficult your life has been. I'm not trying to damage your pride by any means, but please let me feel useful. Your mother was my star pupil, and I was very fond of her. I would do anything in my power to help her daughter."

I felt very flattered by Dr. Tweedle's speech. Even though I felt terrible, I let him lead me into Mr. Murray's. Maybe Mr. Withermyer wasn't so far off believing Dr. Tweedle showed favoritism toward me.

Dr. Tweedle looked so happy as we walked through the aisles of the women's section.

"I always wanted a daughter just like you," he commented, making me feel special. Dr. Tweedle had helped me learn about the pixie world, and I supposed he was like a father figure to me. I told him so, and the smile on his face beamed brighter.

When I had picked out several dresses, Mr. Murray opened a dressing room, so I could try them on. I stepped out of the dressing room for each dress to get Dr. Tweedle's opinion. It felt like a dream to try on all these clothes.

Dr. Tweedle insisted on trying multiple colors and styles. I loved the midnight blue and the emerald green dresses. I had never worn something so exquisite in all my life. When I tried on the deep red traveling gown, Dr. Tweedle applauded and dictated I find a hat to go with it. While I tried on clothes, Dr. Tweedle searched the racks and brought back more options. I couldn't believe how many clothes he was having me try on. Of course, they were the perfect fit, all of them being made out of pixie material.

"Dr. Tweedle, I've tried on so many things," I stated as I stepped out of the dressing room wearing a casual pink skirt and a white short-sleeved blouse.

"That looks lovely on you. The pink skirt goes very well with your complexation," he replied. "We must add it to our purchase."

I looked toward the stack of clothing Dr. Tweedle was too eager to buy. I couldn't allow him to spend any more money on me.

"Dr. Tweedle, you've done enough. I cannot allow you to have me try on anything else. You've been generous enough as it is," I said.

"Jane, it's not a problem," Dr. Tweedle declared. "However, if it's making you uncomfortable, I'll just purchase what we have here. I didn't mean to make you feel self-conscience or insult you in any way. I just want to help."

"Thank you so much. This truly does mean the world to me.

I can't thank you enough for buying these clothes. I just feel like I should do something to earn them."

"Jane, I believe you have earned them. You're doing a fantastic job at the academy. I'm hoping you will be able to acquire an internship in your last few years of school. Continuing to do well with your education is enough of a payment to me," Dr. Tweedle said kindly.

I blushed and muttered another string of thank-yous before disappearing back into the dressing room. I changed out of the skirt and blouse and then hurriedly dressed. Dr. Tweedle had already taken the other clothes to the counter and held out his hand for the skirt and blouse.

I couldn't help but feel terrible as the amount was totaled. Dr. Tweedle didn't seem to mind as he handed over the appropriate kryptos and coodles without a blink of an eye. My new clothes were then packaged into bags, which Dr. Tweedle grabbed from the counter.

"Thank you again, Dr. Tweedle, though I feel the word is an inadequate description for the gratitude I feel," I said as he helped me into the carriage.

Dr. Tweedle chuckled. "You can stop thanking me. I'm happy to help."

I sat quietly, resisting the urge to thank him again. Dr. Tweedle snapped the reins, and the horses began moving forward. He then lifted his hand to check his watch.

"Oh my, the day has just flown by! I'm so sorry we've missed lunch. How about an early dinner? It is almost 3:30 now."

"I wasn't very hungry for lunch anyway," I commented.

Dr. Tweedle steered the horses up the winding road. I was surprised when he pulled them to a halt in front of the Leaf and Lily Inn.

"Why are we stopping here?" I asked, confused.

"Mrs. Irene Dimple makes the best meals in all of Jewel Caverns.

I thought we could eat in the tavern of the inn. I don't think Irene will be very busy at this time. Plus, I'm sure she'd love to see you."

"That sounds wonderful! When I was here in August, she was very busy. It'll be so good to see her now," I replied.

Dr. Tweedle came around to my side of the carriage again and extended his arm to me. He held the door open, and I entered the Leaf and Lily Inn. The inn smelled like warm cinnamon, and I took a deep breath, thoroughly enjoying the scent. Mrs. Dimple stood behind the counter, and she looked up as we came in.

"To what do I owe this surprise?" she asked excitedly as she rushed toward us. She threw her arms around me, pulling me into one of her huge hugs.

"Dr. Tweedle brought me to the Jewel Caverns for some supplies," I stated, hugging her back.

Irene then turned to hug Dr. Tweedle. "It's so good to see you too," she said.

"I'm sure you've heard, but I've closed the academy this week due to the code red. I wasn't going to allow Jane to return home, so she's staying at the school. We decided to make a trip here," Dr. Tweedle said.

"Well, come on in. I'll assume you're here for dinner. I've only got one other table so far this evening, so I should be able to chat for a while," she said, leading us toward the dining area.

Irene got us settled in at a booth and handed us menus. She moved off to inquire after her other customer, giving us time to look over the selection. I paged through the menu and decided on a bowl of potato soup and some freshly baked rolls. My mouth was watering just thinking about Irene's cooking. Her food was the best I had tasted by far. Dr. Tweedle couldn't have picked a better place.

Irene was back in a few moments with drinks, and she took our orders. Afterward, she disappeared into the kitchen.

"Are you happy about my choice for dinner?" Dr. Tweedle asked as he straightened his suit coat.

"Yes, sir. The Leaf and Lily has the best food I've ever tasted. Thank you for such a lovely day," I told him.

"You don't have to thank me. Promise me you won't utter it again for the rest of the evening," he said with a smile.

"I don't know if I can make that promise. It's a tough one to keep. You've been so good to me, sir. Not many people treat me so kindly."

Dr. Tweedle looked sad for a moment, but then he raised his glass with a smile. "To one of my best students. May happier days come her way."

I raised my glass as well and took a sip.

Soon Irene was back at our table with my soup, fresh rolls, and Dr. Tweedle's baked chicken breast. I was surprised the Leaf and Lily wasn't very busy, but we were eating an early dinner.

When Irene came back, she slid into the booth next to me.

"How is the Jelf Academy?" she asked me.

"It's terrific. I'm learning so much this year," I replied, spooning another mouthful of soup.

"Jane is at the top of her class. She's one of the best students," Dr. Tweedle commented.

"That's great, Jane. It sounds like you've taken after your mum," Irene said with a huge smile.

"We played Dyfalu Llun the other night, and Jane is quite the artist," Dr. Tweedle said.

"I would expect so!" Irene said excitedly. "Rachel was the best at Dyfalu Llun. We played all the time when we were in school. Rachel had a certain way of drawing things. She always got people to guess correctly. I don't believe I was the worst in our group of friends, but I was nowhere near the best."

"It seems like my mother excelled at everything," I said, feeling excited that we were talking about my mom.

"Oh, sure. It always seemed like whatever Rachel tried, she

excelled at it. If it didn't work on her first attempt, she would practice until she got better at it," Irene said.

"Yes, your mother was quite extraordinary. The teachers were convinced there was nothing she couldn't do, myself included."

"A lot of students were jealous of her. Rachel was so smart and was at the top of almost every class. She had such a kind heart and would go out of her way to help anyone in need. On top of all that, she was one of the most beautiful girls," Irene said. "I really miss your mother."

A sad silence fell over the table. Both Dr. Tweedle and Irene seemed lost in memories I could only dream of having. Irene reached up and wiped a tear from her eye.

"I'm sorry, I didn't mean to become so melancholy," she said.

"That's okay. I love hearing about my mom," I told them.

"Well, one thing Rachel didn't have was a dragon who grew attached to her," Dr. Tweedle said lightly.

"A dragon?" Irene questioned, turning to look at me.

"Yes, my dragon didn't fly away with the rest of them when it came time to release them into the wild. She refused to leave me."

"That's so strange! I've never seen that happen before!"

"No one has seen it happen before," Dr. Tweedle commented.

"Jane, you're definitely special then! The dragon must have sensed something in you!"

"I don't know why Thistle stayed. Maybe she just really liked the school's barn," I replied, embarrassed. I didn't know why everyone thought I was so special.

"Looks like you have another trait of your mother's. She was always so modest," Irene said with a sigh. Dr. Tweedle nodded in agreement. "So, besides the dragon, is anything else exciting happening at the academy?"

I really couldn't think of much I would consider exciting. I couldn't exactly talk about Robert, and I didn't want to bring up my fight with Josefina. I described what I was currently learning in my classes, and Irene made comments about what she remembered from her school days. While I continued eating my soup, Irene and Dr. Tweedle discussed the government. Apparently, with Edmond O'Donoghue missing, it was the first time the government had enacted the code red. Irene looked terrified as they continued to talk, and I knew it was because the W.A.S.P had murdered her husband. I wondered if Dr. Tweedle would allow me to return to the manor for the weekend.

When we were almost done with our meal, Irene had to leave the table to take care of arriving customers. There seemed to be many now that the dinner hour had arrived.

Dr. Tweedle pushed his empty plate to the middle of the table.

"Are you finished and ready to head back to the academy?" Dr. Tweedle asked.

"Yes, thank you. My soup was delicious."

Dr. Tweedle raised his hand in a stopping motion and then laughed. I realized I had just thanked him again. We rose from the table and said goodbye to Irene.

"Oh, Jane," she cried as she pulled me into an embrace. "It was so good to see you. I can't wait until you come back."

"I'm so glad Dr. Tweedle brought me here today," I replied after being released from Irene's hug.

Dr. Tweedle said his goodbyes, and we left the Leaf and Lily Inn. He steered the horses back onto the road and back to the entrance of the Jewel Caverns. It had been such a nice day. Dr. Tweedle had been so good to me. No one had ever bought me so many gifts before. I felt like I owed Dr. Tweedle so much, and I had no idea how to repay him. Hopefully, one day, I could figure out how to.

29
A Tea Leaf Prediction

THE CODE RED was lifted the following day and replaced with a code orange. Dr. Tweedle decided to reopen the academy on Monday and reluctantly allowed me to return to the manor that weekend. Life at the Jelf Academy resumed its normal pace. I plodded along with my studies, the end of the year quickly approaching. Josefina was still not talking to me, but I was relieved she made it back to the school safely. We both continued to avoid each other, and with the finals right around the corner, it was easy to do.

Josefina constantly disappeared to study with the girls, but I wasn't sure what help they offered her. I decided to study with Taylor, both concerned with the Charms final. Last year, Mr. Withermyer's final tested us on several charms we'd learned throughout the year. He randomized the tests so students in different classes couldn't report what charms were on the exam. To have any hope of passing, you had to study and practice all the charms you learned for the year. I didn't think Mr. Withermyer was above pulling material from last year.

Ms. Crescent's final was also going to be a difficult one because we had to read our tea leaves for her. This would entail memorizing all the symbols in our textbooks since we wouldn't be allowed to reference them during the test. Taylor and I had requested tea leaves from the kitchen so we could practice without looking in our books. We spent most of our evenings drinking tea and deciphering the messages afterward.

I wasn't sure what Mr. Laruse's final would consist of since most of the events we learned to predict couldn't be simulated. I was hoping his test would be multiple choice. Mr. Collyworth's test was most certainly going to be multiple choice with an essay at the end of the exam. Mr. Collyworth would give us four essay topics to look over, and he would put a choice of two to pick from on the test. Mr. Collyworth's tests were predictable, so I felt better about the History final.

Taylor and I studied the entire week leading up to finals. Sometimes we were joined by Miguel and Andrew. Miguel had begun speaking with Josefina again. I figured it was easier for him to forgive her because she was his twin sister: his other half. He couldn't stand Marley, Candi, and Bellony, so he kept his distance.

I was stunned by how quickly the week of finals arrived. The end of the year always seemed to go by at an alarming rate. The Charms final was at the beginning of the week, and I didn't know whether to be terrified or relieved to get it out of the way early.

I entered the Charms classroom and swore I felt my legs shake beneath me. It didn't seem as if I had much time to study. The exam time was longer than a regular class, so Mr. Withermyer would pick something complicated. I glanced through my materials before the bell rang because we would no longer be able to use our books once the exam started.

Josefina came into the room and actually glanced at me before taking her seat. I could tell how nervous she was, so I took a deep breath and leaned toward her.

"Good luck," I whispered to her.

At first, I didn't think she would answer me, but then she murmured, "You, too."

We had finally shared our first words in months. Suddenly, I felt better about taking the Charms final. If Josefina was willing to talk to me again, things wouldn't be so bad.

Mr. Withermyer rose from his desk and paced to the center of the room.

"Everyone, settle in so we can begin. Just like last year, you will complete a true or false section. Once you have it completed, turn it in and begin on the assigned charm. Remember, you will not be able to use your books or any charms you've created previously. As soon as I'm done passing out the questions, you may begin."

Mr. Withermyer passed out the exam, and when he finished, he projected the words *illuminating charm* onto the blackboard. I remembered this charm consisted of melting four metals and then solidifying them with an *ice charm*. It was one of the most complicated charms we learned this year.

Looking down at the true or false portion, I put the *illuminating charm* to the back of my mind and focused on the questions in front of me. Mr. Withermyer was a fan of trick questions, so I needed to read slowly and carefully. For several of my answers, I had to erase them because I reread the statement and found one of the ingredients to be wrong. I felt relieved when I finished because I could focus on the *illuminating charm*. When I turned in my paper, Mr. Withermyer's green eyes stared right through me before he took the paper out of my hand.

Trying not to be intimidated, I returned to my seat and opened my pixie dust case, pulling out the *illuminating* and *ice charm* ingredients. After melting the metals, I remembered to mix the copper and silver first and then add the gold, followed by the platinum. I worked quickly and efficiently to get the *ice charm* ready and added more marble than what the charm called for. When my ice had formed, I placed my combined bowl of metals on it and even packed some of the ice around the edges. When my metals solidified, the next part of the charm would be physically demanding. I had to grate the solid nugget down into pixie dust. Checking my time, I was happy to see I had more than enough.

When I completed the charm, I was delighted with how the process had gone. I was fairly certain I had completed it correctly. Collecting my *illuminating charm* dust, I poured it into a vial and labeled it. I noticed I was one of the first to finish the test.

Taking my labeled vial to the front of the room, I handed it to Mr. Withermyer. He took it from me and then nodded to the classroom door, signaling that I would leave.

Since none of the regular class schedules applied for the week of finals, I returned to my room to study for Zodiac Signs. I decided to concentrate on compatibility since Mrs. Harris had focused on that the most. I sat reading my Zodiac book until lunch, and it wasn't until then that I realized Josefina hadn't come back to the room after Charms. Feeling disheartened, I walked down to the dining hall. My disappointment continued when I saw Josefina seated at the table with the girls. When I grabbed my lunch, she didn't even turn to look at me as I sat down.

Miguel and Andrew arrived at the table, and Miguel began talking about the Charms final right away.

"I knew he would choose a multistep charm for us. Mr. Withermyer knows how to make things difficult, and those true or false questions were horrendous. I took forever on that part because I had to read so slowly," Miguel complained.

"What final do you have next?" I asked.

"Earth Catastrophes, and because I have no idea what I'm doing, I'm going to have to make something up."

"Yes, I know how you feel. That test is one of my last ones," I replied.

"You might be lucky because you'll have more time to think of something," Andrew said.

"Since History is tomorrow morning, do you want to go over notes tonight?" Miguel asked me.

"That would be great. We can go over those memorization techniques you created and look at the essay topics again," I replied.

"What's your next final?" Andrew asked as he stabbed a forkful of salad.

"Zodiac Signs. I hope Mrs. Harris' test isn't too bad. She always explains her subject fairly well."

When I arrived at the Zodiac Signs classroom, Mrs. Harris stood in the middle of the circle of desks with a stack of papers in her hand. I greeted her and went to my usual seat beside Taylor. Taylor looked exhausted. I wondered what final she had this morning. Josefina arrived just before the bell rang, refusing to say anything to me as she slid into her seat. Harris walked around the circle of desks, laying the papers face down in front of us.

"When I tell you, you may flip the test over and begin. I hope learning about zodiac signs has been fascinating to you over the past two years. Many of you may know that Zodiac Signs is a first- and second-year course. Hence, this is your final Zodiac test. I hope you retain what you've learned in this class. You may now begin," Mrs. Harris concluded.

I flipped my paper over to find multiple-choice questions. Slowly, I worked my way through them, making sure they weren't worded in a way that would make me pick the wrong answer. Fortunately, Mrs. Harris was not like Mr. Withermyer, and her test contained nothing of the sort.

On the last page of the test, there was an essay question. At first, I was worried, but I smiled once I read over what Mrs. Harris was asking. The essay question asked why we agreed or disagreed with the traits of our sign. Since she had made us write the same essay earlier this year, I was able to breeze through it. By the time I finished the test, I felt confident I had done an excellent job.

Taylor was finished at about the same time as me, so we left the classroom together.

"Miguel mentioned studying for History tonight. I don't know if you took that final yet," I told her as we walked up the stairs.

"No, I didn't. I had Magical Creatures this morning," Taylor said.

"Was it difficult? You look exhausted," I replied.

"No, it wasn't. Mrs. Rowley had examples of animals which you have to name and then answer questions about what they eat or what kind of habitat they live in. I was just up late last night studying."

"You're more than welcome to join us after dinner to study History," I told her as we reached the fifth floor.

"Okay, I'll find you after dinner," Taylor promised as she headed toward her room.

I didn't expect Josefina to come back to the room before dinner, so I decided to take care of Thistle early since I had plans later. Thistle was always happy to see me. I made her perform a few tricks before giving her dinner so I could see what she remembered. Over the past month, she had excelled at following commands and typically performed them as soon as I instructed her. I briefly petted her, talking about the finals I had taken and the tests I still had. Since she had hatched, I tried to make her understand I would be going away for a while but would return. I prayed to the gods she would be fine spending the summer here without me.

After dinner, Taylor joined Miguel, Andrew, and me in the library. We spent the evening exchanging notes and quizzing each other for hours. Miguel knew the most and hardly ever missed a question. We went over pixie gods and the ancient Greek and Roman cultures. After studying with Miguel, I felt better about tomorrow morning's test.

The following morning, I left the History classroom smiling. All the multiple-choice questions seemed to be what we had studied in the library. The last essay question had been about the pixie gods and goddesses, which I ended up focusing more on Karenza since she had been the goddess I wrote my paper on. I had three out of six finals now in my past, but I still had to get through Predicting the Future today. There were so many symbols for tea leaf reading that I was afraid I wouldn't remember them all.

Miguel was already at the lunch table when I arrived. He had flown through the questions, and I was positive he hadn't missed any.

"How do you think you did?" Miguel asked when I sat down.

"I think I passed, thanks to you," I smiled.

"Don't give me too much credit. I knew you'd do fine."

It wasn't much longer before Andrew joined us, and Marley, Candi, and Bellony huddled to their side of the table. I noticed Josefina wasn't with them. She hadn't had a moment without the girls since our disagreement, so her absence was strange.

"Miguel, where is Josefina?" I asked, alarmed.

"She contacted me a few moments ago and told me she won't be coming to lunch. Her History final is this afternoon, so I'm sure she'll be mentally bothering me while I'm taking my Zodiac Signs test," Miguel replied.

She could have studied with us last night, but she was too busy focusing on helping her friends with their finals. Shaking my head, I finished my lunch. The time had come to decipher some tea leaves. I hoped I wouldn't choke on my tea before the reading.

When I got to the second floor's east wing, I heard my name being called. I turned to see Dr. Tweedle heading in my direction.

"Jane, may I have a moment?" he called.

I moved to the side of the hallway and waited for him to reach me. He had a concerned expression on his face as he drew level with me. A sliver of fear nagged at my mind, but I managed to smile at him.

"Good afternoon, Dr. Tweedle."

"Jane, I don't want to keep you because I know you have a final to get to, but would you be able to stop by my office when your test is over?"

"Of course. Is there something wrong?" I asked.

"I don't want you to be late. We'll be able to talk later. It's nothing to think about at the moment. Just focus on your test." With that, he turned around and headed back in the direction of his office.

The fact he hadn't exactly answered my question wasn't lost on me. Nervously, I continued down the hall to the Predicting the Future classroom. What could Dr. Tweedle possibly want to talk about? Had the W.A.S.P. discovered some new information? My mind jumped to all sorts of scenarios. How could I concentrate on my final now?

The Predicting the Future classroom was dark, and a strange smell of incense filled the air. I yawned as I walked to my seat, instantly feeling tired. I needed to think about tea leaf symbols and push thoughts of Dr. Tweedle from my mind. I wished I didn't have this final, so I could go directly to Dr. Tweedle and find out what he needed to tell me. My mind felt pulled in a million places. Possibilities kept running through my thoughts, each one worse than the one before.

Taylor came into the room looking just as sleepy as I felt.

"Charms was brutal this morning," she murmured as she sat down on the pillow beside me.

She looked mentally drained, and I felt terrible she had two difficult finals on the same day. When all of the students had filed in, Ms. Crescent rose from her pillow. The beads on her arms clanked off one another, and her long orange skirt hid her bare feet.

"Good afternoon, class," her wispy voice filled the room.

"This is the second year Predicting the Future final. When I call your name, you will join me in my office for a cup of tea. Then you'll proceed to read your future in the tea leaves. I'll start with Mr. James Bucklew," Mrs. Crescent said, disappearing behind the beaded curtain.

Finally, Ms. Crescent called my name, and I was forced to take control of my thoughts. I walked down to the bottom of the auditorium and parted the beads to Ms. Crescent's office. She was seated on her pillow. A short table was next to her with a teapot, a few packets of leaves, and a white teacup.

"You may begin making your tea," she instructed me.

I added a few leaves to the bottom of the cup, then poured out the hot water. Steam rose from the cup, and the tea's aroma filled the room. I blew on the liquid, trying to lessen the heat. After a few moments, I downed the cup of tea even though it scalded my mouth. I wasn't in the mood to wait. I wanted to get this test over with, so I could go to Dr. Tweedle's office.

My mouth felt sore, but I looked down into my cup. At first, I couldn't make out anything, but soon the residue of the tea leaves formed into what looked like three things. On one side of the cup, there appeared to be a wagon. The following image looked like an eight-legged creature, perhaps an octopus, and the third symbol was very small, but I thought it looked like a bat.

Ms. Crescent was leaning forward, so I tilted the cup toward her and began explaining what I saw.

"This looks like a wagon," I started, pointing to the shape. "The meaning of a wagon is a wedding."

I noticed Ms. Crescent was nodding as she stared into my cup.

"My stepsister, Emily, is getting married in a few weeks, so that's probably what the wagon is referring to."

I moved on to the next symbol and pointed it out to Ms. Crescent. "This looks like an octopus," I said, closing my eyes, trying to remember what an octopus meant. "The octopus symbolizes danger," I finally said, recalling my textbook.

I felt a cold sweat break out on the back of my neck and travel down my arms. Did this mean there would be a danger at Emily's wedding? I took a deep breath and gazed at the last symbol: the bat. I knew a bat by itself meant sickness or trouble in the home, but I also remembered that a bat combined with other signs meant something else.

"These leaves look like a bat. I know it means something else when combined with other signs. Give me a moment to think," I said.

Ms. Crescent's eyes went incredibly wide as she looked into my cup. She seemed slightly uncomfortable, and she shifted on the pillow beneath her. I closed my eyes and thought about the page with the word bat. I could almost picture it in my mind. When I finally was able to visualize the page, I shuttered at the other meaning.

A bat combined with other signs was a prediction of death.

30

THE FINAL BETRAYAL

I FINISHED MY READING with Ms. Crescent and rose on shaky legs. How often were tea leaf predictions correct? Sweat started to run down my back. I thought I would collapse, but I managed to make it out of the Predicting the Future classroom. I took a deep breath and leaned against the wall. There would be no avoiding Emily's wedding. I would have to be there.

The thought made me feel incredibly sick. What could happen at Emily's wedding? A thought nagged at my mind. I didn't know all five hundred of Emily's guests. What if she had invited a member of the W.A.S.P.? I wasn't planning on performing magic at the wedding. I was going to be surrounded by humans.

Perhaps I had read the symbols in my teacup completely wrong. Maybe the clump of leaves hadn't been a wagon. Perhaps the octopus could have been a spider, and the bat, a bird. I almost laughed aloud in the empty hallway. Why was I becoming so panicked over a wet clump of leaves that could be interpreted as anything? I was acting foolish. At Emily's wedding, I would stay on the lookout. I would have no reason to use magic. I had probably misread my cup, and the only thing I should be worried about was failing.

Taking another deep breath, I walked down the hall in the direction of Dr. Tweedle's office. My stomach was still churning as my thoughts snapped back to what Dr. Tweedle might have to tell me. Like always, when I arrived outside his office, he knew of my presence and called me inside.

"You asked to see me?" I said, entering the office.

"Yes, Jane. Please have a seat," he said grimly.

Slowly, I walked to the sofa and sat down on its edge. Dr. Tweedle didn't look as if he had good news. He sank into his desk chair and straightened his glasses.

"Jane, is there anything you want to tell me?" he asked.

The question confused me. I hadn't done anything wrong. What was there to tell him?

"No, sir. I don't," I said, confused.

"I figured that's what you would say," Dr. Tweedle said.

"I'm perplexed, sir. I'm not even sure what you're asking about. I'm not trying to be difficult."

Dr. Tweedle took a deep breath and looked me right in the eye.

"Jane, you know that interacting with humans and telling them about pixies is illegal, right?"

His words made my heart freeze in my chest. This was certainly not the conversation I had been expecting.

"Yes," I said slowly, wondering why he was asking me about this. How would Dr. Tweedle even know or suspect anything?

Dr. Tweedle sighed profoundly and crossed his hands on top of the desk.

"Then you would know that you have technically committed a crime by telling the farm boy at the manor about the pixie world," he said, shocking me into silence.

Did he somehow read my mind like he always knew I was outside his office? That couldn't be possible. I had told Robert about the pixie world a long time ago. If Dr. Tweedle could read my mind, why hadn't he confronted me months ago?

"Dr. Tweedle, I… I never meant for Robert to find out," I stuttered, causing Dr. Tweedle to put his head in his hands.

It took him several moments to look at me. "I was hoping what I heard was a lie," he finally said.

"What you heard?" I stammered. How could Dr. Tweedle have heard anything? I had kept Robert a secret, and I hadn't told anyone except…

"Josefina," I whispered.

"Jane, I don't think she came here with any intention of hurting you. At least, I don't believe so despite having noticed you haven't been talking much lately. Josefina told me she was concerned about your well-being. She said she tried talking to you about it, but you didn't want to listen. She hoped I could get through to you," Dr. Tweedle said.

I sat there stunned. How could Josefina do this to me? I had asked her not to tell anyone. How could she betray me again and tell Dr. Tweedle of all people? Just when I thought I could get over the *love charm* incident, Josefina was stabbing me in the back again. Only this time, the knife was so much bigger, and it had pierced me much more profoundly.

So, this was where she had been at lunch instead of studying. Now she had lied along with everything else she'd done. I felt tears burning in the corners of my eyes.

"Please tell me that being romantically involved with him is a lie," Dr. Tweedle sighed.

After a few deep breaths, I looked right into Dr. Tweedle's eyes.

"I love Robert," I said. There was no point in denying it. "We love each other."

Disappointment seemed to leak out of Dr. Tweedle as he slumped forward on his desk. "Why, Jane? Why would you do this? You know how dangerous it is to be involved with a human. You know what the pixie laws state."

"Yes, I know. I've tried to ignore what I was feeling for Robert, but I just couldn't. Robert is a good person, Dr. Tweedle. He would never hurt me," I replied.

"Robert is still a human, Jane. You know, telling a human about the pixie world is forbidden, and as for being romantically involved with one, that is out of the question!"

"Not all humans are members of the W.A.S.P., and not all are evil. My father was a human, and he loved my mother and me very much. Everyone here seems to forget I'm half-human. Does that make me evil?" I asked, feeling frustrated.

"History has shown that pixie interactions with humans have never turned out favorably. The laws are in place for our safety. Jane, I don't want you to get hurt, and I certainly don't want you to get in trouble with pixie authorities," Dr. Tweedle said.

"I can't help that I love Robert. No one has control over whom they fall in love with. My mother fell in love with my father, and I'm sure she couldn't stop it from happening. I know they were happy together. Why isn't love all that matters? Why can't pixies be allowed to love whomever they want?" I could feel tears coming to my eyes.

"I have no power when it comes to the law, Jane. I'm not trying to be cruel but being involved with Robert is not in your best interest. I'm only telling you this because I care about you. Your mother left the pixie world because of your father, and it wasn't long until the W.A.S.P. found her. I couldn't stand it if something like that happened to you, too. Please, Jane. All I'm asking is for you to consider the consequences. Would the loss of your life be worth it? I'm sorry to call you here during finals week when you have so much to concentrate on. Just please think about ending things with Robert. I don't want you to get hurt."

I sat on the sofa, completely stunned. I couldn't even believe this conversation was happening. I opened my mouth to refute him, but after thinking about it, I slowly let it close. No matter what I said, Dr. Tweedle wouldn't listen. He was only concerned about pixie laws. Was this how my mother felt when she talked to Dr. Tweedle about humans? I was sure Dr. Tweedle was only worried about me, and I felt terrible for disappointing him, but he had no right to tell me whom I should love.

I could only bring myself to nod slowly. I could feel the anger burning inside me, but I didn't want to show it. Dr. Tweedle rose from his desk, and I felt myself stand.

"I'm sorry to upset you, Jane. I just want you to know how critical this situation is. Forgive me for pulling you away from your studies," Dr. Tweedle said, dismissing me.

I didn't say anything as I left the office. My face felt extremely hot as I began climbing the stairs to the fifth floor. Robert was supposed to remain a secret. This was all Josefina's fault. How could she do this? Dr. Tweedle wanted me to end the only relationship that made my stay at the manor bearable. Of all people, how could Josefina tell him? Dr. Tweedle was upset and believed I was making the same mistake as my mother. I felt tears burning my eyes, but I refused to let them fall. All I wanted to feel was my anger.

When the door to my room slid open, I was shocked to see Josefina inside. My anger burst forward like water fighting to get through a dam.

"Why did you do it?" I yelled. "Why did you tell Dr. Tweedle about Robert?"

Josefina looked up at me, startled. She had been in the middle of reading a book. Her mouth gaped open, and she stared at me wide-eyed.

When she didn't say anything, I continued. "How could you do this to me?"

"Jane, I wasn't trying to hurt you," she stammered, closing her book.

"Well, you did hurt me. I told you not to tell anyone about Robert!"

Josefina grabbed at her long black braid and looked down at the floor.

"I was worried about you. You wouldn't listen to me when I told you having a relationship with Robert was against the law."

"You were worried about me? Josefina, we haven't spoken in two months! How can you even say you were worried?"

"I am, Jane. I really care about you."

"How can you even claim you do? All you've been worried about this year are those three girls! I barely exist to you!" I yelled.

"I still care about you even though I disagree with what you said about my friends," Josefina said, standing from her desk chair.

"I was only warning you. I'm not the only one who's noticed how those three behave."

"Jane, I'm not going to get into that again. Marley, Candi, and Bellony are my friends, and I'm not going to give them up just because you tell me to."

"I love Robert, and I'm not going to give him up either. However, Dr. Tweedle is demanding I end things with him!" I screamed.

"Robert is a human. It's against the law for you to have a relationship with him. It's so dangerous. You have no idea if he told anyone about what you are," Josefina said, crossing her arms over her chest.

"I know Robert wouldn't tell anyone because I'm the only one he's got at the manor! You have no idea what being at the manor is like! Robert would never hurt me because he loves me. My mother married my father because she loved him."

"And look at how well that turned out," Josefina sneered.

I almost had the urge to smack her, but I held back.

"How dare you say that about my mother! I can't even believe you would say something like that to me!"

"I'm sorry, Jane. I just can't stand to see something happen to you. I knew you weren't listening to me."

"You promised you wouldn't tell anyone! I trusted you would respect me enough to keep my secret!" I replied.

"I do respect you, but I also fear for you. I thought if I told

Dr. Tweedle, he would be able to make you understand why seeing Robert is so dangerous," Josefina said.

"Seeing Robert is not dangerous, but no one seems to understand! Robert is genuinely a great person, and he loves me very much. He would never do anything to endanger me. Why doesn't anyone believe me? Whom I fall in love with shouldn't be anyone's business besides my own. I can't control whom I love! Why can't everyone just be happy for me?"

"Pixies have been attacked and murdered by humans for hundreds of years. We cannot trust them. Humans hate the fact we have magic. Most humans would believe we are demons, something evil they have to destroy. Anyone who interacts with humans is not safe. Jane, please believe me when I say I care, and I'm just trying to protect you," Josefina said.

"How can you make these assumptions? You've never met Robert. You don't know anything about him. How could you possibly know if seeing him would be harmful?" I could feel my voice rising again.

"Jane, I don't know Robert, but I know the outcomes of other pixies who have interacted with humans. All the pixies have ended up dead. How can you question those odds?" Josefina argued.

"You don't know that all pixie-human interactions ended in death, Josefina. You couldn't possibly know about every encounter between pixies and humans. Besides, it's not your choice to make. Loving Robert is my decision, and I'm well aware of what the consequences could be. I don't know how this is anyone's business but my own," I cried again.

"I had the best of intentions when I told Dr. Tweedle. Jane, I still think of you as my friend. I was only looking out for your best interests," Josefina said.

"How could you even call yourself my friend? You betrayed me, Josefina. Friends stand by each other. Friends listen and believe each other. Friends don't lie and go behind the other's back. Most of all, friends keep each other's secrets! You promised not to tell anyone. Why would you betray me? For two months, you ignored me. Best friends don't do that!" I yelled, tears threatening to spill over.

My heart was breaking. Josefina had been my first real friend. I thought I had finally found someone who truly cared about me. I wanted to scream out all my pain and anger so I wouldn't feel so consumed by it. Everything Marie, Emily, and Preston had done to me didn't compare to this. They had never cared about me, and I never felt any connection toward them. Josefina was someone I had cared about and believed in.

"Jane, I'm so sorry. I never meant to hurt you. I never intended to betray you," Josefina finally said.

"There isn't another name for what you did besides betrayal. I thought I could trust you. I would never have done anything like this to you. I thought you were my true friend," I replied.

"Jane, I told Dr. Tweedle about Robert because I care. I am your true friend," Josefina said.

"No, I don't believe so. You are no friend of mine," I retorted. I left the room, slamming the door behind me.

31
Painful Preparations

The last few days of finals passed quickly, officially ending my second year at the Jelf Academy. It had been hard to concentrate on my last two finals when all I could think about was my conversation with Josefina. I couldn't shake the hurt I felt from her betrayal. I knew I had probably hurt her with what I had said, but she stopped being my friend long ago.

All the students of the Jelf Academy were packing their belongings and preparing to leave. I was to meet Dr. Tweedle in a few moments, so I was gathering my things. My small suitcase was much fuller on account of the beautiful clothes Dr. Tweedle had purchased for me. I had just managed to fit the last of my things in the bag when Josefina came into the room.

She crept to her desk with her eyes downcast. We had avoided each other for the last few days, more so than in the previous few months. The tension in the room was so thick I couldn't wait to leave. It was hard for me to gaze upon the person who had betrayed my trust. I slung my small bag over my shoulder and bent down to pick up my suitcase. A horrible pain seized my chest, and I tried not to cry. I could never have predicted this at the beginning of the school year.

Before my tears could fall, I crossed the room and headed for the door. Just as I walked by Josefina, she raised her eyes to look at me. I could see the sadness in her chocolate brown eyes, and for a short second, I almost apologized for what I said. Then, her betrayal ripped through my mind, hardening my eyes. I walked by her without saying a word.

The hallways were aflutter with students preparing to depart from the Jelf Academy. I dodged my way around the clutter in the hall and headed for the stairs. I hadn't spoken to Dr. Tweedle since his confrontation. I wasn't sure what to expect when I saw him again. He was waiting as he had hundreds of times before. I moved past a few students to cross the room to him.

"Ready to head back to the manor?" he asked me.

All I could manage was a nod as he took my small suitcase from my hand. I didn't feel like talking. Dr. Tweedle must have sensed how I felt because he remained silent until we reached the carriage.

"Don't worry about Thistle. I promise I'll take good care of her while you're away. I think she'll stay at the Jelf Academy for the summer," he commented.

"Thank you," I murmured. I had said my goodbyes to Thistle this morning, and I hoped she understood. I felt horrible about leaving her even though I knew she would be in good hands with Dr. Tweedle and Mrs. Rowley. If she flew away while I was gone, I would be devastated. I couldn't lose another friend. I reached up and wiped at a stray tear before Dr. Tweedle could notice.

Dr. Tweedle climbed up into the carriage beside me and cast the *teleportation charm*. In a flash, we were down the road from the manor. Instead of snapping the reins, he turned to look at me.

"Jane, before I deliver you to Marie for the summer, I need to talk to you," he said.

My eyes gazed at my lap. What did he have to talk about now?

"While you are at the manor, I want you to be careful. The W.A.S.P. has been very active lately. I want you to do everything you can to stay safe. Promise me you'll carry your pixie dust case with you just in case anything happens. If you encounter trouble, use whatever charms you can think of until you can run away. If something happens, you can use a *calling charm* to contact me, and I'll come for you.

"Also, I hope you thought about our conversation from a few days ago. Please understand that ending things with Robert is for your own good. I know it hurts right now, but in the long run, you'll understand. I need to know you are safe. Promise me you'll do this," Dr. Tweedle said.

"Okay," I lied. "I'm sorry to have disappointed you, sir."

I didn't say anything else. Dr. Tweedle couldn't force me to lose Robert. No one could tell me whom I should love. When he came to pick me up in a few months, I would tell him my relationship was over. I would keep Robert a true secret and tell no one about him. I'd finish my education at the Jelf Academy in three years. Then I would do the same thing my mother had done. Robert and I would disappear so we could be together. For now, I would pacify Dr. Tweedle.

"Thank you, Jane. I appreciate you considering my warnings. I'm not disappointed in you. I'm only concerned about your safety," Dr. Tweedle replied, snapping the reins. "I know it's hard to think about now, but time heals everything."

The horses slowly made their way up the drive. The barn came into view, and I could see its chipped red paint even from this far away. The person I loved more than life was probably inside, and he would remain my little secret. The house rose in front of us as grand as ever. Perhaps this summer wouldn't be as bad as the last one.

Dr. Tweedle pulled the horses to a stop at the front stairs. Grabbing my small bag from the floor, I threw it over my shoulder.

I managed to climb down before Dr. Tweedle could come around to assist me. He did grab my suitcase and handed it to me.

"Well, I guess this is goodbye for another summer," he said sadly. "Remember, you can contact me at any time."

Before I could respond, he pulled me into an awkward hug. Guilt nibbled at the back of my mind from the lie. Dr. Tweedle cared about me, and I knew he was genuinely concerned.

"I'm going to miss you, Dr. Tweedle," I said, feeling tears on my eyelashes.

"I'm going to miss you, too. Don't worry; these three months will go by faster than you know, and you'll be back at the Jelf Academy," he said, breaking away from me.

"Goodbye, Dr. Tweedle. I'll see you in August," I replied as I turned to the stairs.

"Be safe, Jane," he called as he climbed back into the carriage.

I set my suitcase down at the top of the stairs and waved to Dr. Tweedle as he spurred the horses into motion. Once he was out of sight, I took a deep breath and pushed the front door open.

I was in the middle of climbing the staircase when Marie burst into the front hall. Her gray eyes met mine, and she sneered.

"Jane, I see you've finally arrived home. Quickly take your filthy things up to the attic and then come to Emily's room at once. We have to finalize the wedding's seating chart, and there are too many names for our delicate hands to write," Marie said.

I marched into the attic and placed my belongings down beside the mattress. Creating Emily's seating chart seemed like the perfect form of torture to begin my summer. I would be writing over five hundred names for the third time. Couldn't this wedding be over already? I was looking forward to not having to deal with Emily every day.

When I entered Emily's bedroom, Marie and Emily were already on the settee in the sitting area. Sprawled on the coffee table was a stack of paper and a pen. I gulped when I saw the amount of paper. Crossing the room, I bowed to Marie and Emily and took my place in the abandoned armchair. I leaned towards the table, picking up the pen to indicate I was ready.

"For the wedding, we will have forty-two tables, each with twelve people seated at them. We can begin with my family table," Emily said, and I balked at the number of tables I would be drawing up.

"Drake and I will be seated at a bridal table by ourselves, so mother and Preston will be seated at the table closest to mine," Emily said.

She proceeded to rattle off names of aunts and uncles I had only seen at the manor a few times. I followed her instructions completely, afraid to mess up. Finally, she had given me all twelve names. One down and forty-one to go.

As it turned out, Emily's family table was the most straightforward. Marie and Emily bickered about who should be placed with whom. I now understood why a stack of paper had been on the coffee table. After I would write down names, one of them would change their minds, and I would have to start all over again.

"Put Mrs. McGowan with Mrs. Stewart," Emily would instruct, and as soon as I would write down the names, Marie would speak up.

"No, no, no, Emily, don't you remember? These two women can't possibly sit together. They're still fighting about whose son is more successful. They won't want to sit at the same table!"

Emily would just giggle. "You're right, mother. I completely forgot."

I would be forced to discard the table diagram and begin again. I knew they had probably planned this dialog just to have me redo every table at least once. It wasn't long before my hand began to cramp. I listened to their arguments and their complaints about Mr. Doyle's mother.

"We should seat her in the back of the room," Emily laughed.

"No, that would be obvious. We need to find a way to insult her subtly," Marie amended.

They talked about asking the florist to leave the thorns on Mrs. Doyle's corsage or spelling her name wrong for her place card: simple mistakes they could easily blame on the help. I was sure Emily would do all of these things.

By the time we had gotten to the last few tables, I had sworn my hand was frozen around the pen. I didn't think I'd be able to lay my fingers straight again. Grabbing another piece of paper, I awaited instructions for the next table. Marie and Emily looked over the remaining names on the guest list. None of the remaining people knew each other, so Emily and Marie had me change the last few tables again until they were satisfied. Relieved to be finally finished, I laid the pen down and stretched my fingers out, feeling the pain in my joints.

"Now that the seating chart is complete, Jane can begin writing out the place cards," Marie said with an evil smile.

I tried not to look upset about this announcement. How much longer would my hand have to suffer in the name of this wedding?

"All of the place cards are in the office, so you can take this list and get started," Emily said with a laugh as she shoved the papers toward me.

I took the list from her and left Emily's room. As I walked, I flexed my fingers. I wrote slowly so I didn't mess up the place cards. When I entered the office, I found the cards stacked high on the desk. Making my way across the room, I placed the list of names on the desk and picked up my second pen of the day. Just a few more days and Emily would have her own house with her own servants to bother.

My hand protested as I began. I tried to ignore the pain, pushing forward. I put a dot by each name I completed. With each mark, I was a step closer to the end.

I was startled an hour later when Marie came into the office.

"Stop what you're doing and help Ellen in the kitchen! Don't you know what time it is?" she barked.

"No, ma'am. I'm sorry," I replied as I placed the pen down on the list to mark my place.

Hurriedly, I darted down the hallway. Ellen was in the middle of roasting a leg of lamb when I entered the kitchen.

"Where have you been? Didn't you know it was dinner time?" Ellen asked.

"I'm sorry. Marie had another task for me," I said.

"You can start by cutting up those potatoes," Ellen said, indicating the bag of potatoes on the counter.

I pulled out the cutting board, grabbed a knife, and began chopping. Once they were all evenly sized, I added them to a frying pan. At least helping out with dinner allowed me to have a break from the place cards.

While the potatoes were cooking, I busied myself with setting the table. I placed the dishes at the usual settings and double-checked the silverware placement. When everything was neatly arranged, I returned to cooking. The potatoes were getting soft, so I left the lid off, so they could brown a bit. As soon as they were finished, I spooned them into a bowl. Ellen was cutting meat off the leg of lamb and arranging it on a platter.

When she was finished, we took the food into the dining room. As silent as mice, the family had taken their seats at the table. Once I had placed the potatoes down, I ducked back into the kitchen to grab the basket of rolls. Preston already had potatoes all over his face by the time I came back into the dining room. I wondered how he would eat at Emily's wedding.

Ellen and I began cleaning up what we could so I would only have the dinner plates and platters. It was rare for her to help me like this, so I thanked her profusely. Every once in a while, I had to dart back into the dining room to fill up the water glasses.

Ellen left the kitchen once we had gotten everything done.

Now all I could do was sit and wait until dinner was over. I wished I could have been working on the place cards while I waited, but I knew Marie would be mad if I wasn't waiting on them. I kept checking the kitchen clock, watching the hands move ever so slowly. It didn't seem like the family would be done early this evening.

The back door swung open, and Robert entered the kitchen. I lifted my finger to my lips and looked toward the dining room, so he would know to keep his voice down.

"Looks like they're taking their time tonight," Robert whispered after he had crossed the room and kissed me.

"I'll bet they're making sure I have to wait for them before I can get back to my other project this evening," I whispered back.

When he looked confused, I explained about the place cards.

"Marie and Emily had me writing out the seating arrangements this afternoon. They changed their minds at least once for every table, and I had to do them again."

"At least they aren't having the wedding here. We would be killing ourselves to set up everything."

I nodded in agreement. I was actually surprised Emily hadn't thought about it. I was sure she would be hell-bent on killing me on her wedding day. Robert took a seat at the kitchen table and grabbed hold of my right hand. Slowly, he squeezed my hand and massaged circles with his thumbs. It felt good, and I was extremely grateful he had thought to do it.

"At least I have you for the summer, not just the weekends," Robert whispered as he continued to squeeze. "How were your final tests?"

"I hope I passed. It was hard to concentrate towards the end of the week because of Josefina."

"Why? What happened?" Robert asked, looking concerned.

"Josefina told Dr. Tweedle about you," I replied.

"Are you in trouble? Did he kick you out of the school?"

"No, nothing like that. He wants me to end things with you.

Don't worry, Robert. I could never leave you. I'd rather them expel me. When he retrieves me at the end of the summer, I'll just lie and tell him I did what he asked."

"Why would Josefina do something like that?" Robert asked, shaking his head and looking down at the table.

"I don't know. She claimed she cared about me and was only trying to protect me. Every pixie thinks all humans are dangerous. She thinks you're going to get me killed."

"Well, that's completely ridiculous," Robert muttered. "I would never do anything to hurt you."

"I tried to tell them, but they wouldn't listen. Josefina and I had a huge fight."

"That's terrible, Jane. I'm so sorry to hear that," Robert replied as he continued to stroke my sore fingers.

Slowly, I rose from the table, my hand slipping from his. "I have to check on the family," I whispered, backing away from the kitchen table.

When I peeked into the dining room, the chairs were empty. Quickly, I went about gathering dishes. I needed to get back to the office as fast as possible. Robert jumped into action and helped me with the dishes and the wiping down of the countertops.

"Thank you so much, Robert. You didn't have to help me," I said.

"You always say that. When will you realize I do it because I want to," he replied, kissing my cheek.

"I have to get back to writing out those place cards."

"I could help you. You know my writing is decent," Robert offered.

I shook my head. "I can't let you. Marie and Emily are home for the evening, and I think they would notice you were in the office."

"That's right," Robert sighed. "I wish I could help. Why don't you come by the barn when you're finished if you can get out? I'll rub your hand again."

"Thank you again, Robert. I appreciate it," I replied with a wink.

"I would do anything for you," Robert said, grabbing my hands and pulling me into a kiss.

It was hard pulling away from him, but I had to finish the place cards before Marie yelled at me. Quickly, I rushed back into the office and resumed where I had left off. Robert's face swam in my mind, and I concentrated on the hand massage I might receive later. My hand flew over the parchment, writing name after name. Everything began to flow together. When I got to Mr. Doyle's mother, I made sure to spell her name correctly. No matter what Emily wanted, I wasn't going to be rude. If she wanted to change the place card, she could do it on her own.

The hours passed along with the names. This time I was certain I wouldn't be able to straighten my fingers after this. Every so often, I would stop between names and try to flex my hand, pain traveling down to my fingertips. After several sharp breaths, I would begin again. When I had written the last name, I couldn't believe my torture was over, and I looked through the entire list just to make sure.

I already knew what my next task would be, so I grabbed the pages with the seating chart and began grouping names together. Searching through the desk drawers, I found a container of rubber bands. I collected each person's name for every table and used the rubber bands to keep them together. This took me almost an hour to complete, but at least Marie and Emily wouldn't be able to command me to do it later.

It was very late by the time I had finished up in the office, but I didn't care. I knew Robert would be awake waiting for me. Slowly, I snuck out of the office, pausing every so often to listen to the quiet of the house. Once I had escaped the front door and made my way across the lawn, I began to breathe easier.

Robert was indeed waiting for me. I climbed up the ladder to the loft and threw myself into his arms.

"Let me see your hand," he murmured as he pulled me down, my head resting on his right shoulder.

Robert began the massage as he held me close. I finally felt myself beginning to relax. This was, without a doubt, my favorite place to be. I felt the muscles in my hand starting to loosen, and all the tension seemed to flow out of my body.

"I wish I would have been able to help you," he said again.

"Well, you're helping me now," I replied as I snuggled closer.

His right hand began stroking my hair, his touch sending chills down my spine. This had to be what Speura felt like.

"How much does Emily still need to do before the wedding?" Robert asked.

"I'm not sure since I've been at the academy. I'll bet she'll give me plenty to do," I replied.

"Isn't that what stepsisters are for?" Robert joked.

I scowled up at him. "You know I'm not part of their family even though I'm the only real Fitzgerald in this house. I hope she doesn't entrust me with any sisterly duties. For one, I don't want to be responsible for the train on her dress."

"Why's that?" Robert chuckled.

"She ordered the longest train possible, and it's cumbersome. I should know since she made me hold it for her dress fittings."

"I don't believe Emily would give you any task that would be considered an honor. I'm sure she'll have someone else assist her," Robert assured me.

"I'm just wondering what torture she'll put me through. I know she will have a fit over her hair and makeup. I'll have to do it until she is satisfied, and if that makes her late to the altar, she'll blame me."

"Don't worry about that now. We'll deal with the wedding day when it comes. Remember, I will be there to help you in any way I can. I won't let you be blamed for any mistakes. I'll fix them before they even notice," Robert said as he began massaging up my arm.

"You're right, Robert. At least I'll have you by my side to weather this storm. I'll be watching out for you as well. If I see Mr. Wicker, I'll make sure you steer clear of him."

"Thank you. I hope I won't have to see him if five hundred guests attend. If I do, I'll be okay. You've given me strength over the past two years, and I can face the demons of my past because of you. You've made me a better person, Jane. I can honestly say you've saved me. I was dead before I met you, and you've made me come alive. You are the light in all my darkness," Robert said, kissing the top of my head.

"Robert, you've been my light, too. The manor was awful before you came. I didn't have anyone who cared about me. I had nothing to live for. I'm so lucky to have you in my life. I love you, Robert."

"I love you, too, Jane. Just think, after the wedding is over, you won't have to be Emily's slave anymore," he chuckled into my hair.

"This wedding can't come soon enough," I mumbled, holding Robert tighter. Being next to him was the best place I could possibly be.

32

THE WEDDING DAY

THE MORNING OF Emily's wedding came faster than I expected. Ellen woke me by bringing up a large tub of slightly warm water. Marie had drilled into my head the night before what today's events included. She warned me that if I did anything to spoil Emily's special day, she would have me whipped and thrown out of the house. Everything had to run according to plan.

I hurriedly heated the water for my bath and stepped in. I scrubbed my skin and hair and leapt out of the water to grab my ragged towel. I dressed in the outfit Marie had picked. As an afterthought, I slipped my pixie dust case into one of the deep pockets. I wasn't going to be foolish and not heed Dr. Tweedle's warning. My prediction in the tea leaves still haunted me, nagging at the back of my mind.

I pulled out my mother's combs and brushed through my blonde hair. Then, I began tightly braiding it into a French braid. Once my hair was secure, I left the attic and braced myself for the long day ahead.

Ellen was rushing around the kitchen when I arrived. I grabbed the teapot and filled it. Knowing Emily, she would want tea with her breakfast. While I waited for the water to boil, I prepared Emily's breakfast tray with toast, a hardboiled egg, and some chopped fruit. The whistle of the teapot startled me, and I jumped to remove it from the stove. Grabbing a teacup, I placed some tea leaves in the bottom and poured out the hot water. I squeezed a lemon into the tea and added sugar. With the tray full, I lifted it and left the kitchen.

Slowly, I climbed the stairs, carefully holding the tray level. When I reached Emily's room, I knocked on the door before entering. Emily was face down on her pillow, still asleep. I laid the breakfast tray on the coffee table and walked to the bed.

"Emily," I whispered as I gently touched her shoulder. "It's time to wake up."

She didn't stir at first, so I tried again. Suddenly, she rolled over, flailing her arms, almost hitting me in the face. I managed to spring back just in time.

"What do you want?" she demanded when she finally opened her eyes.

"Today is your wedding day. You have to get up," I replied.

She rolled over with a chuckle. "I suppose I do. Where's my breakfast?"

"The tray is on the coffee table."

"What are you standing there for? Bring it to me and then open the drapes," she snapped.

Once I had handed her the tray, I worked on opening the long red curtains. The morning sun streaked into the room, illuminating everything. Emily blinked rapidly and raised a hand to her eyes. She complained about how bright the room was. I ignored her, making my way to the bathroom to fill the tub. When I returned to the bedroom, Emily picked at her food and frowning.

"I'm not very hungry," she stated, picking up her teacup.

"Are you finished?" I asked, coming around to the side of the bed.

She thrust the tray at me in answer and crawled from the bed. As she stalked toward the bathroom, she undressed, throwing her nightgown and underclothes on the floor. Emily hadn't eaten much. Most of the fruit was left, so I popped a few pieces into my mouth, relishing the sweetness on my tongue. The only thing Emily finished was the cup of tea. When I looked into the bottom of the cup, I could make out the shape of a leaf in the remaining debris. The leaf symbolized new life, which was a fitting fortune for Emily.

Leaving the tray to clean up later, I headed into the bathroom to help Emily. She had climbed into the tub already. Her long black hair felt silky in my hands as I gently rubbed the soap into her scalp. Emily didn't yell at me as she usually did. She seemed lost in thought, and I wondered if she was nervous. Getting married was stressful, especially in front of over five hundred people.

After handing Emily the washcloth, I stepped back to prepare a dry towel. As she stepped out and rubbed herself dry, I went into her closet to find her undergarments. I helped Emily into her corset, pulling as tightly as I could. I had never seen the finished dress on her, and I wasn't sure how it fit.

Once the corset was tied, she draped a robe over her shoulders and sat at her vanity.

"My hair has to be perfect, Jane. Nothing can be out of place," she snapped at me as I began brushing the long black strands. "I want my hair off my neck and in a fancy braid. Don't braid all my hair. Just a few small braids will do."

I started parting her hair and clipping sections so they were out of my way. Then, I started a fishtail braid that began on the left side of her head and swooped toward the back. Taking the remaining hair, I twisted it and pinned it into a side bun.

Emily scrutinized her hair in the mirror when I finished.

"The front is okay, but I want the back to be higher," she complained.

I began unpinning and reworking her hair upward. I was glad she hadn't asked me to redo the braid, though it was still possible for her to demand it of me. Once I had finished again, I handed her the hand mirror so she could see the back of her head.

"Now the bun is too high," she complained, pouting her thin lips.

Quickly, I moved into action, knowing I had a few hours left to finish Emily's hair and makeup before I had to get her into her dress. I moved the bun down a bit and pinned it in again, hoping I had completed it right this time. Emily grabbed the mirror off of me with a sigh.

"This will have to do," she said with a slight smile. I could tell she liked her hair but didn't want to compliment me.

She thrust the mirror at me, and I laid it down. Then, I pulled out the makeup case from the drawer and placed it on the vanity.

"I want a very natural, virginal look," Emily sneered. "Don't make me look like a clown or a harlot."

I had never done her makeup garishly. Whatever impression her personality suggested was not my fault. I found several light browns for her eyes and a few pale pinks to dab on her lips. Slowly, I began to apply the color to her eyes, taking my time to get the lines straight. Emily was staring at herself the entire time in the mirror behind me. I knew she was trying to find something to complain about.

I made sure her gray eyes stood out, and her pale cheeks looked slightly rosy. I was surprised when she remained silent. I must have done an excellent job if she couldn't find something to say. Once I had placed the light pink on her lips, I stepped away from the mirror so she could fully see herself.

"I guess this will have to do, too," she stated as she gazed at my excellent work.

Emily stayed seated at her vanity while I cleaned up in the bathroom. I collected all the towels and drained the water in the tub. I also mopped the droplets from the floor that had splashed when Emily stepped out of the tub. When the bathroom was in a suitable condition, I went into Emily's closet to pull out her wedding dress. The dress was cumbersome, and I tried to hold it up from the floor. Using a tiny bit of magic, I was able to take some of its weight from my arms.

Carefully, I laid the dress across the sofa. Emily stood from the vanity chair and began pacing the floor. With bated breath, I lifted the dress, removing it from the hanger. I held it for her, and she stepped into the opening. Now began the part I was dreading. Grabbing at the first set of buttons, I pinched the dress together and started. I prayed to the gods that Emily's dress would fit.

When I made it halfway up the back, I had to pinch the material tighter. Thankfully, the corset made it possible for me to finish with the rest of the buttons. I grabbed hold of the pink sash and made a pretty bow on the back of the dress. I breathed a sigh of relief. Dealing with Emily and Marie would have been a disaster if the dress wouldn't fit.

Emily swirled in front of the floor-length mirror, admiring herself. I straightened the train on the back of the dress and then moved to hang up Emily's robe she had haphazardly thrown onto the floor. Suddenly, Marie burst into the room. She was wearing a lilac dress with a white sun hat. It was odd seeing her in light purple. Marie never wore a light shade of anything. The dress must've been made especially for Emily's wedding. I wondered who had the pleasure of getting Marie ready. I was surprised Marie hadn't demanded I split my time between them.

"My darling daughter!" Marie cried, crossing the room to Emily. "I can't believe you're getting married today."

Emily continued to stare at herself in the mirror and didn't turn to look at her mother.

"Emily, turn around so I can look at you. I want to make sure everything is perfect." Marie pointedly turned her cold gray eyes on me.

Emily finally spun around, and I moved to fix the dress's train again.

"My hair and makeup will have to do. I'm sure we'll have to leave soon," Emily said, rolling her eyes and sighing.

"Yes, I suppose it will," Marie replied, looking her over. "If only your father could be here to see this."

Emily rolled her eyes again. "Is it time to leave?"

I checked the clock on top of the mantle. It was a little after 12:30. The wedding was scheduled to begin at 2:00.

"We might as well get you downstairs and into the carriage. We don't want to be late. Jane, help carry Emily's train down the stairs. Then, come back up here and quickly clean up this mess," Marie barked, indicating the breakfast tray.

"Yes, ma'am," I said as I bowed to her.

Slowly, I followed Emily out her bedroom door. I was relieved when we got to the front entryway, and I could lay the train down. Once Emily was situated, I ran back up the stairs to do as Marie commanded. When I entered Emily's room, I checked for anything else that needed to be straightened before I left.

The family was gathered in the entryway when I came down with the tray. Preston was wearing a suit and had his wild red hair combed neatly. He played with his top hat, throwing it in the air and catching it as it came down. Marie and Emily stood a few feet away from him, their backs straight and noses pointed to the sky.

As I walked by, I heard Emily mutter something about Preston walking her down the aisle. I wondered how he'd behave for his part in the wedding. Quickly, I entered the kitchen. I hurried to wash the plates and put them away. Just as I was finishing up, Robert walked in the back door.

"I hope I'm not too early," he said, crossing the room to me.

"No, you're right on time," I said, taking in his nice clothing. His auburn hair was brushed back from his face, and his brown eyes gazed at me. "Emily is ready to board the carriage, though I don't know how they'll all fit inside with that long dress."

"I prepared horses for two carriages," Robert stated as he pulled me into an embrace. "How I wish we were getting married today instead of Emily."

I felt my cheeks going red. "Certainly, you wouldn't want to marry me dressed like this," I said, gazing down at my servant gown.

"I would marry you dressed in rags," Robert said, his mouth covering my lips.

Slowly, I backed away from him when the kiss ended. "I love you, Robert. I should get back. Marie probably thinks I'm moving too slowly."

Robert squeezed my hand. "Okay. I'll see you around the front," he replied, ducking out the kitchen door.

Preston was still throwing his hat into the air when I returned. Marie and Emily looked annoyed.

"It took you long enough in the kitchen," Emily remarked.

"I'm sorry," I replied, opening the front door for them.

Waiting in the turnaround were two carriages. The coachman opened the door to the first one, and I went around Emily to lift her train.

"Emily will be riding alone. Preston and I will be in the second carriage," Marie commanded as I helped Emily down the front steps. I wasn't going to ask where Robert and I were supposed to sit.

I lifted the train of Emily's dress higher as she placed her foot onto the step of the carriage. I noticed Robert opening the door to the other carriage and helping Marie inside. Once Emily had taken a seat, it was challenging to fit the remaining train inside.

"Be careful with that! I don't want my dress ripped or soiled before making it to my wedding!" Emily snapped.

I did the best I could to gather Emily's train without wrinkling it. Carefully, I situated it inside the carriage and then stepped back so the coachman could close the door.

Unsure of what to do next, I wondered where my place would be.

"Jane," Robert called. "You may sit next to me while I drive this carriage." He indicated the carriage containing Marie and Preston.

I hurried over, and Robert helped me up into the driver's seat. He took the reins for the team of horses and turned to me with a smile.

"I was given orders to follow the other carriage to the Doyle mansion," Robert explained.

I nodded as I secretly brushed his hand with mine. Robert's smile became even more prominent, and he quickly squeezed my hand. The coachman of the carriage in front of us cracked the reins, and Emily's team of horses surged forward. Robert moved to do the same, our carriage following suit. The sun shone brightly through the leaves of the trees, and the air smelled fresh. It was a beautiful day. My heart beat rapidly in my chest as both carriages exited the manor's drive. We were on our way to a wedding.

33

THE DOYLE MANSION

THE LARGE HOUSE loomed before us as the horses turned up the drive. We had arrived at Mr. Doyle's mansion. I couldn't take my eyes from the rising structure. The house was massive. I had always thought my father's house was incredible, but the Doyle mansion had to be double, if not triple the size.

The turnaround driveway was also enormous. Several carriages could fit across the road comfortably. I noticed a road just as significant led down to one of the largest barns I'd ever seen. Carriages were being driven in that direction after the guests had been dropped off at the front door. The size of the mansion's property seemed to go on forever. Now I could see why Emily insisted her wedding be held here instead of at the manor. I was sure it was her way of bragging since she would be living here.

Robert slowed the horses as our carriage pulled around to the front door. He hopped down from his perch and opened the door for Marie and Preston.

"Robert," Marie called sharply. "Park the carriage and then come back up to the house. You're also going to be serving today.

Jane, don't help Emily out of her carriage until the last of the guests arrive. No one must see her!"

Preston took his mother's arm and guided her into the house as Robert jumped back on the carriage. I watched as he steered the horses down the road and went to stand beside Emily's carriage. Several more carriages pulled up the drive to let the guests off as I waited. The women's dresses were exceedingly extravagant, and the gentlemen appeared to be in their best suits. They all gazed at Emily's carriage with interest, knowing that the bride was inside. I remembered to smile as guests looked my way.

After a few moments, I heard the sound of Emily's voice. Carefully, I opened the carriage door a sliver to peek in.

"It's hot," Emily whined. "I don't want to stay in here a moment longer."

"I'm sorry, miss, but you don't want to ruin your entrance, do you? I'm sure you don't want the guests to see you before you walk down the aisle," I replied.

"I don't give a damn!" Emily swore. "My hair will look hideous if I stay in this carriage any longer!"

Thankfully, I was saved by the coachman. "My pocket watch says it's only a few minutes before two. You better get her inside," he said.

Nodding, I opened the carriage door as far as it would go and grabbed the train of her dress. Holding it up, I moved out of the way so Emily could descend. She grabbed onto the coachman's hand, and soon both her feet were on the ground. Emily cast an irritated look at me as if it were my fault she had been stuck inside the carriage. She marched to the front doors, and I hurried along behind her.

The inside of the Doyle mansion was even more elaborate than I imagined. It was so well decorated for the home of a bachelor. I assumed Mr. Doyle's mother had something to do with the décor. Emily hustled through the front entryway and toward a hallway that led to the back of the house. She was moving so fast that I had a hard time keeping up. I didn't want to tug on the train. The room at the end of the hall was a parlor with huge windows that faced the back of the house and a door that led out onto a terrace. I could see a gazebo next to a pond. Rows of chairs lined the path to the gazebo, and I could make out the silhouette of two men standing beneath the gazebo's awning. The scene was absolutely spectacular, making me feel a tad envious. Emily's wedding was going to be beautiful. The pond, the gazebo, and the trees in the background looked so picturesque.

A couple of handmaids rushed to Emily's side as soon as they saw her.

"Jane, you are no longer needed," Emily snapped. "The wedding reception is going to be on the western terrace. Go there and help set up. Make everything look perfect." She waved a hand at me as the other women stepped up to take my place.

I stood in the parlor, transfixed as the two women fixed Emily's veil and then trailed behind her down the terrace steps. At the bottom of the stairs stood Preston. Emily took his arm, and he led her to the beginning of a very long aisle. I watched until Emily made it to the gazebo and was handed over to Mr. Doyle. From this moment, Emily was no longer my problem, I thought with a smile. Now, all I had to do was find the western terrace.

I exited the parlor onto the south-facing terrace and turned right. I hoped the decks were somehow connected. When I came to a set of stairs, I ascended them to see dozens of tables sprawled before me. This had to be the right place. Many servants rushed around each table, setting out place settings. Unsure of what to do, I searched for a friendly face. Suddenly, I heard my name being called, and I turned.

Robert was moving through the crowd toward me with a stack of paper in his hands.

"Jane, I'm so glad I found you. The servants here have given us the task of putting the place cards on the tables. Since you helped Emily design the floor plan, you probably know this better than I do," Robert stated, handing me the stack of diagrams I had drawn up for Emily.

Robert grabbed my elbow and led me over to a table with all the cards I had written. Quickly, I jumped into action, giving Robert stacks of names and table numbers, while I took a handful and headed to the other side of the terrace. Robert and I worked well together, and soon all forty-two tables had the proper names assigned to them.

With that completed, Robert approached the head maid for our next assignment. We were shown into the kitchen area and instructed to plate hors d'oeuvres with several other servants. There was such a wide selection of appetizers. They all looked delicious. I plated the cucumber tea sandwiches, scallops wrapped with bacon, and fabulous smelling garlic bruschetta. My mouth watered since I had eaten only a few pieces of Emily's left-over fruit.

Robert winked at me and quickly popped one of the scallops into his mouth. I tried to stifle my laughter. The other servants didn't appear to have noticed. Looking at Robert, I winked and also grabbed one of the scallops. I placed it into my mouth when I was sure no one was looking. The flavor of the bacon was excellent. Having it wrapped around the scallop was one of the best things I had ever tasted. Whoever the Doyles' chef was, they had done a magnificent job. Robert and I shared a smile, both of us co-conspirators.

Not long after, we heard noises coming from the direction of the eastern terrace. The wedding was officially over, and the guests were making their way to the reception space. Emily was now the new Mrs. Doyle. Per instruction, Robert and I grabbed a tray of hors d'oeuvres and went out onto the terrace. We circled the large crowd of people and came back to the kitchen when our trays were empty.

As I took my next tray out of the kitchen, I moved toward the back of the terrace. I could see the sprawling lawn, the pond, and the gazebo from this position. Emily and Mr. Doyle were having their wedding photographs taken in the gazebo. I could make out Marie, Preston, and the older Mrs. Doyle standing close by. Turning my focus from them, I rounded the terrace again.

It wasn't long before Emily and Mr. Doyle were announced into the reception space. Emily had a smug look on her face as she was escorted to their table. Marie, Preston, and the elder Mrs. Doyle followed the couple across the terrace. Marie's sharp eyes darted from table to table, probably ensuring everyone was placed precisely where they were supposed to be. All the servants stood along the wall as we waited for the newlyweds to take their seats.

Once the happy couple had finished toasting the champagne, I was forced into the kitchen to begin bringing out the salads. Every guest was served a Jackson salad, followed by a spring vegetable consommé. Emily and Mr. Doyle had decided on a small cut of filet mignon, a half lobster tail, and a side of mashed potatoes with asparagus for the entrée. Mr. Doyle had spared no expense when it came to the food.

Everything appeared exquisite. Carefully, I balanced several plates on the large round tray and used a bit of my magic to keep the tray stable. I hated to use magic at all, but no one would be able to tell I was doing it. It was better than dropping the food on the floor.

I raced back and forth from the kitchen with tray after tray. My arm was beginning to feel sore. Even though some other servants and Robert were assisting me, five hundred salads, soups, and entrées were undoubtedly a lot. At one of the tables in the back, I noticed Mr. Wicker. I decided to serve his table so Robert wouldn't have to. Even though the man gave me the chills, I would do anything to keep him away from Robert.

I planned to quickly set his salad down and head back to the kitchen, but his hand shot out and grabbed my wrist as I reached to place the plate down. Thankfully, my magical concentration on the tray kept it upright, or I would have dropped it.

"I know you," he growled, glancing up at me.

"Yes, sir. I work for Mrs. Fitzgerald," I stammered.

"Yes, I know you work there. I saw you last year. That's not what I'm talking about!" Mr. Wicker said harshly. "I know I've seen you before then."

"I'm sorry, sir. You must have me confused with someone else," I replied, trying to pull my wrist from his grasp. Other guests at his table were beginning to stare at us. Mr. Wicker must have noticed, too, because he finally let go of me. Feeling shaken, I quickly retreated to the kitchen.

My heart was racing, but I collected my next full tray of salads and continued to serve. This wasn't the first time Mr. Wicker had claimed he had met me before. I knew I hadn't met him before he came with Robert. Maybe he was becoming senile. I shook off the chill he had given me and continued with my work. I wasn't going to let the ravings of an old man get to me.

Once the first course was passed out, we retreated to the kitchen to prepare the trays with soup. I was given the job of ladling soup into bowls, and Robert placed them on trays. The other servants worked on the same task since there were multiple pots of soup. After the trays were prepared, I went back onto the terrace to collect the salad plates and replace them with soup.

We followed the same pattern with the remaining courses. I intentionally stayed away from Mr. Wicker's table and let the other servants take care of him. When dinner was complete, Mr. Doyle and Emily rose from their table, and the head chef rolled the wedding cake to the middle of the terrace. The cake was just as elaborate as the rest of the wedding. Six three-tier cakes surrounded a raised pedestal, which rested a larger four-tier cake. Mr. Doyle and Emily stepped up to the display to cut their wedding cake.

Dragon Scales

The crowd applauded as the happy couple shared the first piece of cake. As the chef wheeled the remaining cake back into the kitchen, I followed the rest of the servants to start plating the dessert. Robert winked at me from across the tables. I could feel my cheeks reddening, but I subtly smiled at him. I turned to serve the next table when I realized it was Mr. Wicker's. His cold eyes were staring right at me, and I shuddered. As quickly as I could, I passed out the cake. The entire time, his eyes never left me. My skin felt like it was crawling.

While the guests enjoyed their desserts, the servants concentrated on cleaning up the dishes from dinner. The head maid had handed both Robert and me a rag. We began drying dishes the other servants gave to us, then stacked them on an empty table. The work was monotonous, but I tried not to think about what I was doing and kept my limbs moving.

Robert and I were given a break from washing the dishes to collect the dessert dishes. I tried not to look at Mr. Wicker, though I could feel his eyes on me. I couldn't imagine how Robert lived with that man for most of his life. Shuddering again, I collected the last of the plates and returned to the kitchen.

While we were in the middle of washing dishes, I heard music coming from the terrace. A band had started playing. It sounded like a waltz, and I wondered if Mr. Doyle and Emily were having their first dance. The muscles in my neck, back, and legs were starting to hurt from working on my feet all day, but I pushed through, finishing with the dishes. Afterward, the head maid instructed us to carry drinks around the dance floor for the thirsty guests.

I exited the kitchen again with a tray full of drinks, and I saw most of the guests dancing in the ample open space. The women's beautiful dresses swirled in time to the music as the couples circled the floor. As Emily and Mr. Doyle spun in the center, Emily's white dress glowed in the light of the setting sun. Emily's wedding day would be over in a few hours, and I would be free of her.

For the next hour, I continued to circle the western terrace. Robert and I shared secret glances as the night went on. He would subtly make faces or mouth I love you. I couldn't wait for this night to be over, so I could sneak out to the barn and spend time with him. My mind was already imagining his arms around me as I rested my head on his chest, sharing sweet kisses and discussing our future. I began to smile as I walked back into the kitchen with my empty tray.

"Jane," the head maid called as soon as she spotted me. "Your name is Jane, isn't it?" she asked as she approached me.

"Yes, ma'am," I replied.

She lifted a stack of folded linens from a table and handed them to me.

"I need you to take these to the closet next to the parlor. You can reach it by going onto the west terrace and taking the stairs to the south terrace. You can enter the parlor through the double glass doors. The closet is located in the hallway just outside the room. Do you understand where to go?" the head maid asked.

"Yes, ma'am. I understand how to get there," I stated.

"Okay, off with you then," the maid said with a flick of her hand.

I carried the stack of linens back out onto the west terrace. It was harder to find the stairs that led to the south terrace now that night had fallen. I finally found them and slowly made my way in the dark. Crossing the south terrace, I walked to the glass door I had gone through earlier that day. Holding the linens in one hand, I managed to get the door opened. Before I entered, the hair on the back of my neck stood up, and I shivered. Nervously, I entered the parlor, closing the door behind me. I just wanted to put the stack of cloth where it belonged and get back to the party.

Rapidly, I hurried through the parlor and went out into the hall. It was harder to see in the dark hallway without faint light coming in from the windows, but I could tell there was a closet to the right. I opened it to find similar linens within. As I placed the linens on the empty shelf, I heard the sound of a door opening. The noise had come from the parlor. I stepped away from the closet, feeling confused. Had someone followed me?

Slowly, I closed the closet door. With my heart racing, I turned to head back.

"Hello," I called. "Is someone there?"

A sweat broke out over my body when no one answered. I was sure I hadn't imagined the sound of the door. I had distinctly heard it opening. Silently, I crept down the hall. The darkness of the hallway felt like it was pressing down on me, taking the air from my lungs. Upon entering the parlor, the rest of my breath left my body. Silhouetted in the doorway was Mr. Wicker.

34

Up in Flames

BEFORE MY MIND could comprehend, Mr. Wicker stepped into the parlor and turned the dial of an oil lamp located on an end table. The bright light from the lamp blinded me momentarily as it illuminated the darkness. When I regained my vision, I saw Mr. Wicker's evil smile as he stood next to the end table. His weight shifted as he leaned on his cane.

"I've been thinking about where I've seen you before. After hours of staring at you, it finally came to me," Mr. Wicker gruffly spoke as he rubbed the red gem that crowned the top of his cane.

I stared into his beady eyes, feeling extremely confused.

"You were correct when you said I hadn't met you before," Mr. Wicker continued. "but I have been in the presence of someone who looked exactly like you. Amazingly, I haven't realized it before."

My heart pounded in my chest as Mr. Wicker took a step toward me. "I don't know what you're talking about," I stammered, stumbling backward.

"I'm talking about the person who could only be your mother," he growled with a nasty grin. "You look exactly like her."

Mr. Wicker let out a hideous laugh as he stalked closer. My body felt paralyzed with fear.

"Do you want to know how I knew your mother?" Mr. Wicker asked.

I couldn't find any words. My tongue felt frozen in my mouth. Mr. Wicker's fat lips curled into a disgusting grin. His eyes flowed down my body making goosebumps break out on my arms.

"I knew who she was because I killed her."

Mr. Wicker's words shattered my consciousness.

"I killed her," he repeated, "I'm sure you can guess why."

I felt tears spring to my eyes. I knew what he was going to say, but I didn't want to believe it. This couldn't be happening. My body shook uncontrollably, and I couldn't tell if it was because of my sobs or the shock I was in.

Mr. Wicker twirled the cane in his hand. "Now, if I had to take a guess, I would say you're just like her. Would that be correct?" he snarled as he took another step closer.

My whole body trembled, but I managed to pick up a glass table decoration with my mind. I hurled it at Mr. Wicker, but he dodged it quicker than anticipated. Another ugly laugh escaped his lips.

"Exactly what I expected. You're just another vile, monstrous thing that is a blemish on the normal world. I wish I had realized it sooner. We had suspected the supposedly 'great' Rachel McCalski had a child. My organization has been looking for you for quite some time. I'm sure they will reward me greatly when I tell them I have found and eradicated you."

I picked up another table decoration and threw it in his direction. Even though it shattered against his leg, he laughed loudly.

"Your mother was a tough one, I'll admit. I wasn't able to capture her on my own. Something tells me I won't have that problem with you."

Lifting his cane, he twisted the gem on top. A long metal spike shot out of the bottom. It gleamed in the light of the lamp. Visions of my Predicting the Future final surfaced in my memory. The bat had been a symbol of death. Why hadn't I taken the prediction seriously? The W.A.S.P. had found me, and Mr. Wicker was going to kill me. I had to fight for my life. I wasn't going to accept the prediction as fate.

Focusing all my concentration, I lifted the coffee table and flung it straight for him. The wood splintered as it crashed into him, knocking him to his knees. I began rushing toward the glass door, but Mr. Wicker was faster than I thought possible. He grabbed my arm and flung me backward. I lost my balance and fell onto the floor.

"No more games," Mr. Wicker snarled as he straightened the bottom of his suit coat. "You have no chance of escape. This isn't the first time I've killed one of your kind by myself. Your mind tricks and magic won't help you now."

He moved toward me in slow motion, a look of triumph on his face. My head was throbbing. I must have hit it when I had fallen. My muscles ached as I tried to propel myself away from him. Mr. Wicker raised his spiked cane and thrust it downward. A searing pain shot through my right leg. I let out a scream and looked down. Thankfully, Mr. Wicker had missed and had only grazed my calf, but the cane had gone through my dress, pinning it to the floor. I watched my blood soak onto the fabric. Mr. Wicker's lips spread into a slow smile.

"I'm rather enjoying this," Mr. Wicker said, placing his hands on the top of the cane. My leg throbbed as he yanked upward, pulling the cane out of the floor. With an evil grin, he positioned the cane above my heart. "Goodbye," he howled.

Suddenly, Mr. Wicker was hit from the side. He went sprawling to the floor along with his attacker. Robert was on top of him, the two of them struggling over the cane.

"Run, Jane!" Robert screamed at the top of his lungs.

I struggled to my feet, blood dripping down my leg. I couldn't leave Robert with Mr. Wicker. The two men continued to struggle on the floor. I couldn't use my magic to toss anything at Mr. Wicker for fear I would hit Robert. I had to help somehow.

As quickly as I could manage, I hobbled toward them. Mr. Wicker was trying to throw Robert off, and Robert was fighting to hold Mr. Wicker down. Bending down, I picked up a shard of glass from the broken table decoration I had thrown earlier. Holding it firmly in my hand, I limped forward. Mr. Wicker was flailing his legs, trying to toss Robert. I rapidly brought the piece of glass down unto Mr. Wicker's thigh. He cried out, kicking out his injured leg. His boot caught me square in the chest, and I fell backward onto the floor again.

All the breath left my chest as I landed on the oriental carpet. I lay stunned for several moments. My breastbone felt bruised, and my head felt like it had been split open. When I opened my eyes, I saw Mr. Wicker had managed to get out from under Robert. He was gripping the edge of the sofa table, pulling himself to his feet. Robert was curled in a ball, and his hands appeared to be clutching at his stomach.

"How heroic," Mr. Wicker spat. "My old ward, attacking me to come to the aid of a disgusting pixie. I should never have saved you from the streets. I should have killed you years ago."

Mr. Wicker raised his blooded spike and pointed it at Robert's head. Fear and anger rose inside of me. For the first time since he had cornered me, I found myself thinking clearly. I raised my hands and focused all of my concentration on Mr. Wicker. A great flood of emotion burst in my chest, causing me to send a strong gust of wind in his direction. It swept him off his feet, sending him crashing violently into the back wall of the parlor. His body fell to the floor, and he remained motionless.

My body felt completely drained of energy as I crawled toward Robert. Every muscle felt like it was on fire. Slowly, I dragged my bloody leg behind me as I made it to Robert's curled-up form. I placed my hand on his shoulder and rolled him toward me.

Robert's hands were covered in blood as he held them across his stomach. With horror, I saw Mr. Wicker's cane had left a deep gash across his midsection. All the color had drained from Robert's face, and he looked to be in extreme pain.

"Oh, Robert!" I cried, my hands shaking as I ripped at the material of my dress. I had to get pressure on his wound to try and stop the bleeding. "It's going to be okay. I'm here now."

I managed to rip a decent portion of the skirt. I balled it up, pushing it down on his wound. The puncture wound looked deep. I knew I had to get him help. Every fiber of my being shook as I looked into his eyes.

"Hold this tightly over the wound. I need to find help," I said.

Robert began shaking his head. "Jane," he choked out. "Don't leave me."

"Robert, I have to find someone," I sobbed.

I turned to get up, but Robert's hand shot out and grabbed hold of my wrist.

"Jane, I don't think it will be of any use," he muttered.

"What do you mean?" I wailed, hysteria taking over my body.

"I don't think anyone will be able to help me."

"Robert, no! Don't say that! Please let me find someone who can help. I have to do something." I felt tears flowing down my cheeks.

"Jane," he said, raising his hand to cup my cheek. "It will be okay."

"No, it's not okay. Robert, I…" I stuttered as a sob broke from my mouth.

"You were the best thing that ever happened to me. I'm so glad I had you in my life."

"I can't lose you, Robert. I can't lose another person I care about. Don't leave me." I cried, my tears dripping down onto the very bloody cloth.

"I don't want to leave you, my little pixie, but I fear I don't have a choice on this matter," Robert said softly as tears filled his eyes. "Jane, promise me you'll be brave. Promise me you'll live the life you deserve even if I can't be there."

"My life is nothing without you. You're the only person who truly cares about me. I need you, Robert."

"Jane, I know you are so strong, and I need you to be that for me. You're going to become a wonderful pixie, and I know I'm not the only one who cares about you. I'm sure many people at that school care about you too. I know in my heart you are going to be successful. Jane, you have to promise me you'll do enough living for the both of us," Robert replied, his hand shaking as he caressed my cheek.

"You changed my life. I don't want to live without you," I sobbed.

"You changed my life, too. You made me experience feelings I've never had before and feelings I never thought were possible. Although our time together was short, I'm so happy to have had that time with you. I would never change it for the entire world," Robert said as his hand went to my neck.

I bent over him and pressed my lips to his. All my emotions went into that kiss. If only I could fix him with a kiss. How could I have all this magic but not the power it would take to heal him? How could this be happening to me? Why wasn't I able to do anything?

When our kiss ended, I leaned back to stare into his eyes, the beautiful chocolate-colored eyes I had fallen in love with. A small smile played upon his lips as he looked at me.

"I love you so much, Jane," he whispered.

"I love you too, Robert," I replied as I watched him take his last breath.

My heart felt like it had been ripped out of my chest. I let out an agonizing wail as I fell forward onto his chest. Sobs racked my body as a pain I had never felt before coursed through me. I couldn't see through the torrent of tears. All I could do was be consumed by the horrible pain. I sobbed into Robert's shoulder, the place where I had comfortably rested my head when we spent time together in the barn. I cried until my eyes were swollen and sore. How had this happened? It was all my fault.

If I hadn't gone off on my own, if I would have paid more heed to my tea leaf prediction, if I never loved Robert in the first place, or maybe if I had never been born, Robert would've been safe. My whole world had been shattered, and the 'what ifs' would never change it or make it better. Why did everyone I love leave me?

Perhaps I was cursed, and that was why everyone I loved was doomed to die. I sobbed and screamed for Robert, my father, and my mother. No matter how much I cried, the deep-seated pain in my chest hadn't lessened. My body felt like it was being torn apart, and nothing could be done to put it back together again. I wanted to lay down beside Robert and die, too. Maybe that was the only way to make this horrible pain go away.

For a long time, I stayed beside Robert. I would have stayed there the entire night, but I was startled when I heard a groan coming from the back of the parlor. With horror, I saw Mr. Wicker's form beginning to move. It wasn't long before he was getting to his feet. My body felt tired and broken. I wasn't sure if I even had the strength to fight him off.

Mr. Wicker glared at me with his evil eyes. "You're such a stupid, little girl," he laughed. "You're still here. I would have hunted you down anyway now that I know who you are, but this makes it so much easier." Slowly, he limped forward.

I shuddered as I clung to Robert. Mr. Wicker was going to kill me, and a part of me didn't even care. With Robert gone, I had nothing. Now, my pain could finally be over. I closed my eyes and waited.

Visions of Robert floated in my head. His last words rang out across my mind. Robert wanted me to live. He fought Mr. Wicker so I could live. Robert hadn't wanted me to die by his hands. A face resembling my own floated through my thoughts. Mr. Wicker had killed my mother and taken her away from me. He was the reason for my suffering. Shifting on the floor, I felt the corner of my pixie dust case digging into my side. I had forgotten all about it. I couldn't give Mr. Wicker the satisfaction of killing me, too.

Quickly, I pulled out my pixie dust case and enlarged it. Opening it with my finger, I began sifting through my vials. What could I use to defend myself? My hand settled around the vial of *fire charm* before my mind could even comprehend what I was doing. With every last ounce of energy, I rose to my feet.

Mr. Wicker began laughing hysterically from just a few feet away.

"What do you think you're going to do now, you vile, stupid girl?"

Uncorking the vial, I tossed the entire contents in his direction. I hadn't cared that it would've only taken a small amount of the charm to start a fire. The room exploded into heat and flames. I fell to the floor, exhausted, watching Mr. Wicker's body become engulfed in flames.

"That's for my mother and Robert," I cried out exhaustedly.

Mr. Wicker's screams were unlike anything I had ever heard. The fire spread wildly, and I saw flames erupt in the hallway behind the parlor. I had used so much of the charm that the fire was enormous, and it was burning everything in its path. I leaned back onto the glass door, which now felt cold in comparison to the heat of the roaring fire. I watched until Mr. Wicker stopped moving. I had avenged my mother and Robert, I thought with a sob. I began crying uncontrollably again though I couldn't believe I had any tears left. Exhaustion overtook my body as I reached over to my pixie dust case before the fire could consume it. I didn't know if I would have the energy to leave the parlor. Perhaps I would die here after all.

I laid against the door for several moments as I watched the fire creep closer. This wasn't how I imagined the day of Emily's wedding. Never in my wildest dreams would I have thought everything would end for me on this day. The *fire charm* had been my only defense, and now it would be my undoing. I was beginning to feel dizzy as I choked on the smoke. I closed my eyes to block out the horrible image before me.

Suddenly, the door behind me was wrenched open, and I fell into the cool night air. Someone grabbed me under my arms and pulled me out of the building. I opened my eyes to see the head maid. Once she had drawn me away from the flames, she crouched down and looked into my face.

"Jane, you're going to be okay. Was anyone else inside?" she asked.

"They're gone," I mumbled, surprised by how hoarse my voice sounded.

"Can you stand? We need to move away from the house. The entire structure is going up in flames."

"I'll try," I said weakly, not sure if I would have the energy.

The head maid placed one of my arms around her neck, and she lifted me to my feet. I couldn't put my full weight on my right leg because of the wound from Mr. Wicker's cane, but I managed to hobble down the stairs. She supported me as we crossed the lawn, and she didn't stop until we were almost to the pond.

"You can stay here for the moment. I need to see if my master needs anything," she said before rushing away.

I sank down on the grass as I watched the Doyle mansion burn. The fire seemed to be spreading quickly. I could see flames shooting from the upper floors. On the western lawn, I could make out clumps of people standing back from the burning building. From the direction of the barn, it looked like men were running with buckets, but I was certain it wouldn't be enough water to put out the flames.

My body hurt everywhere, and it even hurt to breathe. I wanted to lay down in the grass, but I was afraid I wouldn't be able to get up. Suddenly, the mansion let off an eerie cracking sound, and the backside of the building began to crumble. I watched as the back walls caved in. Only moments ago, I had been inside. Though my body ached all over, my mind felt numb. I couldn't feel any emotions as I watched the Doyle mansion collapse in front of me. I had cried out all of my feelings, and now nothing was left. The head maid had pulled me from the burning building, but it felt like I had died inside.

THE END

Acknowledgements

First, I would like to thank all my readers! Thank you for your support of *Pixie Dust* and for continuing to read the series. I can't be an author without readers, and I will be forever grateful. Your reviews and comments have boosted my confidence and reassured me that this was what I was meant to do. I'm so glad you are fans of the series, and I can't wait for you to find out what happens next!

Many thanks to my parents for your continued support. I couldn't have done this without you. I appreciate your help advertising my book in person and on social media. I credit you both for my success. Mom, thank you for hauling my books and other book-related crafts to all the vendor shows and book signings. It means so much to me that you've been there for every single one.

Clayton, I don't know what I'd do without you. I want you to know that your life is full of unlimited possibilities. Never be afraid to work toward your goals because you'll be surprised by what could happen! God always helps you get to where you are meant to be, and everything happens for a reason.

To my husband, Christopher, I am so thankful you continue to read my manuscripts. You've been there from the beginning. Thank you for supporting my dream of becoming an author. I'm glad you believe in me.

I am beyond grateful to my family and friends. Your support of this series has been phenomenal! I appreciate all the social media likes and shares, reviews, and passing along my book through word of mouth. Your time and effort are essential to this independent author. Also, thank you to Carly, president of my fan club and biggest fan. Your love for my books puts a smile on my face.

To my editor and friend, Alexandria Groves, I have you to thank for helping me grow as a writer. Your corrections and opinions have helped to improve my novels. I never realized how much I use certain words. Thank you for taking the time to read through what I thought was a mess of a manuscript. I appreciate your honesty and support. I'm evolving into a better writer because of you.

Damonza has done another fantastic job with the cover art and internal formatting. I am so grateful for their exceptional work, and I wouldn't have anyone else designing my covers! To all the employees at Damonza, thank you so much for bringing my fantasy to life. You all are such a pleasure to work with.

I'm also grateful to God and Jesus. I feel so blessed with my creative gifts and the life I was given. Through God, all things are possible, and my faith has seen me through my ups and downs. I believe in your plan and know that sometimes unanswered prayers are actually gifts.

Coming February 2023

Secret Siren

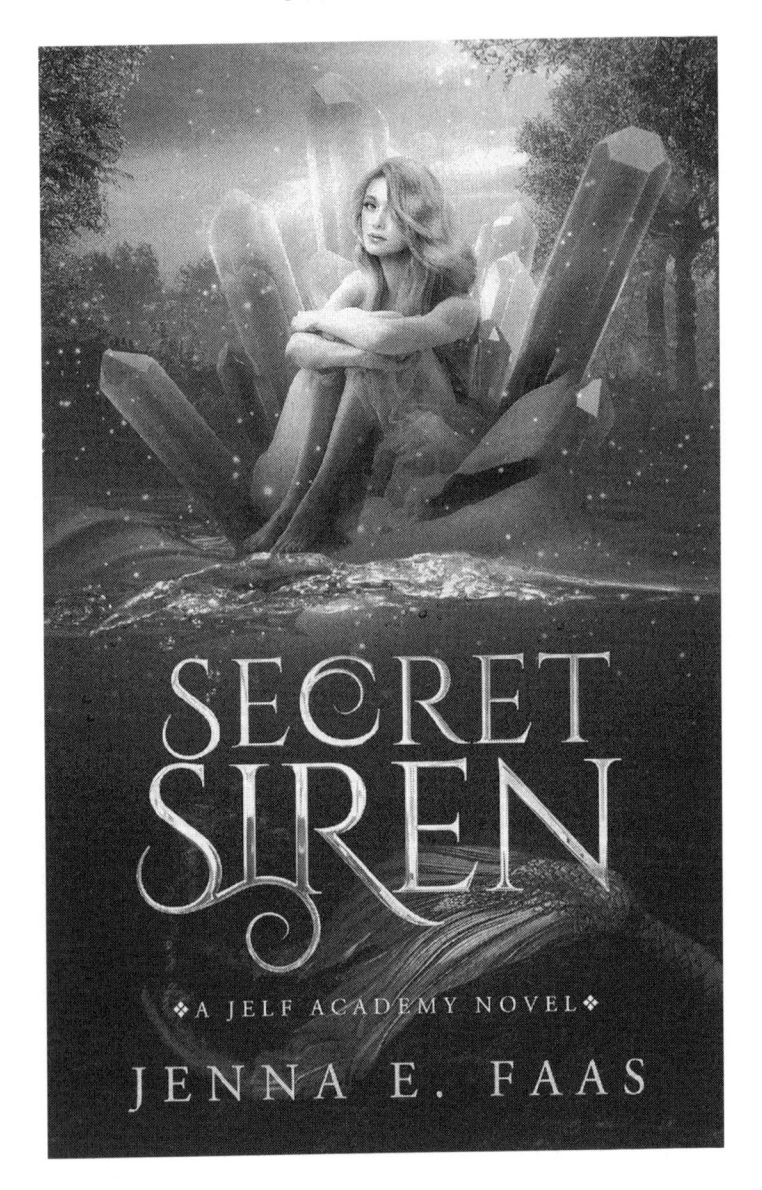

About the Author

Jenna E. Faas is the author of *Pixie Dust*, the first book in the *Jelf Academy Series*. She lives in Pittsburgh, Pennsylvania, with her husband, son, and two Australian shepherds. From the very first time Jenna turned the pages of a book, she was obsessed. As a young girl, she always made up stories, which she jotted down in school notebooks. An avid reader, she would get lost in fantasy and wished magic existed. Jenna began the concept of Pixie Dust when she was seventeen and expanded her creation of the world through her college years. Her bachelor's degree in Geology helped inspire pixie magic since gemstones and minerals are the ingredients to create pixie charms.

When Jenna isn't writing or reading, she enjoys spending time with her family, working on arts and crafts, and singing her favorite songs. She is currently working on the next installment of the *Jelf Academy series*: *Secret Siren*.

Find Jenna on the web at
https://jennaf14.wixsite.com/jennaefaas-author.

Made in the USA
Monee, IL
13 September 2023